TO TEMPT AN ANGEL

She is Angelica Douglas, the Countess of
Melrose. Driven to poverty by the men who
bankrupted her father, forced to support her
family with skillful cheating at cards and dice,
she yearns for revenge. And she is not above
enlisting the aid of a chivalrous, handsome
stranger to get it . . .

He is Robert Campbell, Marquess of Argyll, heir
to the Duke of Inverary. Intrigued to learn
his own father is one of her intended victims,
he decides to keep a careful watch on the
enchanting Angelica. His desire for her is a most
unwelcome complication, for the tragedies of
his first marriage taught him all too well the
damage that love—and its lack—can do. But
when danger begins to stalk them, he realizes
that the best way to protect the stubbornly
independent thief is to marry her.

Now all that remains is to tempt an unlikely
angel to be his bride . . .

Books by Patricia Grasso

TO TAME A DUKE

TO TEMPT AN ANGEL

Published by Kensington Publishing Corporation

TO TEMPT
AN ANGEL

Patricia Grasso

ZEBRA BOOKS
KENSINGTON PUBLISHING CORP.

http://www.kensingtonbooks.com

ZEBRA BOOKS are published by

Kensington Publishing Corp.
850 Third Avenue
New York, NY 10022

All Kensington titles, imprints and distributed lines are available at special quantity discounts for bulk purchases for sales promotion, premiums, fund-raising, educational or institutional use.

Special book excerpts or customized printings can also be created to fit specific needs. For details, write or phone the office of the Kensington Special Sales Manager: Kensington Publishing Corp., 850 Third Avenue, New York, NY 10022. Attn. Special Sales Department. Phone: 1-800-221-2647.

Zebra and the Z logo Reg. U.S. Pat. & TM Off.

First Printing: June 2002
10 9 8 7 6 5 4 3 2 1

Printed in the United States of America

Chapter 1

London, 1812

He knew she was cheating.

Angelica read the suspicion in the man's alcohol-glazed eyes. She was confident of her talent, so being caught didn't worry her, but drunks almost always proved dangerous. With the exception of her own father, of course.

Eighteen-year-old Angelica Douglas wet her lips, gone dry from nervousness, and felt a droplet of perspiration roll slowly down the valley between her breasts. Reaching up, she brushed a wisp of golden hair away from her face and adjusted the wreath of fresh-cut flowers she wore like a crown on her head.

Angelica gave her intended victim a sunny smile and flicked a glance at the group of fairgoers gathered in front of her table. Seated on a stool, she began moving the thimbles around and around on the makeshift table that consisted of a board resting on top of a trestle.

"Stop," the man growled.

Angelica looked at him expectantly.

He pointed at the middle thimble. Angelica lifted it to reveal nothing and laughed with delight.

"Yer cheatin'," he accused her, his foul breath making her stomach queasy.

Seemingly unruffled, Angelica looked him straight in the eye. "Sir, you are a poor loser," she told him in an affronted tone. "Would you care to throw dice instead?"

"I ain't throwin' dice with no girl," the man snapped, and turned to go.

"Afraid?" Angelica challenged him, making her audience laugh with approval. When the man kept walking, she shifted her blue-eyed gaze to those watching and asked, "Would anyone care to throw dice with me?"

"I would love to throw with you," answered a voice in a tone suggesting intimacy.

The crowd parted for the handsomest man Angelica had ever seen. Older than she by ten years at least, the black-haired and dark-eyed English Adonis carried his tall, well-built frame with athletic grace. Though commonly dressed in black breeches and white shirt, the man had the bearing of an aristocrat.

Sacred sevens, Angelica thought, his devilishly good looks startling her. She felt as if Old Clootie, in all his sinful perfection, had stepped out of the crowd to lead her astray.

Towering over her, the man stood ten inches taller than her petite height of five feet, two inches. Angelica tilted her head back to look into his black eyes.

Long moments passed. The sights and sounds

and scents of the crowded Midsummer Fair disappeared as they gazed into each other's eyes.

Recovering herself, Angelica gave him a sunny smile and produced a pair of ivory dice. She offered them to him for his inspection. Their fingers touched as he lifted the dice out of her hand; a jolt of excitement shot through Angelica, and she wondered if he felt it, too.

"I'm Robert," he introduced himself in a husky voice. "What's your name?"

"Angelica."

"Are you a good angel or a bad one?" Robert teased her.

"I was wondering the same thing about you," she answered.

He smiled at that and asked, "How much have you won today, angel?"

"Four pounds."

"Then let's set the stake at four pounds," Robert suggested.

Angelica hesitated and worried her bottom lip with her small white teeth. If she lost the whole day's earnings on one toss of the dice, her family would go hungry. But if she won, she'd have eight pounds for her day's work. Ensuring her own victory wouldn't be difficult, but this man frightened her in some indefinable way.

"Four pounds," Angelica agreed, unable to resist the temptation of doubling her winnings.

"What's your main?" Robert asked, passing her the dice without bothering to inspect them.

"Seven." Tossing twelve or crabs was the only way to lose by choosing seven, but there was no chance of that happening with her loaded dice.

Angelica shifted the dice back and forth in her hands, as if trying to get the feel of them. When she tossed the dice, a four and a three came up.

"Let it ride," Angelica said, casting him a side-long glance, hoping to double the eight pounds.

Robert inclined his head. He placed eight pounds down to match the eight on the table.

"Sacred sevens," she whispered, and tossed the dice. This time a six and a one showed up.

Angelica gifted him with a sunny smile and dragged the sixteen pounds closer. Good Lord, her family could eat on this for a month. If her father didn't steal it for drink . . .

"Do you play?" she asked him, feeling confident.

Robert fixed his dark gaze on hers, and Angelica suffered the uncanny feeling that he knew she was cheating. Then he dropped sixteen pounds on the table.

A four and a three appeared on her next throw. Angelica stared at the thirty-two pounds she'd won. "Let it ride," she said, casting him a flirtatious smile.

Surprising her, Robert dropped thirty-two pounds on the table. Angelica tossed the dice; a five and a two appeared.

"This must be your lucky day," Robert remarked in an amused voice. Carelessly, he dropped sixty-four pounds on the table and challenged her. "Will you let it ride, angel?"

Shocked by the size of his bet, Angelica flicked out her tongue to wet her lips. Should she meet his challenge?

Angelica tossed the dice. A six and a one showed up.

"I'll pass," she announced, dropping the one hundred and twenty-eight pounds into her pocket.

Afraid to look at her victim, Angelica walked away without another word. She hadn't gone more than a few feet when someone grabbed her arm. She whirled around, ready to defend herself.

"May I escort you home?" Robert asked, his smile charming.

Angelica was instantly suspicious. Did he want to steal her winnings? Or was his intention even more sinister? He *was* incredibly handsome, but her family came first. They depended on her for their survival.

"No, thank you," she refused.

"You need protection," he told her. "You carry a great deal of money."

"Who will protect me from you, sir?" Angelica asked, arching a perfectly shaped brow at him.

"You don't trust me?" Robert asked, giving her a lopsided grin.

"I trust no one," she told him. "Especially men I don't know."

"We are merely friends who haven't known each other very long," Robert argued. "I let you cheat me out of a hundred and twenty-eight pounds. The least you can do is allow me to escort you home."

"I never cheat," Angelica insisted, and walked away.

"I suppose you don't lie either," he called.

Angelica quickened her pace. She squelched the urge to turn around to see if he was following her.

Leaving Coram's Field, Angelica slowed her pace and walked west on Guildford Street. Angelica knew she should have looked for her sisters to accompany her home but needed to get away from Robert. Who was this handsome man who'd lost a small fortune to her? She would have liked to know him better, keep company with him, perhaps.

Resentment toward her family stepped out of the shadows of her mind. Why did she need to forgo a normal life in order to support her family? Just once, she wanted someone to take care of her.

And then guilt for thinking such disloyal

thoughts chased the resentment away. A tragic figure in her mind, her father couldn't help his dependence on drink; her aunt certainly couldn't work and had already spent all her money keeping them alive; her sisters were younger and couldn't be expected to do more than help out. Her dreary life wasn't the fault of her family. The men who had ruined her father would pay dearly for their crimes against the Douglas family.

Angelica put her hand in her pocket and touched her winnings. One hundred and twenty-eight pounds would feed them for a long time. Perhaps she could save some of it for their return to Sweetheart Priory, her father's ancestral home in Scotland, the only thing of value they still possessed. If her father didn't steal the money to pay for drink . . .

Glancing at the sky, Angelica wondered if she should have accepted Robert's offer to escort her home. Twilight was just an hour away. Would she make it home before nightfall?

Angelica walked briskly through Russell Square, Montague Place, and Bedford Square. Most Londoners appeared in high spirits, anticipating the celebration of Midsummer. Bonfires would light Primrose Hill that night, discouraging those elegant gentlemen from polite society who wished to duel there.

Then Angelica started down Tottenham Court Road. Here the crowds dwindled until she walked alone.

"Lord, guide me home safely," Angelica whispered, fingering her necklace, the only thing of value she owned.

A gift from her aunt, the fluted diamond globe hung on a gold chain. The pendant's top and bottom were set in gold. Aunt Roxie had insisted the diamond had magical properties that protected its owner from harm.

Unbidden, the image of her handsome victim arose in her mind's eye. Angelica knew she had behaved badly.

Cheating the man out of that much money was sinful, she thought. Her actions mirrored that of the disreputable men who'd ruined her father so many years ago. Perhaps she should return to the fair and give back part of the small fortune to him.

Her need was greater, Angelica told herself. If the man could afford to gamble a hundred and twenty-eight pounds, he could afford to lose it.

Angelica knew the only reason she wanted to return the money was because she wanted to see Robert again. Yes, she was lonely, but she needed no distractions to interfere with her revenge.

"Why are you walking, angel?"

Startled by the voice, Angelica whirled around to see Robert on horseback. Her heart beat faster at the sight of him. Had she conjured the man up by thinking of him? Such happenings were possible.

"I beg your pardon?" she said.

"I asked why you were walking instead of riding," Robert replied.

"I forgot my wings at home," Angelica told him.

"Would you care for a ride?"

Angelica smiled politely and refused, saying, "I never travel with strangers."

"We aren't strangers," Robert said. He gave her a boyish grin and added, "You've just stolen—I mean, *won*—a small fortune from me. The least you can do is allow me to escort you home."

Angelica wanted desperately to ride with him. She wanted to keep company with a gentleman and live a normal life. Sacred sevens, she wanted her *old* life back.

Duty defeated desire.

"Making your acquaintance has been a pleasure," Angelica said, turning away.

"Several people saw you pocket that money," Robert reminded her.

Angelica saw the sense in what he was saying. Yet, she suffered the uncanny feeling that accepting his offer would change her life forever. Would that be a bad thing? She certainly wasn't happy with her present life.

"I live on the far side of Primrose Hill," Angelica said, turning toward him with a smile lighting her face.

Robert dismounted in order to help her up. The sound of a galloping horse broke the silence around them, and they turned in time to see a man on horseback aim a pistol at them.

Robert dove for the ground as the shot rang out and took Angelica with him. She heard their attacker's horse galloping away.

Robert lay on top of her and stared into her eyes. Caught by his dark gaze, Angelica felt her cheeks heating with an embarrassed blush.

"The danger has passed," she managed to whisper, feeling the warmth of his body seeping through her light clothing.

Robert seemed in no hurry to release her. "You've lost your crown of flowers," he said.

Angelica couldn't credit that the man was talking about flowers when they'd nearly been killed. She opened her mouth to tell him to get off, but then he moved.

"I knew someone would try to steal your money," Robert said, helping her rise. He lifted the wreath of flowers off the ground and placed it on top of her blond head, adding, "You look like a flower fairy again."

"What makes you think the assassin was aiming at me?" Angelica countered. "He didn't stop to steal my money. Perhaps he's one of your enemies."

Robert snapped his brows together. She knew from the expression on his handsome face that he thought she made sense.

"I'm an excellent markswoman," Angelica said, pulling her dagger from the sheath strapped to her leg. "If you hadn't thrown yourself on top of me, I could have taken him down. Then we could have questioned him."

Robert burst out laughing. "A knife-wielding angel? Next time I'll let you rescue me," he said, helping her onto his horse.

"I should walk the rest of the way," Angelica said when he mounted behind her. "Being attacked twice in one day is statistically impossible."

"You are the sweetest gambler I've ever encountered," Robert said. Then, "What's your full name?"

"Angelica Douglas." His body pressing intimately against hers made her feel weak. To mask her nervousness, she asked, "What is your full name, sir?"

"Robert Roy."

"Are you joking?" Angelica glanced over her shoulder at him. "Your name is really Rob Roy?"

Robert shrugged. "My father had a keen sense of humor."

"I agree," Angelica said with a smile, "but the joke is on you."

Robert inhaled deeply of her scent, lavender and water lily. She reminded him of a spring day. "Your smile shames the envious sun, angel."

"I love this moment in the year's cycle," Angelica

told him. "Sunshine, flowers, and freedom fill the days."

"Do I detect a philosophical gambler?" Robert asked, amusement tingeing his voice.

Angelica shrugged. "I am philosophical by choice and a gambler by necessity."

A connoisseur of beautiful women, Robert enjoyed the feeling of the angel in his arms as they started down Hampstead Road. She exuded seductive innocence, an aphrodisiac to his senses.

The girl possessed a startlingly perfect face and flawless ivory skin, and full lips that begged to be kissed. Thick golden hair, streaked with paler shades of blond, framed her face and cascaded almost to her waist.

Crowning her head, the wreath of fresh-cut flowers gave her an ethereal appearance. He could almost see this flower fairy cavorting like a nymph through the woodland.

Hers was a haunting beauty that had beckoned to him from the first moment he'd seen her at the fair. Why would such a woman waste her time running a thimblerigger's game? Most gentlemen of his acquaintance would have parted with a fortune to keep her as a mistress. She would produce beautiful babies, too.

Robert stiffened when he realized his thoughts had drifted to babies. Thinking of babies always darkened his mood, like a cloud blocking the sun.

Well, he needn't concern himself with babies. He planned never to marry again.

"Is something wrong?" Angelica asked without turning around.

Her question yanked him back to reality. "No, angel, I merely suffered an unpleasant thought."

"What was it?"

"Nothing important."

Angelica glanced over her shoulder at him. "You mean it is none of my business?"

"Precisely."

Robert halted his horse when they reached the two-hundred-and-sixteen-foot summit of Primrose Hill. He gazed down at the tiny hamlet of cottages with their pale pink, lemon, and sage stucco fronts trimmed with white like frosted cakes.

"Pretty, isn't it?" Robert remarked.

"Everything looks pretty from this height," Angelica replied with a rueful smile.

"A cynical angel?" he teased her.

"Look back at London," she said.

Robert tugged on the reins to turn his horse around and looked over her head. Beyond the sloping meadow lay London with its distant landmarks—Westminster Abbey, Saint Paul's Cathedral, the Tower of London.

"You can't see the squalor," Angelica said softly, "but it exists."

"It's not all squalor."

"I agree with you, but most Londoners do not live on Park Lane," she said.

"A *bitter* cynical angel?" Robert said, turning his horse around.

"There is much in life to cause bitterness unless one is a member of the Quality," Angelica informed him.

"Do you actually believe the Quality lead perfect, happy lives?" he asked.

"None of them need to scratch like barnyard chickens for their next meal," she answered.

Robert couldn't argue with that. "What is beyond the hamlet?" he asked, changing the subject.

"Saint John's Wood."

Robert nudged his horse forward. Slowly, they descended Primrose Hill to the hamlet below.

"Stop here," Angelica said when they reached the last cottage.

Robert halted his horse in front of a pale pink cottage trimmed in white. He dismounted and then lifted her down from the saddle.

"Angelica, darling," a woman's voice called. "Thank God you're home."

Though she appeared to be in her early forties, a youthful beauty still clung to the woman hurrying toward them. Auburn-haired and brown-eyed, the woman was voluptuous of figure. When she smiled to acknowledge his presence, two adorable dimples adorned her cheeks, making her appear even younger.

"What's the problem, Aunt Roxie?"

"Your father is a bit under the eaves," her aunt told her. She flicked a quick glance at Robert and added, "He drank my lavender perfume."

Angelica raced inside the cottage. Robert followed her through a large common room into an inner chamber where an older man lay on a cot and moaned as if in agony.

"He's poisoned himself," Robert said, taking charge. "Fetch me an empty bucket and a jar of heavily salted water."

"What are you going to do?" Aunt Roxie asked, hurrying into the tiny bedchamber.

"Help me get him into a sitting position," Robert ordered, ignoring her question.

On either side of the cot, Robert and Aunt Roxie pulled the man up until his back was against the wall. He opened his eyes, looked at Robert, and mumbled, "Magnus? Is it you, Magnus?"

The words startled Robert. His own father was named Magnus, and some people said he looked like his father as a young man. How could this desperate alcoholic know his father?

"Graham, he's not Magnus," Aunt Roxie was telling him. "He's—" She looked at him.

"Robert," he supplied.

Graham Douglas moaned and clutched his stomach. "Roxanne, it is Magnus," the old man insisted breathlessly.

"He is *not* Magnus," Aunt Roxie replied.

"You cannot win an argument with a drunk," Robert told her. "I'll answer to Magnus if it will help him."

"What a sweet boy," Aunt Roxie said as Angelica returned with the salted water and empty bucket.

Robert lifted the bottle out of her hand and put his left arm around the older man's head in order to force his mouth open. He poured some salted water into his mouth and clamped it shut, forcing him to swallow.

Robert repeated this procedure again and again until the bottle was empty. Then he grabbed the bucket and planted it in the man's lap.

"What do we do now?" Angelica asked, her anxiety apparent in her voice.

"We wait," Robert answered, his gaze fixed on her father. He reached out to grab the back of the man's head and force it forward until he'd vomited everything in his stomach. Then he handed the bucket to Angelica.

"You'll soon feel better," he told the older man, helping him to lie down on the bed.

"I already do," Graham Douglas replied, patting his hand. "I knew you'd come to help me, Magnus."

"Graham, he is not Magnus," Aunt Roxie repeated.

"Roxanne, you've always been a good sister and remained loyal to me," Graham Douglas said. "You were there the day I fell off the horse, weren't you?"

"Yes, I was," Aunt Roxie answered with a nod of her head.

"You were there the day my sweet wife died," he rambled on.

Aunt Roxie nodded her head again. "A sadder day I've never seen."

"And you were here today to help me in my distress."

Once again Aunt Roxie nodded.

The older man's expression changed. "Roxie, you're a damned jinx," he announced.

Robert chuckled, and Angelica smiled. Aunt Roxie rolled her eyes heavenward and then sat on the edge of the bed to take her brother's hand in hers.

Angelica touched Robert's hand and gestured to the outer room. He inclined his head and followed her out of the bedchamber.

The cottage's large common room served as both kitchen and drawing room, with a hearth on each end, one for cooking and the other for warmth. On the kitchen side of the room was a large steel cage, its door ajar. Two doors led to other bedrooms. On a table beside the settee sat a Celtic harp, a flute, and a violin with accompanying bow.

"Thank you for saving my father's life," Angelica said.

"No thanks are necessary, angel."

Her next words came out in a rush, as if she were confessing a crime. "My father suffers from an affliction and was desperate for alcohol."

"I didn't think he was attempting suicide," Robert assured her, and she seemed to relax. He gestured to the musical instruments, asking, "Do you play?"

"The harp is mine," she answered.

"I should have known an angel would prefer the harp," he teased her.

"A long time ago we had an enormous harp, but we needed to sell it," Angelica said, a wistful note in her voice. "Perhaps the harp only appeared enormous because I was a little girl."

"I wish I could have seen that," Robert said, stepping closer.

"You've never seen a floor harp?"

Her question brought a smile to his lips. "I meant, I wish I could have seen you as a little girl."

She blushed with obvious embarrassment.

Robert couldn't credit what he was seeing. How many years had it been since he'd seen a sincere blush stain a woman's cheeks?

"Hello, hello, hello."

Robert stared in surprise as the owner of the voice walked into the room. Approximately three feet long and weighing fifteen pounds, a bird crossed the room toward them. Its head and back were blue, its underside gold, and its eyes green.

"Hello, Jasper," she greeted the bird. "I missed you."

Angelica scratched the bird's head, making him trill with pleasure. Then she warned, "Don't put your fingers near him until he knows you better. Macaws can take a finger off with one bite.

"Say hello to Robert," she told the bird.

"Hello."

"Hello, Jasper," Robert said, amused to be speaking to a bird.

The macaw cocked his head to one side and repeated, "Hello."

"Good-night time," Angelica said, crossing the room to the cage. "Come."

"Good night," Jasper said, walking to the cage.

He stopped in front of the door, turned around, and crossed the room to Robert, saying, "Hello."

Angelica laughed. "Good night, Jasper."

This time the macaw went into the cage. Angelica shut the door and covered the cage with a blanket.

"Good night," the macaw called.

"Good night." Angelica looked at Robert and said, "I won him in a card game."

"Who is this Magnus your father mentioned?" Robert asked.

"Magnus Campbell, the Duke of Inverary," Angelica answered, and there was no mistaking the bitterness in her voice.

"Your father is acquainted with a duke?" Robert asked in surprise.

"My brother is the Earl of Melrose," Aunt Roxie answered, walking into the common room.

Robert was even more surprised by that announcement. He glanced around the common room, unable to credit the fact that an earl lived in this poverty.

"Darling, we've fallen upon hard times," Aunt Roxie explained.

"We did *not* fall," Angelica corrected her aunt. "We were pushed, and the Duke of Inverary is one of the men who pushed us."

"How did the duke push you into . . . your current condition?" Robert asked. "Who are the other men involved?"

"Ours is a long story," Angelica told him, placing her winnings on the table.

"I'm in no hurry," Robert replied, masking his curiosity with nonchalance.

"Another time," Angelica said in refusal. "I'll tell you the whole story when I have written the final page."

Robert cocked a dark brow at her. "Are you planning revenge, angel?"

The door burst open suddenly, ending their conversation. Two young women hurried inside. Both appeared younger than Angelica. One had black hair and limped and the other was a redhead, yet the three sisters resembled one another.

"Robert, I present Samantha." Angelica gestured to the ebony-haired girl. "And this is Victoria. Sisters, meet Robert Roy."

"Rob Roy?" Samantha exclaimed with a smile.

"You must be joking," Victoria said.

"Mind your manners," Aunt Roxie admonished them. "Ladies of quality do not insult guests."

"Ladies of quality do not run a thimblerigger's game," Angelica told her aunt.

"Nor do they pick pockets," Samantha said, emptying her pockets of coins.

"And they do not engage in disreputable activities," Victoria added, placing her own day's earnings on the table. "You know, dear aunt, disreputable activities like telling people's fortunes, calling up the dead in a seance, or selling love potions."

"Hush, darlings, we need the money," Aunt Roxie replied. "I do what I can to help out."

Angelica gestured to Robert, saying, "Let's walk outside."

Once the cottage door closed behind them, Robert asked, "Your sisters are pickpockets?"

"I'm afraid so," she answered.

"And your aunt is a charlatan?"

"Aunt Roxie is no charlatan," Angelica told him. "She has a special gift."

Robert tried hard not to laugh in her face but couldn't quite suppress his smile. "Do you actually believe in that?"

"Yes, I do," Angelica said. "I possess a similar, albeit undeveloped, gift."

"The sight of you did bewitch me," Robert said, gifting her with his devastatingly charming smile.

Angelica stared in the direction of Primrose Hill. "Samantha limps because one of her legs is slightly shorter than the other," she said without looking at him. "A wealthy gentleman, one of the men who ruined my father, ran over her with his carriage. We couldn't afford a physician to set the broken bone."

"I'm sorry," Robert replied.

"That happened a long time ago," Angelica told him. "Victoria has a problem with letters and numbers."

"What do you mean?"

"She can't read properly or cipher numbers," Angelica said, turning toward him. "Other than that, the Douglases are a normal family."

Robert laughed. "I'll come by tomorrow to check on your father."

"You want to consort with people like us?" Angelica asked.

Robert leaned close, his face merely inches from hers, and said in a husky whisper, "I'd love to consort with you."

Ever so gently, Robert drew her into his embrace. His face hovered above hers for the briefest moment and then descended as he moved one hand to the back of her head to hold her immobile.

Their lips met in a chaste kiss. When she relaxed in his arms, Robert changed the tempo of the kiss. His lips on hers became ardent and demanding; his tongue persuaded her lips to part, tasting the sweetness beyond them.

And then it was over.

Robert drew back and studied her expression,

knowing she'd just experienced her first kiss. He traced a finger down her silken cheek and rubbed his thumb across her lips.

"May I have my watch back now?" Robert asked, gazing deeply into her disarming blue eyes.

Angelica blushed. "I-I don't know what you mean."

"You lifted the watch out of my pocket when we were attacked," Robert told her.

Angelica reached into her pocket and produced the watch. "It looks like real gold," she remarked, passing it to him.

"It *is* real gold."

"How can you—?"

Robert planted a quick kiss on her lips and then whistled for his horse, grazing a short distance away. The horse returned to his side in an instant.

"You certainly have trained him well," Angelica said.

"I have a firm hand but can be a generous master," Robert said suggestively.

"I will never call any man my master," she informed him.

"We'll see."

Robert mounted and pulled on the reins to turn the horse around. Whistling a bawdy tune, he started down the road through the hamlet. He knew she was probably watching him but would not turn around to wave good night.

Angelica Douglas was unexpectedly spectacular, a seductive angel, a rare woman of courage and loyalty. Albeit an incorrigible cheater at games of chance.

Though her father had fallen upon hard times, she was still an aristocrat. The father's loss of fortune served Robert's purposes; he planned to make that magnificent angel his mistress.

That thought made Robert smile with pleasure. He decided to go visiting in the morning before he called on Angelica. He needed to know what the Duke of Inverary had done to Graham Douglas.

Keeping a mistress who wanted revenge against his own father could undoubtedly complicate his life. Somehow, he would atone for whatever his father had done to the man.

Chapter 2

People were staring at him.

Sauntering along Park Lane to his father's townhouse, Robert waved at Lord Wiltshire, driving by in his carriage. The older gentleman tipped his hat and shifted his gaze.

No one of any importance ever walked anywhere, but Robert only lived two town houses away from his father's. What was the sense in bringing out a carriage to travel less than a block?

Robert smiled inwardly. His neighbors, including Lord Wiltshire, weren't surprised by his walking. They had become accustomed to that oddity. What surprised them today was his attire.

Clad in black breeches and the slightly wrinkled shirt he'd worn the previous day, Robert walked as proudly down Park Lane as an emperor in his new clothes. Missing were the requisite jacket, cravat, and hat.

"Why are you dressed like that?"

Robert narrowed his gaze on his father's majordomo, a man he'd known his entire life. Apparently, he'd surmised correctly that by wearing this outfit he'd appear a common man, which was what he wanted Angelica Douglas to believe.

"Mr. Tinker, I haven't asked for your editorial comment about my attire," Robert said, brushing past the man. "Where is my father?"

"His Grace is working in his office," Tinker answered, staring in distaste at the wrinkled lawn shirt and breeches.

Robert turned toward the stairs. He would have gone directly to his father's office, but a woman's voice stopped him.

"Wait a minute, Robert. I want to speak to you."

Robert turned toward the voice and watched his sister-in-law walking into the foyer. Christ, he always felt as if she was lying in wait for him. He had hoped to avoid seeing her, but that was not to be.

"Excuse me, my lord," Tinker said, turning away. "I'll inform His Grace that the Marquess of Slovenly has arrived."

Venetia Emerson Campbell, his brother's widow, was lovely, with her chestnut hair and perfect oval face. She had a small nose and inviting lips and soft brown eyes; but shallowness, spitefulness, and greediness marred her beauty.

Wearing a sapphire blue riding habit that accentuated every alluring curve, Venetia walked across the foyer slowly and gracefully. Robert knew her hip-swaying gait was for his benefit. She'd been trying to trap him into marriage since their respective spouses had died.

"Why are you dressed like that?" Venetia asked, echoing the majordomo's words.

"What's wrong with my clothing?" Robert asked with an easy smile.

"Shame on you," Venetia scolded him gently.

"The Marquess of Argyll should dress properly. I hope no one saw you."

"I'm incapable of living up to your standards," Robert said.

Venetia smiled winsomely and stepped closer. "I'd lower my standards for you," she said, her intimate tone and the look in her eyes suggesting more than his choice of attire.

Robert took a step back. "I wouldn't want you to do that," he said, forcing himself to smile. Then, "I purchased Colin a pony yesterday. Was it delivered?"

"Yes. That was thoughtful of you," Venetia answered. "Colin has begun to think of you as the father he never knew. What a pity that Gavin didn't live long enough to know his own son."

"Accidents sometimes happen," Robert replied. He hoped she wouldn't mention Louisa. Talking about his deceased wife brought back unpleasant memories. How Venetia could speak without emotion about her own sister's untimely death always amazed him.

"I'm riding with Lady Griffiths in Hyde Park," Venetia said. "Would you care to join us?"

"Dressed as I am, I would only embarrass you," Robert said, refusing her invitation.

"Changing won't take long," Venetia countered. "I'll wait."

"I haven't the time."

"Will you return later for Colin's birthday celebration?" she asked.

"I wouldn't consider missing my nephew's fifth birthday," Robert said.

"Later we can attend the Randolphs' ball," Venetia said with a smile.

"I have a previous engagement," he told her.

Her smile disappeared. "With that mistress of yours?"

Robert heard the jealous tone in her voice. "Excuse me," he said. "I must speak with my father." He turned to leave the foyer, but Venetia stopped him in his tracks.

"My sister has been dead for four years," she called. "When will you cease mourning her passing?"

Robert stared at her for a long moment. "One of us should mourn her," he said finally, and left the foyer.

Good God, he wished his sister-in-law would leave him alone, Robert thought as he hurried up the stairs and then walked down the corridor to his father's study. Venetia wanted him merely so she could become a duchess when his father died. She and his nephew would never want for anything. Why did Venetia feel the need to torment him with her presence? She'd been trying unsuccessfully to seduce him into marriage for years.

Without knocking on the door, Robert walked into his father's study. He gazed for a long moment at the older man and decided that his father had aged since Gavin's passing.

The study was a man's room. His father sat behind an enormous mahogany desk. High windows behind the desk allowed sunlight to bathe the chamber. On one side of the room was a marble hearth and mantel, above which hung a portrait of Robert's deceased mother.

Bookcases had been built into the walls, and above them perched portraits of every Campbell laird since the beginning of time. His father had even commissioned an artist to paint the images of ancient ancestors from descriptions only.

Robert had always loved this chamber. As a boy,

he would stare at the faces of these long-dead Campbells and wonder what they would think of him. When his father passed away, the awesome responsibility of being Campbell laird and the Duke of Inverary would fall upon his shoulders. A daunting prospect for a boy.

"Come in," the Duke of Inverary said dryly. He dropped his dark gaze to his son's attire, and his lips quirked in a smile. "I suppose you were turning heads on Park Lane."

Robert shrugged and sat down in a chair in front of his father's desk. He smiled sheepishly, thinking his father had the unique talent of making him feel like a boy.

"Wool and grain prices have dropped again," Duke Magnus said without preamble. "Someone keeps undercutting our prices."

"Alexander Emerson still blames me for Louisa's death," Robert said.

"Colin will inherit if you don't marry and sire an heir," his father said, leaning back in his chair. "Why would Alexander undercut his own nephew's profits?"

Robert waved away his father's silent offer of a drink. "Alexander's bitterness prevents him from seeing beyond his own revenge," he said, unconcerned. "Let him have his way for now. When he does us real damage, I'll put an end to it. Speaking of grain, I still believe we can make a fortune by distilling Scotch whiskey for commercial sale."

"I'm listening," Duke Magnus said.

"No one can make a whiskey to compare with ours," Robert continued, leaning forward in his chair. "Only in Scotland can be found spring water that rises through red granite and then passes through peat moss."

"But is commercial distillation feasible?" his father asked.

"I have several men working on inventing a machine for continuous distillation," Robert told him.

"Let me know if these inventors of yours come up with something," the duke said. Then he changed the subject, asking, "Are you entering the London Golf Match this year?"

Robert relaxed back in his chair. "I wouldn't miss the thrill of golfing down Pall Mall and St. James's Street."

"Ah, if only I were twenty years younger," his father said. After a silent moment, he changed the subject again, remarking, "By the way, Charles Emerson broached the matter of a possible match between you and Venetia."

"No," Robert said, his tone emphatic. He knew his father too well to believe this was a casual conversation.

"Louisa has been dead for four years," his father argued.

"Damn it! I know how long she's been dead," Robert snapped, his patience strained by his father's echoing of his sister-in-law's words. "I have lived with it every day."

"Remember to whom you are speaking," the duke admonished him.

"I apologize."

"You cannot blame yourself for Louisa's passing," the duke said.

"Father, I do not wish to speak about this," Robert insisted.

"You need a wife and children," Duke Magnus pressed on.

The image of Angelica Douglas arose in Robert's mind's eye. Her mane of streaked blond hair, her heavenly blue eyes, her inviting lips—a seductive angel with loaded dice.

"I need no wife or children," Robert said gruffly, realizing in embarrassment that his father was staring at him. "Colin will be my heir."

"If Venetia remarries or returns to her father's home, the Campbell heir will be controlled by others," his father argued.

"Venetia won't leave."

"How can you be certain?"

"Venetia enjoys the accommodations and status of being a Campbell," Robert said with a cynical smile. "We are one of the richest families in Britain." Without preamble, he asked, "What do you know about the Earl of Melrose?"

"Graham Douglas?" Duke Magnus said in obvious surprise. "We were the best of friends, but I haven't seen him in ten years. Why do you ask?"

"What happened to your friendship?" Robert evaded the question.

"Nothing happened," the duke answered. "Melrose and his family disappeared about ten years ago. Emerson told me Graham was living in Europe. I searched for him, but—"

"I found him," Robert interrupted.

Obviously shocked, Duke Magnus rose from his chair. "Where is he?"

"Relax, Father."

"I want to know everything," Duke Magnus said, taking his seat again.

"I want to know how Melrose lost his fortune," Robert said. "Did he drink it away?"

"Graham never touched alcohol," his father told him. "He always said it clouded his mind. I was in Scotland at the time Graham suffered his loss, but heard later that several men, including Charles Emerson, had swindled a great deal of money out of him. With his fortune made, Emerson managed to gain the Winchester title. Later Emerson purchased Graham's estate for a piddling sum."

"And you allowed Gavin and me to marry into a family like that?" Robert asked, surprised, leaning forward in his chair.

"Gavin was in love," Duke Magnus said with a shrug. "I could no more prevent his marriage than I can get you into one. Now, where can I find Graham?"

"Seeking him out would not be a good idea," Robert told him. "The man is an alcoholic and living in poverty."

"I cannot believe—"

"I met his oldest daughter at the fair yesterday," Robert continued, his voice softening at the thought of Angelica Douglas. "She was running a thimblerigger's game and cheating outrageously at dice."

"Oh, I must help them."

"I'll help her."

Duke Magnus cocked a dark brow at his son. "Her?"

The old fox certainly picked up on that slip of the tongue, Robert thought. "Angelica Douglas seems to be the head of the family."

"She can't be more than eighteen years old."

"Her father is in no condition to take care of anyone," Robert said. "I'll let you know when he's sobered up. Perhaps then—" His voice trailed off.

"Angelica was a lovely child," the duke said with a smile of remembrance. "Is she still pretty?"

"Beyond pretty," Robert answered, rising from his chair. "I promised to visit today. Her father nearly killed himself yesterday by drinking a bottle of lavender perfume."

Duke Magnus winced. Then he remarked, "You seem interested in the girl."

Robert refused to reply. Without another word, he crossed the study to the door.

"You must be interested if you won't respond to me," his father called.

Robert heard the laughter in his father's voice. "Remember, Your Grace, make no matches for me."

A few miles and a world away from Park Lane, Angelica fed Jasper a breakfast consisting of sunflower seeds, peanuts, and fresh water. She left the cage open and then turned toward the window. Sunlight streamed into the room, promising a perfect summer day.

"Great grunting shit," Jasper swore loudly. "Drink, drink, drink."

Angelica looked over her shoulder at the macaw. The bird had learned the most vulgar words and phrases from her father.

"Great grunting . . . drink, drink, drink."

When the bird repeated its words, an idea popped into Angelica's mind. She hurried across the chamber to the pot used for hiding money. Lifting the plant, she felt inside.

The pot was empty. One hundred and twenty-eight pounds plus her sisters' earnings had disappeared.

"Aunt Roxie," Angelica called.

"Roxie! Roxie!" Jasper mimicked her.

"Good morning, darling," Aunt Roxie said, breezing out of her chamber. "I sent Samantha and Victoria to search for chickweed, larkspur, and other necessary midsummer herbs. I feel my clients will need some advice today."

"The money is missing," Angelica announced.

"I managed to hide a hundred pounds in my chamber before your father confiscated it," her aunt told her, pouring tea into a cup.

"Where is my father?" Angelica asked, irritated that he'd stolen her hard-earned money.

"Graham went to find himself a bottle of peace," Aunt Roxie answered. She shrugged and asked, "What could I do, darling? I didn't want him poisoning himself again."

Angelica opened her mouth to reply, but the sound of horses drew her attention. She crossed the room to the window and said, "You have a customer—Lucille Dubois."

Aunt Roxie wrinkled her nose in distaste. Then she pasted a dimpled smile on her face and opened the door for her guest. "Mademoiselle Dubois, what a wonderful surprise."

Dark-haired, green-eyed, and voluptuous, Lucille Dubois walked into the cottage and glanced with disdain around the cramped quarters. With her was her four-year-old daughter, Daisy.

"Madame Roxanne, I desperately need a reading and a potion to bring—I mean, keep my lover content. Can this be done?"

"Of course, darling," Aunt Roxie drawled. She smiled winsomely and added, "However, it will be expensive."

"The money will be well-spent," the woman replied.

"We require privacy," Aunt Roxie said to Angelica. "Take Daisy into the garden."

Angelica grabbed her harp and smiled at the little girl. She held out her hand, saying, "Come with me, Daisy."

Daisy accepted her hand without hesitation and

held up a small basket. "I've brought Jasper some green apples."

"Jasper adores green apples," Angelica said.

"Take the bird with you," Lucille ordered.

Followed by the macaw, Angelica and Daisy walked outside and around the cottage to the small garden. When Angelica breathed deeply of summer's intoxicating scent, Daisy imitated her.

"Sit here beneath this oak tree," Angelica said, plopping down on the ground. She reached for the girl's arm to help her down.

"Ouch!"

"Did I hurt you?" Her touch on the girl had been light.

"My arm hurts," Daisy said.

Angelica set the basket down in front of Jasper, who immediately began crunching on the crisp green apples. Then she reached for the sleeve of the girl's gown and pushed it up.

Purple bruises ran up Daisy's right arm. Her left arm had the same discoloration.

"Did you fall?" Angelica asked.

"No," Daisy answered, gazing at her through enormous dark eyes that seemed vaguely familiar.

"Did you bump into something?"

"No."

"How did you get hurt?"

Daisy shrugged.

"You can share your secrets with me," Angelica coaxed her.

"Lucille says I'm the naughtiest girl," Daisy told her.

"Lucille?"

"*Mother* makes Lucille feel old," Daisy whispered, as if divulging a secret.

What kind of woman deprived her own child of the right to call her mother? Angelica wondered.

Daisy needed a mother, not someone she called Lucille.

"Did Lucille give you these bruises?" she asked.

Daisy looked away, saying, "I don't remember."

Bull's pizzle, Angelica thought, with anger swelling inside her. How could any woman injure her own child? The harlot was unnatural. But what could she do to prevent such cruelty from happening again?

"Lift your chin for me," Angelica said, picking a daisy from the grass. She held the flower under the girl's chin and said, "Oh, I see that you adore butter."

Daisy laughed and clapped her hands together. "How did you know?" she cried.

"If this daisy reflects yellow beneath your chin," Angelica explained, "then you love butter."

"Let me try." Daisy held the flower under Angelica's chin and exclaimed, "You love butter, too."

"Yes, I do. Shall I play my harp?" Angelica asked. "Or do you want to lay on our backs and see the cloud pictures in the sky?"

"Daisy, darling," Aunt Roxie called from the window, "Lucille is leaving now."

"I wish I could stay here forever," Daisy said, throwing herself into Angelica's arms. "Then I could look at cloud pictures every day and listen to your harp every night."

"I wish you could stay here, too," Angelica said, rising from the grass. "But Lucille would miss you."

Taking the girl's hand in hers, Angelica escorted her around to the front of the cottage. She hesitated for a moment and then asked the other woman, "Would it be possible for Daisy to spend the day here? You could send your carriage for her after supper. Or tomorrow morning, perhaps?"

Lucille Dubois stared at Angelica as if she'd

grown another head. Looking down her nose at her, she said, "Daisy's father is an important man. She couldn't possibly pass the night in this hovel."

Angelica flinched as if she'd been struck. Then she felt her aunt's hand on her shoulder, calming her.

"Get in the carriage," Lucille ordered her daughter.

"But I want to—"

Lucille grabbed the girl's upper arm and gave her a violent shake. "What did I tell you about being naughty? If you cry, I'll give you something more to cry about."

Daisy scrambled to climb into the carriage. The little girl gave Angelica a forlorn look.

"We'll play next time," Angelica assured her. Watching the carriage retreat down the road, she whispered, "I despise that bitch."

"Thinking about the uncontrollable is a waste of time, darling," Aunt Roxie said.

Angelica nodded. She knew her aunt was correct but couldn't recapture her earlier good mood. Her father's drinking and Lucille Dubois's cruelty had destroyed it.

"Please take Jasper inside," she said. "I want to be alone."

"Of course, darling," Aunt Roxie said. "Come, Jasper."

Frustrated by her inability to help the little girl, Angelica returned to the garden and sat beneath the oak tree. She leaned back against its massive trunk and felt its comforting strength.

Angelica wished there was something she could do for Daisy Dubois. She could only imagine the miserable life the girl endured with that woman. Pretty gowns and fashionable addresses could never replace a mother's love.

Trying to soothe herself, Angelica began to play her harp. The serenade, an atmospheric bath of sound, grew and faded and then grew again. Her song evoked a celestial wind, a broad expanse of blue sky, a bubbling brook winding its way through a valley.

"You play like an angel."

Surprised, Angelica looked up and then smiled. There stood Robert Roy, a devastating smile lighting his face.

He *is* Old Clootie, she thought. Only the devil could be that handsome.

Angelica patted the ground beside herself in invitation, and he accepted. She began to doubt her own common sense when she realized that the side of his muscled thigh touched hers.

Sacred sevens, she thought, shivering from the heat coursing through her body. Why did this stranger affect her so intensely?

"How is your father?" Robert asked.

"He has recovered sufficiently to steal my money and take himself drinking," Angelica answered, a rueful tone in her voice.

"I'm sorry."

"Apologizing is unnecessary," she told him. "My father's illness is not your fault."

"Whose fault is it?" he asked, his black gaze holding hers captive.

Angelica wondered how much to tell him. He had saved her father's life and let her win a large sum of money. Judging from his attire, he wasn't a rich man. And yet, he did possess the bearing of a gentleman.

She decided to trust him. Perhaps Robert Roy could help her scheme for revenge. He could gain entry into more places than she.

"Five men are responsible for my father's illness," Angelica said. "Magnus Campbell, Charles Emerson, Alasdair Trimble, Henry Drinkwater, and Archibald Mayhew."

"Archibald Mayhew is dead," Robert told her.

His announcement surprised her. Who was this Rob Roy, a man in wrinkled clothing, to know members of the upper class? Was he a gentleman who'd fallen upon hard times? If that were true, why had he been willing to lose a hundred and twenty-eight pounds to her?

"Archibald has a son, Mungo," Robert added.

"Then Mungo Mayhew will pay for his father's sins," she replied.

"That doesn't seem fair to me," he said. "Do you pay for your father's sins?"

"Every day of my life," Angelica answered bitterly, gazing into his black eyes.

Robert inclined his head. "What is your plan?"

"I intend to pauper them at the gaming table," Angelica announced.

Robert laughed. "You mean cheat them at the gaming table," he corrected her.

"I am willing to do whatever it takes," she told him.

"Ladies are not allowed in gaming halls, angel," Robert reminded her.

"You could gain entrance in my place," Angelica said, touching his arm. She rushed on before he could refuse. "You carry yourself like a gentleman, and I could share all my knowledge with you."

"What knowledge?" Robert asked, smiling.

"I could teach you to cheat without getting caught." She glanced at his wrinkled attire and added, "Obviously, you have fallen upon hard times, too. Not only would I be willing to give you twenty percent of whatever you win, but you would carry that knowledge with you for the rest of your life."

Robert stared across the garden and appeared to be pondering her proposition. Finally, he looked at her and said, "Fifty percent."

"Twenty-five percent."

"We have a deal."

"I need to fetch my dice and cards," Angelica said, rising. "You'll stay for dinner, of course."

Robert stood when she did. "I have a previous engagement but will return tomorrow."

"I understand," Angelica said, unable to hide her disappointment.

"How about sealing our bargain with a kiss?" Robert asked, stepping closer.

Angelica felt a heated blush rising upon her cheeks. She glanced in the direction of the cottage and stammered, "My aunt—"

"Your aunt is not watching," Robert said, taking another step toward her.

Angelica stepped back and felt the trunk of the oak tree preventing further retreat. Trapped against the tree, Angelica had no way or desire to escape.

Robert captured her lips in a kiss that stole her breath away and made her senses reel. His insistent lips parted hers, and his tongue explored the sweetness of her mouth, sending ripples of desire dancing down her spine.

Without taking his lips from hers, Robert traced a finger down her silken cheek. He slid his hand down the column of her throat and then lower. His caress on her breast was seductively light.

Angelica moaned low in her throat. Unaware of what she was doing, Angelica entwined her arms around his neck and returned his kiss in kind.

"Swear that you won't go to the fair or engage

in any gambling," Robert whispered against her lips.

"I promise." Angelica closed her eyes for another kiss.

"Until tomorrow, angel," Robert said, and planted a chaste kiss on her lips. He turned away, whistled for his horse, and left the garden.

Angelica leaned back against the oak tree. Closing her eyes, she raised her fingertips to her lips and tried to recapture the incredible feeling of his lips covering hers.

"Bravo, darling," Aunt Roxie called from the window. " 'Twas well done of you."

Angelica groaned and burned with shame. Her aunt had witnessed her wanton behavior and sounded as if she actually approved.

Oh, Lord, Angelica thought. This mysterious stranger had kissed her, and she'd enjoyed it, had even wanted more. Did he affect every woman that way? Only her? How would she ever face him again?

And then a smile touched her lips. When he returned, she would pretend nothing had happened between them. She only hoped that he would kiss her again.

"Don't worry, darling," Aunt Roxie called from the window. "The man is hot for you."

Chapter 3

He wanted to kiss her again.

Sitting in the Campbell box at the Royal Opera House, Robert smiled at the bent of his thoughts. He couldn't get her out of his mind and wanted to do more to his Primrose Hill angel than kiss her. Feeling their naked bodies entwined and pressed intimately together appealed to him. He could hardly wait to initiate her into the ways of carnal love and mold her into whatever pleased him.

Robert smiled with anticipated satisfaction. How many men of his acquaintance were fortunate enough to deflower their mistresses?

"The woman on stage is dying," Duke Magnus whispered. "Why are you smiling?"

Robert glanced at his father and assumed a suitably somber expression. He always attended the opera alone to think and disliked being bothered. Tonight, he'd been saddled with his father and his sister-in-law.

Without taking her gaze off the stage, Venetia

leaned close and whispered, "I hope you'll reconsider and come to Lord Randolph's with us. My father and brother are meeting us there."

Robert stared through the semidarkness at her perfect profile. He dropped his gaze to her cleavage and knew her display of flesh was for his benefit. Her flawless ivory skin looked soft and oh-so-inviting.

"I've made other plans," Robert said, standing, deciding he'd had enough of the opera. He nodded to his father, left the Campbell box, and walked outside.

The warm night seemed almost magical. A low mist clung to the ground and swirled around his legs, but stars shone overhead.

"Mack, take me home," he instructed his driver.

Robert leaned back in his carriage. He wasn't tired at all and knew he would never sleep, but going to White's for a nightcap held no appeal to him. He wanted only one thing at the moment.

The ride to Park Lane took fifteen minutes. When the carriage halted, Robert climbed into the front seat and lifted the reins out of his driver's hands.

"What are you doing?" Mack asked in surprise.

"I'm going to visit a friend."

"If you start driving yourself," the man complained, "I'll soon be unemployed."

"I'm giving you a paid holiday," Robert told him. "Make the most of it."

"Thank you, my lord." Mack climbed out of the carriage.

Robert drove in the direction of Primrose Hill. He knew he was behaving like a schoolboy, but he'd never felt this way about any woman. Too bad her father had bankrupted the family. If circumstances had been different, he would have married his angel in a heartbeat. On the other hand, marriage might tarnish her allure.

After midnight, Robert stopped his carriage in front of the pink stucco cottage. Staring at the darkened windows, Robert wondered what Angelica was doing at that moment. Was she dreaming of him?

In spite of a few eccentricities, Angelica Douglas had more honor and gentility in her little finger than any woman of his acquaintance. At the tender age of eighteen, she bore the heavy burden of her family's survival and wore this cloak of duty with grace. She was more than worthy to be his mistress, and he knew she was a woman who would never stray into another man's arms.

Robert closed his eyes and conjured her hauntingly lovely image. Her blue eyes made him feel as if he were drowning in a Highland loch, her full lips begged to be kissed, and her streaked blond hair topped with that crown of flowers had lent her an ethereal, otherworldly appearance.

"Bull's pizzle!"

The voice in the darkness sounded exactly like his sweet angel's.

"Darling, a lady never—"

"Be quiet!" The voices emanating from the garden belonged to Angelica and Aunt Roxie.

"We need the money," a third voice argued.

"Samantha is correct," said a fourth voice.

The sisters, Robert thought. Just what in hell was happening back there?

Robert climbed out of the carriage and walked silently around the side of the cottage. He saw the soft glow from a lantern as he neared the garden. Pausing at the corner of the cottage, he watched them for a moment.

"How disrespectful to poor Mr. Lewis," Aunt

Roxie said, shaking her head in obvious disapproval.

"I don't give a fig about that," Angelica snapped. She rounded on her sisters and asked, "Do you want to hang on Tyburn Hill?"

"What is the problem?" Robert asked, stepping into the garden.

All four women cried out in surprise. Angelica and her sisters drew their daggers.

"It's Robert."

"Sacred sevens, what are you doing here?" Angelica asked.

"You've been on my mind all day," Robert said easily, walking toward her. "I couldn't wait until tomorrow to see you."

"How sublimely romantic," Aunt Roxie sighed, making her two younger nieces giggle.

Robert placed the palm of his hand against Angelica's burning cheek. She was blushing again.

"Can I be of service?" he asked.

"Mr. Roy, you are heaven-sent," Samantha said.

"We need help with Mr. Lewis," Victoria added.

Confused, Robert stared at them blankly. Then he glanced at the ground and spied a corpse in burial clothes.

"Good God, what is this?" he demanded.

"This is Mr. Lewis," Angelica told him.

"I don't care what—"

"Girls, I forbid you to sell Mr. Lewis to those surgeons," Aunt Roxie interrupted.

"Sell him to—?" Robert rounded on Angelica and asked, "Have you robbed a grave?"

"Mr. Lewis will bring us good money," Victoria argued. "Ten pounds, at least."

"We misjudged his weight and had the devil of a time dragging him here," Samantha added. "How will we get him to the surgeons?"

"We could have managed if you didn't have that damned limp," Victoria told her sister.

"If it weren't for me," Samantha countered, "you would still be trying to read those tombstones."

Ignoring her sister, Victoria turned to Robert, asking, "May we use your horse?"

"Everyone will go back inside the cottage," Robert ordered, taking charge of the situation. *"Now."*

"What about Mr. Lewis?" Aunt Roxie asked.

"Mr. Lewis isn't going anywhere," Robert told her.

Aunt Roxie, Samantha, and Victoria marched around the cottage to the front door. Behind them walked Robert and Angelica, carrying the lantern.

"I'm sorry you had to witness this," Angelica said. "I had nothing to do with Mr. Lewis's abduction."

"Be thankful I drove out here tonight," Robert said, "or the lot of you would have hanged." Once inside the cottage, he ordered, "Sit down, ladies."

Aunt Roxie and the girls sat on the settee in front of the summer-darkened hearth. Only Angelica remained standing.

"Hello," the macaw called from inside his blanket-covered cage.

"Good night," Angelica called to the bird.

"Good night."

Robert ran a hand through his black hair and wondered what kind of an asylum he'd stepped into. No wonder the earl had lost his fortune. The whole damned Douglas family was mad.

Robert turned to Angelica, whose gaze was fixed on his formal evening attire. She looked surprised.

"Your revenge requires that I renew some old acquaintances," he said by way of an explanation. Without giving her a chance to think, he asked, "Where is your father?"

Angelica shrugged. "My father won't return until he needs drinking money."

Though it made him uncomfortable, Robert decided to play the role of father. He turned to raven-haired Samantha and asked, "How old are you?"

"Seventeen," she answered.

"And you?" he asked the flame-haired Victoria.

"Sixteen."

"Have either of you ever witnessed a hanging?" Robert asked, his voice filling with anger. "Let me tell you what happens to a—"

"Please don't," Aunt Roxie cried. "My nieces are delicate creatures who couldn't endure the shock, and speaking of vile things will bring us bad luck."

Robert inclined his head and then turned his attention again to the delicate creatures who'd dragged Mr. Lewis out of his coffin. "Hanging is an unpleasant death."

"The money is worth the risk," Samantha told him.

"We were lucky no one else tried to steal Mr. Lewis," Victoria agreed with her sister. "There are organized gangs that steal bodies, you know."

"You little blockheads, the anatomical schools are in session from October to May," Robert informed them. "There's no demand for corpses in the summer."

Aunt Roxie burst out laughing. Angelica covered her mouth with her hands and tried to stifle the laughter bubbling up in her throat.

Robert flicked a glance at her but managed to maintain a stern expression. "Samantha and Victoria, go to your room, and do not dare show your faces until morning," he ordered.

The two younger Douglas girls rose from their

chairs and headed for their bedroom. After she'd passed him, Victoria stuck her tongue out at his back.

"We'll need a shovel to put Mr. Lewis back into his grave," Robert told Angelica.

"We left ours there," Samantha called from the doorway. "We couldn't manage the shovel and Mr. Lewis."

"Take the lantern," Robert ordered Angelica.

"What shall I do?" Aunt Roxie asked.

"Guard those two miscreants."

Stepping outside the cottage, Angelica glanced sidelong at Robert. Almost magically, he had appeared to rescue her and her family.

"We'll drive into the garden," Robert told her. "I don't want anyone to see me loading Mr. Lewis into my carriage."

"Thank you," Angelica said, touching his arm. "I appreciate your help."

"Damsels in distress are my specialty," he said, smiling at her in the darkness.

Robert helped her onto the carriage and handed her the lantern. Climbing up beside her, he drove the carriage into the garden.

"Leather seats?" Angelica remarked. "How did you manage—?"

"I borrowed it," Robert said, helping her down. "Bring the lantern over here."

Angelica held up the lantern. She expected him to lift Mr. Lewis into his arms. Instead, he began undressing the old man.

"What are you doing?" Angelica asked in a horrified whisper.

"Being caught with a corpse is not illegal unless it's dressed in burial clothes," Robert told her without looking up.

Bull's pizzle, Angelica thought. Her first sight of

a man's nakedness would be dead Mr. Lewis. Oh, she could cheerfully choke her sisters and sell *their* bodies to the surgeons.

"We'll bury these in the garden when we return," Robert said, setting the man's clothing aside.

Angelica refused to look at Mr. Lewis's naked body. She blushed when she heard Robert chuckling at her reaction and was glad the darkness hid her embarrassment.

"The graveyard awaits us," Robert said, setting the body inside the carriage.

"I don't find this situation particularly amusing," Angelica said primly, settling herself atop the carriage and taking the lantern out of his hand.

"Someday, angel, we'll laugh about this night," he replied, climbing onto the driver's seat beside her.

Angelica marveled at the quietness of the night. She'd never been out this late. The only sound was the horses pulling the carriage down the road.

A few minutes later, Robert halted the carriage outside the graveyard. He leaped off the driver's seat and then helped Angelica down.

Robert lifted the dead man out of the carriage. After positioning the body over his shoulder, he turned toward the graveyard. A low mist blanketed the ground. Only the tops of the tombstones were clearly visible at a distance.

"I don't like this," Angelica said, frightened by the sight of the graveyard. "Let's leave him here."

"If we did that, the authorities would investigate," Robert told her. "I think we had better put Mr. Lewis back where he belongs."

"Spirits roam at night," she argued. "What if his spirit—?"

"Pass me the lantern. I'll go alone."

"And leave me here?"

"I haven't mastered the trick of being in two places at once," Robert said with laughter lurking in his voice.

Angelica realized she'd be safer with him than waiting alone. Summoning her courage, she squared her shoulders and ordered, "Lead the way."

"You have the lantern," he reminded her.

Angelica held up the lantern and forced herself to step into the graveyard. After wandering around for several minutes, she found the opened grave. Beside it lay her sisters' shovel.

Robert set Mr. Lewis down and rested his shoulder for a moment. Then he lifted the lantern and said, "Shit."

"What's wrong?" Angelica asked, beginning to panic.

"Your sisters dug out the entire grave," he answered.

"How else could they abduct Mr. Lewis?"

"Professionals only dig the top of the grave and then pull the body out by the shoulders," Robert explained.

"How do you know?"

"I have friends in low places."

Without bothering about the casket, Robert pushed Mr. Lewis into the opened grave and picked up the shovel. Then he began tossing dirt onto the corpse.

"Why don't we put him inside the coffin?" Angelica asked.

"I assure you, angel, Mr. Lewis doesn't know the difference," he replied, and tossed another shovelful of dirt onto the man.

"I'm sorry my sisters disturbed you, Mr. Lewis,"

Angelica said, fingering her diamond pendant for protection. "Please accept my apology."

Robert burst out laughing.

With her hands on her hips, Angelica rounded on him and asked, "What do you find so amusing? Sacred sevens, the plague must bring tears of mirth to your eyes."

"I never heard anyone apologize to a dead man before," Robert told her. "I find your kindness endearing."

"Thank you."

In silence, Angelica watched him work. Though their task was morbid, she couldn't help but admire the way he looked by lantern light. Those borrowed evening clothes fit him as perfectly as if they'd been custom-made for him.

A perfect specimen of manhood, Robert Roy had dropped into her life like Prince Charming coming to her rescue. Perhaps someday, when her revenge was complete, they could have a life together. She had no dowry and never expected to catch any man's attention.

"Thank you, God," Angelica whispered her thought out loud.

"Did you say something?" Robert asked, and held the shovel out to her.

"No," she answered, blushing.

Without complaint, Angelica took the shovel out of his hand. She pitched it into the mound of earth and then tossed the dirt with such ferocity that she toppled headfirst into the grave.

Robert laughed and pulled her out, saying, "You don't know your own strength, angel."

Angelica smiled in spite of being covered with dirt. Robert lifted the shovel out of her hands and finished filling the grave. Together, they replaced the flowers the mourners had left for Mr. Lewis.

"Thank you for your help," Angelica said, settling herself onto the carriage again.

"The pleasure was mine."

The sky had lightened considerably by the time they reached the cottage. Dawn was only moments away.

First Robert and Angelica disposed of Mr. Lewis's burial clothes. Then they watered the horses.

"Is there anyplace we can wash?" he asked.

For a long moment, Angelica worried her lip in indecision. She should probably retire now and send him home, but she couldn't bring herself to part from him.

"There is a stream on the other side of the woods," she told him.

"We don't need the lantern," Robert said, glancing up at the brightening sky. "We do need soap, though."

Surprising them, a cake of soap flew out of a bedroom window. "Darlings, wash the grime away before you come inside," Aunt Roxie called, her smile feline in the growing light.

Robert chuckled. "I think your aunt likes me."

Already walking toward the woodland, Angelica blushed and said nothing. Her aunt was an incorrigible matchmaker, bent on seeing her penniless nieces well-placed in marriage.

Oak and beech trees stretched their ancient limbs and thrust green fingers skyward. Lush foliage in every shade of green lay on either side of the well-worn path, and wildflowers mingling with moss scented the air in the woodland. Emerging from the woods, Angelica saw that the morning mist on the stream was beginning to dissipate.

Graceful willows with drooping limbs dotted the banks of the stream, and Angelica reached out to touch one. "I love these trees," she murmured.

Robert and Angelica sat down at the stream's edge to remove their boots and stockings. He stood first, pulled his shirt over his head, and then dropped his breeches.

Sacred sevens, the man is naked, Angelica thought, staring with wide eyes at his backside. He looked nothing like Mr. Lewis.

Mesmerized by his masculine beauty, Angelica admired his broad shoulders, his tapered waist, his tight buttocks. What would it feel like to have his strength pressing her down? She snapped her eyes shut when he moved to turn around.

"Were you planning on bathing," Robert asked, "or blushing yourself clean?"

Angelica heard the laughter in his voice, but her mind remained humiliatingly blank. No witty reply slipped from her lips, nor could she summon the courage to look at him.

"You're naked," she said in a choked whisper.

"Yes, I am," he agreed. "Do you bathe with your clothes on?"

Angelica shook her head but kept her eyes shut.

"There's nothing to fear," Robert assured her. "The cold water will probably shrivel me."

"What do you mean?"

Robert chuckled. "Never mind, my innocent angel. I'll sit in the water so my privates aren't exposed."

Angelica opened her eyes when she heard the splash of water as he sat down. She couldn't suppress a bubble of laughter when she saw him sitting in the stream and smiling at her.

"Your turn, angel."

Angelica stood slowly. She dropped her skirt and pulled her blouse over her head. "Please close your eyes until I'm sitting in the water," she said. "Your watching me disrobe makes me feel . . ."

"Embarrassed?"

"Quite."

Robert closed his eyes. He'd assumed she would wear her chemise, but if she was willing to strip down to nothing, he wasn't going to stop her.

A long, silent moment passed. He heard her wade into the water and then plop down beside him.

"Sacred sevens," Angelica cried. "The water doesn't cover—"

Robert opened his eyes. Her perfectly rounded breasts with their pink-tipped nipples rose above the water.

She moved to shield her breasts from his view, but Robert stayed her hand. "Let me see your beauty," he said, his voice husky.

"I'm not beautiful," Angelica said, but dropped her arms. She stared at him through disarming blue eyes large with wonder.

"You are incredibly beautiful," Robert whispered, lowering his head. He covered her mouth in a gentle, persuasive kiss.

Angelica relaxed against him and surrendered to him.

She's ripe for me, Robert thought, slipping his right arm around her shoulder.

He slid the tip of his tongue across the crease between her lips, which parted for him. He kissed her lingeringly, his tongue exploring the sweetness of her mouth.

With his left hand, Robert caressed her breasts. He ran his fingers across her nipples and teased them into aroused hardness.

"Your nipples are sensitive, a sure sign of a passionate nature," he whispered, hearing her ragged breathing. "Do you like my touch, angel?"

"Oh, yes," Angelica said on a sigh. She reached

up and caressed the hand that was bringing her such pleasure.

"Lady, you are exquisite," Robert said, standing and lifting her into his arms.

Noting her dazed expression, Robert kissed her again and then carried her out of the water. Gently, he placed her down on a blanket of grass and lay down beside her.

Robert circled her nipple with one long finger. Then he dipped his head and kissed her again.

Pausing a moment to gaze at her expression, Robert knew the angel in his arms was neatly caught by these new, exciting sensations. Her nipples hardened beneath his gaze, and he leaned down to catch one in his mouth, making her moan.

"What are you going to do?" Angelica asked in a breathless whisper.

"I'm going to taste your beautiful breasts," Robert answered thickly, and flicked his tongue out to tease a nipple. He slid his hand down the length of her silken body to caress the inside of her thighs, whispering, "I'll make you quiver for me."

Angelica moaned and turned in his embrace, his touch and his words making her senses reel. Her young body on fire, she was powerless to resist. For the first time in her life, she experienced the incredible sensation of masculine hardness touching her feminine softness.

"You are wet for me, angel," Robert said, sliding his finger to her dewy pearl. "I want to join our bodies and make us one."

Robert kissed her thoroughly, stealing her breath away. His hands caressed her flesh while his lips moved down the column of her throat and beyond. Catching a nipple with his mouth, Robert suckled and nipped and licked it. Then he lavished the same attention on its mate, igniting a throbbing heat between her thighs.

"I want you," she breathed.

"Spread your legs for me," he whispered, his lips returning to hers.

Without hesitation, Angelica did as she was told. Robert kissed her and inserted one long finger inside her.

She moved in surprise, impaling herself on his finger. He groaned, feeling her wet softness throbbing against his finger.

"Relax, angel," Robert whispered. He kissed her again and inserted a second finger inside her, murmuring, "You are so wonderfully tight."

He dipped his head to her breasts and suckled her aroused nipples. His fingers began to move rhythmically, seductively, inside her.

Robert felt her relax. She began to move her hips, enticing his fingers deeper inside her.

"You were created for passion," he said in a husky voice.

Angelica moaned low in her throat. Her hips moved faster and faster.

Removing his fingers, Robert knelt between her thighs. The knob of his manhood slid back and forth, teasing her dewy pearl in a seductive assault, making her moan.

With one powerful thrust, Robert pushed himself inside her and broke through her virgin's barrier. She cried out in surprise, and he lay still for several moments.

Judging her accustomed to the feel of him inside her, Robert began to move seductively, enticing her to move with him. Caught in the midst of swirling passion, Angelica instinctively wrapped her legs around his waist and moved with him, meeting each of his magnificent thrusts with her own.

Suddenly, unexpectedly, Angelica exploded as wave after wave of throbbing sensation washed over her. Knowing she'd found fulfillment, Robert groaned and shuddered and poured his seed deep within her.

Robert rolled off her, pulled her into his embrace, and kissed her. Finally, he stood and offered her his hand.

When she accepted it, Robert pulled her up and yanked her against the long, muscular planes of his body. He kissed her again and again, one kiss melting into another.

When he released her, Robert scooped up her chemise and drew it over her head. After patting it into place, he reached for her blouse.

"You don't need to do that," Angelica said, embarrassed to meet his gaze.

"I want to dress you," Robert told her. "It pleases me." After helping her into her blouse and skirt, he dressed himself.

Hand in hand, they retraced their path through the woods. He guided the horses around the cottage to the front door.

"I'll return later after you've slept," Robert said, and planted a chaste kiss on her lips. "Why do you look so glum, angel? Do you regret what we have shared?"

Angelica blushed. She'd just experienced one of life's milestones, and he spoke so casually.

"Angel, I want no secrets between us," Robert coaxed, lifting her chin. "Tell me what is wrong."

"My virginity was the only thing of value I possessed," Angelica whispered to his chest. "And—"

"Virginity is decidedly overrated," Robert interrupted. "From now on, I am going to take care of you and your family."

Angelica visibly relaxed and dared to meet his

gaze. "When will we be married?" she asked, giving him a sunny smile.

"I have no intention of marrying again." Robert pulled her close, saying, "I want you to be my mistress. I can afford to—"

Whack! He never saw her right fist coming.

"I am the daughter of an earl and will never be any man's mistress," Angelica told him.

"You're tired and need sleep," Robert told her, squelching the urge to rub his smarting cheek. "I'll return later. You do still want revenge on those men, don't you?"

"You aren't welcome here."

"I saved your father's life and your sisters from a hanging," he reminded her.

"Save yourself the trip," Angelica said before disappearing into the cottage. "I won't open the door."

Chapter 4

She opened the door.

Alone in the cottage, Angelica sat at the table and practiced her card shuffling. She wished the day had been cooler. Then she could have donned a long-sleeved gown and practiced slipping cards out of her sleeve.

Angelica smiled when she glanced across the room at the settee. The slanting rays of the afternoon sun fingered the cottage's common room with light and shadow, as if angels plucked the strings of a harp.

Her smiled disappeared, though, when she recalled Lucille Dubois's words to her about the cottage being a hovel. She preferred to think her home reflected genteel poverty rather than squalor.

Angelica tried hard to banish Robert from her thoughts. What she had done with him at the stream was immoral and unforgivable, and she'd succumbed so easily to his advances. She knew he had a bad opinion of her. He'd asked her to be his mistress, hadn't he?

Well, the dirty scoundrel had better think again about his proposition. She was an earl's daughter, not a scullery maid.

Angelica sighed. She was the impovished daughter of a bankrupt, alcoholic earl, and an expert cheat at the gaming tables. Sacred sevens, she'd been working a thimblerigger's game when Robert had first seen her. No wonder he'd assumed she was free and easy.

"Hello, hello, hello." Jasper drew her from her thoughts.

"Hello, Jasper." Angelica set the cards aside and reached down to scratch the macaw's blue head, making it trill with pleasure.

Bang! Bang! Bang!

"Is anyone home?" The voice belonged to Robert Roy.

Angelica rose from her chair and walked to the door. "Who is it?" she asked.

"Robert."

"Go away," she told the door.

"I apologize for my behavior this morning," he called.

He didn't sound especially sorry, Angelica thought. "Apology accepted," she replied. "Now go away."

"I've brought you a gift," Robert coaxed.

Payment for services rendered, Angelica thought. Then she called, "The only gift I want is for you to go away."

"Away, away," Jasper mimicked her.

"What about your revenge?" Robert asked.

"I don't need you for my revenge," she answered.

"Angelica, open the door," Robert ordered in

a stern voice, his growing frustration apparent. "Or I'll—" He let the implied threat hang in the air.

"Or you'll do what?" Angelica challenged him. "Steal my virginity?"

"I'll . . . I'll huff and puff and blow your house down," he called.

Angelica burst out laughing. She opened the door.

No longer dressed in elegant evening attire, Robert Roy smiled with boyish charm. He held out two roses, one red and one white.

"Love and unity?" Angelica asked, referring to the language of flowers as she lifted the roses out of his hand.

Robert shrugged. Nailed to the wooden door frame above his head was a plant. "What is this?" he asked.

"Wolfsbane to keep you away," Angelica answered, and gave him a sunny smile.

Robert grinned. "It didn't work."

"Neither did this," Angelica replied, reaching into her pocket for a bit of rolled leather.

"What is that?"

"Wolfsbane seed wrapped in lizard's skin is supposed to empower its bearer with invisibility," Angelica told him.

Robert burst out laughing. "May I come in?"

Angelica inclined her head. She stepped aside to allow him entrance.

"Hello," the macaw called.

"Hello, Jasper."

"Great grunting shit," the bird said. "Drink, drink, drink."

"Jasper learned vulgar expressions from my father," Angelica said with an embarrassed smile, a high blush staining her cheeks. She gestured toward the table, saying, "Sit down here."

"Where is the earl?" Robert asked.

Angelica placed the two roses in a glass and sat down opposite him, saying, "My father hasn't returned yet."

"Where are your sisters and aunt?" he asked.

"They've gone out to discover whether there's been any gossip about Mr. Lewis today."

"So we're alone," Robert said, relaxing visibly.

"What happened between us this morning will never happen again," Angelica told him, her blue gaze narrowing on him. "Do you understand?"

"Would you leave me without hope, angel?"

"Yes, I would."

Robert lifted the cards off the table and shuffled them. "What will you do with the winnings from your revenge?" he asked, changing the subject.

"I intend to move my family to Scotland," she answered.

"Scotland?" Robert echoed in obvious surprise.

"My father owns Sweetheart Priory," Angelica told him. "He's forbidden by law to sell it."

"I thought you would move to Park Lane and flaunt your riches," Robert said with a smile.

Angelica laughed at the idea. "What do you do for money, sir?"

"What do you mean?"

"How do you earn your keep?"

"Oh, this and that," he answered with a shrug. "I almost forgot."

Robert rose from the chair and walked outside. Returning a moment later, he held up a green apple. "For Jasper."

"Hold it out to him," Angelica said.

Instead of returning to the table, Robert sat on the settee in front of the hearth. "Come, Jasper," he said, holding out the apple.

The macaw approached him cautiously. Quickly

but gently, the bird lifted the apple out of his hand. Then it shifted the apple from its mouth to its claws and began crunching away.

"Mmmmm," Jasper said.

"He appears to be eating by hand," Robert said with a smile. He glanced over his shoulder at her, saying, "We'll be more comfortable on the settee."

Angelica did not want to sit beside him on the settee. There was danger in being so close to him. And yet, the man was so incredibly handsome.

Reluctantly, Angelica rose from her chair and crossed the room like a woman going to the gallows. She sat down, her body stiff and poised to bolt if he tried to touch her.

"Relax, angel," Robert said. He drew her back against the settee, but his arm remained around her shoulders.

Angelica fixed her gaze on Jasper, the sight of the green apple reminding her of Daisy Dubois. "I would like your advice," she said, turning to him.

"About what, angel?" he asked.

"One of my aunt's clients brought her little girl with her yesterday," Angelica explained. "The poor child had bruises on both arms."

"And?"

"I'm certain the mother inflicted them on her," Angelica continued. "What would you do?"

"I would mind my own business," Robert told her.

"But the child—"

Robert placed one finger across her lips and said, "Angel, you have enough problems without borrowing another's."

"I cannot bear to see children suffer," Angelica told him.

"You have a good heart," Robert said. "Perhaps

when your revenge is complete, you'll have enough money to take the child away from the mother. Until then—"

"I suppose I am in no position to feed another mouth," Angelica replied. She stared into the darkened hearth, and her thoughts traveled through space and time to her own childhood. "You may not believe this, but my father was kind and sensitive and sober before my mother died.

"Every night my father would tell me a story. My favorite was the one about whom I would marry." She smiled with remembrance. "He said I needed to content myself as a duchess instead of a princess. He and his so-called friend, the Duke of Inverary, had decided that I would marry the duke's oldest son. Why are you looking at me so strangely?"

"I had no idea I was in such exalted company," Robert answered.

"The higher one flies, the farther one falls," she replied.

"I am sorry for your loss, angel."

"I don't mind not becoming a duchess," Angelica said with a sad smile, her blue eyes glistening with unshed tears. "I only miss my father and . . . and feeling safe."

Robert lowered his head and pressed his lips to hers. His kiss was long, slow, and healing. Loss and the need to feel loved made Angelica yield to his advances. She entwined her arms around his neck and returned his kiss in kind. Only the exquisite feeling of his touch on her breasts brought her back to reality.

Angelica drew back. "I told you this would never happen again," she said, and there was no mistaking the anger in her voice and her gaze.

"Listen to your body, angel," he said in a husky whisper.

"I want you to leave now," Angelica said, though her heart ached for him to stay.

"I was married briefly," Robert said, ignoring her words. "Louisa was carrying my child when she—" He hesitated. "—when she died."

His revelation surprised Angelica, her heart wrenching at his obvious pain. No wonder the man was reluctant to marry.

"I am sorry for your loss," she said.

"Thank you, angel." Robert gave her a sad smile. "Shall I leave now, or would you like to sit at the table and teach me how to cheat?"

"Let's sit at the table," Angelica answered, trying to cheer him.

Together, Robert and Angelica returned to the table. When he helped her into her chair, Angelica felt like a Park Lane lady.

Again, Robert sat in the chair opposite hers. He lifted the cards and started to shuffle them.

"Cheating at dice is easier," Angelica said, reaching out to stay his hands. "Besides, hazard is played for high stakes at Crockford and White's."

Angelica stood and disappeared into her chamber. When she returned a moment later, she carried a small wooden box and set it down on the table between them.

With a mischievous smile, Angelica lifted the top off the box to reveal two dozen pairs of dice. "Loaded dice have heavy metal inserted into the dots, while crooked dice land on certain faces more often."

Angelica knew from his expression that she had surprised him. "I prefer loaded dice," she said, and lifted several pairs out of the box. "Dice can be made from ivory, wood, stone, glass, amber, or metal. I always carry several different kinds so I'll be prepared, no matter what."

Robert grinned at her. "Angel, you amaze me."

"Thank you."

"How do you introduce these into the game?" he asked.

"Sleight of hand."

"How does one cheat at cards?"

"Ah, that is a bit more difficult," Angelica told him. "You must remember what cards have been played and always keep extra cards on your person. Sleight of hand is also useful."

"How unfortunate that you were born female," Robert said, laughing. "If you'd been born male, you'd be the richest man in London."

"Or England," she added.

The door crashed open. Her father staggered into the cottage, muttering, "Great grunting shit, I need a drink."

Angelica bolted out of her chair. "Papa, where have you been?" she asked, hurrying to his side.

"Looking for peace," Graham Douglas answered.

"Let me help you to your room," Angelica said, taking hold of his arm.

Her father paused at the table and looked at Robert, who'd stood when the older man had entered. "You haven't aged a day, Magnus," the earl said.

"My lord, you mistake me for another," Robert replied.

"Ah, Magnus, you can't fool me," Graham said, and then turned to Angelica. "I'm tired, little girl."

"I'll help you to bed." She put her arm around him and guided him to the bedroom.

"I've a mighty thirst," he told her. "Is there anything to drink?"

"Water."

"Great grunting shit." Her father lay on his bed

and then called out to her, "Child, leave the door open. Magnus has an eye for the ladies, and I don't want him dishonoring you."

Angelica left the door open. When she looked at Robert, she was startled by his forbidding expression. Was he angry with her? She couldn't help the fact that her father had returned. He did live here.

"What is wrong?" she asked.

"It's a little late for the earl to think about protecting your virtue," Robert answered, his cold gaze fixed on the doorway to his room. "Your father had an obligation to protect you. His neglect of his duty has left you and your sisters vulnerable."

"That's unfair," Angelica protested, coming to her father's defense. "My father has troubles."

"Everyone has troubles," Robert replied. "I didn't drown myself in alcohol when my wife died."

"Perhaps you possess more inner strength."

"Perhaps you are correct," Robert said, his gaze on her softening. "I'm leaving now."

Angelica nodded but was unable to hide her disappointment.

"I promise to return tomorrow," Robert told her. He produced a leather pouch and emptied its contents, twenty pounds, on the table.

"I don't want your money," she said.

"Take it," he ordered. "I want you to promise me you won't gamble today."

"I promise."

Robert leaned close and planted a chaste kiss on her lips. "I'll see you tomorrow."

Angelica nodded and walked outside with him. She smiled when he whistled for his horse.

"Remember, angel," Robert said after mounting his horse, "no graverobbing tonight."

Angelica watched him ride down the dirt road toward Primrose Hill. She knew she shouldn't have let him kiss her again. Her duty to her family was more important than her desire for love. What power did this Robert Roy possess that his mere touch made her forget both her duty and her revenge?

Too bad they hadn't met under different circumstances. Angelica sighed. As long as she was wishing, she might as well wish her father had never lost his fortune, her mother was still alive, and the duke's son had come courting and fallen in love with her.

With a heavy heart, Angelica walked back inside the cottage. Playing her harp would make her feel better.

"What are you doing?" Angelica cried when she spied her father lifting the twenty pounds off the table.

"I need a drink," her father answered.

Blocking the door, Angelica stood her ground. She refused to let him steal their money and kill himself with drink.

"Papa, put the money back."

"I need a drink," he repeated. "It dulls the pain."

"You do *not* need a drink," Angelica insisted. "That won't bring Mother back from the dead."

"Stand aside," he ordered.

"No."

In one swift motion, Graham Douglas reached out and shoved her so hard she fell to the floor. Instinctively, Angelica drew the dagger she kept strapped to her leg.

"Would you murder your own father?" the earl demanded, standing over her. "You have the look of your mother but none of her gentleness." And then he disappeared out the door.

Angelica lay on the floor where she had fallen.

Suddenly, the burden of her life seemed too heavy to endure a moment longer. She rolled onto her stomach and wept . . . for her father, for her family, for the fairy-tale life with a duke's son that would never be.

Her aunt and her sisters arrived home a few minutes later and found her there. "Angelica, darling," her aunt cried. "Are you ill?"

Angelica rolled over and looked at them through tear-swollen eyes. She shook her head and tried to explain. "R-Robert—"

"Did Robert dishonor you?" Aunt Roxie asked.

"Yes, but that was this morning," Angelica answered, rising from the floor with the aid of her sisters.

"Why, that's wonderful news," Aunt Roxie gushed with excitement.

"What did it feel like?" Victoria asked.

"Don't be a twit," Samantha scolded her younger sister. "Lovemaking with a man like Robert Roy would be paradise on earth."

"This subject is unseemly for girls your age," Aunt Roxie told them. She smiled at Angelica, saying, "You'll marry, of course. Events are progressing as I saw in my vision."

"You had a vision?" Samantha echoed.

"What did you see for me?" asked Victoria.

Aunt Roxie gave them a quelling look.

"The man does *not* want to marry me," Angelica told her aunt. "He asked me to be his mistress."

Aunt Roxie dismissed that with a wave of her hand. "Darling, watch what a man does, not what he says."

Angelica gave her aunt a skeptical look. Robert had certainly seemed emphatic about his desire not to marry her.

"I can see that you don't believe me," Aunt

Roxie said, and then she laughed. "Think, darling. Haven't I already buried three husbands? I needed them to marry me before I could bury them."

"And you wasted all your inheritances keeping us alive," Angelica added.

"Oh, pish, the money was well spent," Aunt Roxie replied. "Once all of you are married, then you'll take care of me." She gave Angelica a puzzled look, asking, "If Robert seduced you this morning, why did you wait until tonight to fall on the floor and weep?"

"I wasn't weeping for Robert," Angelica told them. "Papa pushed me out of his way and I landed on the floor. He stole the money Robert left for us."

"Oh, the man adores you," Aunt Roxie exclaimed, clapping her hands together.

"What about Papa?" Angelica asked.

"I can do nothing for Graham," Aunt Roxie said, losing her smile. "His fate was written before he was born."

"What do you mean?" Angelica asked.

"I don't know absolutely everything," Aunt Roxie answered. "The good news is our visit with Mr. Lewis last night has gone undetected." She smiled brightly at her three nieces, saying, "Let's make supper, my darlings."

Two hours later, Angelica sat in front of the hearth and played her harp. Accompanying her were Samantha on the violin and Victoria on the flute.

With her eyes closed in relaxation, Aunt Roxie sat on the settee and enjoyed the soothing bath of sound they created. Their serenade evoked a morning breeze, dancing wildflowers, rustling leaves.

Angelica stopped playing when she heard the

knock on the door. Aunt Roxie and her sisters looked at the door in surprise. No one ever visited them. Robert had left only a few hours earlier; he wouldn't be returning this soon.

"Don't open the door," Angelica ordered when her aunt rose from her chair.

Aunt Roxie gave her a confused look. "Why not, darling?"

"I have a bad feeling," Angelica answered. "Let's pretend we aren't home."

"We cannot change what will be." Aunt Roxie opened the door and said, "Parson Butterfield, what a surprise."

Bull's pizzle, Angelica thought, flicking a glance at Samantha and Victoria. Her sisters' indiscretion of the previous night had been discovered.

"What is this?" Angelica heard her aunt saying.

Parson Butterfield stepped inside the cottage and gestured to someone behind him. A moment later four men appeared, carrying an unconscious Graham Douglas.

"Papa," Angelica cried, hurrying across the room. "Bring him this way."

The four men placed her father on his bed and immediately left the room.

While her sisters watched, Angelica lightly tapped her father's face, saying, "Wake up, Papa. Wake up." She looked in confusion at the parson and asked, "What's wrong with him?"

"He's dead."

"Dead?" Angelica cried.

She glanced at her sisters. Their complexions had paled to a ghostly white. Her aunt, more experienced with loved ones dying, shook her head sadly.

"Now my poor brother has what he's wanted since the day your mother died," Aunt Roxie said.

Angelica felt torn. Though saddened by his unexpected passing, relief at being freed from the terrible burden of her father's affliction shot through her. In the next instant, guilt replaced her relief.

Angelica leaned close and kissed her father's forehead. "One day soon, you and Mother will be buried on your own land," she whispered. "I promise you that."

Turning to the parson, Angelica asked, "What happened?"

"I don't know," Parson Butterfield told her, shaking his head. "He just dropped dead at my feet."

"How horrifying for you," Aunt Roxie sympathized. "You will do the funeral in the morning?"

Parson Butterfield nodded. "Is there anything else I can do?"

"As a matter of fact, I need a favor," Aunt Roxie said, casting the parson an ambiguous smile. She looped her arm through his and steered him toward the door. "An old friend of mine, a man of some importance, lives in London. Could you possibly deliver a message for me?"

Parson Butterfield hedged. "Well, I—"

"I'm certain the Duke of Inverary will be grateful to you for delivering my letter," Aunt Roxie said.

"The Duke of Inverary?" Parson Butterfield echoed in surprise.

Aunt Roxie nodded.

"You will *not* write to that man," Angelica ordered.

Her aunt glanced over her shoulder and gave her a frigid glare. "Don't listen to my niece," Aunt Roxie told the parson. "Grief for her father's passing steals her common sense."

"That is to be expected," Parson Butterfield replied.

Aunt Roxie gave him a dimpled smile. "Until tomorrow morning, then."

"I've a mind to murder those men who murdered Papa," Angelica said after the door closed behind the parson.

"I'll help," Samantha said.

"So will I," added Victoria.

"Swallow your tongues," Aunt Roxie said. "Whatever we send out returns to us tenfold."

Chapter 5

"Bull's pizzle," Angelica grumbled, recalling her aunt's words of wisdom. If what we sent out to others returned to us tenfold, those men who had ruined her father would surely be burning in hell. Especially Charles Emerson, who had swindled an honest man, and Magnus Campbell, who had failed to help a friend in trouble.

Angelica glanced at Aunt Roxie, who sat beside her in the garden the following afternoon. Her sisters had disappeared into the woodland, probably intending to wade in the stream's cooling waters.

Her father was dead and buried, Angelica thought, yet the world kept spinning as if nothing momentous had happened. The sky was a blanket of blue, the sun shone brightly, the old oak offered shade from the day's warmth.

Angelica closed her eyes and tried to block out the beauty of the day. The Duke of Inverary still sat in his mansion on Park Lane. Charles Emerson still owned the lands he'd stolen from her father. Trimble and Drinkwater still enjoyed the fruits of their dishonesty. Only Mayhew had gone to meet his Maker.

Where was justice for the Douglas family? She had no faith in the law; she would make her own justice, and woe come to anyone who stood in her way.

Angelica lifted her harp onto her lap and began plucking its strings idly. The plucking became a haunting melody that conjured a solitary bird flying overhead, the sins of old age, tears on the heather.

"You are a very beautiful bird," Aunt Roxie crooned to Jasper. "The ladies of the ton would love to wear those blue and gold feathers in their hair. And your owner is now the Countess of Melrose. That makes you a special macaw."

"What did you say?" Angelica asked.

"I was speaking to Jasper," her aunt told her.

"Yes, but what did you say?"

"I said that you are the Countess of Melrose." That surprised Angelica. "I am?"

"Darling, our family's ancient charter stipulates that if there are no males in direct descent, then the eldest daughter assumes the Melrose title," Aunt Roxie informed her.

"A penniless countess?" Angelica said. "That's laughable."

Angelica closed her eyes again, leaned back against the oak, and pretended to relax. Her mind raced faster than a highwayman chased by soldiers. If she could raise enough money to purchase decent clothing, the Countess of Melrose would have more gambling options open to her.

She could pretend to be newly arrived from

Europe. With a letter of introduction from her aunt, she would present herself . . . where?

Angelica decided she would present herself to the Duke of Inverary and pretend he'd done nothing wrong. She would use his influence to get the first four villains, and then she would turn on the duke. After that, she would get even with Robert Roy. If he hadn't left that money on the table, her father might still be alive.

With her mind set on justice, Angelica relaxed against the oak's trunk. A smile touched her lips when she thought of putting her scheme into action.

"Darling, I do not like that smile," Aunt Roxie said. "What are you planning?"

"I don't know what you mean," Angelica said, fixing an innocent look on her face.

Aunt Roxie narrowed her gaze. "I mean—"

"Hello? Is anyone home?" called a voice.

"Hello, hello, hello," Jasper called.

Robert Roy appeared around the side of the cottage. "I thought I heard an angel playing her harp," he said, crossing the garden toward them.

Reaching into his pocket, Robert produced a green apple. He held out the apple to the macaw, and Jasper lifted it out of his hand and shifted it to his claws.

"Say 'Thank you,' " Robert told the bird.

"Thank you," Jasper said, making him smile.

Robert looked at her black gown and then raised his eyes to hers. "Is something wrong?" he asked.

"We buried my father this morning," Angelica answered, rising from her seat on the grass beneath the oak.

Robert looked surprised. "I am sorry for your loss."

"Are you?" Angelica asked, her gaze on him

cold. She knew she was wrong to blame him because of the money he'd left on the table, but she was unable to control the urge to lash out at someone.

"Do you believe I wished for your father's death?" Robert asked, his surprise evident in his voice.

"My father might be alive," she told him, "if you hadn't left that money on the table."

"Angelica," her aunt cried.

"Your father drank himself to death without my help," Robert told her. "Apparently he wanted to die ... Good-bye, Angelica." With those final words, Robert turned and left the garden.

"Apologize," Aunt Roxie ordered.

Angelica looked at her aunt and then hurried after Robert. What had she done? No one had forced the poison down her father's throat; he'd done that to himself.

"Wait, please," Angelica called, rounding the cottage.

Robert turned around. With the misery of the world etched across her features, Angelica halted mere inches from him.

"I didn't mean what I said," she told him. "Please, forgive me."

Without saying a word, Robert opened his arms, and Angelica flew into his embrace. She buried her face against his chest and wept, his arms around her offering comfort and safety.

When her sobs subsided and then ceased, Angelica looked up at him. She shifted her gaze to the handkerchief he offered.

"It's clean," he said, making her smile.

"I feel so guilty," she told him, her voice raw with emotion.

"I accept your apology."

"I don't feel guilty about you," Angelica said, making him smile. "I feel guilty about my father."

"There is nothing you could have done," Robert said, holding her close.

"You don't understand," Angelica replied, misery swelling inside her chest, making breathing almost painful. "When Parson Butterfield told me my father was dead, I felt . . . *relieved.*"

Robert tightened his hold on her. He tilted up her chin so he could gaze into her tear-filled eyes and spoke soothingly. "You took good care of your father and are *not* relieved that he is dead, only that a heavy burden has been lifted from your shoulders." He planted a kiss on her forehead. "Believe me, love. Your heart is too gentle to wish anyone dead."

"That isn't what my father said," Angelica told him. "His final words to me were that I looked like my mother but possessed none of her gentleness."

"The alcohol was speaking, not your father," Robert replied.

"I suppose you could be correct."

"I want you to get some rest," Robert told her. "Tonight I'll take a couple of my friends to the graveyard to guard your father."

Angelica became alarmed. "I thought corpses weren't in demand at this time of the year."

"That didn't stop your sisters," Robert reminded her, a smile flirting with his lips.

Angelica reached up and placed the palm of her hand against his cheek. "Thank you."

"Do you feel better now?" Robert asked, turning his head to kiss the palm of her hand.

"No, but I'm certain I will someday," she answered with a rueful smile.

Angelica watched Robert ride down the dirt road to Primrose Hill. For the first time since she'd met him, he turned in the saddle and waved before disappearing from sight.

In spite of seducing the virginity from her, Angelica thought, Robert Roy was truly heaven-sent. He cared about what happened to her and her family. Yes, he had seduced her before mentioning his aversion to marriage, but other than that one lapse, he'd been completely honest with her. How ridiculous that an expert cheat like herself should value honesty and loyalty above all else.

Long after the sun had set, Angelica sat with her sisters in front of the hearth and told them her plans for revenge. Jasper had long since been put to bed, and Aunt Roxie was floating in and out of her bedchamber. She seemed in high spirits for a woman who'd buried her brother only that morning.

"Aunt Roxie, what are you doing?" Angelica asked finally.

"I'm packing a few of my belongings," her aunt answered.

Her reply confused Angelica. "Are you going somewhere?"

"Yes, I am," her aunt answered with an ambiguous smile, and disappeared into her chamber.

"Do you think Papa's death has unbalanced Aunt Roxie?" Samantha whispered.

"Aunt Roxie has always been a bit unbalanced," Victoria answered.

Angelica smiled at that. "We need to walk to the graveyard now."

"Why?" Samantha asked.

"I want to be certain that Robert hasn't forgotten his promise to guard Papa," Angelica answered.

"He said there was no demand for corpses at this time of year," Victoria said.

"That didn't stop you," Angelica replied, echoing Robert's words.

Samantha and Victoria rose from the settee. Angelica stood when they did and glanced at her aunt's closed bedchamber door. She caught her sisters' attention and shook her head.

The three sisters tiptoed out of the cottage, stopping only to light a lantern. The night was warm and hushed and eerily dark since no moon shone overhead to help the lantern light their way. Ten minutes later, the girls arrived at the graveyard.

"I don't see any lantern light," Angelica said, disappointed. "Robert must have forgotten."

"Perhaps he's been delayed," Samantha suggested.

"I bet he's on his way," Victoria added.

"We'll guard Papa until he arrives," Angelica said.

"Can we guard him from here?" Victoria asked. "You know I don't like the dark or graveyards."

"You weren't afraid when you abducted Mr. Lewis," Angelica reminded her.

"Yes, she was," Samantha said. "I had the devil of a time getting her inside. Tory jumped at every little noise and gave me the creeps."

"We're going inside," Angelica told her youngest sister. "You can wait here alone in the dark or come with us."

"Lead the way," Victoria said.

Though reluctant to enter the graveyard at night, Angelica forced herself to step inside and hold the lantern high. She walked the breadth of the graveyard to where they had buried their father beside their mother.

"You don't trust my word, angel?" asked a voice in the darkness.

Angelica gasped in surprise, as did her sisters.

She smiled when Robert appeared in the light cast by the lantern. "You're alone?" she asked.

Two other men stepped into the light. "These are my friends, James Armstrong and Adam St. Aubyn."

"I am pleased to meet you," Angelica said. "These are my sisters, Samantha and Victoria."

"We've heard good things about you," James Armstrong told her.

"Yes, we certainly have," Adam St. Aubyn agreed.

Angelica tried to think what good things Robert could have said about her. She'd cheated him out of more than a hundred pounds, enlisted his aid in burying Mr. Lewis, given him a lesson on cheating, and—and surrendered her virginity to him. Feeling her face heat with a blush, Angelica was relieved that the night masked her embarrassment.

"I appreciate your help," Angelica managed to say. "Would you like us to leave our lantern?"

"We covered our lantern when we saw your light coming down the road," Robert told her. "Come on. I'll walk you to the gate."

With her sisters in the lead, Angelica and Robert crossed the graveyard. At the gate, Robert kissed her hand and said, "While I'm guarding your father, I'll need to sleep during the day. I'll come by the cottage in a couple of days."

"I'll miss you," Angelica said before she could stop herself.

Robert planted a kiss on her lips and said, "I'll miss you more."

Two mornings later, Angelica slept later than usual and awakened with a smile on her lips and Robert on her mind. *I'll miss you more.* The memory of his words warmed her heart.

Angelica wondered where he lived and what he did when he wasn't with her. Though she'd only known him for a few days, she could not imagine life without Robert Roy.

Is this love? she wondered.

"Angelica, darling, come here," Aunt Roxie called from the common room.

"I'm coming." Angelica pushed blond wisps of hair out of her eyes and rose from the bed.

Without bothering to cover her nightshift, Angelica opened the bedroom door and walked into the common room. Aunt Roxie, Samantha, and Victoria were staring out the window.

Puzzled, Angelica hurried across the room. "Sacred sevens, what is that?" she gasped.

Aunt Roxie smiled. "That is the Duke of Inverary's answer to my message."

Parked in front of their cottage was the ducal coach, a barouche drawn by four pure white horses. On the door of the barouche had been painted the Campbell crest, a gold boar's head with silver tusks and a red tongue. Behind the coach was a cart used to haul goods.

"I'll be a rat's arse," Victoria murmured.

Wearing the black and green Campbell livery, a coachman approached their door. "Are you the Countess of Melrose?" he asked Aunt Roxie.

"No, my niece is the countess," Aunt Roxie answered, touching Angelica's shoulder.

The coachman bowed to Angelica and said, "The Duke of Inverary requests the honor of your presence at his home."

Who did the Duke of Inverary think he was? Angelica thought with mutiny in her heart. The bloody King of England? If His Grace believed she would set one foot inside his home, then he was as mad as King George whom, everyone knew, conversed with trees.

"Tell His Grace that the Countess of Melrose

does not take orders from him," Angelica said, a mulish expression on her face.

The coachman seemed at a loss. "My lady, I cannot possibly return—"

"Excuse us for a moment," Aunt Roxie interrupted the coachman.

Aunt Roxie grabbed her arm and forced her farther into the common room. "Pack your bags," she ordered in a whisper. "We are being driven out of poverty."

"I won't go," Angelica insisted.

"I thought you wanted revenge on those men who stole your father's fortune," Aunt Roxie countered. "What better way to get at them than by becoming the Duke of Inverary's house guest?"

"But the duke—"

"—had nothing to do with your father's troubles," Aunt Roxie finished for her.

"What about Robert?" Angelica asked.

Aunt Roxie gave her an ambiguous smile. "Don't worry about him, darling. I promise His Grace will know how to find Robert Roy. If you don't believe me, leave the man a note."

Angelica hesitated in indecision. She supposed this was the best way to get to the men who'd ruined her father. But what if Robert Roy refused to disturb her at the duke's residence? She might never see him again.

"Think of your sisters' future," Aunt Roxie said, as if she'd read her thoughts. "With the duke's sponsorship, Samantha and Victoria will make good matches."

Angelica saw the sense in what her aunt was saying. She would leave Robert a note, telling him where she'd gone, and pray that he would come for her.

One last thought occurred to Angelica. "What about Jasper?" she asked.

Aunt Roxie gave her a feline smile. "Why, darling, Jasper will accompany us."

Angelica knew when she'd been bested. Reluctantly, she nodded and said, "Very well, but I won't like it."

Two hours later the Douglas family, including Jasper, sat inside the luxurious ducal coach. Angelica slid her hand across the black leather seat and murmured to herself, "Softer than a lady's lap."

"Driving down Park Lane again feels wonderful," Aunt Roxie gushed, gazing out the window.

"Wonderful," Jasper repeated. "Wonderful."

Angelica smiled at her aunt's delight and glanced at Samantha, who rolled her eyes. Victoria giggled.

The coach halted in front of an elegant brick town house. A moment later the coachman appeared and opened the door to help each of them down.

Last to leave the coach, Angelica warned, "Do not touch me or the bird unless you wish to lose a finger."

The coachman stepped back instantly.

Angelica placed a hand around the back of the macaw's head, securing its lower mandible. With her free hand, she secured the bird's wings. Only then did she climb out of the coach, her sisters' hands ready to steady her.

"Mr. Tinker, you haven't aged a day," Aunt Roxie cried.

Angelica turned toward the mansion to see the Campbell majordomo. Wearing a broad grin, the man rushed down the stairs to escort her aunt inside.

"Lady Roxanne, you are even more beautiful than I remember," the majordomo said.

"You old rascal," Aunt Roxie replied, giving him a dimpled smile. Over her shoulder, she called, "Come, girls."

The mansion's foyer was imposing, classically inspired with marble statuary and elaborately carved cornices. Its ceiling had been decorated with delicate rococo ornamentation.

"Please, come with me," Tinker said, walking toward the stairs. "His Grace asked me to escort you to his study as soon as you arrived." The major-domo looked at Angelica and asked, "Where shall I put the bird, my lady?"

"Jasper stays with me," she told him.

The majordomo nodded. With him in the lead, they climbed the stairs. Its main feature was the wrought-iron balustrade lit by a tall, round-headed window gracing the landing.

"I was sorry to learn of the earl's passing," Tinker said, leading them down a long corridor. He knocked on a closed door.

Angelica wet her lips nervously when she heard a man's voice bidding them enter. She could hardly believe she was about to meet one of the devils she was determined to pauper.

And then the majordomo opened the door. With her aunt in the lead, Angelica and her sisters walked into the duke's study.

The chamber reeked with masculinity. On one side of the room was a marble hearth and mantel. Portraits of important-looking men topped bookcases that had been built into the walls.

A rogue's gallery, Angelica thought, realizing the portraits were Campbell lairds. And then she dared to look at the man rising from his chair behind a mahogany desk that was bigger than her bed at home.

Despite his age, the Duke of Inverary was an

attractive man. Tall and well-built, the duke had black hair, graying at the temples, and dark eyes. He seemed oddly familiar.

"Roxanne, I've missed you," the duke said, walking around the desk to take her aunt's hands in his. Then, instead of kissing her hand, he pulled her aunt close for a hug and kissed her cheek.

"Darling, you cannot imagine how many times I've thought about you," Aunt Roxie drawled, obviously pleased with his greeting. "But Graham—" She shrugged. "My brother was a proud man, too proud to ask for help."

"The help should have been offered," Angelica spoke up, a bitter edge to her voice. "A true friend helps without being asked."

"And these are Graham's daughters," the duke said, ignoring her remark.

"The mouthy one is Angelica," Aunt Roxie said, giving her a warning look.

"Ah, yes, the Countess of Melrose." The duke smiled warmly and asked, "What have you there, Lady Angelica?"

"Jasper, my pet macaw," she answered. "Do not touch him or he'll bite off your finger."

"What wonderful protection," the duke said smoothly.

"Great grunting shit," Jasper shrieked unexpectedly.

Aunt Roxie looked ready to swoon. Samantha and Victoria dissolved into giggles. Even Angelica managed a smile.

"He has quite a vocabulary," the duke remarked.

Jasper cocked his blue head to one side and said, "Hello."

The Duke of Inverary smiled and turned to her sisters. "And these pretty girls are . . . ?"

"Samantha and Victoria," Aunt Roxie supplied.

"I am pleased to make your acquaintances," the duke said. "Make yourselves at home." He turned to Roxie, saying, "I have London's most fashionable dressmaker coming here tomorrow to outfit the four of you with new wardrobes. Now, you must be tired after your long ordeal. Tinker will show you to your rooms."

Angelica started to turn away when the majordomo opened the door for them, but the duke's voice stopped her. "I would like a private word with you, Lady Angelica," he said. It was a command, not a request. "Tinker will return for you shortly."

"Mind your manners, darling," Aunt Roxie said, giving her a pointed look.

"Please sit down," the duke said when they were alone.

With malice in her heart, Angelica set the macaw down on the upholstered chair in front of the desk and then sat in another chair. She gave the duke a sunny smile and said, "You don't mind if Jasper sits there, do you?"

The Duke of Inverary inclined his head. "Where does he usually perch?"

"Jasper has a cage," Angelica answered. "However, macaws need companionship, so I doubt placing the cage in my bedchamber will be healthy for him."

"I will instruct Tinker to purchase a cage for every room," the duke said expansively.

"He'll need blankets and perches and toys to go with each cage," Angelica added.

"I'll leave it to you to tell Tinker what will make your pet happy."

Angelica fixed her gaze on his and said, "My cottage is what will make Jasper happiest."

The Duke of Inverary appeared unruffled by her

statement. He leaned back in his chair and studied her until she began to fidget uncomfortably.

"You are even prettier than I remember," he said finally.

"I don't recall meeting you," she replied. "Though you do seem vaguely familiar, as if I'd seen you somewhere recently."

"I have sensed a certain hostility emanating from you since the moment you walked through that door," the duke remarked. "I have opened my home to you. Why don't you like me?"

"You betrayed my father," Angelica accused him, staring him straight in the eye. "I intend to make you regret that, Your Grace."

Unaccountably, a smile flirted with the corners of his lips. "I see you have inherited dear Roxie's fierce spirit," the duke said. "I must correct your misconceptions, though. Your father was the dearest friend I ever had, and I would never betray him."

Angelica opened her mouth to refute his statement, but the duke raised his hand to let him finish.

"I heard Graham had gone to Europe," the duke told her. "I had every intention of helping him." He paused to run his hand through his hair and then added, his frustration evident in his voice, "I searched for years."

Angelica dropped her gaze to the carpet. His sincerity confused her, but she had no experience with sophisticated deceivers. Should she give him a chance or not?

"I will allow you to prove the veracity of your words," Angelica said, raising her gaze to his, heedless of the rude way she was speaking to a duke. "I will give you the opportunity to help him now by helping me exact revenge on the men who ruined him.''

The Duke of Inverary snapped his brows together. "Do you know who these men are?"

"Alasdair Trimble, Henry Drinkwater, Archibald Mayhew, and Charles Emerson."

"Archibald Mayhew is dead."

Angelica arched a blond brow at him. "The son will pay for the father's crimes."

The duke inclined his head, but his expression remained bland. "Getting even with Charles Emerson is out of the question," he told her. "His daughter is my son's widow and the mother of my only grandchild."

Angelica said nothing. She stared at him, an expression of contempt etched across her features.

"How were you planning on getting even, child?" the duke asked.

"Please call me 'my lady,' " Angelica drawled, in a frigid imitation of her aunt.

"I beg your pardon, my lady."

Angelica inclined her head like a young queen granting a courtier a favor. "I am planning to pauper them at the gaming table."

That made him smile. "So Graham taught you to gamble?"

"Unlike my father, *I* make my own luck," Angelica told him. "Honest luck is decidedly overrated, not to mention unreliable."

"I can gain you access to those men," the duke said. "Even Charles Emerson."

Angelica's smile could have lit the whole mansion. He had redeemed himself.

"You have a charming smile and should use it more often," the duke told her. "Am I forgiven?"

"Promises are easily broken, Your Grace," she reminded him.

The Duke of Inverary inclined his head. Then he rose from his chair, signaling an end to their interview.

The door burst open suddenly. "What is so urgent, Father?" asked a familiar voice.

Angelica whirled around in her chair as Robert Roy marched across the study toward them. *Father?* she thought in surprise. *The Duke of Inverary was Robert Roy's father?*

Angelica rose from her chair and closed the distance between them. His expression told her that her presence was as surprising to him as his was to her.

"What are you doing here?" Robert demanded.

"I was going to ask you the same thing," Angelica replied.

"Allow me to introduce my son, the Marquess of Argyll, Robert Roy Campbell," the Duke of Inverary said with laughter lurking in his voice.

Tinker returned at that moment, asking, "Shall I escort her ladyship to her chamber now?"

Both Angelica and Robert ignored the duke and his majordomo. Angelica recognized the anger in Robert's gaze but couldn't understand why he was angry with her. He was the one who had lied, not she.

"Were you thinking to force me into marriage?" Robert demanded, a hard edge to his voice.

Chapter 6

"I wouldn't marry you to save my life," Angelica said, an expression of contempt etched across her face. Without warning, she slapped him hard and added, "I despise liars."

Suppressing the urge to touch his smarting cheek, Robert couldn't credit that the chit had slapped him again. This time she'd done it in front of his father and Tinker. A servant, for God's sake. The girl's rough upbringing had made her prone to violence.

"Do cheaters get to heaven before liars?" Robert asked in a sarcastic tone, cocking a dark brow at her.

Angelica gave him a scathing look and turned away. "Mr. Tinker, please escort me to my chamber," she said. "Come, Jasper."

Glorious in her fury, Angelica held her head high and followed the majordomo out of the study. Behind her hurried the macaw, calling, "Good night."

"You are an insensitive blockhead," Duke Magnus said as soon as the door closed.

"What the bloody hell do you think you're doing?" Robert snapped, ignoring his father's insult.

"I'm setting things right," Duke Magnus said, sitting in the chair behind his desk. "Sit down, and refrain from speaking to me in that disrespectful manner."

"Did she show up on your doorstep or did you send for her?" Robert asked, sitting across the desk from his father.

"I sent for the Douglas family," Duke Magnus replied.

"How did you find them?" Robert asked. "Did you have me followed?"

"In her infinite wisdom, Lady Roxanne sent me a message as soon as Graham passed away," his father told him.

"The aunt is a disreputable charlatan," Robert said.

"I will not listen to a word against Roxanne or her nieces," Duke Magnus said. "I owe this to Graham." His next words nearly toppled Robert out of his chair, "In my younger days, I foolishly let Roxanne get away from me. I won't let that happen again."

"What do you mean?" Robert demanded. His father sounded as if—

"Once the Douglas girls are settled," the duke answered with a smile, as if tickled by the prospect of shocking his son, "I may consider remarrying."

Robert couldn't credit what he was hearing. Had his father lost his wits?

"You ruined my plans," Robert told him.

"What were your plans?" Duke Magnus asked, raising his brows, looking very much like his son.

Robert had the good grace to flush. "I planned to make Angelica my mistress and would have supported her family."

"Son, money does not make a woman a lady," Duke Magnus told him. "Some wealthy ladies are born whores, while some penniless paupers are queens and should be treated as such." His father smiled like an old fox. "That lovely young woman, the Countess of Melrose, is an aristocrat in her heart as well as in fact. If you desire her, you'll need to court her affections and marry her."

Robert refused to allow his father to trap him into an unwanted marriage. He'd done that to him once, when he was still young enough to be intimidated by a father who was a duke, an important peer of the realm. The end result was Louisa's suicide. She hadn't wanted the marriage either and certainly hadn't wanted to bear his children.

"Father, your ploy won't work," Robert informed him. "I have no wish to marry again."

Duke Magnus shrugged his shoulders, as if the matter was of no importance. Then he changed the subject, saying, "One of our ships was pirated."

That startled Robert. "Which one?"

The Tempest."

"I suppose all the commodities were lost," Robert said.

"On the contrary, *The Tempest* was nearly at home port," his father answered. "The cargo had been delivered, but we did lose all the money."

"Did you speak to Captain Taylor?" Robert asked.

Duke Magnus nodded. "Taylor reported the theft this morning as soon as they'd docked."

"I have a few questions for him, too," Robert said.

A knock on the door drew their attention, and then Tinker entered. "Lady Roxanne is on her way down, Your Grace," the majordomo informed him.

"Thank you, Tinker."

"I'll leave you," Robert said, starting to rise.

"Stay where you are," the duke ordered, motioning him to sit down.

A moment later, Aunt Roxie breezed into the study. Both father and son stood when she entered.

"Hello, darlings," Aunt Roxie called, giving them a dimpled smile.

She sat in the vacant chair in front of the duke's desk. The men sat when she did.

"Have you suffered an accident?" Roxie asked Robert.

Her question confused him. "I beg your pardon?"

"One side of your face is quite red," she said.

"I bumped into Angelica's hand," Robert told her, making his father chuckle.

"Angelica does possess a fiercely passionate nature," Aunt Roxie remarked. She gave him a dimpled smile and said, "I knew who you were almost from the moment I saw you."

Robert's lips quirked as he struggled against a smile. "How did you know?"

Roxie cast the duke a flirtatious look and drawled, "Why, darling, you are almost as handsome as your father."

"Thank you, I think."

"Angelica will *not* become your mistress," Aunt Roxie informed him, speaking in a hushed tone.

"If you think to entrap me, my lady," Robert informed her, "I must tell you I have no intention of marrying Angelica. Or anyone else, for that matter."

Aunt Roxie waved her hand, dismissing his

announcement as unimportant. "Angelica will marry someone else. All my lovely nieces will make good matches."

Robert sat up straighter and stared at her. Budding jealousy bloomed inside his chest. "Whom did you have in mind for Angelica?"

"No one in particular," Aunt Roxie answered with a shrug. "I'm positive that once Angelica is out and about, she will be popular with the opposite sex and besieged by dozens of offers for her hand in marriage." She glanced at the duke, asking, "Don't you agree, Your Grace?"

Duke Magnus nodded. "With their beauty and intelligence and my new wardrobes and dowries, I plan to secure the best matches possible for your nieces."

"The Douglas sisters are not your responsibility," Robert said, irritated that his own father would thwart his desire to make Angelica Douglas his mistress.

"I plan to become their legal guardian," Duke Magnus announced. "Even now my solicitor is drafting the document."

"That is unnecessary," Robert said, surprised.

"Sponsoring his beautiful daughters is the least I can do for Graham," his father replied.

"You haven't forgotten your promise to help with Angelica's plans for those men?" Aunt Roxie asked, turning to Robert.

"I doubt that Angelica wants my assistance," he answered, rubbing his cheek.

"Darling, do not be absurd," Aunt Roxie replied with a throaty chuckle. "Angelica needs you as much as you need her."

Robert would have argued the point of his needing anyone, but the lady turned to his father, asking, "Your Grace, how shall we explain our unexpected arrival to society?"

"Call me Magnus," his father said, and winked at her.

Aunt Roxie gave him a feline smile and blushed as if on cue. His father dropped his gaze to her ample bosom, and she dropped her gaze demurely.

Robert nearly burst out laughing. He couldn't credit their byplay. His father seemed completely smitten.

"I suggest we say that Graham recouped his financial losses while abroad but refused to return to England because of his bad experiences at the gaming tables," Duke Magnus said. "The Douglas family passed the last ten years traveling between Italy and France."

"Magnus, darling, we have arrived without gowns, furs, and jewels," Aunt Roxie reminded him.

"I intend to remedy that situation," the duke replied.

"I know you will," Aunt Roxie said, "but how will we explain arriving in England in our paupered condition?"

"You were traveling to England on board our ship, *The Tempest*," Robert suggested.

"What an outstanding idea," Duke Magnus said with a broad smile.

Seeing the lady's confused expression, Robert explained, "*The Tempest* was recently pirated on its way to port."

"What wonderful news," Aunt Roxie exclaimed. Her expression changed faster than an eye can blink. "I mean—I'm so terribly sorry."

"Don't worry," Duke Magnus said.

"If you will excuse me," Robert said, standing, "I'd like to speak with Captain Taylor."

"You will return for tea?" his father asked. "Or dinner, perhaps?"

"I've already made other plans," Robert lied, a feeling of being trapped sweeping through him. What his father had in mind was a date for tea today, dinner tomorrow, and the altar the day after that. If he wasn't careful, he'd find himself married before Parliament broke for autumn's grouse-hunting.

Robert left his father's study and hurried down the stairs, anxious to be away. When he reached the bottom step, though, Tinker was just opening the front door for Venetia, who was returning from a ride in Hyde Park.

"Robert," Venetia called, her expression brightening as soon as she saw him. "What a wonderful—"

"I haven't the time," Robert growled, brushing past her. But he felt no relief when he'd escaped his father's mansion. Robert mounted his horse. He planned to ride east to the docks and speak with Captain Taylor; instead, he rode west in the direction of Primrose Hill.

Twenty minutes later, Robert halted his horse outside the now-familiar pink stucco cottage. He stared at the cottage but thought of Louisa and her suicide. Perhaps if he'd been more attentive, she would still be alive. Neither of them actually wanted the union, but he'd had no idea that doing his father's bidding by marrying her would cause her untimely end. She must have been unspeakably unhappy but masked it well.

Robert became fully aware of his surroundings. He dismounted and walked toward the cottage. The wolfsbane, intended to keep him away, still hung overhead. Reaching the door, he lifted the latch and walked inside.

The cottage seemed eerily quiet and empty without Angelica. Robert lifted a parchment off the table and read: *Robert: I am staying at the Duke of Inverary's on Park Lane. Come for me there.*

Angelica hadn't known who he was, Robert realized. She hadn't been trying to trap him into marriage at all. If he hadn't been so angered by the sight of her sitting in his father's study, he would have realized her innocence from her expression of surprise.

What had he done? Robert thought, feeling a twinge of remorse. He'd lashed out at her in anger and humiliated her. His father was correct; he was a blockhead.

How could he make this up to her? Of course he would assist her in her plans for revenge. He also owed her an apology for his bad behavior and an explanation of why he'd lied, if he could think of a reasonable excuse for it. Then he would court her and see where their relationship went.

With his mind settled, Robert turned to leave. He opened the door, only to find his path blocked by a beautiful, ebony-haired woman.

"You're here," Lucille Dubois exclaimed. "I thought the potion hadn't worked."

"What are you doing here?" Robert demanded. Were his former mistresses now following him around London? How would he explain that to Angelica?

"I want to see Madame Roxanne for another reading," Lucille answered.

"Reading?" Robert had no idea what she meant.

"A reading of my future," Lucille said. "I see that her first reading was correct, though. Are you here for a reading, too?"

"Don't be ridiculous," Robert snapped, and tried to brush past her.

Lucille stayed him with a gloved hand. "When are you coming back to me?" she asked, her voice a mere whisper. "No woman could ever please you as I do."

Robert dropped his black gaze to her cleavage. Memories of shared pleasure hit him like an avalanche. His former mistress had a perfect body and exquisite breasts. He recalled the moments he'd enjoyed burying his face between those perfect mounds of flesh, the unexpected pleasure of suckling upon her dusky nipples when she'd carried his child deep within her body.

Reaching up, Robert let one long finger glide down the valley between her breasts, nearly exposing them. He heard her sharp intake of breath and felt her, almost imperceptibly, press herself against his hand.

"Lucille, I am *not* continuing our relationship," Robert said, his hand dropping away from her body.

"You miss my bed," Lucille said, pouting prettily. "And I yearn to feel you inside me again."

"Are you wet for me now?" Robert asked, his voice husky.

Wearing a feline smile, Lucille suggested, "Slip your marvelous fingers up the front of my gown and find out for yourself."

"No, thank you," he refused in a clipped tone.

"Daisy is four years old and wants to meet her father," she said, her irritation apparent.

"Be thankful that I take responsibility for my sins, and I'm rich enough to be generous," Robert replied.

"But you've never even seen her," Lucille argued.

"I have no intention of seeing the child whose

existence caused Louisa's suicide," Robert told her.

"Do you blame Daisy for your wife's death?"

"No, I blame myself." At that, Robert closed the cottage door behind himself and headed for his horse.

"Oh, I must speak to Madame Roxanne about this," Lucille exclaimed, and knocked on the door.

"Madame Roxanne doesn't live here anymore," Robert called. He reined his horse away and rode in the direction of London.

Angelica slept through tea but awakened in plenty of time to prepare herself for her first dinner at the Duke of Inverary's mansion. Opening her eyes, she felt momentarily confused by the unfamiliar chamber but then remembered the day's events. She sat up, pushed her blond hair away from her face, and inspected the chamber, which had been decorated in white, gold, and shades of blue.

The bed was larger than her whole chamber at home, its canopy, curtains, and counterpane matched and complemented the room's wallpaper and paintwork. A thick blue, gold, and ivory carpet hugged the floor, and an upholstered chaise in a flowered print and two matching winged-back chairs perched together near the hearth. Following her instructions, a servant had set Jasper's cage near the privacy screen on the opposite side of the room from the windows.

Angelica rose from the bed. She wandered across the chamber to see the view from the windows, a rear garden and courtyard.

"Hello," Jasper called from inside his cage.

Angelica crossed the room to let the macaw out. "Hello, Jasper," she said. "Are you ready to eat?"

"Eat," the bird shrieked.

Angelica rinsed her face at the washstand. Crossing to the dressing table, she saw that her brush and toilet articles had been placed there. She brushed her golden hair, weaved it into one thick braid, and then circled it into a knot at the nape of her neck. After donning her black gown again, she gazed at herself in the cheval mirror and decided she looked too pale. Pinching her cheeks gave them a hint of color.

She'd lost her old life, her mother, and her father, Angelica thought. Now she'd lost the only hope she'd spied in years, Robert Roy. Oh, how that devious Campbell must have enjoyed his prank on her.

There was one thing she would never lose—her desire for revenge. She must never let others make her doubt herself or distract her from her revenge. She needed to hold on to the hatred. Here, at the Duke of Inverary's, she was merely days or weeks from completing the task for which she'd prepared herself all these years. Neither Robert Roy Campbell nor anyone else would stand in her way. She'd come this far and would go the rest of the way.

Angelica turned slowly in a circle and realized what was missing. Without her sisters, the chamber seemed empty. Thankfully, she still had Jasper to keep her company.

"Come in," Angelica called, hearing the knock on her door. She smiled when she saw her sisters.

"Hello," the macaw said.

"Hello, Jasper," Samantha and Victoria said in unison, and then laughed.

"I was just thinking how much I missed you," Angelica told them.

"We missed you at tea," Samantha said.

"Isn't this exciting?" Victoria exclaimed, pushing a fiery curl out of her eyes. "I never imagined that people lived in such luxury."

"My bed is bigger than our chamber at home," Angelica said. "If you get lonely, don't hesitate to crawl into bed with me."

"How hard the past ten years must have been for Aunt Roxie, who lived with this luxury until she used her money to keep us alive," Samantha remarked.

Angelica nodded and added, "Don't forget Father and Mother."

"Strange, but I have trouble remembering what Mother looked like," Samantha said.

"I understand," Angelica said, reaching out to touch her sister's hand.

"Aunt Roxie's chamber is at the far end of the corridor near the duke's," Victoria said. "You don't think that she and the duke—?"

"Aunt Roxie has been without a husband for a long time," Angelica replied. "Perhaps she's lonely, too."

"Even dukes must get lonely sometimes," Samantha said. After a moment of silence, she added, "We are supposed to pretend that we're newly arrived from Europe. Our father died recently, and we've spent the past ten years traveling between Italy and France."

"We are exceedingly wealthy," Victoria informed her. "Father recouped his financial losses."

"Unfortunately, our ship was pirated," Samantha told her, "and we lost all our clothing and jewels."

"What a wonderful story," Angelica said, laughing. She became serious when she told them, "Robert Roy is actually the duke's son."

Victoria nodded. "Aunt Roxie told us. Shall we go downstairs now?"

"We're meeting in the small drawing room before dinner," Samantha said, already limping toward the door.

"Come, Jasper," Angelica called.

"You're taking Jasper to dinner?" Samantha asked in obvious surprise.

"Jasper dines with us at home," Angelica replied, and gave her sisters a mischievous smile.

Victoria giggled. "I can hardly wait to see Aunt Roxie's expression when Jasper takes his place among the Quality."

The first thing Angelica noticed when she walked into the drawing room was an enormous birdcage, complete with perches, food dishes, and toys. The second thing she saw was the chamber's understated opulence.

The small drawing room was bigger than the entire Douglas cottage. Crimson Spitalfields silk hung on the walls to the dado, complemented by diamond and octagonal shapes on the gilded ceiling. The carpet had been designed in large octagonal patterns of crimson, gold, and blue. The furniture was oversized mahogany, and there was an elegant Grecian couch upholstered in crimson velvet. A settee and chairs sat in front of the hearth, above which hung a portrait of a distiguished gentleman.

"Hello," Jasper shrieked.

Aunt Roxie appeared scandalized. "You've brought Jasper to dinner?"

"Don't worry about it," Duke Magnus told her. "Macaws need companionship." He turned to Angelica, saying, "Tinker has purchased several cages. Jasper will be pleased and you, too, I hope."

"Thank you, Your Grace," Angelica said with a sunny smile. "I appreciate your generosity."

"I want you to meet my daughter-in-law, Venetia, and hope you'll be friends," Duke Magnus said. "Venetia, this is Lady Angelica, the Countess of Melrose, and her sisters, Ladies Samantha and Victoria."

Angelica turned her attention to the young woman who stood beside him. Venetia Emerson Campbell was a curvaceous brunette with a flawless face.

"We are pleased to make your acquaintance," Angelica said, speaking for her sisters. She had the sudden feeling that the other woman was eyeing her critically, looking for flaws.

"I'm terribly sorry for your loss," Venetia said.

"Thank you, Lady Venetia," Angelica said stiffly, noting that the other woman had failed to call her *my lady*, as befit a countess. "Losing our father was an unexpected shock."

"The earl's death was sudden?" Venetia asked.

"Riding accidents *are* sudden," Duke Magnus said, giving Angelica a pointed look.

Venetia blushed prettily. "Oh, I'd forgotten what you'd told me." She looked at Angelica, asking, "And then your ship was pirated?"

Angelica inclined her head in the affirmative. She didn't like this woman but felt uncertain whether the dislike stemmed from her being an Emerson. The woman's questions seemed designed to catch them in a lie.

Venetia shuddered delicately. "I cannot begin to imagine how frightened you must have been."

"I understand you have a young son," Angelica said, changing the subject. When the other woman nodded, she added, "I love children and look forward to meeting him."

"Hello," shrieked Jasper.

"I'm positive Colin will be intrigued by a bird that talks," Venetia said.

"Never put your hands near Jasper," Angelica warned. "Macaws can bite the finger off a man."

"Is it safe to be near him?" Venetia asked, taking one step back.

"Yes, of course."

"Wherever did you get him?"

I won him in a card game, Angelica thought. "Prince Rudolf purchased Jasper for me when we visited a carnival near Lake Como," Angelica drawled, recalling a name she'd once read in *The Times*.

"Prince Rudolf?" Venetia echoed, clearly impressed.

Lying is fun, Angelica decided. "Rudy was such a sweet man, but I knew I could never be happy living in Russia."

Angelica glanced at Aunt Roxie. *Bravo* was etched across her aunt's features.

"A Russian prince proposed marriage?" Venetia echoed again.

Angelica opened her mouth to embellish her lie, but Jasper shrieked, "Hello."

"Hello," said a familiar voice.

Angelica turned to see Robert, magnificent in evening clothes, walking across the room toward them. Her heart ached at the sight of his dark handsomeness.

"I'm surprised to see you," Duke Magnus said.

Robert inclined his head at his father but walked directly to Angelica. "I wanted to attend the countess's first dinner in England," he said smoothly, raising her hand to his lips.

Angelica was stunned. Not only was Robert

behaving exactly the opposite of what she'd expected, but he was lying on her behalf.

"You've already met?" Venetia asked.

"We met this morning in my father's study." Robert kissed Aunt Roxie's hand and nodded at her sisters.

Sacred sevens, Angelica thought, watching him perform. If the scoundrel thought to take up where he'd left off at the cottage, he had better think again.

"Look at the beautiful bird Prince Rudolf gave Lady Angelica," Venetia said.

With laughter lurking in his dark eyes, Robert looked at Angelica and said, "Prince Rudolf must be a generous man."

Angelica shrugged. "Unlike other men of his ilk, the prince had no ulterior motives."

Robert raised his brows and asked, "To what ulterior motives do you refer?"

"Prince Rudolf wanted Lady Angelica to marry him," Venetia spoke up. "Can you imagine she passed up the chance to be a princess?"

"Moscow is very cold in the winter," Angelica said.

Robert fixed his black gaze on her. Slowly, almost leisurely, he let his gaze slide down her body, perusing every curve.

"Ah, but cold nights incite warm cuddling beneath the furs," Robert said in a husky voice, his gaze returning to hers.

Angelica blushed a vivid scarlet. Flustered, she glanced at Venetia and was surprised to see the other woman staring at her, an angry glint in her eyes.

So, Venetia wanted Robert? Full-bodied jealousy swelled within Angelica's breast.

The duke cleared his throat and said, "I believe it's time for dinner."

Robert grabbed Angelica's hand and hooked it through the crook of his arm. "Allow me the pleasure of escorting you, Countess."

"Thank you, my lord," Angelica said. With Venetia in mind, she gave him a sunny smile. "Come, Jasper."

Angelica was at a loss for words as they descended the stairs to the first floor. Robert had gone from seducing her to accusing her of entrapping him in marriage to kissing her hand. Trying to understand him was giving her a headache.

And then Angelica spied the enormous birdcage in the grand foyer. "Another cage for Jasper?"

"I believe you'll find cages all over the house," Robert said. "Father wanted your pet to feel at home."

Angelica was surprised to find another birdcage in the dining room. From behind her, she heard Venetia saying, "We're dining with a bird?"

"We want the countess to feel at home, don't we?" the duke said.

Venetia did not reply.

The dining room was like nothing Angelica had ever seen. The forty-foot table had been created in solid mahogany, as was the sideboard, and three crystal chandeliers hung overhead.

With place settings for seven, the dining table held a soup tureen and cover dishes. The service was Wedgwood, and there were silver knives and forks and spoons with ivory handles. A silver tea urn graced the mahogany sideboard.

"Ah, seven place settings," Angelica remarked, glancing sidelong at Robert. "My lucky number is seven."

"The bird isn't actually going to sit at the table with us?" Venetia asked.

"Of course not," Angelica answered. She opened the birdcage and placed Jasper inside, where there were bowls of nuts, chopped green apples, and fresh water.

Dinner at the Campbell mansion was a feast. First they were served tomato soup enriched and garnished with a swirl of cream and chopped green herbs. Cool raw cucumbers contrasted with cayenne pepper sprinkled on top. Next arrived mushrooms stuffed with garlic, shallots, parsley, and breadcrumbs and doused with olive oil. The two main courses consisted of succulent salmon cakes on a bed of sorrel, enriched with cream and beaten eggs and grilled lamb chops served with new potatoes, cauliflower, and carrots.

"Your son isn't joining us for dinner?" Angelica asked Venetia, trying to keep her mind off Robert, sitting beside her.

"Colin always dines with Mrs. Honey," Venetia answered. "Mrs. Honey has been the Campbell nanny for years and years. As a young girl, she cared for Robert." She was silent for a moment and then added, "Colin has begun to think of Robert as his father."

Angelica cast a sidelong glance at Robert, who was frowning at his sister-in-law. "I'm sure the marquess will be a wonderful father," Angelica replied.

"Dearest Roxanne, I'd like to plan a small party," Duke Magnus said, changing the subject. "Would you like to help?"

"I'd love to help plan your party," Aunt Roxie drawled. "In fact, there is nothing I'd rather do more."

"Nothing?" the duke asked.

"Almost nothing," Aunt Roxie amended, giving him a flirtatious smile.

"Do you think Prince Rudolf will follow you to England?" Venetia asked. "How exciting that would be."

"I beg your pardon?" Angelica asked, her gaze and attention on Robert's long fingers.

"Prince Rudolf won't come for Angelica," Samantha spoke up.

"Brokenhearted, the prince left Italy," Victoria added, and winked at Angelica.

"That is too bad," Venetia said. "Robert, would you care to accompany my family and me to Lord Murray's ball tonight?"

"No, thank you," Robert refused. "I'm meeting friends at White's."

"Adam St. Aubyn and James Armstrong?"

Robert nodded.

"Adam St. Aubyn is the Marquess of Stonehurst," Venetia explained, looking at Angelica. "James Armstrong is the Duke of Kinross."

Angelica nearly choked on her lemon barley water. Two marquesses and a duke had been guarding her father's grave the other night.

"You won't mind if I desert you for the evening?" Venetia said to Angelica. "My father and brother will be here shortly, and I'd love for you to meet them."

Angelica smiled politely but said nothing. She could hardly believe she was about to meet Charles Emerson, the man who'd ruined her father. She glanced at Robert, who was watching her intently, and then dropped her gaze to her plate lest he read the emotion in her eyes.

After dinner, they retired to the small drawing room. Venetia went to her chamber to make final preparations for Lord Murray's ball.

"I took the liberty of having the servants bring your instruments here," Duke Magnus said. "I hoped you would play for me."

"We'd love to play for you," Angelica said.

Closing her eyes in order to keep Robert out of her thoughts, Angelica placed the harp on her lap. Samantha with her violin sat beside her on the settee and Victoria with her flute stood beside them. The three sisters played a spritely tune, their melody evoking sparkling water, fingers of dancing sunbeams, and hummingbirds.

Duke Magnus, Aunt Roxie, and Robert clapped when the three sisters ended their song. Aunt Roxie beamed with pride and called, "Bravo, my darlings."

"Bravo," shrieked Jasper, making everyone laugh.

Tinker walked into the drawing room at that moment and announced, "Your Grace, the Earl of Winchester and his son."

Angelica whirled in the direction of the door. Her breath caught in her throat, her heartbeat quickened, and her hands trembled with anticipation.

"Easy, angel," she heard Robert say.

And then Charles Emerson walked into the drawing room.

Chapter 7

He wasn't what she'd expected.

Bland in appearance, Charles Emerson was short and thin. The only hint of his villainy were his small brown eyes, which contained no expression, and his ingratiating smile as he crossed the drawing room to Duke Magnus.

Men who groveled always proved untrustworthy, Angelica thought, scrutinizing his every movement.

She slid her gaze to his son. Alexander Emerson was unexpectedly blond, tall, and well-built—the opposite of his father in appearance.

With a sickeningly ingratiating smile, Charles Emerson shook the duke's hand and flicked a disinterested gaze over her and her sisters. His blank gaze became an expression of surprise when he recognized Aunt Roxie, who offered her hand like a queen to a courtier.

"Lady Roxanne, I am surprised to see you," Emerson said, bowing over her hand.

Aunt Roxie gave him a feline smile. "I'm sure you are, Chuck."

"Now, Roxanne," he said with a smile that did not reach his eyes, "I dislike that name."

"I know," she replied, making the duke smile. "Is Graham here, too?"

"Graham passed away recently."

"I am sorry for your loss," Emerson said, a suitably somber expression on his face.

You don't know the meaning of sorry, Angelica thought, *but I intend to teach you that hard lesson.*

She flicked a glance at the son and was surprised to see him staring coldly at Robert. Why would Alexander Emerson hate Robert Campbell?

"Charles, meet Angelica Douglas, the new Countess of Melrose," Duke Magnus said, gesturing in her direction. "These two lovely ladies are her sisters, Samantha and Victoria."

"I knew your father well," Charles Emerson said, turning to her. "Did Graham ever mention me?"

"I'm sorry, but my father preferred never to speak of England after my mother passed away," Angelica told him.

"I can understand why," Emerson replied. "Graham and I suffered an unpleasant experience. We lost a fortune in a business deal. Luckily, I managed to recoup my losses as, obviously, your father did as well."

"My father's fortune passed to me," Angelica said, feeling the strain of being polite to a man she would prefer to murder. "I never speculate in business, though I do admit a fondness for games of chance. I'm particularly partial to dice and love to see them roll across the table. One never knows what numbers will come up."

"Then we shall contrive to keep you amused while you are in England," Emerson replied.

Angelica smiled brightly, but her thoughts were black. She sensed that he couldn't wait to get her at the gaming table and steal another fortune.

"How long do you plan to remain in England?" Emerson asked, turning to her aunt.

"Indefinitely," Aunt Roxie replied.

"I have invited the Douglases to live here," Duke Magnus said. "I intend to see Graham's daughters settled into happy and advantageous marriages."

"You always were the kindest of souls, Your Grace," Emerson replied.

Silent until now, Jasper walked out of his cage, calling, "Hello."

"What is this?" Emerson asked.

"Jasper is my pet macaw," Angelica told him. "A gift from Prince Rudolf."

"What an unusual and colorful bird," Emerson remarked. "Is it friendly?"

"Quite." Angelica heard Robert clear his throat but refused to warn the villain about the macaw's bite.

Emerson moved to touch the bird.

"Don't touch it," Robert ordered.

Emerson wasn't fast enough. Frightened by the stranger, Jasper nipped the earl's finger.

"It bit me," Emerson exclaimed, holding up his index finger. A dot of blood stained it.

"Bad bird," Angelica scolded, struggling against a smile. She rose from her chair, ordering, "Come, Jasper." The bird followed her across the room to the cage.

Closing the door behind it, Angelica turned around and, wearing a sunny smile, said, "No harm done, then."

"That bird is a menace," Charles Emerson said, his anger apparent, as he wrapped his finger in his handkerchief.

"Do not disparage my pet," Angelica ordered like a queen, forgetting to play the sweet, naive role.

"Child, I am the Earl of Winchester," Emerson said, flushing with anger. "Assume a proper tone when you address me."

"*I* am the Countess of Melrose," Angelica countered, arching a blond brow at him. "I will address you however I please."

"You should respect your elders," he said.

"Being an elder only means you will die sooner," she told him.

Robert burst out laughing. "Well said, angel."

Angelica smiled at Robert and realized she'd made a terrible blunder by antagonizing Emerson. He would never roll dice with her if she provoked him into anger.

"I apologize for failing to warn you about Jasper," Angelica said, changing her tone of voice. "He is friendly once he knows a person."

That seemed to appease the Earl of Winchester. "I accept your apology," Emerson said, and then smiled. "Perhaps you would like to attend tonight's ball with my family?"

His invitation surprised Angelica. Did the man who'd ruined her father think to befriend her? Or was he trying to make amends for his rude words? After all, he wouldn't be able to get her to the gaming table if she disliked him.

"My nieces and I will be housebound for several days," Aunt Roxie said, saving her from answering.

"Our guests lost their gowns, jewels, and furs to pirates while sailing to England on board *The Tempest,*" Robert said, looking at Alexander Emerson.

"I hadn't heard about that," Alexander replied stiffly, his dislike of Robert apparent.

Venetia appeared in the drawing room at that moment. She looked enchanting in a petal pink silk gown.

Charles Emerson bowed over Angelica's hand, saying, "Meeting you has been a pleasure, my lady."

"Thank you," Angelica replied without returning the compliment.

"You are even lovelier than the last time I saw you," Emerson told her aunt.

"I know, darling," Aunt Roxie drawled. "Good to see you again, Chuck."

"Good evening, Your Grace," he said, inclining his head to the duke.

"Good evening, Charles."

Emerson smiled at his daughter and escorted her out of the drawing room. Alexander Emerson paused to cast Robert a final glare and then followed them out.

Depleted of energy, Angelica sank down on the settee beside her sisters and touched her diamond pendant. She'd waited years to confront the man who'd ruined her family. Charles Emerson didn't look like the monster she'd imagined, and that made him dangerous.

"Well done, darling," Aunt Roxie said.

"I applaud your restraint," Robert said.

Victoria giggled. "I couldn't believe you let Jasper bite the bastard—I mean, villain."

"I wish I had warned him," Angelica said. "Now Emerson will be on guard."

"I doubt that," Duke Magnus told her. "Despite his villainy, Charles Emerson is a stupid man who underestimates others."

Robert perched on the arm of the settee beside Angelica. "I would guess that Emerson is plotting the most expedient way to steal your fortune, best-ing you at the gaming table or marrying you off to his son.''

Glancing at him, Angelica fixed her gaze on his leg and recalled how well-muscled his thighs were, how his back muscles rippled, how he felt on top of her, pressing her down on the grass. She shifted her gaze to the hearth. There was danger in his nearness. In spite of her fondness for him, Angelica refused to forgive him for his lies or his cruelty that morning.

"Where did the son get his blond hair?" Samantha asked.

"I suppose his mother was blond," Duke Magnus answered.

"Suppose?" Samantha echoed.

"Emerson's wife was already deceased when I met him," the duke said. "Roxanne, do you know anything about her?"

"I never met the woman," Aunt Roxie answered. "She must have been blind to marry him."

Precluding further conversation, a dark-haired boy ran into the drawing room and headed straight for the duke. Duke Magnus laughed and lifted the boy onto his lap. A graying, middle-aged woman rushed into the drawing room, then stopped short.

"I'm sorry, Your Grace," the woman said, obviously flustered. "I'm not as fast as I used to be."

"Don't worry, Mrs. Honey. I wanted Colin to meet my guests," Duke Magnus told her. "Colin, this beautiful woman is Lady Roxanne, and these are her nieces." He gestured to them, saying, "Ladies Angelica, Samantha, and Victoria."

Colin bowed first to Aunt Roxie before giving Angelica and her sisters the same honor. Then he ran to his uncle and hugged him.

The boy had black hair and dark eyes. When he smiled, as he did now, Angelica saw the uncanny resemblance to his uncle and his grandfather. Thankfully, she saw nothing of the Emersons in his appearance.

"I'm pleased to meet you," Angelica said. "How old are you?"

Colin stared at her for a moment and then answered, "I am five." He held up his hand to emphasize his age. "You're very pretty," he added, reaching out to touch her blond hair.

Robert grasped the boy's hand, saying, "Colin, you are entirely too young to try your hand with the ladies."

"Hello," the macaw called from his cage.

Colin whirled toward the voice. His mouth dropped open when he spied the vibrantly colored bird.

"That is my pet macaw, Jasper," Angelica said. "Would you like to meet him?"

Without taking his eyes off the bird, Colin nodded and held his hand out to her. Angelica smiled and rose from her seat. She escorted the boy across the chamber and then crouched down to be eye level with him.

"Hello," Jasper said.

"The bird talks," Colin whispered.

The macaw cocked his head to one side and said, "Hello."

"Say hello to Jasper," Angelica coaxed the boy.

His grip on her hand tightened. "Hello, Jasper."

"You must never put your hands near Jasper because his teeth are very sharp," Angelica instructed the boy. "He can bite your finger off. Do you promise not to touch him?"

"I promise," Colin said, and nodded solemnly.

"Drink, drink, drink," the macaw said.

"Jasper wants a drink," Colin told her.

"That is my father talking," Angelica said with a rueful smile.

Colin looked around and then asked, "Where is your father?"

"He's gone away to heaven," she answered.

With a maturity beyond his years, the five-year-old touched her cheek and said, "My father went to heaven, too."

"Mrs. Honey, I believe it's time for Colin to retire," Duke Magnus said.

"I don't want to retire," Colin protested.

Angelica feigned a yawn. "Oh, I am so tired," she said. "I believe I'll retire, too. Would you care to walk upstairs with me and Jasper?"

Colin nodded, his black eyes gleaming with excitement. Angelica stood, opened the cage, and then took the boy's hand in hers.

"Come, Jasper," she called.

With Mrs. Honey in the lead, Angelica and Colin walked out of the drawing room. Jasper followed behind them.

Angelica didn't spare a glance at Robert but felt his gaze on her. Relief at escaping his scrutinizing gaze swept through her as soon as she left the drawing room.

Sitting in front of the darkened hearth in her chamber for a long time, Angelica considered the abrupt changes in Robert's behavior. The only thing she understood was that he'd lied about his identity. Life had seemed simpler before he became the Duke of Inverary's son. She'd grown fond of Robert Roy and would have been happy living in poverty with him. The Campbell name, status, and wealth complicated matters.

Guilt stabbed at her heart when she glanced at the luxurious chamber. How dare she feel relieved by her father's passing. Her father and mother had lived their entire lives surrounded by wealth like this. To have it stolen away had killed both of them.

Angelica thought of Aunt Roxie, and love swelled in her heart. Her aunt had enjoyed a life of privilege and wealth and had sacrificed it to keep them alive. Somehow, she would repay her aunt for her loyalty and unselfishness.

As if her thoughts had conjured the woman, Angelica heard a rapping on her door and then her aunt asking, "Darling, are you awake?"

"Come in," Angelica called, rising from her chair. She hurried across the chamber and threw herself into her aunt's arms.

"What is this?" her aunt asked.

"I love you, Aunt Roxie."

"I knew that, darling."

"When my revenge is complete, I'm going to marry a wealthy gentleman and take care of you forever," Angelica promised.

"Men don't come any wealthier than the Campbells," Aunt Roxie said, giving her a dimpled smile. "One day you will be mistress of all this."

"I would not count on that happening," Angelica told her.

"I saw it in a vision," Aunt Roxie insisted. "You handled Robert spectacularly tonight. I couldn't have done any better. He left disappointed beyond belief. Men love challenges, you know. Keep up the good work."

"I'll try," Angelica replied, confused by her aunt's praise.

"Beware Venetia," her aunt warned. "She's an Emerson and not to be trusted."

Angelica smiled. "Thank you for worrying about me."

"I'll say good night, then." Her aunt kissed her cheek.

"Good night," the macaw called.

"Good night, Jasper," Aunt Roxie answered.

After her aunt had gone, Angelica covered the birdcage with a blanket and climbed into bed. She wanted to think about the day's events and her aunt's vision, but weariness claimed her in a deep, dreamless sleep.

The next morning, Angelica awakened refreshed and hungry, her nervousness having stolen her appetite the previous evening. She had felt uncomfortable at dinner, with Robert sitting beside her and Venetia watching every move she made.

After completing her morning toilet, Angelica uncovered the macaw's cage and said, "Hello, Jasper."

"Hello."

"Do you want to eat?" she asked, opening the cage door.

"Eat."

With the macaw trailing behind her, Angelica walked down the corridor to the stairs. The hour was relatively early, and she look forward to breakfasting alone and thinking about her aunt's vision. She wondered briefly why she hadn't missed her sisters' company during the night but decided she'd been too tired to care about anything except sleep.

Angelica smiled to herself when she walked into the dining room. Except for the majordomo, the chamber was empty.

"Good morning, Mr. Tinker," she said, opening the door of the birdcage for Jasper.

"Good morning, my lady," Tinker greeted her. "I have already placed Master Jasper's breakfast in his cage."

"Call him Jasper," Angelica said with a smile.

"All his friends do." She closed the cage door behind the macaw.

Angelica walked to the sideboard and helped herself to a Geneva roll with butter, a slice of ham, and a spoonful of scrambled eggs. When she sat down at the table, the majordomo appeared at her side and placed a cup of coffee beside her plate.

"*The Times,* my lady," the majordomo said, setting the newspaper down beside her.

"Thank you, Tinker." Angelica opened the paper and read while she ate. She never noticed the newcomer.

"Good morning, angel. I was hoping you'd be here."

Angelica looked up, though she recognized the voice, and saw Robert standing in the doorway. Her heart ached at the sight of his rugged handsomeness, but she steeled herself against him. The man was a liar and a fraud.

You are a cheater and a fraud, an inner voice told her.

"Good morning, my lord," Angelica said, watching him cross the dining room to the sideboard.

"Call me Robert," he told her, filling his plate. "Nothing has changed."

A great deal has changed, she thought.

When he sat down beside her, Angelica gestured to the forty-foot dining table and said, "There are a dozen seats. Why must you sit so close?"

"I want to speak to you without shouting."

"Speak about what?"

"I want to invite you to ride with me in Hyde Park," Robert said.

"No, thank you," Angelica refused, her gaze on the newspaper. "I have an appointment with the dressmaker this morning."

"Look at me, angel."

Reluctantly, Angelica turned her head and gazed into his dark eyes. There was as much danger in his intense gaze as there was in sitting so close to him.

"I apologize for my behavior yesterday," Robert said. "Your presence in my father's house surprised me."

A smile flirted with Angelica's lips, but she wasn't about to forgive him so easily. "I don't believe Mr. Tinker heard you as well as he did yesterday in your father's study. Isn't that right, Mr. Tinker?"

"I beg your pardon?" the majordomo asked. "I wasn't listening."

Angelica smiled at Robert.

Robert inclined his head, but his expression told her that he'd prefer to throttle her. He cleared his throat and said in a loud voice, "I apologize for my behavior yesterday." Then he called over his shoulder, "Did you hear that, Tinker?"

"Yes, my lord."

"You haven't apologized for lying," Angelica said. "Nor have you given me a reason for your lies."

"I wanted to become acquainted with you without my name getting in the way," Robert told her.

Angelica arched a brow at him. She lowered her voice to a whisper and blushed when she said, "I believe we are intimately acquainted."

Robert gave her a wolfish smile. "The Campbells are one of the wealthiest families in Britain," he said. "I needed to be certain you liked me for myself and not my money."

"I don't like you at all," she told him.

"You don't mean that, angel."

"I see the Campbells are long on money and short on modesty," Angelica replied.

"All I meant was that a man in my position needs

to be careful," Robert said. "Besides, your intention to rid the world of Campbells held my tongue."

Angelica didn't know whether to forgive him or not. She was attracted to him, and other than his lying and one lapse into pigheadedness, he had been kind to her.

"I will consider forgiving you," Angelica told him.

Robert inclined his head. Lifting the newspaper off the table, he said, "Let me know when you have decided."

"I was reading that paper," she told him.

"A marquess takes precedence over a countess," he replied, and returned his attention to the newspaper.

Angelica resumed eating but shot him an occasional sidelong glance. Was he just going to ignore her until she forgave him?

When he burst out laughing, Angelica rounded on him. "Are you laughing at my expense?" she demanded.

"Yes, I am." Robert dropped the paper on the table and pointed to an article.

Angelica leaned close and read:

Recently arrived from the Continent, Russian Prince Rudolf attended Lord Murray's ball last night and captured the admiring eye of those ladies in attendance. Perhaps the dashingly handsome prince will take an English bride?

"Sacred sevens," Angelica exclaimed in horrified dismay.

"What were you saying about lying?" Robert asked with a smile.

"Very funny."

"Give over, angel," Robert said. "Let's retire to my father's study and practice our strategy. You do want revenge, don't you?"

Angelica inclined her head but asked, "What will I do about Prince Rudolf?"

Robert couldn't contain his smile. "With any luck, angel, your paths will never cross."

"I'll get my dice and meet you in the study," Angelica said, rising from her chair.

Robert stood when she did. He crossed the dining room and opened the macaw's cage.

"Come, Jasper," Angelica said.

The macaw followed them out of the dining room. When they reached the second floor, Robert said, "Come, Jasper."

Angelica watched in amazement as the macaw followed the marquess down the corridor to the study. The bird had never obeyed any stranger before. Turning away, Angelica hurried upstairs to fetch her gambling paraphernalia.

Walking into the duke's study a few minutes later, Angelica saw Robert sitting in his father's chair. Beside him on the desk perched Jasper.

Angelica left the door open to discourage any advance he might be plotting. Robert had pulled another chair close to the front of the desk.

"Sit down," Robert said, gesturing to the chair.

Whoever sat in the duke's chair had control, Angelica decided. "I want to sit behind the desk," she said.

"I'm already sitting here," Robert replied.

"I liked you better when you were Robert Roy," Angelica told him.

Robert grinned. "I liked you better before you became a countess."

Angelica gave him a grudging smile. She looked

around and then suggested, "Why don't we call a truce and sit in front of the hearth?"

"An excellent idea."

Robert pulled a table close to the settee and gestured to her. Angelica sat down and then realized he was going to sit beside her. The chair in front of the desk would have been safer.

"Who is she?" Angelica asked, looking at the portrait hanging over the mantel.

"My mother."

"She was very beautiful."

"Thank you."

Angelica gave him a sidelong glance and said, "Too bad you resemble your father."

"Are you implying that my father is less than handsome?" Robert asked in an affronted tone of voice.

"No, I didn't mean—"

Robert laughed. "I know what you meant."

"Who are all these men?" Angelica asked, gesturing to the portraits covering the walls above the bookshelves.

"Every Campbell laird since the beginning of time hangs in this chamber," Robert told her.

"A rogue's gallery?"

He nodded. "An intimidating sight for a young boy."

"I cannot imagine you being an intimidated young boy," she said.

Robert shrugged. "We'll start with unloaded dice," he said, producing his own and passing them to her.

"Shall I throw first?" Angelica asked, inspecting them out of habit.

When he inclined his head, Angelica shifted the dice back and forth in her hands, as if getting the feel of them. "Seven is my main," she said, and threw the dice. A two and a two showed up, her chance to continue.

Again, Angelica tossed the dice. This time a six and a six showed up.

"Winning is more difficult when you don't cheat," Robert said, scooping the dice off the table.

"What's your main?" she asked.

"Seven."

Robert shook the dice in his hands and tossed them on the table. A six and a one appeared face up.

Again, Robert tossed the dice. They landed on four and three.

"My luck seems to be changing," Robert remarked. "How about a kiss if I win again?"

"Winning is its own reward," Angelica said primly.

"A kiss would be a wonderful incentive."

"Oh, very well."

Robert tossed the dice. A five and a two appeared.

Angelica grabbed the dice off the table and inspected them. "These dice are loaded," she said in surprise. "How did you make the switch?"

Robert smiled. "I listened carefully during my last lesson."

"I had a feeling you were going to do this," Angelica lied, too proud to admit she'd been bested at her own game. "Cheating successfully in a situation like this is easy. It becomes a bit more difficult when your opponents are alert and bound to call you out if they catch you."

Robert leaned close. "Are you angry because I beat you?"

"You did *not* beat me," she said, refusing to meet his gaze.

"I never would have taken you for a poor loser," he said, close to her face.

"I am not a—"

Unexpectedly, Robert drew her into his embrace. Mesmerized by his intense gaze, Angelica was caught by the gleam of desire in his dark eyes.

Robert's face hovered above hers for the briefest moment and then descended as one of his hands held the back of her head. Their lips touched in a kiss.

When she relaxed in his arms, his lips on hers became demanding, stealing her breath away. His tongue persuaded her lips to part and then explored the sweetness of her mouth.

The intoxicating feel of his mouth on hers made Angelica melt. She reveled in these exciting feelings and returned his kiss in kind.

"Hello," Jasper shrieked, startling them.

Robert and Angelica turned toward the open door. Looking none too happy, Venetia walked across the study toward them.

"There you are, my lady," Venetia said.

With a high blush staining her cheeks, Angelica rose from the settee and faced the other woman. Robert stood when she did.

Venetia looked from one to the other and then said, "The dressmaker has arrived."

"I'll take my leave," Robert said to Angelica. "I'll see you this afternoon for tea." And then he left the study.

Silently cursing him for leaving her to face Venetia, Angelica started to leave the study. Venetia put her arm out in a gesture for her to stop.

"I met a friend of yours last night," Venetia said.

Angelica stared at her blankly.

"Prince Rudolf was at the ball."

Knowing she was caught in a lie, Angelica did the only thing she could do. She stared at the other woman and tried to outface her.

"Prince Rudolf is in England?" Angelica asked, forcing herself to smile.

Venetia nodded but watched her closely. "He can hardly wait to see you again."

Her statement surprised Angelica. "There is no point in my seeing him. I would only break his heart again."

"You should have married the prince," Venetia told her. "There is nothing in England for you."

Angelica stared at her in confusion. "I don't understand."

"Robert already has a mistress," Venetia informed her. "His father and mine desire a union between Robert and me."

Angelica felt as if she'd been kicked in the stomach but managed to keep her face exprssionless. Robert had a mistress and planned on marrying Venetia?

"I wish you well, Lady Venetia," Angelica said, summoning all the dignity she could muster. "Come, Jasper." At that, she quit the study.

Chapter 8

"I have Angelica exactly where I want her."

Sitting in his own study two houses down from his father's, Robert looked across the desk at his friends, James Armstrong and Adam St. Aubyn. He watched them exchange smiling glances.

"What do you find amusing?" Robert asked.

"I thought you wanted the lady in your bed," James answered.

"You said you wanted to make her your mistress," Adam added.

"I did until my father intervened," Robert replied, and sipped his whiskey. "Now she's living beneath the umbrella of his protection."

"Are you certain Angelica Douglas doesn't have *you* where she wants?" James asked.

That remark didn't sit well with Robert. No woman had ever engineered him into anything he didn't want, and he had no intention of allowing Angelica Douglas to achieve what no one else had.

"What I meant was, Angelica and I have called

a truce and are concentrating on her revenge again," Robert amended himself.

"Do you love her?" Adam asked baldly.

"I want her," Robert answered.

"You've already had her once," James said. "Why don't you move on to the next lucky woman?"

"If I did that," Robert answered, "my father would marry her off to someone else."

"And the problem with that is . . . ?" Adam asked.

"Angelica Douglas is an Original," Robert told them. "No man of my acquaintance is worthy of her."

"Except you?"

Robert smiled, as if the other man had asked a stupid question. "I am more than worthy of her."

"How does the lady feel about you?" Adam asked.

"Angelica adores me," Robert answered. "She melted in my arms this morning. That is, until Venetia walked into the study."

At that, his friends burst into laughter. "I wish I had been there," James said to Adam.

"Seeing the object of her desire embracing another woman must have made Venetia decidedly unhappy," Adam replied.

"She will survive," Robert told them. "I refuse to sacrifice myself so that she can become a duchess."

"What did Venetia do when she found you and Angelica together?" James asked.

"She announced that the dressmaker had arrived," Robert said with a shrug. "I left at that point."

"You abandoned Angelica to the wrath of Venetia?" Adam asked. "I'd give a fortune to have witnessed that confrontation."

"Venetia is only my former sister-in-law," Robert

replied, unconcerned. "What could she possibly say? Besides, Angelica Douglas can take care of herself."

"What have your investigators discovered about the man who shot at you?" James asked, changing the subject.

"Nothing, but I'm positive the man was after Angelica's winnings," Robert replied, refilling their glasses with whiskey.

"The culprit was shooting at you, not her," Adam disagreed.

Robert sipped his whiskey and said, "No one hates me enough to hire an assassin."

"What about Alexander Emerson?" James countered.

Robert shook his head. "Alexander doesn't have the stomach for murder."

"He doesn't need stomach if he hires an assassin," Adam replied.

"Alexander Emerson is too honest to hire anyone to do his dirty work," Robert told them.

"Too bad he doesn't speak that highly of you," Adam said.

"You sound as if you like him," James remarked.

"Alexander is undercutting my prices," Robert said. "He could be behind the piracy of *The Tempest.*"

"What does your father say about the attempt on your life?" Adam asked.

Robert rose from his chair and walked to the window overlooking the rear garden. Though not furnished as grandly as his father's, the house was his own domain. Once he'd married, Robert had felt that he and his wife needed their privacy. Besides, he took enough orders from his father without living with the man. When his father passed on, he would consider moving into the ducal mansion.

Gazing out the window at the garden and courtyard below, Robert felt a sudden surge of remorse when he looked at the gazebo he'd built for Louisa. It seemed lonely without her. He hadn't loved her but had wanted to make her happy. When she told him how much she loved the gazebo at his father's country estate, he'd built a replica of it right here in London.

Strange, he had thought little about Louisa and their unborn child in almost two weeks. Angelica Douglas had replaced his deceased wife in his thoughts. Did that mean he loved her?

Banishing both women from his thoughts, Robert turned to his friends and admitted, "I haven't mentioned the incident to my father."

"His Grace could have some good ideas about who it could be," James said.

"Or how to protect yourself," Adam added.

"My father would hire an army of bodyguards," Robert told them. Then he changed the subject, asking, "Do either of you have any suggestions on how to bring Angelica together with her intended victims?"

"Invite them to dinner," James suggested.

Adam smiled. "Think of it as the last supper before financial ruin."

"Not one of them would dare to refuse an invitation from the Duke of Inverary," James said.

"That's a sterling idea." Robert glanced at his watch and said, "Let's walk to my father's house for tea with the ladies. We can discuss this with my father."

Adam St. Aubyn rose from his chair. "I can hardly wait to see Angelica Douglas melt at the sight of you," he said.

"Scoff if you want," Robert replied, "but you'll see a woman enthralled when she looks at me."

"A woman enthralled?" James echoed, and then laughed.

"Watch what I do," Robert told them jokingly. "You'll enjoy better luck with the ladies."

James Armstrong and Adam St. Aubyn looked at each other and laughed. "Modesty becomes you," Adam remarked.

"I can hardly wait to see a master at work," James said, and headed for the door.

At the duke's residence, the enthralled woman sat alone in her chamber and fumed with anger. Venetia's announcement had given Angelica a headache, and she'd begged off tea with the others, promising to attend supper.

How dare Robert seduce her and invite her to become his mistress when he already had a mistress and a fianceé, too. Did the man ever rest, or did he spend his days traveling around London, futtering whomever he desired at the moment? She thought she'd been insulted by his asking her to be his mistress, but this was simply unforgiveable.

Angelica suffered the urge to pack her belongings and return to the cottage near Primrose Hill. She didn't think she could bear seeing Robert with Venetia.

Too bad she needed him for her revenge. Even in death, her father was forcing her to accept responsibility for him.

Angelica felt a pang of guilt. Her father and her mother were dead and needed to be avenged. The fault did not rest with them, but with the men who'd put them into early graves.

When her revenge was complete, she would use her share of the winnings to leave London and her painful memories. Her sisters could marry wealthy men and care for Aunt Roxie.

"Yes?" Angelica called, hearing a knock on the door.

"Yes?" Jasper mimicked her.

"My lady?" The voice belonged to Mr. Tinker. "Lady Roxanne has asked that you attend her in the drawing room on a matter of importance."

"Thank you, Mr. Tinker." Angelica checked her appearance in the cheval mirror and smoothed the skirt of her gown. "Stay here," she told the macaw.

Wondering what was so important, Angelica walked down one flight of stairs. When she entered the drawing room, her heart sank to her stomach, but she managed to keep her face expressionless.

Robert stood there, along with his two friends from the graveyard. He surprised her by crossing the chamber and asking, "How does your head feel?"

"I beg your pardon?" Angelica said, her tone and her gaze frosty.

"Your aunt said you suffered from a headache," he said.

"Oh, that." Without answering his question, Angelica brushed past him to join the others. She sat beside her sisters on the settee and smiled at James Armstrong and Adam St. Aubyn.

"My lords, I want to thank you for your assistance the other night," Angelica said.

"You are welcome, my lady," James replied.

"We are glad we could be of service to you," Adam said.

"To what assistance do you refer, darling?" Aunt Roxie asked, clearly confused.

"They helped Robert guard father's grave," Angelica told her.

"How generous to help us in our hour of grief,"

Aunt Roxie told them. She looked at Robert, adding, "But I thought you said—"

"Robert noticed that being out of season did not stop us," Samantha interrupted her aunt.

"So he took precautions," Angelica added.

"What are you speaking about?" Duke Magnus asked.

"We abducted Mr. Lewis from his grave," Victoria answered. "Robert buried him again."

The duke looked shocked. "You robbed a grave?" he echoed in obvious disbelief.

"Believing we were in dire financial straits, my misguided sisters sought the help of Mr. Lewis," Angelica explained, trying to be delicate. "In life, he always liked us, so they assumed he would wish, in death, to help."

James and Adam burst out laughing, earning a censorious glare from Angelica. That only made them laugh more.

"The ladies didn't realize there is no demand for corpses in the summer," Robert told his father.

Wearing a disapproving expression, Duke Magnus looked at each of the girls in turn. Angelica felt like crawling beneath the settee. She folded her hands in her lap and stared at the crimson, gold, and blue carpet.

"Roxanne, I hope you did not encourage or condone this behavior," Duke Magnus said.

"No, darling, I insisted they return Mr. Lewis to his—his new home," Aunt Roxie replied.

Feeling a presence beside her, Angelica shifted her gaze to the left. Robert perched on the arm of the settee, so close to her, she could have pinched his thigh.

Angelica refused to acknowledge his presence. Instead, she looked at her aunt and asked, "What was the important matter you wished to discuss?"

Duke Magnus answered her question, saying, "Robert suggested that I host a dinner party and invite those men you want to meet."

"That's a wonderful idea," Angelica said with a grateful smile. Finally, after all these long years, her revenge was about to begin.

"James, Adam, and I can ruin three in one night," Robert told her. "That would leave only Emerson."

"You told your friends about my plans?" Angelica asked, rounding on him. Only a dead man would have missed her displeasure.

Robert shrugged. "They want to help you get justice."

"Absolutely not," Angelica said, rising from the settee.

Robert seemed surprised. "Why not?" he asked.

"First of all, you had no right to tell anyone what my plans were," Angelica said, her expression battle-ready, her voice rising with her anger. "Besides that, I want to take care of them one at a time, so I can savor their ruination."

"Well said, Angelica," Duke Magnus spoke, drawing her attention. "We have another matter to discuss. Your aunt and I believe Victoria should take no part in this. We'll give her a come-out ball in another year or two."

"She's only sixteen," Aunt Roxie said.

"That is unfair," Victoria protested. "Samantha is only one year older."

Angelica glanced at her youngest sister and then returned her attention to the duke. "Victoria is an adult and will attend all social events with us."

"That is most unwise," Duke Magnus said.

"With all due respect, Your Grace, *I* am the head of the Douglas family and will decide what Victoria may do," Angelica told him. She turned away, adding, "Excuse me, please. I really do have a headache now."

Leaving the drawing room, Angelica marched down the corridor to the stairs. Sacred sevens, she thought. How could Robert have betrayed her trust so easily? He had no right to—

"What the bloody hell is wrong with you?" Robert demanded, grasping her arm and whirling her around.

Angelica shifted her gaze from his dark eyes to the hand holding her arm. "Remove your odious paw from my person," she ordered coldly.

Robert snapped his dark brows together at her tone. Instantly, he dropped his hand.

"You are the blackest scoundrel I have ever met," Angelica told him. "I know about your mistress and your plans to marry Venetia."

"Are you jealous?" he asked.

"Don't be absurd," she snapped.

Robert gave her a lazy smile. "I have no mistress," he told her, "nor do I plan to marry Venetia."

"Your history of lying precedes you," Angelica said with a look of contempt.

"I thought you forgave me for that," he said, assuming an injured air.

"Forgiving does not extend to forgetting," she countered.

"What about your revenge?"

"What about it?"

"Don't you want my help?"

"Go home and practice," Angelica told him. Purposefully, she looked him up and down, as if he were dirt beneath her feet, adding, "When you can successfully cheat me, then you will be ready."

"I already cheated you, angel," Robert reminded her.

It was the wrong thing to say.

"I *let* you cheat me," Angelica said in a tight voice, fighting the urge to slap him. "When you can cheat me while I am cheating you, then you will be ready."

"That is illogical," Robert said with a smile, heedless of the warning signs in her expression.

Angelica lost the battle for control of her emotions. She slapped him hard, surprising him. Without another word, she turned away and walked down the corridor.

When she neared the stairs, she heard James Armstrong saying, "You have the lady where you want her?"

"I can hear the wedding bells now," Adam St. Aubyn remarked.

"No, no. That's the sound of crashing crockery," James replied.

Angelica smiled to herself. She walked up the stairs, out of earshot, and began to worry about how the marquess would retaliate for striking him.

Sacred sevens, why had she done it? Certainly not because he'd managed to beat her at dice.

She was jealous, Angelica realized in surprise. She loved Robert Campbell in spite of his lies. Well, her love for him was something he would never know. After her revenge was complete, she would leave London. Eventually, she would find another man to love.

Thank heavens for her aunt's example. Aunt Roxie had loved three men enough to marry them, proving there was more than one love in a woman's life.

Angelica refused to speak to the marquess for a week. Keeping her silence wasn't easy, though. If nothing else, the man was persistent.

Robert arrived to breakfast with her the morning

after she slapped him and kept up a ridiculous one-sided conversation. When he invited her to ride in Hyde Park, Angelica left the dining room and retreated to her bedchamber.

On the second day Robert came to tea, and the third day saw him at the dinner table. When the fourth day dawned, Angelica breakfasted alone in her chamber. Fearing she'd meet him, she skipped afternoon tea and pleaded a headache at the dinner hour.

When she awakened on the fifth day, Angelica knew two things for certain: She was hungry, and she had never felt so confined in her life. Her bedchamber was a luxurious cell. Why should she be imprisoned because the Marquess of Argyll was a womanizing liar?

"Darling?"

Angelica heard her aunt call and the soft rapping on her bedchamber door. "Darling, are you awake?"

"Come in, Aunt Roxie," she said.

The door opened. Her aunt carried a bouquet of royal blue and soft azure forget-me-nots.

"The marquess sent you these," Aunt Roxie said, handing her the flowers.

His message was obvious. Lifting the bouquet out of her aunt's hands, Angelica asked, "What marquess?"

"Give over, darling," Aunt Roxie said. "You cannot believe how distraught with remorse Robert is about your misunderstanding."

"You are correct," Angelica replied. "I cannot believe Robert is distraught with remorse."

Aunt Roxie gave her a dimpled smile. "Don't make him wait too long," she advised, and then left the room.

When teatime arrived, Aunt Roxie returned to

her chamber. This time she carried a bouquet of crimson-tassled love-lies-bleeding blossoms surrounded by greenery.

"The marquess sent you these," her aunt said.

Angelica lifted the bouquet out of her aunt's hand, a reluctant smile flirting with the corners of her lips. Did the marquess actually want to make amends, or was his pride merely hurt? If only she knew the truth.

"In the language of flowers, love-lies-bleeding means 'hopeless, not heartless,' " Aunt Roxie told her.

"Thank you, Aunt Roxie."

"I never noticed how stubborn you are," her aunt remarked. "No offense, darling."

"None taken."

"If you refuse to speak to him," Aunt Roxie warned, her exasperation apparent, "you'll never become mistress of all this." For emphasis, she gestured around the richly appointed chamber.

"I'll never become mistress of this even if I do speak to him," Angelica replied.

"We'll see about that," Aunt Roxie said with an ambiguous smile.

"Auntie dearest, the marquess has a mistress and plans to marry Venetia," Angelica informed her.

"Who told you that?"

"Venetia."

"I warned you not to trust her," Aunt Roxie replied. "That extends to listening to her lies." Her aunt put her arm around her and said, "Darling, dangers surround us in every direction now that we've taken our rightful place in society. Never remove that diamond pendant I gave you. Its magic will protect you from those who seek to do you harm."

"What do you mean?" Angelica asked as her aunt crossed the chamber to the door.

Aunt Roxie smiled at her and said, "Understanding is unnecessary; believing is everything." And then she vanished out the door.

Alone again, Angelica sat in front of the darkened hearth and considered her aunt's words. Could she be correct about Venetia? Had the other woman lied in order to discourage her?

Robert had been kind and generous to her family. Perhaps she would send him a note in the morning, asking him to call upon her. She would make him squirm and then forgive him.

Angelica knew one thing for certain: She couldn't spend the rest of her life hiding in her chamber.

"Come in, Aunt Roxie," she called a short time later, hearing a knock on her door.

Carrying a long box, her aunt breezed into the room. "How did you know it was me, darling?"

"I have the Sight."

"What a tease you are," Aunt Roxie said, passing her the box. "The marquess sent you this."

Angelica opened the box. Inside lay one perfect red rose entwined with one perfect white one.

"A symbol of unity?" Angelica said, laughing.

"The marquess adores you."

"The marquess adores *all* women."

"Give the man another chance," her aunt advised.

"I've already given him another chance," Angelica said. She sighed, adding, "I will consider it just for you."

The next morning Angelica went down to breakfast and helped herself to eggs, ham, and a roll. Then she sat down alone at the table. The wonderful thing about rising early, she decided, was enjoying a leisurely breakfast and reading *The Times* without having to make conversation.

A footman appeared at the door and handed an envelope to the majordomo who, in turn, delivered it to Angelica. He told her, "The courier has instructions to wait for an answer."

"Thank you, Mr. Tinker."

Angelica knew who it was from before she opened it. The message said: *Will you meet me in my father's study at noon to dice? If you win, I'll leave you alone; if I win, you'll speak to me again.*

"Tell the marquess I said *yes*," Angelica called to the courier.

"Very good, my lady."

Angelica had a second cup of coffee and thought about Robert. His ploy was so transparent. He thought she would be unable to resist a challenge at the gaming table. Obviously, he planned to use his loaded dice and win their game. She planned to let him.

When she descended the stairs to the duke's study at noon, Angelica left her loaded dice behind in her chamber. She needed to pretend to play in earnest. The man had his pride, and she had no wish to injure his feelings. Angelica cared deeply for him and believed the marquess cared for her, or he would not have been so persistent.

Robert was waiting for her. Heartbreakingly handsome in his crisp white lawn shirt and black waistcoat, he sat behind his father's desk, reading some documents. He smiled when she entered and rose from his chair, saying, "Good afternoon, my lady."

"Good afternoon, my lord," Angelica said, and then closed the study door to give them privacy. She walked across the study, saying, "Thank you for the flowers."

"You are welcome. But where is Jasper?"

"I left him upstairs," Angelica answered, halting in front of his father's desk. She suffered the sudden feeling that more than the furniture separated them.

"You wanted no distractions?"

"Precisely."

"Where would you like to sit?" he asked, gesturing around the room.

She pointed to the chair behind the duke's desk and answered, "I want to sit there."

"I've already set up a table in front of the settee," Robert said. "I believe we'll be more comfortable there."

Angelica inclined her head like a young queen granting a favor. She crossed the study and sat on the settee.

"Do you have anything up your sleeves?" Robert teased, sitting down beside her.

"Your suspicion wounds me," Angelica said.

"Then you know how I feel," Robert replied. "But I forgive you."

"*You* forgive *me*?" she echoed in disbelief.

"I forgive you for believing Venetia's lies," he told her, "but I understand that my previous lies contributed to your lack of faith."

Angelica gave him a long look and then said dryly, "How generous of you to forgive me."

"Shall we play?" Robert asked, and gave her a boyish grin. He produced the dice and handed them to her, saying, "You throw first."

Angelica lifted the dice out of his hand. Ever so slowly, she turned each die over and over and carefully inspected them to be certain they hadn't been loaded.

"Don't you trust me?" Robert asked with laughter lurking in his voice.

Angelica gazed at him from beneath the thick fringe of her golden lashes. "No, I don't," she answered.

"Your distrust hurts me deeply," Robert told her, touching his heart. "The winner will be two out of three games?"

Angelica nodded in agreement. "My main is seven," she said, and tossed the dice. A two and a two showed face up, giving her another chance to throw.

Again, Angelica tossed the dice. This time they landed on four and two. She tossed once more. A one and a one showed, which meant she gave up her throw to him.

Robert lifted the dice off the table. He shifted them back and forth in his hands, saying, "Seven is my main."

The dice landed on six and three, giving him another chance. The second toss landed on four and two. Three and four showed on his third toss, giving him a one-game lead.

Smiling broadly, Robert lifted the dice and shook them in his hand. Then he passed them to her, saying, "Try again, my lady."

"You're certain?" Angelica asked. Technically, the winner tossed again.

Robert inclined his head. "I want to be fair."

Angelica paused and inpected the dice again. When she tossed, they landed on five and four. She cast the dice three more times before they showed six and six.

"Sacred sevens," Angelica muttered. Winning without cheating was difficult in the extreme. Oh, how her poor father must have suffered as he lost his fortune to Emerson and the others.

Robert lifted the dice off the table and shook

them in his hands. He tossed three times before the dice landed on four and three.

"And now, my lady, will you honor me with a victory kiss?" he asked, pocketing the dice.

"You've won the honor of speaking to me," she answered, and gave him a sunny smile. "Nothing more, nothing less."

"As you wish, my lady." Then Robert asked, "Are you enjoying your new life of luxury?"

Angelica paused for a brief moment and then sighed. "If it weren't for my revenge," she answered honestly, "I'd pack my belongings and return to Primrose Hill."

His expression registered surprise. "Tell me why," he said.

"Life before Campbell mansion was infinitely more interesting," Angelica told him. "I'm bored to tears."

Robert laughed. "Thankfully, you're not bored to death."

"Who will you ruin tomorrow night?" she asked, leaning close.

"I think Alasdair Trimble will be easiest," Robert told her, leaning back and resting his arm on the settee behind her.

Angelica smiled with anticipation. "Alasdair Trimble, it is."

"I'll catch Henry Drinkwater at the Emersons' ball next week," Robert said. "I suppose I can catch Mayhew at White's."

"I can't watch if you do that," Angelica complained. "I want to see these villains squirm."

"Bloodthirsty, aren't you?" Robert stood then, saying, "I do have paperwork waiting for me at home."

Angelica was unable to keep the disappointed

look off her face. Reluctantly, she rose from the settee.

"Would you care to accompany me and tour my house?" Robert invited her. "I live two doors down from here."

I would love to tour your house, Angelica thought. Instead, she said, "No, thank you. The Countess of Melrose has a reputation to protect."

"Will you walk me to the foyer?"

"Yes, of course."

Arm in arm, Robert and Angelica left the duke's study. They walked slowly down the corridor to the stairs as if neither wanted to separate.

"Why didn't you use your loaded dice on me, angel?" Robert asked as they reached the foyer.

"I left them in my chamber."

"By design or accident?"

"Design."

"Are you implying that you wanted me to win?" Robert asked.

"Well, I thought I'd use yours," Angelica answered, giving him a flirtatious smile, "but you kept switching them on me."

Robert burst out laughing.

From the corner of her eye, Angelica spied Tinker opening the front door and heard the major-domo saying, "I hope your ride was—"

"I've changed my mind about that kiss," Angelica said, throwing herself into Robert's arms.

She drew his head down to hers, pressed her lips to his, and kissed him as if she would never let him go. Robert put his arms around her and returned her kiss in kind.

"Are you certain you won't accompany me home?" he whispered against her lips.

"I'm positive," she answered, albeit reluctantly.

"Until later, my lady." Robert stepped back and

lifted her hand to his lips. Turning away, he crossed the foyer to the door, saying as he passed her, "Good day to you, Venetia." And then he disappeared out the door.

Seeing the murderous gleam in the other woman's eyes, Angelica gave her a sunny smile and said, "Don't send those wedding invitations out just yet." Without giving the brunette a chance to respond, she hurried up the stairs.

"Bravo," Aunt Roxie said, watching from the first landing.

"I learned my tricks from an expert," Angelica said, and winked at her.

"Thank you for the high praise, darling."

Chapter 9

She felt like a princess.

Alone in her chamber, Angelica stood in front of the cheval glass and inspected herself. She could hardly believe the image was her own. Never had she worn so fine a gown.

Created in ice blue silk, it had a low-cut bodice and short Spanish shoulder sleeves. Her blond mane had been confined at the back of her neck in a knot. On one side of her coiffure, she wore a white rose, flowers in a lady's hair being all the rage this season. Or so her aunt had informed her.

Angelica studied herself from every angle. She looked like a princess, which was exactly what she wanted. She needed to look like a wealthy young woman on this important evening, the night she began to exact her retribution for crimes against the Douglas family.

Was Robert Campbell destined to be her prince and slay the dragon named Emerson?

Angelica smiled at the absurd bent of her

thoughts. Robert Campbell was no prince, merely a disreputable marquess.

And you love him.

The unexpected thought startled her. Yes, she loved him, but he would never know. That knowledge in his hands would only cause her heartache.

Angelica forced herself to think of the mission instead of the man. She had no intention of allowing Robert to have all the fun. While he was ruining Alasdair Trimble, she would study the others and decide which of them would gamble against her another night.

Participating was preferrable to watching, and Angelica felt certain that ruining her victims herself would give her infinitely more satisfaction. Or should she save her skills for the blackest villain of all, Charles Emerson?

Touching her diamond pendant, Angelica hoped the evening would go smoothly and her aunt was correct about the diamond's protection. She glanced at her hands and realized her nervous anticipation was making them tremble. The night she had dreamed about for years had arrived.

A knock on the door drew her attention. "Come in," she called.

"Come," Jasper mimicked her.

Samantha and Victoria walked into the chamber. Samantha wore a pink satin gown, and Victoria was dressed in the palest shade of yellow.

"Hello," said Jasper.

"Hello," the sisters chimed together, crossing the chamber to inspect their older sister.

"You look beautiful," Samantha said.

"You look beautiful, too," Angelica replied. She turned to Victoria and said, "You look lovely and so grown up. The pale yellow complements your hair perfectly."

"I thought I would look like a carrot-topped daisy," Victoria admitted with a smile.

"We can thank Aunt Roxie's impeccable fashion sense for choosing good colors for us," Angelica said. "I just wish we could wear mourning clothes for Papa."

"Wearing black won't bring Papa back from the dead," Samantha said. "We honor him more by getting even with those men. We're meeting in the drawing room."

"Are you ready?" Victoria asked.

Angelica shook her head. "I need a few minutes to focus on my mission. I'll be along shortly."

"Never forget that you are a countess with an impeccable pedigree," Samantha said.

"Don't worry, Angel," Victoria added. "Consider this evening as the beginning of the most elaborate fraud we've ever concocted. These people are no match for us."

Angelica laughed and hugged her youngest sister. "Tory, I love your optimism."

"Will Jasper be accompanying us?" Victoria asked.

"Robert advised me to leave Jasper upstairs," Angelica answered. "If he should bite someone's finger off, the gambling would come to an abrupt halt."

"That sounds wise," Samantha said, limping toward the door. "We'll see you downstairs."

After they'd gone, Angelica lifted her gown and placed her last-resort dagger in the sheath attached to the garter strapped on her thigh. She didn't expect any trouble, but, considering whom she was meeting, felt vulnerable without it.

Angelica stood in front of the cheval glass again to take one final look at herself. Both of her sisters were correct—she was a countess and a fraud.

Taking a deep breath, Angelica willed herself to calm down. "Wish me luck," she called to the macaw.

"Luck," Jasper called.

Angelica opened the bedchamber door, stepped into the corridor, and gasped in surprise. Robert stood there, leaning against the wall opposite her door.

"What are you doing?" she asked.

"Waiting for you," he answered, with a devastatingly charming smile. "I was beginning to fear you would hide in your chamber after all my careful planning."

"I've waited too long to miss this evening," Angelica replied.

"You are simply perfection," Robert said, dropping his gaze to her body. "Your bodice is cut too low, though."

He likes the gown, Angelica thought. "Distracting Trimble will help you," she told him.

"Hell, *I'm* distracted," Robert said, and offered her his arm. "May I escort you, my lady?"

Angelica gave him a sunny smile and slipped her hand through the crook of his arm. "Our unsuspecting victims await us, my lord," she said, her blue eyes sparkling with excitement.

The guests had assembled in the small drawing room where Duke Magnus was playing the host. Angelica fixed a warm, welcoming smile on her face as they crossed the room to the settee and chairs in front of the hearth.

"Here she is," Aunt Roxie announced.

Though every person in the room turned to watch her, Angelica never hesitated or lost her gracious smile. She felt calm, yet excitement coursed through her body, the same feeling she had when she gambled.

"Lady Angelica, may I present Baron Alasdair Trimble and his wife Mary," Duke Magnus made the introductions. "Alasdair, this is Graham's oldest daughter, the Countess of Melrose."

Angelica turned her sunny smile on the baron and his wife. Both of them were middle-aged and graying; the baron was as fat as his wife was skinny.

Like a princess, Angelica offered the baron her hand and inclined her head at his wife. "I am pleased to make your acquaintance," she said.

"The pleasure is ours, my lady," Baron Trimble replied.

Touching her arm, Duke Magnus introduced Angelica to his other guests. Henry Drinkwater was thin to the point of emaciation; his wife Wilma was extremely round and appeared to be wearing every piece of jewelry she owned. Standing with Venetia, Mungo Mayhew had the biggest beak of a nose she'd ever seen and beady eyes that remained fixed on her cleavage.

Ignoring Venetia's glare, Angelica greeted their final two guests, James Armstrong and Adam St. Aubyn. "Good evening, my lords."

"Good evening, my lady," James said, lifting her hand to his lips.

Adam inclined his head, saying, "You look lovely as usual."

"Shall we go down to supper?" Duke Magnus said.

Leaving Mungo to escort Venetia and his friends to escort the Douglas sisters, Robert reached for Angelica's hand and placed it on his arm. "Allow me to escort you to supper," he said.

Angelica leaned close as they descended the stairs and whispered, "I wouldn't wish to be near Mayhew when he sneezed."

Robert laughed. "You cannot imagine the size of his handkerchiefs," he said, lowering his voice.

"How large are they?"

"He uses his old sheets."

Duke Magnus sat at the head of the table in the dining room, and Aunt Roxie, glorious in red, sat to his right. Robert escorted Angelica to the chair on the duke's left and then sat down beside her. Opposite them had been placed Alasdair Trimble and his wife. Henry Drinkwater and his wife sat beside Robert. Appearing distinctly unhappy, Venetia and Mungo Mayhew had been relegated to the end of the party, beyond the Douglas sisters and Robert's friends.

"How kind of you to invite us to dinner," Mary Trimble said in a voice smaller than her body.

"I haven't entertained for a long time," Duke Magnus told the woman. He reached out to touch Aunt Roxie's hand, adding, "Now that Lady Roxanne and her nieces are here, I am planning to host many dinner parties and balls. As a matter of fact, my first ball will be on July twenty-third. We hope you will attend."

"We are honored to have been chosen as your first guests," Alasdair Trimble said, reaching for the rolls and butter. "We would never decline an invitation from you, Your Grace."

Mr. Tinker supervised the footmen serving dinner. A rich French cucumber soup, enriched with egg yolks and cream, arrived first, and was followed by dandelions dressed with crisp bacon and a sharp vinaigrette. Next came meadow mushrooms, baked with a stuffing of garlic, shallots, parsley, and breadcrumbs and then doused in olive oil. Asparagus with melted butter arrived with the baked Dover sole and a plump chicken, roasted to perfection.

There were wine for the gentlemen and lemon barley water for the ladies.

Mary Trimble talked more than she ate. "How old are your sisters?"

Angelica wanted no one to exclude Victoria from the social scene so she lied, "Both are eighteen."

"*Both* are eighteen?" the woman echoed, appearing confused. "How old are you, if you don't mind my asking?"

Angelica gave the woman a smile filled with sunshine. "I'm eighteen."

"All three of you are eighteen?"

"I will be nineteen in a few months," Angelica replied. "Samantha and Victoria recently became eighteen. My sisters are twins, you know."

"They don't even have the same hair color," Mary Trimble said, looking dubious.

Angelica glanced sidelong at Robert. He wasn't smiling. In fact, he appeared distinctly displeased.

"My nieces are fraternal twins," Aunt Roxie spoke up, looking down the table at the other woman. "The birth of identical twins is rare. Isn't that correct, Your Grace?"

Duke Magnus nodded. "So I'm told."

"Baron Trimble, what do you do for entertainment?" Angelica asked, leaning foward slightly to give him a better view of her cleavage.

Trimble fixed his gaze on her breasts as if they were two tasty morsels being offered to him as a treat. He seemed at a loss for words but found his voice at last, saying, "I enjoy a turn at the gaming table."

Angelica peeked at Robert. He had developed a twitch in his cheek muscle. "Do you dice, Baron?" she asked.

"Yes, I do."

"I love to watch the dice roll across the table,"

Angelica gushed. Then she added, "Perhaps we could toss together later." Only a dead man would have missed the suggestion in her voice.

Duke Magnus coughed, and her aunt smiled. Baron Trimble appeared ready to swoon. Angelica didn't bother to look at Robert. She knew he would be unhappy with her behavior.

"Ladies do *not* toss dice," Mary Trimble told her.

"My sisters and I possess very Continental attitudes," Angelica told the woman.

"You can watch the men throw dice later," Robert said. "How about it, Trimble?"

"I'd love a few games of chance," the baron replied. "With Lady Angelica watching, I feel confident of winning."

"How are our commodity investments, son?" Duke Magnus asked, changing the subject.

Angelica glanced at Robert, who frowned at his father and pretended deafness. Duke Magnus missed his son's warning look.

"I asked what commodities are doing well," the duke repeated in a louder voice.

Baron Trimble chuckled. "Your Grace, the marquess doesn't want to answer in front of us and give away a hot tip."

"Robert, where is the harm in our guests investing in a profitable commodity?" Duke Magnus asked.

Robert appeared decidedly uncomfortable. He hesitated briefly and then said, "Leeks and salt."

"Leeks and salt?" the duke echoed in apparent surprise.

Grim-faced, Robert nodded and lowered his voice. "Shortages are expected, and prices will soar."

"Use that information as you wish," Duke Magnus told the baron. "Refrain from spreading it around, or none of us will make a profit."

"You can depend upon me," Trimble replied.

Leeks and salt? Angelica thought in bewilderment. How many people ate leeks? Wasn't the ocean filled with salt?

Mr. Tinker and a small army of servants served dessert. There were seasonal fruits, cheeses, lemon sponge cake with whipped cream on the side, and sherry syllabub.

"Lady Angelica almost married Prince Rudolf," Angelica heard Venetia telling those at her end of the table. "Can you imagine any woman disappointing a prince?"

"Oh, my, she actually refused a prince?" Wilma Drinkwater exclaimed.

"A wife should make her husband happy," Aunt Roxie spoke up. "If Angelica wasn't happy living in Russia, she would never have made Prince Rudolf happy."

"I liked Rudy too much to make him unhappy," Angelica said.

"How magnanimous of you," Wilma Drinkwater said.

Mary Trimble nodded in agreement. "Most women would have accepted his offer and, once married, refused to live in Russia."

"My dearest niece is much nobler than most women," Aunt Roxie told them.

"Whoever would like to hear Venetia's pianoforte come along to the music room," Duke Magnus said as dinner ended. "Those who prefer gambling can accompany Robert to my study."

Duke Magnus and Aunt Roxie escorted the Drinkwaters and Lady Trimble to the music room. With obvious reluctance, Samantha and Victoria accompanied them, along with Venetia and Mungo Mayhew.

"I'm going to watch the dicing," Angelica announced, slipping her arm through the baron's.

Reaching the study, Angelica sat down at the desk beside Trimble. She wanted to be near the baron in order to distract him.

"I really would like to play," Angelica said.

"Ladies in England do not dice," Baron Trimble said, echoing his wife's words.

"Ladies on the Continent dice," Angelica told him, leaning close to give him another peek at her cleavage. She was so close he could have tweaked her nipple, and she expected him to start drooling any moment.

"What else do ladies on the Continent do?" Trimble asked in a choked voice, his gaze fixed on the swell of flesh above her low-cut bodice.

"Naughty things," she whispered, casting him a flirtatious smile.

Angelica glanced at Robert, who was staring at her. Only a dead woman would have missed his irritation. She caught Adam's eye and glanced over her shoulder toward the hearth.

"Dicing bores me," Adam said, taking her hint. "How about a game of cards?"

"Let's play faro," James said, taking his cue, and led the way across the chamber to the settee.

"You'll bring me luck," Trimble told her, patting her hand, apparently emboldened by her forwardness.

Angelica felt contaminated by his touch. She battled the urge to wipe his touch off on the skirt of her gown. Instead, she gave the baron a smile filled with sunshine and inched closer.

Robert produced a pair of ivory dice and handed

them to the baron, saying, "Shall we set the stake at a hundred pounds?"

"That is so much money," Angelica said, hoping she sounded suitably impressed.

"A hundred pounds is nothing, my dear," Trimble bragged. Looking at Robert, he said, "My main is—" The baron paused to ask her, "What is your favorite number from five to nine?"

Sacred sevens, Angelica thought, *the man is a bloody fool.* She smiled sweetly and told him nine, one of the worst mains a gambler could choose.

"My main is nine," he announced.

Trimble tossed the dice, and they landed on four and four. Again, he threw the dice. This time one and one showed, and he gave up his turn.

"My main is seven," Robert said, and threw the dice. They landed on four and two. He tossed again and lost his turn when they landed on two and one.

Angelica looked at him in surprise. She'd been expecting him to win. Where were his loaded dice?

"Shall we double the stakes?" Robert asked.

Trimble nodded and tossed the dice, which showed three and two. He threw the dice three more times before they landed on one and two.

Robert lifted the dice and tossed. A three and a three showed face up. Again he threw the dice, landing on a five and a four. His third toss produced one and one.

Angelica suffered the powerful urge to tell the marquess to get his loaded dice. However, years of gambling had taught her to keep her face expressionless.

"Shall we double our stakes?" Robert asked, passing the baron the dice.

Trimble glanced at Angelica. He dropped his

gaze to her breasts and found bravado. "Let's triple the stakes."

Robert smiled and inclined his head. "Certainly, sir."

Back and forth the dice went between the two men. Each time the dice returned to the baron, Robert offered to double or triple the stakes, and the fat man readily agreed.

Angelica tried to catch Robert's attention. She wanted him to move in for the kill, but he ignored her. She glanced at the baron. Sweat had broken out on his upper lip, and he patted his forehead with his handkerchief.

Robert glanced at her finally and said, "Wish me luck, my lady."

"Good luck, my lord."

Robert threw the dice. A four and a three showed face up, making him the winner of a hundred thousand pounds.

Trimble looked ready to swoon. "It's only pocket money," he said, glancing at her. "My dear, would you care to—?"

"No, I would not." Wearing an expression of contempt, Angelica stood and left the study. She would let the marquess deal with collecting the money.

Angelica went to her bedchamber. She needed a few minutes to collect herself. Strange, she didn't feel as satisfied as she had anticipated she would.

"Hello," Jasper called.

Angelica crossed the chamber and covered the macaw's cage with a blanket, saying, "Good night, Jasper."

"Good night."

Angelica stared out the window at the night and hoped the baron had more than a hundred thou-

sand pounds. Suddenly, she didn't want innocents
to suffer as her family had.

Taking a deep breath, Angelica left the chamber.
She didn't want to arouse the other guests' suspicions by disappearing for the evening after Trimble
suffered his loss.

Angelica walked down the stairs. She could hear
her sisters playing their instruments but didn't
think her rioting nerves would allow her to play
the harp.

Worrying her bottom lip, Angelica stood in indecision outside the drawing room and considered
returning upstairs. Then she spied Robert walking
down the corridor and hurried toward him.

"Where did you go?" he asked.

"I needed to get away."

"The Trimbles have gone," Robert told her,
holding his hand out to her. "Let's return to my
father's study."

Angelica gave him a wan smile and placed her
trembling hand in his. The warmth and strength
in his hand comforted her. "I never realized that
achieving my revenge would affect me like this,"
she said.

They sat together on the settee in front of the
darkened hearth. The only light was the candle on
the desk.

Angelica knew she shouldn't be sitting alone with
the marquess at this late hour, but he'd just
brought down one of her father's enemies. She
didn't have the heart or the inclination to leave
him.

"We make a good team, angel," Robert said,
leaning back and resting his arm on the settee
behind her.

"Your delay gave me a nasty fright," Angelica

admitted. "By the way, I want to invest some of our winnings in leeks and salt."

Robert laughed. "Angel, do you actually believe investing in leeks and salt could be profitable?"

Angelica smiled with understanding. "How fortuitous that your father asked about commodities."

"Fortuitous my arse," Robert replied. "Father and I planned that whole scenario."

"I couldn't have done a better acting job," Angelica said. With a worried expression, she turned to him and asked, "Will Trimble's family suffer in poverty now? I wouldn't want any innocents to suffer as I did."

"I knew you would feel that way," Robert said, dropping his hand to her shoulder. "I have friends in banking who investigated what Trimble was worth ten years ago. He will retain what he had then. With interest, of course. Does that make you feel better?"

Angelica nodded. "If I stole everything, I would be as evil as he."

"What do you want me to do with the money I've won?" Robert asked, his hand on her shoulder beginning a slow caress.

"Keep it," Angelica said absently, her mind focused on his hand. She knew she should leave, but—

"Keep it?" he echoed.

Angelica smiled at his surprised expression. "My revenge has never been for profit but rather justice for the wrong done to my parents."

"How noble of you," Robert replied, "but I insist the money go to your family."

"Very well," Angelica agreed. "Invest half in your companies. Then divide the remainder into four equal shares and bank it for my aunt, my sisters, and me. By the end of a year, our investments with the Campbells should be showing us a profit."

Robert smiled. "Why do you want to invest in my companies?"

"Everyone in Scotland knows the Campbells are always on the winning side," Angelica answered. She arched a blond brow at him. "I trust that extends to financial enterprises."

"Thank you for the praise," he said.

"I meant to insult you," she said. "The Campbells aren't the most despised family in Scotland for no good reason."

Robert burst out laughing. "As you can see, angel, I've been trying to make amends for my ancestors' misdeeds. What are you planning to do with your share?"

"I'll set half aside for gambling and give the other half to the poor," Angelica told him.

Again, surprise registered on his face. "You'll give it away?"

"Is there anything wrong with helping the poor?" Angelica asked, a note of challenge in her voice.

"My lady, your generosity is commendable," Robert said, leaning closer. "You are an Original."

Angelica placed the palm of her hand against his cheek. "Thank you," she said in a voice barely louder than a whisper.

Turning his head, Robert planted a kiss on the palm of her hand. Angelica leaned temptingly close.

"Kiss me," she said on a sigh, yearning to feel his warm lips pressed to hers.

Her invitation was irresistible.

Robert inched closer, his mouth capturing hers in a smoldering kiss. He slipped his tongue past her lips, tasting the sweetness beyond them.

Entwining her arms around his neck, Angelica caught fire and surrendered to him. She returned his kiss with equal ardor, and together, they lay on the settee.

Robert slid his lips to the delicate column of her throat, leaving a fiery trail of kisses. He slipped his thumb inside the top of her low-cut gown and pulled it down, baring her breasts to his gaze.

Angelica moaned throatily. She arched her breasts forward, offering herself to him.

"Your breasts are beautiful," Robert whispered thickly, his fingers caressing her aroused nipples. "I can make you wet merely by suckling upon them."

Robert dropped his mouth to her breasts and drew enticingly upon her nipples. Angelica moaned and squirmed as a throbbing heat ignited between her thighs, and she arched herself toward him.

Without taking his mouth from her nipples, Robert lifted the skirt of her gown and caressed the inside of her thigh. His fingers slid to the juncture between her legs, and he stroked the jewel of her womanhood, wet and swollen beneath his touch.

Angelica moved her hips and felt her tension building to unendurable heights. With a soft cry, she melted against his gently tormenting fingers and then floated back to reality.

Opening her eyes, Angelica saw Robert watching her. She blushed with embarrassment and nearly swooned when she heard someone opening the study door.

"Lord Robert, are you in there?" The voice belonged to Tinker.

Ignoring her pleading expression, Robert looked over the back of the settee and called, "I'm here, Tinker."

"Your guests are leaving," the majordomo told him. "I believe Lady Angelica has already retired."

Robert grinned at the man. "Lady Angelica is here, too."

Only silence met Robert's announcement. Too mortified to show herself, Angelica yanked up the top of her gown but refused to move. How could she ever face the duke's retainer again?

"His Grace thought you and Lady Angelica would like to bid your guests a good night," Tinker said.

"I'll be down directly," Robert told the man. "I'm unsure about the lady, whose complexion is crimson with embarrassment."

Angelica had a sudden wish for death, either hers or his. And then she heard the majordomo say, "She could do a lot worse."

"Thank you for the compliment," Robert replied.

"Don't let it go to your head."

Robert grinned and then looked down at her, saying, "He's gone now."

"How dare you?" Angelica said. "I hope you haven't ruined my reputation." She sat up and adjusted the skirt of her gown.

"You're wearing a dagger," Robert remarked.

"I felt vulnerable without it," Angelica said, standing. She gestured to the settee and added, "This will never happen again."

Robert grinned. "You said that the last time."

"Sacred sevens, you are incorrigible." At that, Angelica marched out of the duke's study, feeling Robert's gaze on her as she walked the length of the corridor to the stairs.

When she reached the foyer, Angelica refused to look at the majordomo. Duke Magnus and Aunt Roxie stood with James Armstrong and Adam St. Aubyn. The others had already taken their leave, and Venetia had followed the Douglas sisters upstairs.

"One victim down and three to go," James said to Angelica, who managed a smile for him.

"I wish you would allow us to help," Adam said. "Robert is having all the fun."

"I was thinking the same thing," Angelica replied.

"What will you do with your winnings?" Duke Magnus asked.

"Lady Angelica is investing most of it in Campbell companies." Robert spoke up before she could answer.

"Angelica, darling, why are you flushed?" Aunt Roxie asked, her voice filled with concern. "You aren't becoming ill, are you?"

"I'm a little warm," Angelica told her aunt, glancing at the majordomo, who avoided looking at her. "The excitement, you know."

"Adam and I are going to White's for a nightcap," James said.

"I'll join you," Robert said. He grabbed Angelica's hand before she could step back and lifted it to his lips, saying, "Until tomorrow, my lady."

"Good night, my lord." Intending to go to her chamber, Angelica headed for the stairs as Tinker closed the door behind the three friends.

A loud boom sounded outside the mansion.

Angelica paused, thinking it sounded like a gunshot, and then heard a second noise from outside. She whirled around and ran across the foyer.

Tinker had already opened the door. Duke Magnus and Aunt Roxie had rushed outside.

"He's been shot," James shouted.

Robert lay on the stairs. Adam was pulling Robert's jacket off to reveal his white shirt, its left sleeve slowly turning red from his blood.

"Sacred sevens," Angelica cried, pushing past the duke and her aunt. She knelt beside him.

"It looks worse than it is," Robert told her. Then he looked at his friends, asking, "Help me up?"

"Let's get him inside," Duke Magnus ordered. "Tinker, send for my physician."

"There's no need for a physician," Robert said.

"You've been shot," Angelica screamed in a panic.

Robert grinned at her as his two friends sat him down on a chair in the foyer. "The bullet grazed my upper arm," he said as they removed his shirt. "Tinker, fetch warm water, bandages, and whiskey."

The majordomo returned in a very few minutes, and Angelica knelt beside the chair to wash the bloody wound. Taking the bandages from the majordomo, she began to wrap his arm.

"This is the second attempt on his life," James told the duke.

"Second?"

"The first was a couple of weeks ago," Adam said.

"Why didn't you tell me?" Duke Magnus asked, clearly displeased with his son.

Robert took a swig of whiskey and answered, "I knew you would hire half of London to guard me."

"You're damned right about that," his father replied.

"Magnus, darling, becoming upset will not help," Aunt Roxie said. "You will hire those bodyguards in the morning."

"I do *not* need bodyguards," Robert insisted.

Angelica reached up to touch his cheek. When he looked at her, she stared into his dark eyes and said, "Someone wants you dead."

Chapter 10

Who wants Robert dead? Angelica wondered, alone in her chamber the next afternoon. Worrying about Robert had stolen her sleep for most of the night, and she'd awakened later than usual. What should have been her first night of triumph had become a nightmare of dread.

Who hated Robert enough to kill him? For some unknown reason, Alexander Emerson despised him. Alasdair Trimble would probably love to see him dead but, in all likelihood, hadn't had the time to hire an assassin. Robert must have other enemies, but she knew so little about him and his businesses. Sacred sevens, the whole of Scotland would love to see the Campbells extinct.

What Robert needed was an amulet to protect him against unseen forces, Angelica decided. She would speak to her aunt at the first opportunity.

The door swung open suddenly, and Aunt Roxie appeared as if conjured by her thoughts. "Good afternoon, darling," her aunt called, crossing the chamber. "You slept late."

"Good day to you," Angelica said. "Do you know where Jasper is?"

"He's visiting His Grace in the study," Aunt Roxie answered. She sat down beside her on the chaise. "Darling, I need a tiny favor."

"It's yours if possible," Angelica said. She smiled when she added, "After all, you *are* my favorite aunt."

"I'm your *only* aunt," Roxie drawled. "I want you to deliver an amulet and a salve to Robert."

Angelica lost her smile as thoughts of their intimate encounter surfaced in her mind. "Can't a servant do that?"

"I've passed the entire morning shopping for the proper amulet, consecrating it with my special magic and then preparing the salve," Aunt Roxie told her. "I'm certain poor Robert would prefer you to tend his wound."

"Won't my reputation suffer if anyone sees me calling upon him?" Angelica asked.

"Nobody knows you, darling." Aunt Roxie chuckled throatily. "Besides, an army of bodyguards in his father's employ surround the poor boy."

Angelica fell silent with indecision. She wanted to see him but felt reluctant to be alone with him because of their encounter the previous evening.

"A countess enjoys more freedom of movement than an untitled miss," her aunt was saying.

Angelica found that difficult to believe. Society's rules applied to everyone, didn't they? "Are you sure about that?" she asked.

"Have I ever given you poor advice?" her aunt countered.

Aunt Roxie had spent her entire fortune keeping

her and her sisters alive. Even though they'd fallen upon hard times, her aunt had insisted that she and her sisters learn the essentials of being a lady. Hence, the sisters had no fear of embarrassing themselves with any faux pas.

"I'm sorry for doubting you," Angelica said, rising from the chaise. "Shall I leave now?"

Aunt Roxie gave her a dimpled smile. "Change your gown, darling, and I'll meet you in the foyer."

Dressed in a high-waisted peach gown, Angelica walked downstairs fifteen minutes later. Her aunt was already waiting for her.

"I adore that color on you," Aunt Roxie said, handing her a package.

"Which house is Robert's?" Angelica asked.

"Two doors down on the left," her aunt told her, brushing a strand of hair off her forehead. "You are my golden girl, with beauty, intelligence, skill, and, most importantly, a generous heart."

"I love you, too, Aunt Roxie."

Angelica walked down the stairs, turned left, and paused. A small group of men loitered in front of the marquess's mansion. She realized the men were the bodyguards hired by Duke Magnus.

"Good day," Angelica greeted them. The men made a path for her, but when she started up the stairs, one of them touched her arm to stop her.

Angelica halted. She looked from his eyes to his hand and then cocked a blond brow at him.

"I'm sorry, miss," the man said, his hand dropping away. "You must state your business here."

Angelica blushed when one of the men said with a chuckle, "You know His Lordship's vices. Why do you think the doxy is here?"

"Why don't you search her for weapons?" another added.

Angelica wished she'd worn her last-resort dagger. Before speaking, she gave each of the men a withering look. Finally, she turned to the man who'd dared to touch her, saying, "I am the Countess of Melrose and have come at the Duke of Inverary's request. If you don't believe me, walk two doors down and ask him."

The man had the good grace to flush; the others laughed at his expense. "I'm sorry, my lady," the man apologized. "His Grace instructed us to be thorough in protecting the marquess."

"Apology accepted, sir," Angelica replied. "However, thoroughness does not imply lewdness."

Angelica turned her back on them and walked up the stairs. She reached out and banged the knocker against the door.

A tall, dignified-looking man with graying hair opened the door. He looked her up and down and, apparently, decided her business was legitimate. "Please, come inside," he said, and stepped back to let her pass.

Shrugging off the feeling that she'd seen this man before, Angelica walked inside and heard the door close behind her. The marquess's foyer was less imposing than his father's. Along with marble statuary, carved cornices, and rococco ornamentation were several pieces of potted greenery that softened the overall atmosphere of the reception hall. There were a synonium plant with heart-shaped leaves, a double ivy topiary, and a six-foot dracaena plant.

"Whom may I say is calling, my lady?" the major-domo asked with a polite smile.

"The Countess of Melrose," she answered.

The man lost his smile. "The Countess of Melrose is deceased," he informed her. "You are an imposter."

"I beg your pardon?"

"I was previously in the Earl of Melrose's employ and know his wife is deceased," the majordomo told her. "I don't know what you want, but you must leave at once."

Angelica said nothing but stared at him for several long moments. "Webster?" she said finally. "Is it you?"

The man seemed taken aback. "How do you know my name?" he demanded.

"Don't you remember Angelica?" she asked. "Is Mrs. Sweeting here, too?"

"Lady Angelica, is it really you?" he asked with a surprised smile.

Angelica hugged her father's former majordomo. Then she asked, "Mrs. Sweeting?"

Webster shook his head. "The Duke of Inverary purchased her a cottage on the outskirts of London and pensioned her off. Later, the marquess persuaded her to leave retirement to assume a position with one of his acquaintances. Your father—?"

"—passed away recently," she told him.

"I am truly sorry," Webster said. "His Lordship was a kind and decent man. You wish to see the marquess?"

"I've brought him a couple of items from Aunt Roxie," she answered.

Webster grinned broadly. "How is Lady Roxanne?"

"My aunt enjoys the best of health and is still as beautiful as ever," Angelica answered. "We are guests of the Duke of Inverary."

"Come with me," Webster said. "The marquess is working in his study."

Angelica followed the majordomo up the stairs. The balustrade was a dark mahogany, and a round-headed window graced the landing, along with a potted wisteria tree.

"How does the marquess manage to keep these plants alive inside the house?" she asked.

Webster paused. "His Lordship requisitioned several dozen pieces of greenery created with bark and silk."

Angelica reached out and touched a lavender wisteria flower. "Sacred sevens, it *is* silk," she said with a smile.

"His Lordship says a man should be well-planted," Webster told her. "He enjoys gardening and wanted to bring the outdoors inside his home."

His revealing statement about the marquess heartened Angelica. A man who cared for plants wasn't beyond redemption.

Reaching the study, Webster knocked on the door and, hearing the marquess call out, entered the room. "The Countess of Melrose has arrived for a visit."

"Send her in," she heard him say.

Robert stood when she walked into the study and gave her his devastatingly charming smile. He seemed sincerely happy to see her.

"Welcome to my home," Robert greeted her. "If I had known being injured would bring you here, I would have hired the assassin myself."

"If I had known a bullet would make you so agreeable, I might have pulled the trigger myself," Angelica quipped, making him smile. "How does your arm feel?"

"I can handle the pain," he answered.

"I've brought you some things from my aunt," she said, crossing the study.

Like the Duke of Inverary's, the marquess's study faced the rear garden, and bookcases had been built into the walls. An enormous oak desk stood in front of the high, round-headed windows that allowed ample sunlight into the room. The chamber's only ornamentations were a thick, red Persian carpet, a mosaic of a lion and a lioness, made from thousands of colored tesserae, hanging over the mantel, and a giant alabaster statue of Atlas holding up the world, perched on top of a black marble pedestal.

"What about your reputation?" Robert asked, walking around the desk.

Angelica dismissed his question with a wave of her hand, saying, "Aunt Roxie explained that a countess enjoys more freedom of movement than an untitled miss."

Robert smiled as if she'd said something wildly amusing. "I'm glad your aunt explained the situation to you," he said. "Now, what have you brought me?"

"An amulet for protection and a salve for your wound," she answered, setting the package on his desk.

Angelica opened the box containing the amulet and smiled at her aunt's extravagance. Attached to a heavy gold chain was a replica of Wotan's Cross, a cross inside a circle. The circle and the cross were made of gold, and a blue topaz sat inside the center of the cross.

"What a handsome pendant," Robert said.

"Topaz with gold is powerful protection against envy, intrigue, disease, injury, sudden death, and lunacy," Angelica told him, placing the gold chain with the pendant over his head to hang around his neck.

"Lunacy?" Robert echoed.

"It is especially effective if worn on the left arm,"

she added, "but I suppose my aunt believed you
would never wear a bracelet."

"Give your aunt my thanks," he said.

Angelica peered up at him. "Wearing topaz also
draws love."

"I hope so," Robert said, putting his arms
around her and pulling her close, his clean scent
of mountain heather assailing her senses, enticing
her to remain within the circle of his embrace.

Slowly, Robert lowered his head until his warm
lips claimed hers in a lingering kiss. When she
returned his kiss, he flicked his tongue out to caress
the crease between her lips.

Remembering their sensuous interlude of the
previous evening, Angelica broke off the kiss and
stepped back. She turned away and walked behind
the desk to gaze at the garden below until she
could compose herself. What power did Robert
Roy Campbell have over her that she would forget
her resolve as soon as he touched her?

Below in the garden, a blond-haired woman sat in
a gazebo and looked toward the house. Not wishing
to get the woman in trouble with her employer,
Angelica turned her back on the window and walked
back to the desk to pick up the jar of salve.

"Sit on the settee and remove your shirt," she
instructed him.

Robert grinned wolfishly. "With pleasure, my lady."

Fixing his black gaze on hers, Robert unbuttoned
his shirt and tossed it toward the desk. It landed
on the chair.

His well-muscled chest mesmerized Angelica,
and she couldn't seem to tear her gaze from it. She
only hoped she could complete her task without
falling prey to his irresistible allure.

Angelica sat on the settee beside Robert and
gingerly removed the bandage on his upper arm.

The wound bled a bit and looked sore but much better than it had the previous night.

"What's in it?" Robert asked as she dipped her fingertips in the salve.

"My aunt simmered certain herbs in oil and then blended it with beeswax," Angelica told him. She touched his wound with her fingertips and felt him flinch almost imperceptively. She hoped she wasn't hurting him too much.

"You have a gentle touch," Robert said in a husky voice. When she snapped her gaze to his, he asked, "What herbs?"

"There are yellow chamoile, leaves of plaintain and woodruff, bark and buds of poplar, and myrrh to seal the wound," Angelica told him. Then she asked, "Who wants you dead?"

"I have no enemies," Robert told her.

"Alexander Emerson dislikes you," she remarked, watching for his reaction.

He didn't seem surprised. "How do you know?"

"I read the hatred in his eyes the night I met him and his father," Angelica answered.

"My former brother-in-law blames me for his sister's death," Robert admitted. "However, Alexander is incapable of murder."

"Underestimating others is unwise," Angelica advised him. She gazed at him through her disarming blue eyes and added, "Your wife suffered an untimely accident, didn't she? Why would he blame you?"

Robert looked away and speculated, "Perhaps if she hadn't married me, Louisa would be alive today."

The obvious pain in his voice tugged at her heartstrings. The marquess had loved his wife and felt her loss keenly.

And where does that leave me? Angelica wondered. She could never compete against a dead woman.

"I suppose we can add Alasdair Trimble to your list of enemies," Angelica said with a smile.

Robert returned her smile. "I suppose we can."

"Along with a host of husbands and fathers?"

"Either you consider me as wicked as Satan," Robert said dryly, "or you give me more credit than is my due."

"Actually, the first time I saw you, I suspected that Old Clootie himself had stepped out of that crowd at the fair," Angelica said, her cheeks pinkening with the admission.

Robert grinned. "Why did you think that?"

Instead of answering him, Angelica picked up the new bandage she'd brought with her and began wrapping it around his arm. "Perhaps I should dice with Drinkwater and Mayhew."

"You will do no such thing," Robert told her, a sharp edge to his voice. "Ladies play whist; they do not dice for high stakes. Ruining those men would mean ruining yourself, not to mention good marriage prospects for your sisters."

"Sacred sevens, that is absurd," Angelica said, wiping the salve off her fingers with an extra piece of gauze.

"I will not debate the point with you," Robert said. "I will ruin Drinkwater and Mayhew. Furthermore, I do not want you distracting them with views of your cleavage."

"I was helping you," Angelica said. "Besides, I am more proficient at cheating than you."

"I appreciate your determination to see this through to a successful conclusion," Robert replied, leaning back. "However, your cheating would create a grand scandal if you were caught." He winced as he lifted his left arm to rest on the settee behind her. "Don't rush home, angel. I could use some company."

Angelica inclined her head. She knew she was in danger by staying, yet she hadn't the heart to leave.

"So, tell me why you thought I was Old Clootie," Robert said.

Angelica stared at his bare chest, the blue topaz sparkling at her from the center of the amulet. Without thinking, she answered truthfully. "I thought no flesh-and-blood man could be that handsome, and Old Clootie had stepped out of the crowd to lead me astray."

"I did," Robert said, taking her hand in his and lifting it to his lips. "I love you in peach; you are tempting enough to eat."

Angelica blushed and dropped her gaze. The hint of a smile touched her lips when she asked, "Do you always compliment the ladies by comparing them to fruit?"

She snapped her gaze to his when she heard him laugh. "What do you find so amusing?"

"Your innocence," he answered, his dark gaze on her softening.

"I was more innocent before I met you," Angelica reminded him, giving him a long look.

With a devastating smile on his handsome face, Robert inched closer, and his mouth descended to claim her lips. Angelica closed her eyes, surrendering to her desires, and their lips touched in a lingering kiss.

When Angelica relaxed in his arms, Robert's kiss became ardent and demanding. Together, they fell back on the settee and kissed for an eternity.

Without taking his lips from hers, Robert slid the bodice of her gown down to free her breasts from their confinement. The gown lifted them high, as if they begged for his touch.

Robert kissed her eyelids, temples, nose, and

throat. He claimed her lips again while his fingertips glided back and forth across her sensitive nipples, which hardened into arousal beneath his touch.

Angelica sucked in her breath at the sensation. His fingers on her nipples ignited a throbbing heat in the secret place between her thighs. Her young body yearned to feel his masculine hardness filling her, making her complete; instinctively, she moved her hips in a sensual invitation as old as time itself.

Slowly, enticingly, Robert slid his lips down the delicate column of her throat to her breasts. He flicked his tongue across her nipples, making her moan with pleasure.

"Yes, oh yes," Angelica murmured, clasping his head to her breast.

Robert fixed his mouth on a breast and drew tantalizingly upon its nipple. Capturing it between his teeth, he nipped it gently, spurred on by her moans of pleasure. He licked her nipple again and teased it with his teeth. At the same time, he slipped his right hand down her body and lifted the skirt of her gown to caress the inside of her thigh.

"I love your breasts, with their sensitive nipples," Robert whispered.

Angelica moaned low in her throat and thrust her breasts out. Embracing him, she pulled him tighter and panted, "Touch me, touch me all over."

In answer, Robert drew hard on her engorged nipple and slid his hand to the juncture between her thighs. Angelica spread her legs for him, and when he caressed the jewel of her womanhood, she began to move her hips in rhythm with his fingers.

"You are swollen and wet for me, my love," Robert whispered thickly.

"Only for you," Angelica breathed, her young body inflamed by his touch and his words.

Sliding down her body, Robert used his fingers to tease her nipples while his mouth found the jewel of her desire. He licked and nipped her female button while holding the tips of her nipples between his thumbs and forefingers and squeezing gently, his hands mimicking what his lips had done.

Angelica felt her tension building and cried out as wave after wave of exquisite pleasure crashed over her. She clung to him as if she would never let him go.

Robert rose up between her thighs and pushed himself inside her. He grinded himself deep within her trembling body and rode her hard until they cried out their pleasure and then lay still. The only sound in the chamber was their labored breathing as they floated back to earth.

Reality returned in the form of shame and guilt. Now sated, Angelica realized what she had done. Again. Her behavior was appalling. Ladies did not abandon themselves to their desires, especially unmarried ladies.

She was a countess but no lady. Did she suffer some defect of character? Would she behave this disgracefully with all men, or only Robert? Was she a born wanton? Were sexual desires to her what sweets were to a fat woman?

Her previously privileged life had prevented her from truly fitting into a life without wealth. Had her exposure to a rougher class of society tarnished her somehow? Sacred sevens, where in God's great universe did she belong?

When Robert lifted himself off her, Angelica pushed the skirt of her gown down and then covered her breasts. Rising from the settee, she turned her back to him and wandered across the chamber to the window while she composed herself physically and emotionally.

Angelica tried in vain to rid herself of the tousled look by pushing her blond hair back away from her face. Her gaze drifted to the garden below. The gazebo was empty, the blonde having taken herself back to work.

When she turned away from the window, Angelica saw Robert watching her. She squared her shoulders and crossed the study to stand in front of him.

"*This* will never happen again," Angelica said, gesturing to the settee.

Robert grinned. "You're repeating yourself, my love."

Without warning, Angelica slapped him. Playing the wanton was bad enough, but she refused to be mocked.

"Why did you do that?" Robert asked.

"I despise men who smirk," she told him.

"I wasn't smirking," he said.

"Bull's pizzle."

Robert grabbed her upper arms and yanked her against his unyielding body. With his lips hovering above her, he said, "I've changed my mind, angel."

"What do you mean?" Angelica asked in confusion.

"Almost being killed has made me aware of my mortality," Robert told her. "I want to marry you and make a dozen babies."

What about love? Angelica thought, stepping back two paces, her heart wrenching at his omission. By sheer force of will, she kept her tears from flowing.

"I've changed my mind, too," Angelica said, her smile filled with sunshine. "I wouldn't marry you to save my soul from eternal damnation."

Chapter 11

"*You're rejecting me?*"

Robert couldn't credit what he'd heard. This must be some mistake or a joke. No woman had ever refused his advances, never mind that he was offering the chit a high-ranking title and vast wealth, in addition to his numerous physical and intellectual attributes.

"Don't look so surprised," Angelica said. "I've built up an immunity to your charms, my lord, as one does with the measles."

Robert stared at her in disbelief. She seemed to be enjoying the moment. "Are you comparing me to a childhood disease?" he asked, unamused by her wit.

Angelica smiled at that.

"You were purring in my arms not ten minutes ago," Robert said, wiping the smile off her face. He felt some satisfaction when her cheeks pinkened with her embarrassment. "*You* asked *me* to marry you only two weeks ago."

Her blush deepened into a vibrant scarlet. She recovered herself, though, saying, "Now that I know you better, I've changed my mind."

"Any woman in England is mine for the asking," Robert told her, insulted by her remark. He knew it was the wrong thing to say as soon as the words slipped from his lips.

Angelica drew herself up to her full height of five feet two inches. A mulish expression appeared on her face.

"Any woman *except me,*" Angelica told him, and turned to leave.

Robert moved when she did. He stood in front of the closed door and blocked her exit. Relaxing back against the door's solid wood, he folded his arms across his chest.

"Let me pass," she said.

"No, and if you strike me again," he replied, "I'll take you across my knee."

Angelica arched a blond brow at him. "Are you keeping me prisoner?"

"What an excellent idea," Robert said, his smile growing into a broad grin.

Angelica assumed a disgusted expression. She rolled her eyes heavenward, as if he was trying her patience.

"I ruined Alasdair Trimble," Robert reminded her, "but you don't seem grateful."

"I am exceedingly grateful," Angelica told him. "However, I could have ruined him myself." She appeared wholly disgusted when she added, "Any five-year-old could have ruined that breast-ogling idiot. What sane person chooses a main on the basis of someone else's favorite number? I cannot imagine how my father lost part of his fortune to the man."

"Have I told you how beautiful you are when

you're angry?" Robert asked. "Your blue eyes blaze with emotion. You're doing it now. Almost the same thing happens when we make love. Your facial expressions and soft moans could incite a holy man to lust."

"You watched me?" Angelica exclaimed, blushing fiercely.

"Watching is part of the fun," he said. "Try it next time."

"There won't be a next time," she informed him.

Robert ignored that remark and asked, "May I escort you to Emerson's ball?"

"No."

"Please?"

Angelica looked surprised by his use of the word *please*. After a moment, she said, "I'll consider your request."

Robert stepped aside to let her pass. "Tell my father to call his watchdogs off," he said as she passed him.

"Tell him yourself." At that, she disappeared out the door.

Robert smiled to himself as he crossed the study to his desk. He sat down and poured himself a whiskey.

His angel's fierce spirit was one of her most endearing qualities. But what the bloody hell did she want from him? A profession of undying love? What a ridiculous—

I love her, Robert realized, surprising himself. He had never loved any woman before, merely accepted their love as his due and taken what he'd wanted. Well, he would never tell the little minx that he loved her. He'd seen too many henpecked gentlemen at White's, trying to escape their wives for an evening to catch a few hours of peace. Their torment always began with the words *I love you.*

Robert picked up a quill and returned his attention to the ledgers. He tried to focus on the column of numbers but saw only his angel, disheveled on the settee.

Five minutes later, Robert threw the quill down. He leaned back in his chair and propped up his legs on the desk.

How could his angel have rejected his offer of marriage? he wondered. Didn't all women want an honorable marriage with a wealthy, titled aristocrat?

Louisa hadn't wanted to marry me, Robert reminded himself, disturbing thoughts stepping out of the shadows of his mind. If she had wanted a marriage with him, she and their unborn child wouldn't be buried in an early grave.

Six days later, as he dressed for the Emersons' ball, Robert was still wondering what his angel really wanted. He'd left her alone since that day at his house in the hope that his absence would make her heart grow fonder.

One thing was certain. He was not going to court his angel or even escort her to the Emerson ball beneath the eyes of his father's watchdogs.

Robert left his chamber and walked downstairs to the foyer. "Are those bodyguards outside?" he asked his majordomo.

"No, my lord, I told them you wouldn't be leaving until later," Webster answered. "I told them you insisted they come inside for supper and took the liberty of serving them in the formal dining room."

Robert grinned. "Webster, you are too amazing for words."

"Thank you, my lord," the majordomo replied. "A hefty raise would be welcome."

"We'll discuss that in the morning," Robert said.

"Take care of yourself tonight, my lord," Webster said, opening the door.

Robert paused, saying, "Why, Webster, thank you for your concern."

"You are welcome, my lord," the man said. "I wouldn't wish to be unemployed."

Robert climbed into his carriage, calling, "Let's go, Mack."

Two minutes later, his driver parked the carriage in front of his father's mansion. Before his driver could open the door, Robert leaped out and hurried up the stairs. He didn't want to appear a coward; but, on the other hand, he had no wish to see his own blood splattered across his father's front stairs.

"Good evening, my lord," Tinker greeted him.

"Good evening."

"His Grace and Lady Roxanne are waiting in the drawing room," the majordomo informed him.

"Where are the young ladies?" Robert asked.

"Primping."

Robert walked up the stairs to the second-floor drawing room. After an absence of six days, he could hardly wait to see his angel.

"Ah, there you are," Duke Magnus said when he walked into the drawing room.

Robert lifted Lady Roxanne's gloved hand to his lips. Gowned in midnight blue, she wore sparkling diamonds in her upswept hair. "You are a beautiful midsummer evening," he complimented her. "Midnight blue with glittering stars in the night sky."

"Thank you, darling," Roxanne said. "Your

father keeps showering me with gifts. I must admit I am becoming a tad spoiled."

"You deserve only the best," Duke Magnus spoke up. He turned to his son, asking, "Are you certain attending tonight's ball is wise?"

"Father, your bodyguards are smothering me," Robert said. "I was forced to feed the whole lot of them in order to escape."

"They didn't accompany you?" the duke asked, a hard edge to his voice.

"Magnus, dear, do not upset yourself," Roxanne said. "Robert is a grown man who, I'm positive, doesn't wish to die. Let him decide what is best for himself."

"Lady Roxanne gives good advice," Robert told his father. "You should follow it."

"I'm glad you think so," Roxanne said, giving him a feline smile. "I have advice for you, too."

"Concerning what?" Robert asked. Was he in trouble for seducing her niece?

"I've been hearing stories about your fabled Campbell charm," Roxanne said. "Poor darling, your experience extends only to the myriad willing. No wonder Angelica felt reluctant to accept your proposal."

"You proposed marriage?" his father asked in obvious surprise.

Robert looked at his father, saying, "The lady refused my offer."

Duke Magnus chuckled. "Then follow Roxanne's advice."

"To tempt an angel into marriage, darling, a man needs a strategy," Roxanne told him. "Lucky for you, I am an expert strategist and willing to help."

Robert stared at her in insulted silence. "I do not need help with women," he said.

"We aren't speaking of women, only my niece," Roxanne told him. "If you change your mind— Ah, here are my three lovely nieces."

Robert turned around to see the Douglas sisters walking across the drawing room. Samantha looked lovely in a deep pink gown, while Victoria's ice blue gown artfully complemented her fiery tresses, but his attention was drawn to his angel in red.

Angelica's red gown was low cut, and the bodice molded tightly to her figure. She wore a single white rose in her blond hair, swept away from her hauntingly lovely face and woven into a knot at the back of her head. White gloves covered her bare arms, and she carried a reticule and a circular fan painted in swirls of red, gold, and white.

"I've never seen more beautiful young women," Robert said, smiling. He cast a sidelong glance at Lady Roxanne, who smiled and nodded at the "fabled Campbell charm."

Angelica smiled almost shyly at him. "Thank you for the pretty compliment, my lord."

"May I escort you to the ball?" Robert asked. "I assure you, the others will follow directly behind us."

Angelica inclined her head, as if granting him a favor. "You may, my lord."

"I must be the luckiest man alive to escort three beautiful women," Duke Magnus said. "Shall we go?"

"Remember, my darlings, friends may come and go in society, but enemies tend to accumulate," Aunt Roxie said. "Do *not* dance more than twice with any man below the age of fifty, and that includes the Duke of Inverary."

"Now, Roxanne, you know that I am fifty-five," Duke Magnus said with a smile.

"You are? Oh, darling, your youthful vigor and

incredible handsomeness make you seem much younger," Aunt Roxie drawled, making her nieces giggle.

Once outside, Robert helped Angelica into his carriage and then climbed in beside her. "Grosvenor Square," he called to his driver.

"How does your arm feel?" Angelica asked.

"Much better," he answered. "I'm certain I'll be able to ruin Drinkwater or Mayhew tonight."

"Where are your bodyguards?" she asked.

"I ditched them."

"Are you certain that's wise?" Angelica asked, giving him a worried look.

"I cannot pass the next forty years hiding in my home or surrounded by my father's bodyguards," Robert told her. He smiled and added, "It's good to see you again."

"Where have you been for the past six days?" she asked.

Robert took advantage of this opening to make her wonder about him. "Keeping myself busy."

"Doing what?"

"This and that."

Robert smiled inwardly. He could see that his answers didn't sit well with her and hoped she was jealous of this time spent away from her. He would show Lady Roxanne what real strategy was.

The carriage came to an abrupt halt. Without waiting for his driver, Robert opened the door and climbed down. Then he turned to assist Angelica.

Sacred sevens, Angelica thought, frowning when she looked toward Charles Emerson's mansion. Her aunt should have warned her.

"What's wrong?" Robert asked.

Angelica heard the concern in his voice, glanced at him, and then stared at the mansion again. "This house belonged to my parents," she answered. "I lived here until I was eight."

"I'm sorry, angel," Robert said, placing his hand on the small of her back. "I didn't know. Do you still want to go inside?"

Angelica forced herself to smile when she answered, "I am fine, only startled to realize Emerson lives in my house."

"Trust me, love," Robert said. "The Douglas family will own this house again one day."

Duke Magnus, Aunt Roxie, and her sisters had alighted from the duke's carriage. Robert and Angelica waited for them before walking upstairs.

"Sisters, take a long look at this house," Angelica said. "We lived here until father lost his fortune."

"That dirty Emerson bastard," Victoria exclaimed. "I'd love to slit his throat."

"Tory, your language and thoughts are unbecoming to a lady," Aunt Roxie scolded her youngest niece.

Samantha touched Angelica's arm and turned to look at the street through the long line of carriages waiting to deliver their passengers. "Is this where the carriage struck me?" she asked. "The memory of that day is hazy in my mind."

"Yes, I remember that day," Angelica told her.

"Was it Emerson's carriage?"

"I don't know."

Samantha turned to her aunt, asking, "Did Emerson hit me with his carriage?"

"My darling, tonight is not the right time to speak of such things," Aunt Roxie answered.

"Samantha needs to know," Angelica said.

"Yes, Emerson struck you," Aunt Roxie told them. "I'm positive he never meant to hurt a child. The incident was an unfortunate accident."

"I hate all Emersons," Victoria said.

"So do I," replied Samantha.

With a dangerous glint in her blue eyes, Angelica touched her sister's hand. "Sam, I promise Emerson will pay for what he did to you."

Duke Magnus cleared his throat. "Shall we go inside?"

Angelica turned to Robert and slipped her hand through the crook in his arm. "Don't look so concerned, my lord," she said, giving him a bright smile. "Emerson is safe for tonight."

With the others in the lead, Robert and Angelica walked up the stairs into the foyer. Excitement coursed through Angelica's body as the sounds of music drifted down from the second-floor ballroom. Tonight she was a princess, and the man beside her was her prince, her champion.

Charles Emerson, his son Alexander, and Venetia stood at the top of the ballroom, where a receiving line had formed. The orchestra played at the opposite end of the room, consisting of a cornet, a piano, a cello, and two violins.

The Emerson majordomo announced the Duke of Inverary and his party first. Then it was their turn.

"The Marquess of Argyll and the Countess of Melrose," the majordomo announced, joining them together in Angelica's mind.

Surprisingly, many in the crowd turned to watch them enter the ballroom. "I feel so conspicuous," Angelica whispered, a placid expression pasted on her face.

"When you've got it, darling, flaunt it," Robert drawled in a good imitation of her aunt.

Angelica laughed. "And do I have *it*, my lord?"

"Angel, you are an Original," Robert answered. "That is spelled with a capital *O*."

"Should we step into the receiving line to greet our host?" Angelica asked.

"I was hoping you would dance with me first," Robert said.

Angelica smiled. "I would much rather dance with you."

Robert led her onto the dance floor, and Angelica stepped into his arms, thankful that her aunt had insisted on teaching her nieces how to dance. As he led her in a sweeping circle around the ballroom, they danced with the ease and grace of a couple who had waltzed a thousand times.

Dancing in his arms felt as natural as breathing. The music and their constant swirling motion conspired with the man to intoxicate her senses.

Robert Roy Campbell reminded her of Lucifer in all his perfection before his fall from grace. His formal black trousers, jacket, and waistcoat combined with his white shirt and tie to accentuate his dark good looks. When he smiled, his teeth appeared strong and straight and almost as white as his shirt.

The marquess was the most handsome man she'd ever seen. How could any woman not be attracted to him? How could she possibly have rejected his marriage proposal?

And then Angelica's gaze swept past Charles Emerson. She would never consider marriage until that villain was in the same condition as poor Mr. Lewis.

"What are your thoughts, angel?" Robert asked.

"I was thinking that I would love to make Charles Emerson and Mr. Lewis neighbors," Angelica answered honestly.

Robert laughed, earning them curious glances from other couples. "If that happened," he replied, "Mr. Lewis might leave his new home and walk to the anatomical schools."

Now Angelica laughed, drawing more curious glances from the waltzing couples. She lost her smile when she added, "I do hope Samantha dances."

"Samantha is almost as lovely as you," Robert said with a puzzled smile. "Why wouldn't she dance?"

"Her limp makes her self-conscious," Angelica told him. "Do you think any gentleman will invite her to dance?"

"Your sister will receive dozens of invitations to dance, angel," Robert assured her. "The receiving line is much shorter now. Shall we pay our respects?"

"I cannot respect that man," she said.

Robert inclined his head in understanding and escorted her off the dance floor. They stood at the end of the receiving line.

"Lady Angelica, how lovely you look tonight," Charles Emerson greeted her.

"I always look lovely, my lord," Angelica replied, wearing a sunny smile. "Thank you for mentioning it, though. How kind of you to invite my family and me."

"The pleasure is mine," Emerson said.

Angelica gazed at him from beneath the fringe of her golden lashes. "Perhaps we'll meet at the gaming table later?" She watched his beady brown eyes narrow, and knew that he'd heard about Trimble's reversal of fortune.

"I must play the gracious host tonight," Emerson replied. "Another time, my lady?"

Angelica inclined her head. "I shall look forward to it."

After leaving the receiving line, Robert led her

in the direction of their relatives. "You will *not* meet Emerson at the gaming table," he ordered in a whisper.

"You have Trimble, Drinkwater, and Mayhew," she whispered back. "I am saving Emerson for myself."

"I forbid it."

"I don't take orders from you."

"We'll see about that."

"You're damned right we will."

Robert ignored her last comment and walked directly toward her sister. "May I have this dance?" he asked.

Angelica felt her heart wrench at the frightened expression on Samantha's face. Murderous hatred for Emerson swept through her like a gust of wind.

"Could we postpone our dance until later?" Samantha asked. "I need to get my bearings in this crowd of strangers."

"I understand how intimidating a gathering like this can be," Robert said smoothly.

"I'll dance with you," Victoria piped up.

"Ladies do not ask gentlemen to dance," Aunt Roxie corrected the girl's behavior.

"I was about to ask you for this dance," Robert said. He took her sister's hand in his and led her onto the dance floor.

When the waltz ended, Alexander Emerson appeared and claimed Victoria for the next dance. Angelica waltzed with James Armstrong and then Adam St. Aubyn, who returned her to Robert for the fourth dance. She kept her gaze riveted on her sister as they swirled around the ballroom floor.

"Watching Samantha won't get her onto the dance floor," Robert said, drawing her attention.

"I'm sorry," Angelica said with a sheepish smile. "You are correct, but I can't help worrying."

"When she's ready," he said, "Samantha will dance."

When the waltz ended, Robert and Angelica returned to their group. Duke Magnus and her aunt stepped onto the dance floor as Alexander Emerson escorted Victoria off the dance floor and then left to speak to his other guests.

It was then that Angelica spied Venetia heading straight for them. With her walked an incredibly handsome gentleman, and Angelica wondered if Venetia had given up on Robert.

"Angelica, I've brought Prince Rudolf to see you," Venetia said, her smile not quite reaching her eyes. "He is an old friend of yours, isn't he?"

Angelica nearly swooned from shock but managed to paste a sunny smile on her face. She glanced at Robert, who was grinning, and then gave the prince her attention.

With his black hair and piercing blue eyes, Prince Rudolf was the kind of man maidens dreamt about. He was as tall as Robert and well built, and had the most charming smile.

"Your Highness, we meet again," Angelica said, deciding the only thing to do was continue the deception and hope the prince was an understanding man.

"So formal a greeting for such an old friend?" Prince Rudolf returned, bowing over her hand, his eyes sparkling with easy camaraderie.

"Seeing you again is good, Rudy," Angelica said, blushing prettily. "You do remember my sisters, Samantha and Victoria?"

"I'm certain I could never forget such lovely young women," Prince Rudolf said smoothly, his gaze fixed on Samantha, making her blush.

Venetia looked distinctly unhappy. She turned

to Robert, saying, "Aren't you going to invite me to dance?"

"Dancing with you is always a pleasure," Robert said, as he escorted her onto the dance floor.

Angelica waited for them to start dancing and then said, "Thank you, Your Highness, for giving credence to my tiny fabrication."

Prince Rudolf grinned. "What was your little white lie?"

Angelica blushed a vibrant scarlet. "I told Venetia that, while living on the Continent, I had declined your offer of marriage."

The prince burst out laughing. "Was I heartbroken?"

"Devastated."

"Your secret is safe with me." Prince Rudolf turned abruptly to her sister, saying, "My lady, will you do me the honor of dancing with me?"

Obviously surprised, Samantha stared up at him. "Your Highness, I-I suffer from an old injury and limp," she said in a soft voice.

"Are you in pain?" the prince asked, appearing concerned.

"No."

"Then you will dance with me," Prince Rudolf said, offering her his hand.

Angelica watched her sister look from the prince's blue gaze to his hand. And then a miracle happened. Samantha placed her hand in the prince's, allowing him to lead her onto the dance floor.

"I need to visit the ladies' resting area," Angelica told her youngest sister.

"I want to stay here in case Alexander asks me to dance," Victoria replied.

"Do not dance more than two times with anyone,

especially an Emerson,'' Angelica warned, sounding like her aunt.

Angelica left the ballroom and, after asking directions from a servant, found the ladies' resting area. Several young matrons, on their way out, greeted her pleasantly, and then she was alone.

Sitting down, Angelica thought about her sister. That Samantha was dancing was a minor miracle, and Angelica would always be grateful to the prince. Now, if only she could teach Victoria to read and cipher numbers.

"Are you upset by the prince dancing with Samantha?" asked a familiar voice. "Or Robert dancing with me?"

"I'm not upset at all," Angelica said, looking in the mirror at the other woman.

"My father promised that you will never be the mother of the Campbell heir," Venetia told her. "My father always keeps his promises."

Angelica couldn't believe what she was hearing. She stood to face the other woman.

"Your father has no control over whom Robert or I marry," Angelica informed her.

"Robert will never marry you," Venetia said.

Angelica could not resist meeting her challenge. "He's already proposed," she announced, and felt a surge of satisfaction when the other woman's expression mottled with barely suppressed rage.

"You scarcely know Robert," Venetia said, a condescending note in her voice. "Let me tell you about him. His first wife was my sister. Louisa committed suicide because he kept a mistress who was also pregnant at the time."

Angelica felt as if she'd been kicked in the stomach. She stepped back two paces. It couldn't be true. Robert wasn't the kind of man who would drive a woman to suicide, especially his own wife, carrying his first child.

"I don't believe you," Angelica said.

"Ask him, then," Venetia countered, a haughty smile on her lips. "His mistress is Lucille Dubois. He sired a daughter on her."

Chapter 12

"Daisy's father is an important man. She couldn't possibly pass the night in this hovel."

The memory of Lucille Dubois's words slammed into Angelica, and she plopped down in the chair. Lucille had been referring to Robert Campbell, the Marquess of Argyll.

Angelica looked at herself in the mirror. Surprise had paled her complexion to a ghostly white, and she willed herself not to look at her badly trembling hands.

"I'm so sorry for upsetting you," Venetia said.

Angelica looked at the other woman in the mirror. Venetia wore the most unrepentant expression she'd ever seen.

"Surely you knew that gentlemen kept mistresses," Venetia said. "Bastards are the byproducts of those illicit unions."

Angelica flinched at the word *bastard*. Daisy Dubois was a sweet child, not a bastard to be scorned by the likes of Venetia Emerson.

"Please go away," Angelica said.

"I only wanted you—"

"I said *get out,*" Angelica snapped, and the other woman made a hasty exit.

She knew that rich gentlemen kept mistresses who bore them children. But she never imagined that Robert—

Angelica remembered the purple bruises on Daisy's arms. What kind of father was Robert Roy Campbell? Did he approve of Lucille abusing his only child, albeit a daughter he would never acknowledge to society?

"Beware, Venetia. She's an Emerson and not to be trusted." Angelica recalled her aunt's warning to her.

Venetia was an Emerson who would do or say anything to get what she wanted. Perhaps she had been lying in order to cause trouble between herself and Robert.

Angelica rose from the chair, pinched her cheeks to bring back her color, and left the ladies' resting area. She would find Robert and ask him to tell her the truth.

Returning to the ballroom, Angelica noted that Victoria was dancing with Alexander Emerson and Samantha was dancing with Prince Rudolf. How many dances did that make? she wondered, noting her aunt's disapproving expression. She wanted her sisters happy but not ruined in the eyes of society.

"I've been looking for you," Robert said, materializing beside her.

Angelica flicked a worried glance at him. "How many times have they danced with those men?" she asked, her gaze on her sisters.

"I don't know," Robert answered. "Who's counting?"

"Society is counting," she told him.

"Society be damned," he said. "Let them enjoy themselves."

Angelica arched a blond brow at him, saying, "Spoken like a man whose place in society is assured no matter how disreputably he behaves."

Robert smiled, apparently deciding to ignore the censure in her voice. "I was about to follow Drinkwater and Mayhew into the gaming room and—"

"Forget the gaming room," Angelica said. "I need to speak to you on a matter of importance. Privately."

Robert inclined his head. "Let's walk outside. There will be other couples in the garden to chaperon us."

Together, Robert and Angelica left the ballroom. Following another departing couple, they wandered downstairs and then stepped outside.

Torches lit the small rear garden for the few couples meandering about, and the sensual scent of flowers wafted through the air, setting the perfect stage for a romantic interlude. Deeply scented pansies, peonies, and that feathered enchantress love-in-a-mist mingled with the heady perfume of lavender, sweet peas, and roses.

"What is more important than your revenge, angel?" Robert asked.

"Did your wife commit suicide?" Angelica asked baldly.

Robert's expression became grim. "To whom have you been speaking?"

"Never mind about that," Angelica said. "Did your late wife—?"

"Louisa is none of your business," Robert interrupted, his anger apparent.

"I need to know."

Robert snapped his brows together. "Why?"

Angelica couldn't give him a reason why. She wanted him to tell her that he hadn't left his pregnant wife to make love with another woman.

"Is Lucille Dubois your mistress?" she asked.

"Who has been whispering in your ear?" he asked again.

"Sacred sevens, answer the damned question," Angelica demanded, losing her temper.

Robert stared at her for agonizingly long minutes. Finally, he told her, "Lucille Dubois is not my mistress."

Angelica relaxed. "Has Lucille ever been your mistress?"

"Has Venetia been poisoning you against me?" he asked.

"Do *not* answer my questions with questions," she ordered.

"I've heard enough." Robert walked away but paused several yards from her, asking, "Are you returning to the ballroom?"

Angelica pasted a mulish expression on her face. "I'll return inside after you answer my question."

Robert walked back to her. "Lucille Dubois was my mistress several years ago," he told her. "Is your curiosity satisfied?"

"Is Daisy your daughter?"

"Who?"

His question surprised Angelica. He seemed sincerely puzzled by the name.

"Lucille's daughter, Daisy," Angelica added.

Surprisingly, he appeared to relax, as if the worst of the storm had passed. His next words shocked her right down to the tips of her toes.

"The girl is my daughter, but I have nothing to do with her," Robert admitted. "I've never even seen her."

"You've never seen your own daughter?" Angelica gasped, stepping back a pace.

"Naturally I accept responsibility for my indiscretions and support the child," Robert explained.

Outrage welled up inside Angelica. Not only was the child abused by the mother but neglected by the father.

"Daisy Dubois is not an indiscretion," Angelica told him in a choked voice. "She's a sweet, trusting, loving child."

Robert narrowed his black gaze on her. "How do you know Lucille's daughter?" he asked.

Lucille's daughter? Angelica wondered. Why did this man distance himself from his own flesh and blood?

"Lucille Dubois is one of my aunt's clients," Angelica answered. "Sometimes she brought Daisy with her to our cottage."

Robert seemed to accept that as plausible. "Now that we have settled your thoughts," he said, visibly relaxing, "let's return inside."

"Nothing is settled," Angelica told him. "Lucille abuses Daisy. The poor child has more bruises on her arms than Wilma Drinkwater has bracelets."

Angelica watched his lips tighten into a grim white line, a sure sign of anger. Finally, she was making him understand what his neglect had wrought.

"Well, what will you do about that?" she asked.

"I'll send Lucille a note with my next check," he answered.

"Sacred sevens, how can you condone your own daughter's abuse?" Angelica asked, losing her temper again, her voice rising in anger. "What a poor excuse for a father you are. I wouldn't marry you for all the king's gold . . . not even if you were the last man in England . . . *in the whole damned world.*"

Robert developed a twitch in his right cheek muscle, which promptly spread to his left cheek. "Lower your voice," he ordered in a harsh whisper. "Unless you want those watching couples to return inside and embroil us in a scandal? Then you would be forced to marry me."

"I don't give a fig about those couples or scandals," Angelica countered, but she lowered her voice to a whisper. "Since you refuse to help, I'll save Daisy from that unnatural woman."

"Leave it alone, Angelica," Robert warned.

"I don't take orders from you," she told him. "I am the Countess of Melrose and do whatever pleases me."

Robert grabbed her wrist in a firm but gentle grasp, saying, "Let's go."

"You're mad to think I'd go anywhere with you," Angelica said, pulling away. "I'm going home."

At that, Angelica whirled away. Heedless of the staring couples, she marched toward the stairs leading to the alley and emerged into Grosvenor Square proper.

"Be reasonable," Robert said, following closely behind her.

Glancing over her shoulder, Angelica gave him a look of contempt. She quickened her pace and managed to put several yards between them.

"You are behaving badly," Robert called in a stern voice.

Behaving badly? Angelica thought in a fury. Was the kettle now calling the pot black? Intending to give the marquess a large piece of her mind, she stopped short midway between the corner of the alley and the carriages parked in front of Emerson's mansion.

At that moment, Angelica saw a man on horseback approaching from the opposite direction. As he passed the gaslight just ahead of her, she spied the pistol in his hand. He pointed it at something just behind her.

Robert!

Angelica reacted instinctively. In one swift movement, she drew her last-resort dagger and threw it at the man.

With a cry of pained surprise, the assailant fired his pistol wildly, missing his quarry, and the horse reared. The man clutched his chest, toppled backward off his mount, and lay still in the road.

Cries of alarm sounded as the coachmen left their carriages and ran toward them. Within moments, Emerson's guests streamed out of the mansion to see what was happening.

Angelica reached the assailant at the same moment as Robert and crouched down beside him. The dagger protruded from the villain's heart. Looking up, she saw James Armstrong and Adam St. Aubyn and said, "He's dead."

"What a marvelous throw," Adam St. Aubyn said.

"Bull's eye," James Armstrong added. "I didn't know you could toss a dagger with such precision, Campbell."

"He didn't," Angelica admitted. "I tossed the dagger, but I was aiming for his arm."

"Now we can't question him, can we?" Robert said in an angry voice.

Angelica snapped her head around and glared at him. "Is this the thanks I get for saving your miserable life?"

"Ladies do not—"

"Futter yourself," Angelica interrupted, making Armstrong and St. Aubyn laugh. She noted the twitch had returned to Robert's cheeks.

"I warned you to keep those bodyguards close," Duke Magnus told his son.

"May I borrow your handkerchief, Your Grace?" Angelica asked.

Duke Magnus produced his handkerchief and handed it to her. Angelica pulled the dagger out of the man's chest and wiped it clean on the duke's handkerchief. She started to pass the handkerchief back to him but thought better of doing so, and tossed it down beside the body.

Looking up, Angelica noticed the shocked expressions on the faces around her. She stood then and, without a glance at Robert, walked in the direction of the carriages, where her aunt and sisters stood with the other ladies.

"Well done, Countess," Prince Rudolf said as she passed him.

Angelica ignored him but stopped when she came abreast of Alexander Emerson. "The next time you try to kill the marquess, be certain to hire a more efficient assassin," she said.

"I thought he was trying to kill me," Alexander replied.

"You had nothing to do with this?" Angelica asked, staring into his eyes.

"No, of course not."

He was telling the truth. She could read it in his expression. On the other hand, he was an Emerson and adept at lying.

"Has someone tried to eliminate you?" she asked.

Alexander nodded. "Twice, at least."

"How provoking." Angelica walked away, wondering who would want both Robert Campbell and Alexander Emerson dead.

"I want to go home," Angelica said, approaching her aunt. "This whole incident has given me an upset stomach."

"Yes, my darling heroine, we'll go home immedi-

ately," Aunt Roxie whispered soothingly, guiding
her toward the duke's carriage. "I wonder how
we'll stop the gossip about this."

Angelica looked at her in confusion.

"Ladies usually do not carry daggers or execute
men, no matter how frequently they are provoked," Aunt Roxie explained.

"You sound like the mad marquess," Angelica
replied.

"I am as sane as you are," Robert said dryly,
materializing beside her. "I want to thank—"

"Stay away from me, you sniveling son of a
swine," Angelica warned, rounding on him. "I
want nothing to do with you."

Angelica climbed into the carriage. She averted
her gaze while the others, excluding the marquess,
climbed inside.

"Someone has been trying to kill Alexander
Emerson," she told the duke as the carriage started
away.

"That is not my concern," Duke Magnus said.

"It should be," she replied. "These assassination
attempts could be related."

Duke Magnus nodded. "You may be correct. I'll
have it investigated."

Late the following morning, Angelica sat on the
chaise in front of the hearth in her bedchamber
and plucked the strings of her harp. She wondered
in frustration who would want both Robert and
Alexander Emerson dead. If she knew them better,
she might be able to guess at a few possibilities;
however, she knew nothing about Alexander and
next to nothing about Robert.

You know you love him, an inner voice told her.

Angelica banished that disturbing thought to the

shadows of her mind. Thinking about him aggravated her. She couldn't condone his never seeing his daughter or his callousness concerning Lucille's abuse of the child.

"Enter," Angelica called, hearing the knock on her door.

"Enter," Jasper called.

The door opened. Samantha and Victoria walked into the room.

"Hello," the macaw called.

"Hello, Jasper," her sisters said in unison, and then sat beside her on the chaise.

"Whom do you think is trying to kill Robert?" Samantha asked.

"And Alexander Emerson," Victoria added.

"I don't know," Angelica said with a shrug. She looked at her youngest sister. "You should not have danced more than twice with Alexander. Sacred sevens, Tory, the man is an Emerson."

"He doesn't seem like a villain to me," Victoria replied. "Besides, Samantha danced more than twice with Prince Rudolf."

"Samantha should not have danced so many times with the prince," Angelica said. "However, refusing a prince's invitation is not an option. I'm afraid Aunt Roxie must be disappointed with our behavior."

"To tell you the truth, I've been bored since arriving at the duke's," Samantha said.

"Except for last night," Victoria qualified.

"We miss the freedom and excitement of our old life," Samantha said.

"You want excitement?" Angelica asked, smiling. When her sisters nodded, she continued, "I have a pressing problem. As you know, Lucille Dubois abuses Daisy. The little girl is Robert's daughter—"

"What?" exclaimed her sisters, again simultaneously.

"I was surprised, too," Angelica admitted. "Robert has never seen Daisy, nor does he intend to see her. I want to steal Daisy and bring her to live with us."

"What about Duke Magnus?" Samantha asked. "Will he allow it?"

"I can handle His Grace," Angelica said with confidence. At their skeptical looks, she added, "His Grace owes us for not coming to Father's rescue, and I intend to use that fact to get what I want."

"We don't know where Lucille lives," Victoria said.

"Good morning, my darlings," Aunt Roxie called, breezing into the bedchamber.

"Darling," Jasper mimicked.

"Hello, Jasper," Aunt Roxie cooed to the macaw. "You beautiful baby bird."

"Hello."

Aunt Roxie turned to them. "Samantha and Victoria, you should not have danced more than two times with the same men. Angelica, your executing that man was quite unladylike, albeit necessary for the marquess's continued good health." She smiled at them, adding, "I'm positive we'll have many callers today, especially in view of the entertainment Angelica provided, but I have instructed Tinker that we aren't receiving visitors."

"Why did you do that?" Victoria asked.

"The unattainable is always more desirable," Aunt Roxie answered, affectionately touching her youngest niece's cheek. "I forget how young you are and how much you need to learn."

"Daisy Dubois is Robert's daughter," Angelica blurted out.

"Yes, I know."

"Why didn't you tell me?"

"You never asked," Aunt Roxie replied, making her two younger nieces giggle.

"I told Robert about Lucille's abuse of his daughter, but he doesn't seem to care," Angelica informed her aunt. "I have decided to rescue Daisy but don't know where she lives."

"I know where she lives," Aunt Roxie said. "I have a plan."

Angelica bit her bottom lip. "Do you think Robert will be angry?"

"He'll be furious," Aunt Roxie answered, giving her a feline smile. "How divinely delicious . . ."

At three o'clock that afternoon, Angelica locked Jasper in his cage and hurried downstairs to the foyer. Aunt Roxie and her sisters were waiting for her.

"See how popular you have become," Aunt Roxie said, gesturing toward the foyer table. Calling cards filled the crystal dish that had been placed there.

Angelica rolled her eyes. "Our association with His Grace has gained us entrée into society."

"Perhaps society wanted another look at freaks," Samantha said, making her sisters laugh.

"Do not disparage yourself and your sisters," Aunt Roxie replied. "Tinker, please tell His Grace—"

"Tell him yourself," called a voice behind them.

Angelica turned around, as did her aunt and sisters. Duke Magnus, Robert, James Armstrong, and Adam St. Aubyn were descending the stairs to the foyer.

"The girls and I are going out in the carriage," Aunt Roxie told the duke.

"Where?" Robert asked.

"Here and there, no particular destination," Aunt Roxie answered. "We'll return later for tea."

"Have an enjoyable outing," Duke Magnus said.

"Angel, I want to speak to you," Robert said.

Raising her disarming blue gaze to his, Angelica said in a haughty voice, "Leave your card with Tinker."

James and Adam burst out laughing, earning themselves a glare from Robert. Duke Magnus coughed, apparently to cover his chuckle, and her sisters giggled.

Angelica turned her back on him and walked out the door. She bit her bottom lip to keep from laughing when she heard Tinker say, "Would you care to leave your card, my lord?"

And then Angelica reached the sidewalk. She climbed into the duke's carriage, and her sisters climbed in behind her.

"We won't be needing your services today," Aunt Roxie told the driver. "I'm driving."

"With all due respect, my lady, I refuse to lose my job over a female's whim," the coachman told her.

"What is your name?"

"Willie."

"Do you know to whom you are speaking, Willie?" Aunt Roxie asked, assuming a haughty attitude. "I am the Countess of Melrose's aunt."

"Do you know who *I* am?" Willie returned. "I am the man in charge of His Grace's carriages, and you aren't taking this one out alone."

Aunt Roxie gave him a dimpled smile and reached for her reticule.

"And I don't take bribes."

"I wouldn't dream of trying to bribe you," Aunt Roxie purred. "I'll give you these coins and allow you to drive us if you promise to remain silent about our destination."

"I can keep a secret but don't want your money," Willie told her.

"Consider it a gratuity for a job well done," Aunt Roxie said, placing the coins in his hand.

Willie nodded. He helped her into the carriage and closed the door.

"Portland Place," Aunt Roxie instructed him. She settled herself into the coach beside Angelica. "When we arrive, you and your sisters will walk down the alley behind the town house and wait outside in the garden. Once inside, I'll tell Lucille that the stars insist Daisy should wait outside while we discuss an important matter."

"What if she sends Daisy to her room?" Victoria asked.

"Trust me, darling," Aunt Roxie said with a mischievous smile. "Lucille will obey what the stars foretell."

"The urgent matter to discuss must be something plausible," Angelica told her.

"How about the fact that someone tried to assassinate Robert?" Aunt Roxie asked. "If he dies, her funds could be terminated."

"I cannot think of a more urgent matter than having one's funds terminated," Samantha said.

Her aunt's remark reminded Angelica that someone was trying to murder the man she loved. She had considered Alexander Emerson the most likely culprit, but now that she knew attempts had been made on his life, she needed to reconsider the whole situation. Not only that, but her argument with Robert and the attempt on his life had destroyed an opportunity to ruin Drinkwater or Mayhew.

"Angelica, are you feeling well?" Aunt Roxie asked, intruding on her thoughts. "You look pale."

"I'm fine," Angelica answered. "I have a butterfly stomach from nerves and my argument with Robert."

"You've suffered from a queasy stomach for several days now," Aunt Roxie said, reaching out to touch her forehead. "You seem a little warm, too. I hope the excitement isn't making you ill."

Fifteen minutes later, Aunt Roxie called out for the carriage to stop and then turned to her nieces, saying, "Hide at the corner of the alley. When you see me go inside, walk down the alley to Lucille's garden."

Angelica, Samantha, and Victoria climbed out of the carriage and hurried to hide. Fingering her diamond pendant for luck, Angelica peered around the corner and watched her aunt climb the front stairs. The door opened before she reached the top, and Lucille Dubois stepped outside, apparently on her way out.

"Madame Roxanne, I've been looking for you," Angelica heard Lucille exclaim. "Where have you been?"

"I must speak to you on an urgent matter," Aunt Roxie answered.

"Come inside," Lucille said, and the two women disappeared into the house.

"She's inside," Angelica told her sisters. "Let's go."

The Douglas sisters hurried down the alley. Entering the Dubois garden, they hid behind an enormous evergreen shrub and waited for the little girl to arrive. Daisy appeared five minutes later in the company of an older woman.

"Her nanny is with her," Samantha whispered. "What will we do?"

"We'll take the nanny with us," Angelica said in a whisper, lifting the edge of her gown to draw her last-resort dagger.

"What if she screams?" Victoria asked.

"I'll threaten her with my dagger before she does," Angelica answered.

"Won't that frighten Daisy?" Samantha asked.

Angelica bit her bottom lip and considered her sister's words. Finally, she lifted her skirt and returned the dagger to its sheath attached to the garter on her leg.

"Stay here until I call you," Angelica instructed them. "The woman won't cry out once Daisy recognizes me."

Angelica stepped out from behind the shrub and started across the garden toward the little girl, who sat on a stone bench with her nanny. "Daisy, I've come to play with you," she called, fixing a smile on her lips.

Startled, the nanny whirled toward her but relaxed when the child cried out, "Lady Angel," and raced toward her. "Have you brought Jasper?"

"No, but my sisters are here," Angelica answered. She gestured to her sisters, who appeared from behind the shrub and crossed the garden.

"Why were you hiding?" the nanny asked, her expression mirroring confused suspicion.

"We didn't want to startle you," Angelica answered, hoping her smile would calm the woman. "My aunt is inside visiting Lucille."

"This is Lady Allegra," Daisy told her, holding a doll out for her inspection. "My father sent her to me, but I wish he brought her himself." She brightened when she added, "Do you want to watch the clouds make pictures?"

"Lady Allegra is quite lovely," Angelica replied, taking a seat beside the nanny while her sisters positioned themselves behind the woman. "Your father loves you very much."

"Yes, he does, but—" Daisy leaned close and whispered, "I've never seen him because he's too important and too busy to visit me."

Angelica felt her heart wrench at the girl's words. She could have throttled Robert and his former paramour.

"Sit on my lap," Angelica said.

Daisy climbed onto her lap and rested her head in the crook of her neck. Angelica put her arms around the girl protectively and glanced over her shoulder to give her sisters a pointed look.

Victoria drew her dagger and touched its cold steel to the back of the woman's neck. At the same moment, Samantha turned her body diagonally to block Daisy's view of it.

"Keep silent and nothing will happen to you," Victoria whispered against the side of the woman's head.

Angelica smiled at the woman's frozen expression. "What is your name?" she asked.

"Ethel Sweeting."

"Mrs. Sweeting?" Angelica echoed in surprise, recalling Webster's information that Robert had brought the former Douglas nanny out of retirement.

Angelica smiled at the woman's blank expression. "Mrs. Sweeting, I am Angelica Douglas. Do you remember me?"

"My Lord, I never thought to see you again," the woman exclaimed. "You are a grown woman. I didn't recognize you." She glanced over her shoulder, adding, "These young ladies must be Samantha and Victoria. How are the earl and countess faring?"

"Both are dead," Angelica answered. "Mrs.

Sweeting, you must have noticed the bruises on Daisy's arms.''

Mrs. Sweeting shook her head in disgust. "I try to protect her as much as I can.''

"I understand," Angelica said, reaching out to touch her arm. "Mrs. Sweeting, we have come to take Daisy away to safety. Will you come, too? Please?"

"You always were an adventurous child, ready to defend the weak and right a wrong," Mrs. Sweeting said. "Kidnapping is a hanging offense, I think.''

"Don't worry about that," Angelica said. "We're taking you to live with us at the Duke of Inverary's mansion. His Grace won't allow the law to punish us."

Mrs. Sweeting glanced uncertainly toward the house. "What about our clothing and belongings?"

"We'll buy you new clothes," Angelica answered. "Once we get Daisy safely away and ensconced in her new home, His Grace will send to Lucille for anything of value you've left behind.''

"Very well, then," the woman agreed.

Angelica looked at Daisy. "Do you want to come and live with me?"

Daisy nodded, rose from her perch on Angelica's lap, and held out her hand. The five of them left the garden and walked briskly down the alley.

Peering around the corner, Angelica watched her aunt descend the front stairs and climb into the carriage. Willie drove around the corner and stopped for them.

Once inside, Angelica took Daisy upon her lap. Victoria sat on the carriage's floor, between the two seats.

"God bless you, my lady," Mrs. Sweeting said when Aunt Roxie gave her a welcoming hug.

"What about Lucille?" Daisy asked, glancing back down the street.

"Never mind about her," Angelica said, keeping her close. "I'm taking you to stay with your grandfather."

Daisy looked astonished. "I have a grandfather?"

"Not only do you have a grandfather, you also have a fairy godmother," Aunt Roxie told her.

"Who is she?"

"Lady Angelica."

Daisy laughed. "She's an angel, not a fairy godmother." She turned to Angelica, asking, "Can we watch the cloud pictures and play your harp?"

Angelica nodded. "I know lots and lots of fun things to do."

When they reached the duke's Park Lane residence, Tinker opened the front door, and they hurried inside. The majordomo appeared puzzled by the sight of the older woman and the child.

"Tinker, prepare a chamber for our guests," Aunt Roxie instructed the majordomo. "They'll sleep in the same chamber. Samantha and Victoria, accompany Mrs. Sweeting to help her settle in. Angelica, you and Daisy come with me."

Aunt Roxie led them upstairs. Angelica and Daisy stopped on the second floor with her, while the others continued up to the third floor. Outside the duke's closed study door, Aunt Roxie whispered, "Wait here until I come for you."

Holding hands, Angelica and Daisy stood in the corridor. After her aunt's initial, "Hello, darling," all was silent for several long moments.

"Angelica did what?" the duke shouted from within the study.

"Is my grandfather a dragon?" Daisy asked, a frightened expression on her face.

Angelica smiled. "There is nothing to fear."

The door opened after a prolonged period of silence. Aunt Roxie beckoned them inside.

"Lady Allegra is frightened," Daisy cried, pulling back. "She doesn't want to meet the dragon."

"I'll hold your hand the whole time," Angelica promised.

Duke Magnus was seated behind his desk. "Well, Lady Angelica, I see that you have taken charge of everyone's life," he said dryly.

"I try to help whenever I can," she replied, and gave him a smile filled with sunshine.

"So, you are Daisy Dubois," the duke said, turning his attention on the little girl.

Daisy looked ready to bolt. Her grip on Angelica's hand tightened.

"Come closer so I can see you," Duke Magnus said.

Angelica forced the child forward a few steps. Daisy dug in her heels, still out of arm's reach of the duke.

"Do you know who I am?" Duke Magnus asked. Daisy nodded.

"Do you know how to speak?"

Daisy nodded again, and the duke laughed. Angelica felt the girl relax.

"Who am I?" he asked.

"Grandfather," Daisy answered in a voice barely louder than a whisper.

"I am your father's father," Duke Magnus told her. "You have your father's eyes."

"I do?"

Duke Magnus nodded. "Do you think you will be happy here?"

Daisy nodded.

"I am very glad you're here," Duke Magnus said, and gave Angelica a look, signaling the interview finished. "We'll speak again at tea."

Angelica led the girl away, saying, "I want to get some green apples. Will you help me feed Jasper?"

Daisy nodded and then asked, "Will I meet my father, too?"

"I'm certain you will," Angelica answered.

"Is he a dragon, too?"

"No, sweetheart. Your father is a horse's arse."

Chapter 13

Angelica Douglas is more obstinate than a donkey, Robert thought in growing irritation, sitting behind the desk in his study. Once she got an idea fixed in her mind, she dug in her heels and refused to budge an inch. The word *compromise* was not in her vocabulary; she saw the world in black and white, with no shades in between.

And I love her.

That disturbing thought stepped out of the shadows of his mind. He scowled at its truth. The last thing he needed in his life was love.

Angelica Douglas was beautiful, fair-minded, and kind; she also aggravated the hell out of him. First, she wanted to marry him; then she wouldn't have him on a golden platter. She wanted him to help her exact revenge on the men who'd ruined her father but didn't want him to go near her anymore.

Robert had never realized how difficult a woman could be. Most women tripped over each other to gain his attention and please him. He was wealthy, titled, and handsome. What was there to reject?

Different from the other ladies of the ton, Angelica Douglas truly cared about people other than herself. So, how could he fault her for caring about a child's welfare?

He had behaved badly last night. What had she done but defend a child and save his life?

Robert knew Angelica was going to do something outrageous about the situation with Lucille's daughter. He only hoped that whatever she did wasn't illegal.

And then he thought about Daisy, the daughter he'd refused to see because her existence had caused Louisa's suicide. Good God, he hadn't even remembered her name.

"... *sweet, trusting, and loving* ..." That was how Angelica had described her.

Did she resemble Lucille or himself? Or perhaps a combination of both?

"... *more bruises on her arms than Wilma Drinkwater has bracelets,*" Angelica had said.

An enormous swell of remorse swept through him. The child had suffered because of his neglect. How could Lucille abuse her own daughter? Or had Angelica been exaggerating?

Robert poured himself a fortifying dram of whiskey, downed it in one gulp, and then rose from his chair. The only way to know if Angelica had told him the truth was to visit Lucille and inspect the girl's arms.

Halfway across the study, Robert paused and looked at the mosaic over the mantel. The lion and his lioness reminded him of Angelica and himself.

Shit, Robert thought in the next instant. He must be in love. He was beginning to think like a blinking idiot.

Turning away, Robert spied Atlas carrying the weight of the world on his shoulders. He felt more like Atlas than that noble lion standing with dignified pride beside his lioness.

Reaching the foyer, Robert instructed his major-domo, "Tell Mack to bring the carriage around."

"Yes, my lord," Webster said. "What shall I do about the bodyguards?"

Robert was about to tell him to distract them but thought of his father and the events of the previous evening. "Tell them I'm going out in the carriage and will need outriders."

Webster looked relieved. He opened the front door and called, "Look sharp. His lordship is going out in the carriage."

"Thank you, Webster," Robert said dryly when the man closed the door.

"You are welcome, my lord," Webster said, and hurried in the opposite direction to find the coachman.

Ten minutes later, Robert sat inside his barouche. Though the afternoon was a rarity of summer perfection, the hood of the barouche was up to discourage another assassination attempt.

"Portland Place," Robert told his man.

"I thought you were finished with that one," Mack said.

Robert narrowed his black gaze on the coachman. "Do your job without comment," he ordered.

Why did his retainers believe they could question his judgment and decisions? Both Webster and Mack constantly gave him their editorial comments concerning his life. No doubt they adored Angelica Douglas, the most unbiddable woman who'd ever crossed his path.

Beautiful, lovable, unbiddable woman, he corrected himself.

Robert glanced out the barouche's window at the bodyguards on horseback, positioning themselves around his carriage. He felt like a bloody spectacle. If Armstrong or St. Aubyn chanced to see him, he'd never live this down.

A short time later, Robert leaped out of the barouche in front of Lucille's town house and hurried up the stairs. He knocked on the door, which opened almost immediately, and walked into the foyer.

"Your lordship," the maid exclaimed. "We weren't expecting you."

"Fetch Lucille to me," Robert ordered.

"Yes, your lordship." The maid hurried up the stairs.

A few minutes later, Lucille appeared at the top of the stairs. She wore a low-cut gown, as if she'd known he would visit and wanted to seduce him.

"You've returned," Lucille greeted him, a smile of welcome on her face as she walked downstairs. "Thank God you're safe."

"I want to see the child," Robert said.

At Lucille's nod, the young woman raced up the stairs again. When she reappeared at the top of the stairs, she called, "Daisy isn't in her chamber."

"Then check the garden," Lucille ordered in an irritated tone.

The maid rushed downstairs. She disappeared down the corridor leading to the back of the house.

"So, you've finally decided to meet your daughter," Lucille remarked.

Robert said nothing. He walked away from her, leaned against the foyer's reception table, and folded his arms across his chest.

"Mrs. Sweeting and Daisy aren't there," the maid said, breathless, returning from the garden. "Nobody has seen them since you sent them outside earlier. In fact, no one remembers seeing them return to the house."

"My God, that woman has stolen my daughter," Lucille cried in a near panic.

Robert shook his head, though the slightest of smiles touched his lips. Apparently, Angelica Douglas had already been there and, somehow, persuaded the nanny to leave with her.

"Do something," Lucille said. "Have your driver fetch the authorities."

"Do you see your income disappearing with your daughter?" Robert asked.

"How can you say that?" Lucille asked in an affronted tone. "I love our daughter more than anything."

"You love your daughter more than anything *except yourself,*" Robert qualified. Turning away, he said, "I think I know where she is."

"I'm coming with you," Lucille said.

Robert stared at her for a long moment. Finally, he nodded and opened the door for her.

Once seated in the carriage, Lucille tried to turn the full force of her charm on him. "I love this barouche," she gushed, leaning forward so he could get a good look at her breasts. "We always took the barouche when we dined out. Remember?"

"Be quiet," Robert snapped, "or I'll dump you out here."

While Robert sat inside the barouche with his former mistress, Angelica and Daisy enjoyed the perfect summer's afternoon within the security of the duke's garden. Mrs. Sweeting, sitting on a stone bench, watched them.

Angelica and Daisy lay on their backs in the grass.

Both woman and child studied the pictures the fair-weather clouds formed against the blue sky.

"There's a flower," Daisy cried.

"I think it's a daisy," Angelica said.

Daisy laughed loudly. Beside them, Jasper laughed in a perfect imitation of the little girl, which made Angelica and Mrs. Sweeting laugh. And that made Jasper continue his laughing.

"You're having fun?"

At the sound of the boy's voice, Angelica sat up and watched Colin Campbell racing across the garden toward them. With him was Mrs. Honey.

"Mrs. Sweeting, I would like you to meet Mrs. Honey," Angelica introduced the two older women.

"I'm pleased to meet you," Mrs. Sweeting said.

"Likewise," Mrs. Honey replied, sitting beside her on the bench.

"Colin, I want you to meet Daisy," Angelica said, giving her attention to the children. "She's your cousin. That's why you both have big, dark eyes."

The little boy bowed from the waist, which made Daisy smile. "I like you," he said, pointing a finger at her.

"I like you, too," Daisy said. "Do you like Jasper?"

Colin nodded.

Daisy clapped her hands together, saying, "I like him, too."

"Colin, sit beside me here," Angelica said. "I want to tell you and Daisy the fingers story."

The boy plopped down beside her. Both children looked at her expectantly.

"Did you know that a family lives in everyone's hand?" Angelica asked.

Both Colin and Daisy shook their heads.

"This is the baby," Angelica told them, holding

her thumb up. "This is the mother," she said, holding her index finger up. "And this is the father," she said finally, pointing her middle finger into the air.

When the two nannies giggled, Angelica glanced at them over her shoulder and smiled mischievously. Colin and Daisy laughed, too, as if they knew what the adults found humorous.

"Enough of the family," Angelica said. "If you want to send someone bad luck, give them the devil's sign." She demonstrated as she explained, "Your thumb pins down the middle and ring fingers, and you point at the person with your index and little finger."

Both children made the sign of the devil. Then Colin cried, "Come, Daisy. Let's run."

The little girl jumped up when he did. Together, the two of them gamboled around and around the garden and gave every plant, flower, and shrub the sign of the devil.

Tinker appeared unexpectedly and crossed the garden toward Angelica. "Excuse me, my lady," the man said. "His Grace wishes to see you and Mistress Daisy in his study."

"Thank you, Tinker," Angelica said, rising from the grass. "Daisy, your grandfather wants us to visit him now."

"I'll be right back," Daisy told Colin.

Followed by Jasper, Angelica and Daisy returned to the house and climbed the stairs to the second-floor study. She paused near the study door, put Jasper in the corridor cage, and then knocked on the door.

"Enter," she heard Duke Magnus call.

Angelica stopped short just inside the doorway and felt the girl's grip on her hand tighten. Not only were Duke Magnus and Aunt Roxie waiting for them, but Lucille Dubois and Robert were also in attendance.

Shifting her gaze from Robert's twitching cheek, Angelica looked at her aunt. Lady Roxanne raised her brows and shrugged her shoulders, but the hint of a smile was on her lips.

"Angelica Douglas has stolen my daughter," Lucille complained. "I'm going to the authorities and *The Times.*" She stopped speaking, as if a thought had just occurred to her, and asked, "What are these peasants doing here?"

"Lady Angelica is the Countess of Melrose," Duke Magnus told her.

"She's poorer than I am," Lucille said, looking bewildered.

"Her finances do not change the fact that she is the Countess of Melrose," the duke replied.

"I don't care who she is," Lucille said. "I want my daughter returned to me. Come here, Daisy."

Daisy's enormous black eyes grew even larger, and her grip on Angelica's hand tightened painfully. She stepped closer to Angelica and refused to budge.

"I said to come here," Lucille repeated in obvious irritation. She turned to Robert, saying, "Do you see what a disobedient child she is?"

Angelica watched Robert drop his black gaze from her to Daisy. She stepped protectively in front of the girl, hiding her from view.

"I'm keeping her," Angelica announced, making the duke chuckle.

"She's *my* daughter," Lucille cried.

"She's mine now," Angelica countered.

Lucille turned to Robert. "Do something."

Robert remained silent for an excruciatingly long moment. Then he crossed the study, ordering, "Step aside. I want to see her."

Angelica remained where she was. Their eyes clashed in a fierce battle of two strong wills. Finally, Angelica inclined her head and stepped to the side, but Daisy moved with her.

"I'm waiting," Robert said, the hint of a smile touching his lips.

Angelica drew Daisy around until the child stood beside her but never let go of the little hand, lest Robert grab her and return her to the ogre posing as a mother. "Daisy, I want you to meet your father," Angelica said. To Robert, she added, "She has your eyes . . . and your sweet disposition, of course."

Duke Magnus laughed out loud. Robert's cheek muscles began twitching again.

Angelica felt a growing fury as she watched father and daughter. Daisy's black eyes, so much like her father's, held a deep yearning; and her expression mirrored her awe at meeting her father.

Robert said nothing. In fact, he inspected the little girl's arms as if she were an object instead of a child. Finally, he turned around to confront the mother.

"How did she get those bruises?" Robert demanded.

"You've seen how disobedient she can be," Lucille defended herself.

"If you ever touch her again," Robert threatened, "I'll cut you off without a penny. Do you understand?"

"Yes," Lucille answered, her anger apparent. "Come, Daisy. We're going home."

Angelica stepped in front of the girl. "You'll take her over my dead body."

Lucille turned to Robert for help. After a momentary pause, he took a step forward.

With her gaze fixed on his, Angelica flicked the

bottom of her gown up and drew her dagger. She held it in a relaxed grip, the blade up and away from her body, its sharp edge ready to slice him.

"I saved your life last night, my lord," Angelica said. "If need be, I'll take it away today."

Duke Magnus shouted with laughter, and then said, "Roxanne, she has your spirit."

"Yes, darling," her aunt replied, "but the girl lacks my subtlety."

Robert turned, saying, "Father—"

"Fight your own battles," Duke Magnus said, cutting off whatever his son had intended to say.

Robert stared tensely at Angelica, and she wondered what he would do. And then he relaxed, and that frightened her more than his anger.

"Countess, may I speak with you privately in the corridor?" Robert asked, the corners of his lips turning up in a polite smile.

Angelica felt uncertain about what to do. She wet her lips, gone dry from nervousness, and said, "Yes, you may." She refused to let go of Daisy's hand, though.

"The girl stays here," Robert said.

"I won't let her go," Angelica told him.

"You don't trust me?"

"Inspiring trust is not one of your talents, my lord. No insult intended."

"None taken."

"I'll guard her," Aunt Roxie said, crossing the chamber to take Daisy's hand in hers.

"Don't let go of Aunt Roxie's hand," Angelica instructed the girl. "I'll return in a few minutes."

Daisy nodded but flicked a worried glance in her mother's direction. "I won't let go," she promised.

Angelica stepped into the corridor. Robert walked behind her and closed the door.

"I appreciate your concern for the child, but you shouldn't have stolen her," Robert said.

Angelica arched a blond brow at him. "I didn't steal Daisy. I rescued her."

Robert smiled at that. "How badly do you want to keep her?"

"What do you mean?" she asked, instantly suspicious. The marquess wasn't above lying to get what he wanted. He'd already lied to her several times.

"From the appearance of the girl's arms, I would hazard a guess that Lucille lacks the maternal instinct," Robert told her. "She sees the child as her source of income." He paused for a moment and then said, "I'll offer Lucille enough money to keep her happy for the rest of her life if you—"

"Why do you want to marry a woman who doesn't love you?" Angelica interrupted. He would never know of her love for him. That knowledge in this scoundrel's possession would be dangerous for her peace of mind. She had no doubt that he would use it against her.

Robert smiled. "I was going to say, *if you spend the day in my bed.*"

Angelica felt as though he'd struck her. When had the marriage proposal become a proposition?

"I refuse to be at any man's beck and call," she told him.

"I didn't ask you for that," Robert replied. "One day in my bed, and you can keep the child."

"Just once?"

Robert inclined his head.

Angelica felt there had to be something more but couldn't imagine what else he had planned. "I cannot be seen going into your house," she hedged.

"I'll wait for a rainy day," he countered. "You

can wear a cloak and cover your head with its
hood."

Angelica remained silent, considering his offer.
If she did this, she would be little better than the
whores she'd met at fairs.

"That poor little girl will need to return to Portland Place," Robert said. "There's no telling what
Lucille will do after this stunt."

"Bull's pizzle," Angelica muttered. The man *was*
Old Clootie, sent to earth to lead her astray.

"I beg your pardon?"

"I'll come to you on the first rainy day," Angelica
agreed.

Robert gave her a devastating smile. "I'll pray
for rain."

Returning to the study, Angelica went directly
to Daisy and grabbed her hand. The little girl wore
an expression of anxiety and trembled with fear.

"Lucille, I want to speak to you in the corridor,"
Robert said.

Lucille crossed the chamber. As she passed her
daughter, Daisy pinned down her middle and ring
fingers with her thumb and cast her mother the
bad luck sign of the devil.

Angelica grabbed her hand, lest Robert notice
and change his mind. She glanced at the duke,
who wore a broad grin.

After placing the little girl in the chair in front
of her grandfather's desk, Angelica walked to the
one nearest the door and tried to hear what was
being said in the corridor. She could hear voices
but couldn't understand the words.

"Are you having fun here?" Duke Magnus asked
Daisy, breaking the silence in the study.

Daisy nodded and said, "This is the baby." She
held her thumb up. "This is the mother." She

held her index finger up. "And this is the father." Up went her middle finger.

Duke Magnus shouted with laughter. Aunt Roxie gave a throaty chuckle and glanced at Angelica, who covered her face with her hands.

"Did you learn that from Lady Angelica?" the duke asked.

"Yes, I did."

"Lady Angelica will be such a good influence on you," Duke Magnus said dryly.

"We saw the clouds make pictures of daisies," she told her grandfather. "Tonight, she will play her harp for me. Won't that be fun?"

"I can hardly wait for the hours to pass," Duke Magnus said. "Has she taught you to dice yet?"

"Lady Angelica, will you teach me to dice?" Daisy called.

"No, Lady Angelica will not teach you to dice," Robert said from the doorway. "That is, she won't if she has any common sense, which is doubtful after the stunt she pulled today." He mocked her with a smile and asked, "Eavesdropping, my dear?"

"I was not eavesdropping," Angelica replied, lifting her nose into the air. "As a matter of fact, you and your former paramour have given me an upset stomach."

"Lucille is gone and won't return," Robert announced. "Unless, of course, she doesn't receive my bank note tomorrow morning."

"How much did it cost you?" Duke Magnus asked.

"A hundred thousand pounds," Robert answered, looking at Angelica. "Lucille will return after she squanders that."

"Perhaps you should have given her a percentage in one of your businesses," Angelica said, rising from the chair and taking Daisy's hand in hers.

"Then she would have received payment quarterly instead of one lump sum."

Angelica could tell by his expression that he hadn't thought of that. What else could one expect from a man who'd never been forced to conserve resources like food in order to survive? "Your father loves you so much that he paid Lucille lots of money to keep you here with us," Angelica told the little girl.

Daisy looked at her father with adoration in her enormous black eyes. Robert ignored her, and Angelica could have carved him up without suffering a qualm.

"Who was that woman I saw leaving?" Venetia asked, walking into the duke's study.

"Darling, that was Lucille Dubois," Aunt Roxie purred.

Venetia appeared shocked and scandalized. "You brought your mistress into this house?" she asked, turning to Robert.

"Lucille is my former mistress," he told her.

"And what difference does that make?" Venetia asked, stamping her dainty foot. "If anyone passing by sees her—" She broke off, noticing Daisy for the first time, and asked, "Who is this?"

Angelica braced herself for the worst. "This is Daisy Dubois," she answered. "I'm keeping her."

"I refuse to live under the same roof with Robert's bastard," Venetia said, turning to the duke. "What will society—"

"Then I suggest you pack your bags and go," Angelica interrupted her.

"If I leave, I'll take my son with me," Venetia told the duke.

"Do not *dare* to threaten me," Duke Magnus said in a deadly voice. "At the moment, Colin is the Campbell heir. He won't be going anywhere with you. I will do whatever I must to keep my grandson with me. My influence exceeds your father's, so looking to him for satisfaction will prove futile." The duke glanced at Daisy and then told Venetia, "You may return to your father's if you wish."

"There's no need for Venetia to leave," Robert said. "Mrs. Sweeting and the child may stay at my house."

Angelica opened her mouth to protest, but Duke Magnus spoke first. "My granddaughter will remain with me," he told his son. "Venetia, perhaps you should return to your father's for a few days. That will give you time to calm yourself without hurting anyone's feelings more than you already have."

"What about my feelings? That woman has turned you against me and ruined my life," Venetia cried, pointing at Angelica. Without another word, she rushed out of the study.

Angelica suffered the sickening feeling that neither Venetia nor Lucille was finished with her. Taking the little girl's hand in hers, she led her toward the door, saying, "This whole affair has upset my stomach. Would you like to take a nap, Daisy?"

"No nap."

"*I* need a nap," Angelica said. "Will you accompany me?"

"I'll sing you to sleep," Daisy said as they walked out of the room.

"She'll make an excellent mother," Angelica heard her aunt exclaim.

"Lady Roxanne, I would like to speak to you regarding that strategy you suggested," Robert said.

"Of course, darling."

And then Angelica and Daisy released Jasper

from his cage and walked out of earshot. "Why is my father angry?" Daisy asked as they climbed the stairs to the third floor.

"He suffers from boils," Angelica lied.

"Does Lady Venetia suffer from boils, too?" Daisy asked.

"No, her bowels bother her."

"Lady Angelica, what are boils and bowels . . . ?"

Chapter 14

It rained the next day.

Angelica awakened early to the rhythmic tapping of raindrops against the window. Recognizing the sound, she hid her head beneath the pillow to block it out; but the thought of making love with Robert kept her awake and filled her with growing excitement.

My immoral behavior is for a good cause, Angelica told herself. *Daisy is worth the sacrifice.*

What sacrifice? You little hypocrite, you want this as much as he does, an inner voice countered.

By eight o'clock, Angelica had already washed and dressed and sat alone in the dining room. On the table in front of her were buttered scones and a pot of tea. She ate her breakfast and perused *The Times*, looking for some mention of her abduction of the Marquess of Argyll's daughter by his former mistress.

The newspaper contained no hint of her felony.

She supposed Lucille was waiting for her fortune to arrive.

The bargain Robert had made with Lucille confirmed Angelica's suspicions about the woman. Thankfully, Daisy need never pass another moment in that woman's company.

A footman appeared in the doorway and handed something to Tinker. The majordomo delivered the missive to her at the table.

Breaking its seal, Angelica read, *Noon?* There was no signature, but she knew the note's sender. She pocketed the missive but felt herself heating with embarrassment, as if the majordomo knew what the note contained.

"Lady Angelica, pardon my boldness, but are you feeling well?" Tinker asked. "You seem a bit flushed."

"I am quite well," Angelica managed to choke out. "Thank you for your concern."

Halfheartedly cursing the marquess for putting her into this untenable position, Angelica left Jasper breakfasting in his dining room cage and returned to her chamber. She sat on the chaise in front of the hearth and considered what she was about to do.

If the Marquess of Argyll thought she would sneak into his house and submit to his every whim like a whore, he was destined for disappointment. She would lay in his bed like a dead woman, or fight him every step—

Sacred sevens, she would *not* fight him, Angelica decided, a soft smile touching her lips. She would teach the arrogant bastard a lesson he'd never forget.

Since he was intent on making her play the whore in order to keep Daisy safe, she would give him a day to remember for the rest of his life. And after that, she would never share anything with him again until the hereafter, when they would burn together in the flames of Hell.

What did she have to lose? Angelica thought. He'd already taken her virginity.

If only she could recall what those streetwalkers at the fair had told her . . .

With her cloak wrapped around her and its hood pulled up to cover her blond hair, Angelica left the duke's residence at five minutes before noon. She dodged raindrops and puddles as she hurried down Park Lane to the marquess's residence.

Angelica stood at the top of the stairs, mentally bracing herself, and reached for the doorknocker. She pasted a bright smile on her face when it opened a moment later.

"Welcome, Lady Angelica," Webster said, stepping back to allow her entrance. "His Lordship is expecting you."

"Good afternoon, Webster," Angelica said, walking into the foyer.

"May I take your cloak?" he asked.

"No, thank you," she answered, and then gestured to the front door. "Where are the bodyguards?"

"They're sitting in the carriages parked across the street," the majordomo told her. "Mrs. Sweeting sent me a note. How kind of you to take her and her charge into your home."

"It's the Duke of Inverary's home and kindness," Angelica replied.

"Quite right," the majordomo agreed. "Please follow me."

Webster led Angelica up the stairs to the third floor and then walked down the carpeted corridor. He stopped in front of a closed door and knocked, calling, "Your lordship?"

"Send her in," she heard Robert say.

Angelica hoped the marquess wasn't waiting in bed. How would she ever face the majordomo again?

"Thank you, Webster," Angelica said, pretending that visiting the marquess in his bedchamber was perfectly agreeable. "That will be all."

"Very good, my lady."

Angelica stepped into the room and let the door click shut behind her. Dressed in black trousers and shirt, Robert stood with his back to her and gazed out the window. He didn't turn around right away, and she admired his broad shoulders and tapered waist.

Crossing the chamber, Angelica thought about this perfect specimen of manhood, pressing her down with his body, imbedding himself deep within her. She felt her knees go weak, the butterflies in her stomach take flight, and a tautness between her thighs. She wanted him.

"Your prayers have been answered," Angelica said, standing behind him.

Robert turned around. His black shirt was partially unbuttoned, and the jeweled Cross of Wotan gleamed at her.

"You're wearing the cross," Angelica said.

"I haven't removed it since you put it there," Robert told her. "May I take your cloak?"

Angelica pushed the hood off her head, revealing her mane of streaked gold hair. "After I've had a glass of—"

"Whiskey, I think," Robert said, and crossed the chamber to the bedside table.

Angelica knew that he could see her nervousness. She glanced out the window to the garden below. Again, that blond woman sat in the gazebo and looked toward the house. Hadn't Robert noticed her? Why wasn't the woman wearing a cloak to protect herself from the rain?

"Why is that woman sitting in the rain?" Angelica asked, turning around.

Robert stood at the bedside table, where a decanter, two glasses, and a bowl of fruit had been placed. He gave her a curious look and poured a splash of whiskey into one of the crystal glasses.

"To what woman do you refer?" Robert asked, returning to her.

"The woman sitting in the gazebo."

Robert glanced out the window and said, "I don't see anyone."

Angelica whirled around. The gazebo was empty.

"I guess she returned to her duties," she said.

Without taking her gaze from his, Angelica lifted the glass to her lips and took a sip. The whiskey burned a trail to the pit of her stomach.

"You don't need to do this," Robert told her, a tenseness in his voice. "I'll let you keep the girl."

The girl? He never referred to Daisy as his daughter. Eventually, she would need to speak to him about that.

Angelica knew that Robert was giving her the opportunity to leave. Accepting his offer never entered her mind.

"A bargain is a bargain," Angelica told him, her blue eyes gleaming with anticipation, the corners of her mouth turned up in a smile. She sensed him relax.

Taking the last sip of whiskey, Angelica passed him the empty glass. She waited for him to set it down and then unfastened her cloak, letting it drop to the floor at her feet.

Robert slid his dark gaze from her face to her body in the high-waisted morning gown. He stepped closer.

"Not so fast," Angelica said, holding out her hand in a gesture for him to stay where he was. "I'm providing the entertainment for today."

Robert inclined his head.

Angelica showed him her back. Glancing over her shoulder, she said, "The buttons, my lord."

Robert gave her a wicked smile and stepped closer. He unfastened the buttons with the practiced ease of a man who had undressed dozens of women.

Turning to face him, Angelica captured his black gaze with her own. Slowly and deliberately, she pushed the sleeves down her arms, and the gown's bodice slid to her waist. Letting it drop to the floor at her feet, she stepped out of the gown.

Angelica stood before him in a sleeveless, nearly transparent silk chemise. "Do you like what you see?"

"Very tempting, angel," he answered, his gaze fixed on her breasts, covered only by a whisper of silk.

Angelica slipped the chemise's straps down her arms, and it, too, fell to the floor. She wore nothing beneath the chemise except the diamond pendant, silk stockings held up by lace garters, and rouge used to accent her nipples.

She caught his heated gaze and asked, "Do you like my breasts?"

"You know I do," Robert said in a husky voice, and stepped forward.

Angelica held up her hand. "You'll need to wait."

"What the bloody hell are you doing?" Robert growled. "If your intention is teasing, then you had better—"

"I simply want to undress you," she interrupted, and smiled at his surprised expression.

Angelica stepped closer. She stared into his dark eyes, unbuttoned his shirt, and pushed it off his shoulders. Then she pressed herself against him and slid her breasts back and forth across his chest. When she heard his sharp intake of breath, she felt immensely pleased with herself.

Almost immediately, Angelica stepped back and whispered, "Stay where you are." She began walking around him, as if assessing his worth. After rubbing her breasts against his back, she embraced him from behind and slipped her hands to his groin.

"So hard for me," she said, and continued her stroll until she stood in front of him again.

Angelica caressed his cheek, her fingers tracing a line down his throat to his chest. She settled her hands on his flat nipples and caressed them with her fingertips.

And then her lips and tongue replaced her fingers. She flicked her tongue back and forth across his nipple, teasing it to aroused hardness, and then she suckled upon it.

Robert drew her up and kissed her with the fiery passion she had ignited in him. One of his hands held the back of her head, keeping her immobile, while the other cupped her buttocks and pulled her against his unyielding frame as he ground his lower regions against her.

Angelica felt her control slipping. She insinuated her hands between their bodies and unfastened his trousers, pushing them down his body until they dropped to his ankles. Hooking her arms around his neck, she returned his kiss with equal ardor. She slipped her tongue between his lips and explored his mouth while savoring the exquisite sensation of their nakedness pressed together.

Releasing him, Angelica stepped back a pace and said, "Touch me."

Her invitation was irresistible.

With a hand on each side of her head, Robert kissed her gently and then, watching her reactions, slid his hands down her cheeks to the slender column of her throat. His touch was a summer's breeze lightly caressing her skin, and Angelica realized, in some distant corner of her mind, how difficult controlling himself must be for him.

Robert caressed the outside of her arms from her shoulders to her fingertips. Lifting her hands, he planted a kiss on each and turned them over to flick his tongue across their palms before letting them drop to her sides.

Slowly, enticingly, Robert slid his fingertips up the inside of her arms. He cupped and lifted her breasts. With his dark gaze fixed on hers, he brushed his thumbs across her rouged nipples and smiled when he heard her audible gasp of pleasure.

"I love your sensitive nipples," Robert said huskily.

Leaning close, Robert placed a kiss on each and then glided his hands down the sides of her body to her gently rounded hips. He traced a teasing line across her legs and caressed her inner thighs, slowly running his fingers up and down them.

"I want to possess you," Robert whispered, one long finger slashing up the soft folds of flesh between her thighs.

Angelica moaned softly, his words inflaming her senses. She grabbed his hands and dropped to her knees in front of him. Taking his long length into her mouth, she sucked it and, at the same time, swirled her tongue around the head of his engorged manhood. She heard his groan of pleasure and then—

Robert pulled back, disengaging himself from her mouth, and yanked her to her feet. "What the bloody hell are you doing?" he demanded.

Angelica stared at him blankly, confused by his reaction. He was angry? Sacred sevens, he wasn't supposed to be—

"I asked you a question," he said.

"What does it look like I'm doing?" she countered.

"Where did you learn that?"

"At the fair."

"At the fair?" he echoed. "Who taught you?"

"The streetwalkers," Angelica answered. "I heard the streetwalkers at the fair talking about— *you know.*" Her cheeks pinkened. "I asked them a few questions, and they told me everything about . . . *you know.*"

Robert threw back his head and shouted with laughter. He laughed so hard he had to turn his back and walk away from her.

"Are you laughing at me?" Angelica asked.

Robert nodded. His shoulders still shook with his mirth.

What had she done incorrectly? His response to her advances had been exactly what the streetwalkers had predicted.

Robert turned and walked back to her. "Come here, angel," he said, opening his arms in invitation. "I want to explain why I laughed."

Angelica gave him a wary look but stepped forward. Walking into his embrace, she decided she liked the feel of his naked skin touching hers.

With one finger, Robert lifted her chin and looked into her eyes. "I laughed because you are so refreshingly innocent."

His remark didn't sit well with Angelica, and

there was no mistaking her displeased expression. She thought she'd been highly seductive.

"You do exhibit a natural talent, though," he amended himself.

Without giving her time to decide if she'd been complimented or insulted, Robert scooped her into his arms and carried her across the chamber to place her on his bed. He lay down beside her and glanced at his groin, saying, "We'll need to start over." Then he pulled her into his arms and kissed her as if he would never let her go.

Angelica returned his kiss, her heart vanquishing her resolve to keep him at bay emotionally. She poured all her love into one stirring kiss that melted into another and then another.

"I love you," Angelica murmured when his lips left hers.

"Lady, you excite me," Robert said, caressing her back and buttocks, pulling her against the long length of him to feel his aroused manhood.

Angelica dropped her hand to his groin. She stroked his manhood with her silken fingers, and he responded by sliding his hand to the soft folds of flesh between her thighs.

Robert slashed a long finger up and down her female's cleft until he found the moist, sensitive nub hidden there. "Do you like that?" he whispered.

"Yes," she breathed, arching herself toward him.

Robert dropped his head to suckle her nipple while his finger continued stroking her in exquisite torment. "Open your eyes," he whispered, gazing up at her, his lips still attached to her nipple and his fingers on her throbbing jewel.

"Tell me what you want," Robert ordered thickly.

"Fill me with your love," Angelica panted.

Robert rose up, spread her legs, and drew them over his shoulders. She lay open to him. With his manhood poised at her moist opening, he pushed himself forward slowly and pierced her body until their groins touched, the length of him filling her completely. He pulled himself out, ignoring her murmured protest, and caressed her wet female's button with his engorged shaft.

Angelica moaned at the exquisite sensation.

"Open your eyes," Robert said, positioning himself to pierce her again. "I want to look into your eyes when I enter you."

Dazed with passion, Angelica opened her eyes and stared into his dark gaze. She fought to keep her eyes open as he slid deep inside her and arched her body to receive him.

"You are so wonderfully tight," Robert said huskily, closing his own eyes first.

He began to move inside her rhythmically, one moment grinding himself into her and the next moment easing up. At the same time, he moved his hand to stroke the nub of her pleasure.

Angelica cried out. Waves of throbbing ecstasy crashed over her, carrying her to a primal paradise.

In answer, Robert let her legs slide down his arms and pulled her close. He groaned and shuddered and fell on top of her, finding his own release as she did.

Rolling to the side, Robert took her with him and kept her locked within his embrace. Completely sated, Angelica rested her head against his chest. Neither spoke, their breathing the only sound in the room.

Angelica recovered herself slowly. The more alert she became, the more her behavior embarrassed her. She felt her whole body heating with a blush. How could she have told the marquess she loved him? Angelica wondered. More importantly, how would she extricate herself from this situation? Should she dress and leave? How could she do that when she wasn't wearing anything and couldn't possibly parade naked in front of him?

"You're still wearing your garters and stockings," he said.

"So I am," Angelica replied in a small voice.

Robert raised himself up on his elbow and loomed over her. He stared down at her for a long moment and then smiled.

What now? she wondered, feeling self-conscious.

"You're blushing," Robert said, his gaze and his hand gliding down the length of her body. "You're blushing all over."

Angelica shifted her gaze away from his, saying, "I should leave now."

"Relax, angel. The afternoon is young," Robert told her. "Roll onto your stomach."

"Why?"

"Do as I say."

Angelica rolled over, and Robert knelt beside her. The bed creaked as he reached for something on the bedside table, and then she felt his hands on her shoulders, kneading her muscles with lotion, gliding his hands across her back.

Sighing, Angelica luxuriated in the feel of his strong hands massaging her, magically erasing her tension. A warm, languorous feeling seeped through her body. By the time he started on her buttocks, her eyelids had grown heavy and then closed.

"Awaken, my sleeping angel," Robert whispered in her ear.

Opening her eyes, Angelica realized that she had dozed off. How long had she slept?

Clutching the coverlet to her breasts, Angelica

sat up and leaned back against the headboard. Still naked, Robert sat on the edge of the bed. On the table was a tray containing a bowl of steaming soup, slices of bread, butter, and jam.

"What time is it?" Angelica asked.

"Two o'clock."

"I need to leave."

"Eat something first," Robert insisted.

"Pass me a slice of bread," she said.

Robert placed a slice of bread onto a plate, asking, "Butter or jam?"

"I want it dry."

Robert cocked a dark brow at her. "Dry bread?"

"The bread will soothe my queasiness," Angelica explained.

He looked concerned. "Are you ill?"

"I ate an early breakfast and missed lunch," Angelica said. "I always feel sick when I miss a meal."

Robert set down the bread plate and lifted the spoon. "Then I insist you eat a little soup," he said, dipping the spoon into the bowl. Holding his hand beneath the spoon lest he spill the soup, he offered it to her, saying, "Open your mouth."

Angelica did as she was told. "Delicious," she said. "May I please have my bread now?"

Robert passed her the bread, and when she'd eaten it, Angelica said, "I really must be going now."

"I'm not finished with you, angel." Robert pulled the coverlet down to reveal her nakedness.

"But I really—"

Robert lay down beside her and drew her into the circle of his embrace. His mouth covered hers in a gentle kiss that soon became demanding. The idea of leaving drifted away as his hands slid down her body.

Breaking their kiss, Robert reached for the crystal dish containing strawberry jam. He dipped one long finger into the jam and held it close to her lips.

"Lick it, angel," he whispered.

Angelica smiled. What new game was this? She flicked her tongue out and tasted the jam.

"That's a good girl," Robert said. "Now lick it off the whole finger."

Angelica grabbed his wrist, holding his hand immobile, and licked the jam off his finger, slashing her tongue this way and that. Catching his dark gaze, she licked his finger in long strokes and then took the tip of it into his mouth to suck it.

"My sweet angel," Robert whispered, kissing the excess strawberry jam from her lips.

Robert dipped two fingers into the jam. Angelica opened her mouth to receive his fingers, but he surprised her by grabbing her wrists with one hand and drawing her arms over her head.

"What are you going to do?" she asked.

"Pleasure you, my lady." Robert touched her lips with his fingers, and she flicked her tongue out to taste them.

"You like licking and sucking me," he said.

"Oh, yes," she breathed, his words igniting a throbbing heat between her thighs.

Tracing a line of strawberry jam, Robert moved his fingers from her lips to her throat and then paused to dip his fingers into the jam again. Teasing her, he swirled his fingers around one of her breasts until the circles of jam reached her nipple. Then he dipped a finger into the crystal dish and topped the nipple with a tiny dollop of jam, its coolness on her nipple increasing the throbbing between her thighs.

"Take me again," Angelica whispered.

"Are you asking or demanding?"

"Please . . ."

Robert smiled. "I'll give you what you want when I'm ready," he said, rubbing his hardened manhood against her thigh.

Dipping his head, Robert licked the jam off her lips, his tongue following the streak of jam down her throat to her breast. In teasing strokes, he flicked his tongue around her breast, licking the jam, and then took her nipple into his mouth and drew upon it, gently at first and then harder.

Angelica moaned and arched herself toward him. Her hips began a rhythmic gyrating movement as she tried to entice him to enter her. By the time he finished decorating her other breast with the jam and tormenting her with his tongue, Angelica was desperate with need.

Robert dipped his finger into the jam again. With one hand he opened her soft folds of flesh, and with the other he smeared her nub with the strawberry jam. Lowering his head, he licked the jam from her pearl.

Angelica lost control. She arched herself into his mouth, surrendering her very being to him as spasms of ecstasy carried her to paradise.

Robert fell back on the bed and pulled her on top of him. "Sit up," he ordered in a voice thick with passion. "Take me deep inside you and let our juices mingle."

Angelica needed no further invitation. She lifted her body into a sitting position and, holding his gaze captive, impaled herself on his aroused manhood until his groin pressed against her sensitive jewel.

Smiling at his groan of pleasure, she whispered, "I love the way you fill me." Then she moved, riding him slowly at first before increasing the tempo.

Angelica raised her arms into the air as she ground herself into him. Never had she felt so gloriously alive. When he caught her nipples between his thumbs and forefingers and squeezed them, she cried out and exploded, her juices flooding his manhood.

Robert flipped her over and rode her hard. Within minutes, he groaned and shuddered and found completeness within her body.

Falling to the side, Robert pulled her with him and said, "Sleep now . . ."

Two hours later, with her tousled mane of blond hair covered by the hood of her cloak, Angelica hurried down Park Lane. She raced up the front stairs of the duke's house and flew into the empty foyer. Relief at making it home undetected washed through her, and she dashed up the stairs to her third-floor bedchamber.

Rounding the corner of the second-floor landing, Angelica nearly collided with her aunt. She cried out in surprise and then laughed.

"There you are, darling," Aunt Roxie said. "I've been looking for you all afternoon."

"I went to visit the marquess."

"The marquess?" her aunt drawled.

"I-I needed to speak to him about Daisy," Angelica lied.

"For so long?"

"Robert challenged me to a game of chess," Angelica told her. Warming to her lies, she added, "Only, I had never played chess before, so he needed to teach me the game."

Aunt Roxie gave her a curious look and asked, "Why do you smell like strawberries?"

"I-I-I spilled strawberry juice," Angelica stammered.

"Starwberry juice?" Aunt Roxie echoed. "Why are you flushed?"

"I ran home," Angelica said. "I'll see you at dinner."

Angelica brushed past Lady Roxanne and raced up the stairs. She looked back once to see her aunt watching her, a feline smile on her face.

Chapter 15

Telling Robert she loved him had been a mistake, Angelica told herself for the hundredth time since leaving his town house five days earlier.

Passing that afternoon in his bed had been ecstasy; Angelica blushed when she thought about what they had done. Now, however, she was paying for that weakness of the flesh.

Each day Angelica had expected Robert to appear at the duke's mansion to see her and Daisy. Especially Daisy, who asked about him constantly.

Although his unspoken rejection hurt, Angelica concluded that she was an adult woman and could bear the pain. Daisy was another matter, however.

If it hadn't been for Robert's absence, life at the duke's mansion would have been heaven. With Venetia's departure, the tension that hung like a cloud over the household disappeared, leaving its occupants lighthearted.

Angelica and her sisters passed each day in the company of Daisy and Colin. Life had become one long game, interrupted by meals and sleep. She and her sisters hadn't spent a day in play since their father had lost the Douglas fortune.

Would Robert speak to her at his father's ball? Angelica wondered, the prospect of seeing him unsettling to her. Even now she heard the musicians in the ballroom, tuning their instruments in preparation.

Pulling on her white gloves, Angelica stepped in front of the cheval glass and inspected her reflection. She'd chosen this particular gown to entice Robert, though she intended to ignore him for the rest of her life.

Angelica was a Greek goddess in her white silk evening gown. The bodice's neckline was square, cut low, and form-fitting. The whole of her bust, shoulders, and arms were exposed as the gown sported a mere strap—a whisper of silk—over one shoulder. She wore silk stockings and evening slippers of white satin with golden rosettes. Around her neck hung her diamond-and-gold pendant. She had pulled her streaked blond hair into an intricate knot at the nape of her neck and adorned it with a sprig of baby's breath.

"Lady Angelica, you look beautiful."

Angelica turned toward the doorway. Daisy and Colin hurried across the bedchamber.

"Hello," Jasper called from his perch inside his cage.

Angelica crouched down to be at eye level with the children. She opened her arms and said, "Give me a kiss."

She hugged Daisy and kissed her cheek. Then Colin received the same attention.

"Won't you get messy?" Daisy asked. "Lucille never let me hug her when she dressed up. She said I would mess her."

"Who's Lucille?" Colin asked.

"My mother."

"My mother doesn't want me to mess her either."

"Lady Angelica, why do you let us mess you?" Daisy asked.

"You and Colin are more important than this old dress," Angelica told her.

Daisy threw her arms around her neck, saying, "I love you, Lady Angelica."

"I love you, too," Colin said, clinging to her other side.

"I love both of you," Angelica told them, putting an arm around each. Then she asked, "Will you sit in my chamber to keep Jasper company?"

Both Daisy and Colin nodded. Angelica could see the gleam of excitement in their eyes.

"You must promise not to open his cage or stick your fingers inside it," she warned.

"I promise."

"I promise, too."

Angelica gave each a kiss on the cheek and stood. "I want you to decide what games we'll play tomorrow." Then she watched them cross the chamber to sit on the floor near the macaw's cage.

Opening the door to leave, Angelica saw Mrs. Sweeting and Mrs. Honey headed down the corridor. "I asked Daisy and Colin to keep Jasper company," she told them. "Please, sit in my chamber until their bedtime."

Angelica walked down the corridor to the top of the stairs. The music grew louder as it wafted up to the third floor.

She wondered if Robert had arrived, and then told herself she didn't care. But the least he could have done was visit his own daughter. Why did he reject his own flesh and blood? Louisa's suicide wasn't Daisy's fault. Why was he punishing the child?

Angelica walked into the duke's study, where she'd been summoned by her aunt. Her sisters were already there, as well as Duke Magnus and Aunt Roxie.

"Close the door behind you," Duke Magnus said.

Angelica did as she was told. With a smile on her face, she crossed the chamber to the desk and stood beside the chair occupied by her aunt.

"I see that my nieces look spectacular," Aunt Roxie said, beaming at them. "I feel that tonight will be special."

"Hopefully, Charles Emerson will lose his fortune tonight," Angelica said, making her sisters smile.

Aunt Roxie patted her hand and replied, "Perhaps the time has arrived to think about something other than revenge."

"Nothing is more important than ruining the villain," Angelica said.

Duke Magnus cleared his throat. "My barrister has completed the document making me your legal guardian," he said, holding up the document. "It's a mere formality." He passed her aunt the quill and set the paper down on the desk in front of her, saying, "Roxanne, you sign first, and then your nieces."

Without reading it, Lady Roxanne took the quill and signed her name. She passed the quill to Victoria, who signed it next, and then Samantha. Angelica took the quill from her sister and started to read the document.

"Darling, just sign the paper," Aunt Roxie said. "We're already late."

Angelica signed her name. Then she passed the

quill and the document to the duke, who walked around his desk.

Duke Magnus offered Aunt Roxie his arm. They followed the three sisters out of the study and walked down the corridor to the ballroom, located on the same floor.

Their group gathered at the top of the ballroom, opposite the musicians at the other end. Two violins, a cornet, a cello, and a piano comprised the orchestra.

No sooner had they entered the ballroom than Venetia walked in and, smiling, crossed the room to them. She looked especially lovely in a sky-blue gown.

"Good evening, Your Grace," Venetia said, ignoring the Douglases. "I came early to act as your hostess."

"That won't be necessary, darling," Aunt Roxie drawled. "I am His Grace's hostess."

Venetia appeared ready to explode, but Duke Magnus said, "Do not even consider creating a scene. Why haven't you visited Colin?"

"I didn't think I would be welcome here," Venetia answered, an expression of hurt appearing on her face.

"You are always welcome in my home as long as you behave civilly," Duke Magnus told her.

The arrival of their first guests precluded Venetia from answering. She stood beside the duke, pasted a gracious smile on her face, and pretended to be the duke's hostess.

Swallowing a smile, Angelica turned away and spied Robert walking into the ballroom. She turned her back and whispered to her sisters, "Remember, no more than two dances with any gentleman."

Samantha and Victoria looked at each other and rolled their eyes.

"I mean it," Angelica warned. She shifted her gaze and found her aunt watching her, a knowing smile flirting with the corners of her lips.

Sacred sevens, did her aunt know how Robert and she had passed the other afternoon? Angelica wondered. Where should she look? If she turned one way, her aunt and Venetia were there; but if she turned the other way, Robert—

"Good evening, Countess."

Angelica turned around and smiled coolly at Robert. "Good evening, my lord."

"I hope you will save a dance for me," he said, a devastating smile on his face.

Angelica felt her heart wrench. The man was too handsome for her peace of mind. If he really cared for her, he would have shown his face before now.

"Countess?"

"I will be happy to save you a dance," she said. "If you will excuse me?"

Angelica tried to brush past him, but he grabbed her arm, asking, "Where are you going?" She shifted her gaze to the hand on her arm. When she raised her gaze to his again, he dropped his hand.

"You aren't leaving on my account?" Robert asked.

"You flatter yourself if you think your presence affects me," she answered. "I simply forgot to brush my teeth."

Angelica walked away from him and left the ballroom. She went to the ladies' resting area and sat down. Her stomach churned, and she longed to return to her chamber. She felt comfortable with the children and out of place with society. Oh, why couldn't Robert have left her alone that day at the fair? She didn't belong with these people, who had never known a day of poverty; she didn't know how to play these aristocratic games. She was the penniless Countess of Nowhere.

Society was not to blame for the way she felt, Angelica knew, pinching her cheeks to regain some color. She had created her own problems by spending an afternoon in the marquess's bed and professing her love for him. Aunt Roxie had always said that men loved challenges. She should have listened to her aunt.

Returning to the ballroom, Angelica saw Robert in private conversation with his father and her aunt. Her sisters were dancing, as was Venetia, and Angelica wondered uncomfortably what she should do.

With no other choice, Angelica walked slowly in the direction of her aunt and the duke. Their conversation ended abruptly when she reached them.

"I hope this is our dance," Robert said.

Angelica inclined her head and stepped onto the dance floor with him. Though her smile remained placid, she felt a hundred butterflies winging through her stomach.

What could she possibly say to him? Angelica wondered. What would she do if he mentioned their tryst?

Robert held her closer than he should have, though she tried to keep her distance. Slowly, she relaxed in his arms as they swirled around the ballroom.

"Making polite conversation is expected while dancing," Robert said. "Unless you want the guests to think we are not in accord?"

"You dance divinely," Angelica told his chest.

"I believe you complimented my chest the last time we danced," he teased her.

Angelica raised her blue gaze to him. "Where

have you been these past five days?" she blurted out, losing conrol of her tongue.

Robert smiled. "Did you miss me, angel?"

"Not bloody likely," she snapped with a smile on her face.

"I'm relieved to see you are your normal ornery self and suffered no ill effects from our activities the other day," Robert said.

Angelica felt embarrassment heating her cheeks. She could only imagine how red her face must be. "Never mention that day again," she whispered.

"I have fond memories of it," he told her.

Of course he had fond memories, Angelica thought. She'd given herself to him completely and professed her love. What had she to show for it? Nothing.

You rescued Daisy, an inner voice reminded her.

"Daisy has been asking for you," Angelica said, changing the subject. "Do you think you could possibly show her a little kindness and pass an occasional hour with her?"

"I can't do that."

"She's only a baby—"

"My gift to Daisy was allowing her to remain with you," Robert interrupted. "She will need to be content with that."

What a pigheaded lout, Angelica thought, her smile never faltering. She inclined her head, accepting his statement. Arguing with him tonight would only harm her new cause, fostering a relationship between father and daughter.

"What are you planning, angel?"

"I don't know what you mean."

"I don't trust your ability to capitulate so easily," Robert said.

The waltz ended. Angelica turned to leave the

dance floor, but Robert stopped her, saying, "I believe this is our dance, too."

"I prefer to sit this one out," she said.

"Are you ill?" Robert asked, his hand on her arm. "Do you feel tired or queasy?"

"I am perfectly well." Angelica couldn't imagine why the marquess was so interested in her health. He didn't even like her.

"I'll ruin Drinkwater or Mayhew tonight," he whispered, close to her ear.

"Don't bother," Angelica said, shrugging out of his grasp. "Ruining them is my responsibility."

"That won't happen tonight," Robert told her. "You aren't wearing sleeves or pockets."

Angelica arched a blond brow at him. "So I'll lose a few coins, which will make them eager to dice against me when I am wearing sleeves."

"I forbid you to dice wearing that gown," Robert said, a scowl appearing on his face.

"You aren't my keeper," Angelica informed him, unable to credit what she'd heard. "And what is wrong with this gown?"

"The gown doesn't cover enough of your skin," Robert answered.

So he *had* noticed her gown, Angelica thought with satisfaction. Imitating her aunt, she drawled, "The most interesting parts are covered, darling."

"Don't *darling* me," Robert said in a harsh whisper. "Every man in this room is ogling you."

"You really should smile, darling, lest these guests belive we are not in accord," Angelica said, glancing around. No one appeared to be paying any particular attention to her.

Drawing their attention, the orchestra stopped playing. The duke stood with her aunt at the bottom of the ballroom. "May I have your attention, please?'' Duke Magnus called out, holding her aunt's hand.

Angelica and Robert looked at each other. She shrugged, indicating that she had no idea what was happening.

"I have excellent news," Duke Magnus announced. "Lady Roxanne has honored me by accepting my proposal of marriage and will become my wife, the Duchess of Inverary."

Angelica dropped her mouth open in surprise. She glanced at Robert, who looked as surprised as she felt.

Everyone in the ballroom clapped in approval. Duke Magnus raised Aunt Roxie's hand to his lips. Looking infinitely pleased with herself, her aunt smiled at the duke.

"I'll be damned," Robert said, a smile touching his lips. "After all these years, the old fox has finally done it."

Angelica wasn't as pleased as the marquess. Though she approved of her aunt finding happiness, Angelica realized that now she and her sisters would be forever linked with the Campbells. The thought of facing Robert and whomever he eventually married made her stomach churn and breathing became almost painful.

"Excuse me," Angelica said, needing to escape.

"Aren't you going to wish them well?" Robert asked.

"I'll speak to them later." Without another word, Angelica left the ballroom. Instead of going to the ladies' resting area, she wandered into the gaming room.

Charles Emerson sat at a table with Henry Drinkwater, Mungo Mayhew, and James Armstrong. Sipping a drink, Adam St. Aubyn stood nearby and watched the four men dicing.

Ladies and gentlemen filled several other tables. Some people diced, while others played cards.

"Lady Angelica, perhaps you would care to dice with us?" Charles Emerson asked, his smile ingratiating.

If only she was wearing sleeves, Angelica thought.

"I'd love to dice, if you're certain the others won't mind," she answered.

Angelica glanced at Drinkwater and Mayhew. Except for James Armstrong, the others were staring at her wolfishly. Did they think she was an easy mark, or was her gown too daringly cut, as Robert had said?

"Join us, Countess," James Armstrong said. "You are so much prettier than these fellows."

James stood and brought an empty chair from another table. Angelica sat down and smiled as winsomely as she could.

"How much are we betting?" she asked.

"Ten pounds per throw," James answered.

That didn't sound too bad to Angelica, even though she was unable to cheat without pockets or sleeves. Besides, she would never try to cheat four men at the same time. If she lost a small amount of money, each of them would be eager to dice with her again.

Adam St. Aubyn placed twenty chips in front of her, saying, "You can reimburse me later."

"Thank you, my lord," she said.

"Gentlemen, shall we say ladies first?" James asked.

The three other men nodded. Everyone, including Angelica, put a chip aside.

"What's your main?" James asked.

"Seven."

Angelica made a show of closing her eyes and shaking the dice in the palm of her hand. She tossed the dice and opened her eyes. A four and a three showed up.

No one was more surprised than Angelica. She clapped her hands together, exclaiming, "I've won."

Each man gave her a chip worth ten pounds and then set another chip aside. She tossed the dice again. This time a four and a two showed up, giving her another chance to throw. The third toss came up three and two, and the fourth showed a six and a one.

Smiling as the four men handed her three chips each, Angelica couldn't believe her good luck. Too bad her father hadn't enjoyed this luck ten years earlier. Life would have been different for her and her sisters.

Thirty minutes later, Angelica had won two hundred pounds from each man. She looked up to see Tinker standing beside her.

"Excuse me, my lady," the majordomo said, passing her a folded piece of paper. "This is for you."

Angelica opened the paper and recognized the handwriting. It said: *Need to speak with you privately. Meet me at the gazebo.*

Angelica stared at the message. It seemed urgent, but what could have happened in the preceding thirty minutes?

She was beating her enemies without cheating. Granted, ruining them would take a long, long time if the bets remained at ten pounds a throw. Still, there was nothing more exhilarating than beating someone you hated.

Torn between staying to gamble and rushing to Robert's side, Angelica didn't know what to do. She hesitated for a moment and then rose from her chair.

"I'm sorry, gentlemen," Angelica said, glancing

with regret at the pile of chips she'd won. "I'm needed elsewhere."

"Aren't you going to give us a chance to recoup?" Charles Emerson asked.

Angelica knew these men would never dice with her again if she didn't give them the chance to recoup their losses. She turned to Adam St. Aubyn, asking, "My lord, will you take my place?"

"I would be honored to represent you," Adam said, stepping forward.

"Good evening, gentlemen," Angelica said, smiling at each in turn. "I hope we can do this again sometime."

Angelica quit the gaming room. She walked downstairs to the first floor and then headed down the corridor that led to the back of the mansion. She stepped outside into the duke's garden.

Accompanied by hundreds of glittering stars, a crescent moon hung in a black sky. Ground fog swirled around her legs up to her knees.

Though torches had been lit, no couples walked about, and Angelica hesitated. The night was quiet, eerily quiet.

Robert needs me, Angelica told herself, and forced herself to step forward. In less than five minutes, she was entering his garden.

In the distance, Angelica could see a figure sitting in the gazebo. "Robert?" she called, her voice sounding loud in the stillness of the night.

And then Angelica realized the figure was the woman she'd seen there before. "Hello," she called. The woman turned in her direction and then vanished.

Frightened, Angelica stopped short. Her heart beat rapidly, her breathing came in shallow gasps, and the hairs on the back of her neck rose up like hackles.

Sacred sevens, the woman was a spirit. Oh, she needed to speak with her aunt.

Intending to return to the duke's town house, Angelica whirled around and ran straight into an immovable object. She screamed, and a hand covered her mouth.

"It's me." The voice belonged to Robert.

Angelica threw herself into his arms and hid her face against his chest. He put his arms around her and held her close, though the safety within his embrace failed to keep her stomach from churning.

"What is wrong?" Robert asked, lifting her chin. "You look like you've seen a ghost."

"I have."

Robert kissed the crown of her head and said, "Angel, ghosts do not exist."

"That's easy for you to say," Angelica replied, her voice muffled against his chest. "You didn't see her."

"I wanted to explain my behavior and speak to you about the girl," Robert said, "but I think you need this more."

Robert tilted up her chin and kissed her. The warmth of his lips seeped into her, calming and exciting her at the same time.

"I'm glad we followed her, Roxanne." This voice belonged to Duke Magnus.

Angelica whirled around. Seeing the duke and her aunt standing there, she dropped her mouth open in surprise. Of all the bad luck—

"Your behavior is unseemly, Angelica," Aunt Roxie reproved her.

"You have placed the lady in an untenable position," Duke Magnus told his son. "You will marry her posthaste."

Angelica was stunned. "But nobody knows I'm here."

"You were seen leaving the ball," her aunt told her.

"What do you have to say for yourself, son?" Duke Magnus asked.

"I have already proposed marriage," Robert answered. "The lady refused."

Duke Magnus shifted his dark gaze to Angelica. "I intend to announce your betrothal to Robert tonight."

Angelica felt trapped, a mulish expression appearing on her face. "I will not—"

"Roxanne, tell her and be done with it," Duke Magnus said, sounding irritated.

Aunt Roxie smiled. "Darling, your tiredness and queasiness can only mean that you are with child."

Her words shocked Angelica. Suddenly dizzy, she swayed on her feet, but Robert steadied her and kept her from falling.

"That is impossible," she whispered.

"Have you been intimate with my son?" Duke Magnus asked.

Angelica couldn't seem to find her voice through her humiliation. She looked from the duke to her aunt, but no words came out.

"We have been intimate several times," Robert told his father. "Five days ago we passed the afternoon in my bed."

Angelica swayed on her feet again. She wished she would swoon to escape this whole situation.

"It's settled then," Duke Magnus said. "You will marry after a short betrothal. I will tolerate no scandal attached to the Campbell heir."

"You have no control over me," Angelica countered, accustomed to giving orders, not following them. "I am a countess."

"I am your legal guardian," the duke reminded her.

Angelica knew when she'd been trapped. It seemed as if the three of them had conspired against her, but she refused to surrender to their wishes so easily.

"I am willing to bargain with the marquess," Angelica told the duke.

Duke Magnus inclined his head. "Do whatever she wants," he ordered his son. "This marriage needs to take place almost immediately."

Robert turned her to face him and asked, "Angel, what is it you want?"

When she raised her gaze to his there was no mistaking the battle lines etched across her face. "I will marry you only if you promise to form a relationship with Daisy."

Robert stared into her eyes for a long moment and then, surprisingly, smiled. "I promise to form a relationship with the child if—"

"Daisy is her name," Angelica interrupted him. "Use it."

Robert inclined his head. "Daisy, then. However, you must promise to forget your revenge."

Conniving bastard, Angelica thought. He knew that giving up the prospect of revenge would be impossible. She had an obligation to her parents.

"No deal, my lord," Angelica said, wiping the smile off his face. "Prepare yourself for another child born out of wedlock."

"Robert, I'm warning you . . ." the duke growled.

"I will not allow my wife to jeopardize her health and her reputation, as well as the health of our child, by proceeding with this scheme for revenge," Robert told his father.

"Darling, be reasonable," Aunt Roxie pleaded with her. "You will become the Marchioness of Argyll, the future Duchess of Inverary. Think of the status, the jewels, the glamour. Your every wish will be granted."

"All but one," Angelica replied.

"You misunderstand me," Robert amended himself. "I will take revenge on Drinkwater, Mayhew, and Emerson in any manner I think expedient. I promise their crimes will not go unpunished."

Angelica knew that was the best she would get. "You have won a bride for yourself," she said.

Robert lifted her hand to his lips. "And a loving wife, I hope."

"Don't press your luck," Angelica said, and brushed past him, intending to return to the duke's town house.

Robert caught up to her and grabbed her hand. When she tried to pull out of his grasp, he said, "We need to play the loving couple, angel."

Angelica made no reply but allowed him to escort her back to the duke's town house.

"I knew they would be fabulous together," she heard her aunt say to the duke.

"Humph," the duke snorted, mirroring her own feelings. "I'll announce their betrothal before supper so she can't change her mind."

Ten minutes later, Angelica stood with Robert at the foot of the ballroom. For the second time that evening, Duke Magnus instructed the orchestra to stop playing. A sea of faces turned to look at them.

"I have additional good news," Duke Magnus announced, beaming with pride. "The Countess of Melrose has accepted my son's proposal of marriage."

A murmur of surprise swept through the crowd. Responding to it, Angelica pasted a bright smile on her face and fixed her blue gaze on Robert instead of their guests. She hoped she looked adoring.

Duke Magnus held up his hand in a gesture for silence. "I realize this is a bit unorthodox, but Robert and Angelica have agreed to marry in three weeks so that my own marriage to Lady Roxanne will not be delayed."

The crowd erupted into conversation. Someone in the crush of people applauded with approval, and others followed suit.

And then the well-wishers surrounded Angelica and Robert. Adam St. Aubyn stood in front of her and lifted her hand to his lips. He winked at her and whispered, "I beat the others. I'll send you a banknote in the morning."

"You keep it," Angelica said, looping her hand through Robert's arm. "I have just caught myself an exceedingly wealthy husband."

When Adam stepped away, Angelica scanned the ballroom and noted Venetia's venomous glare, as well as Charles Emerson's nauseatingly insincere smile. That smile frightened her more than his daughter's expression of hatred.

Chapter 16

The bride wore a frown.

"Angelica, darling, do stop frowning," Aunt Roxie said. "What will our guests think?"

"Would you prefer growling?" Angelica asked, making the duke smile.

"Don't encourage her," Aunt Roxie told the duke. She turned to Angelica, saying, "Today is the happiest day of your life. You should be smiling."

"The happiest day of my life?" Angelica echoed. "You tricked me into marrying a man who hasn't exchanged one word with me in the past three weeks. No visits, no gifts, no notes."

"Perhaps the marquess feared you would cancel the wedding," her aunt said.

"Is that why the marquess didn't bother with a betrothal ring?" Angelica countered. "More likely, the marquess wanted me to cancel the wedding."

"Be quiet," Aunt Roxie snapped, losing patience. "I am tired of listening to you, which is probably what kept the marquess away. You'll need to be more agreeable if you want a successful marriage."

Standing with the duke and her aunt in the nave of the Grosvenor Chapel, Angelica clamped her lips together, and her frown became a scowl. Two hundred of the Campbells' closest friends filled the church for her wedding.

"You look like a princess, except for that grotesque expression," Aunt Roxie said, after circling her with a critical eye. "Your parents would be so proud."

Angelica wore her mother's wedding gown. Elegantly simple, the gown of white silk had been embroidered with hundreds of tiny seed pearls. Its bodice had a squared neckline and long, flowing sleeves shaped like bells. Drop-waisted, the gown flared slightly from her hips.

Around her neck, Angelica wore her diamond and gold pendant, and on her feet were white satin slippers that complemented the gown. A wreath of orange blossoms served as a headdress, crowning the blond hair that cascaded to her waist.

"Child, I do not want either you or my son unhappy," Duke Magnus said, taking her hand in his. "If you prefer not to marry Robert, I'll call off the wedding."

Angelica raised her gaze to the duke's. She loved the marquess and couldn't bring herself to say the words that would cancel this fiasco. How could she bring a child into the world unless she married the babe's father? She had trapped herself into this marriage without any help from her aunt or the duke.

"I'm already unhappy," Angelica said, and then she sighed. "Another forty years of misery won't make any difference. The child will be loved."

"Darling, why are you unhappy?" Aunt Roxie asked, looking concerned.

"I wanted to marry a man who loved me," Angelica answered, a catch of emotion in her voice.

"Is that all?" Aunt Roxie said, and smiled. "The marquess adores you."

"He's never expressed any love for me," she countered.

"Have you expressed any for him?"

"Yes," Angelica answered, wiping the smile off her aunt's face.

"Actions speak louder than words," Aunt Roxie told her. "Watch what a man does, not what he says or doesn't say."

Duke Magnus cleared his throat. "Roxanne, I'll handle this." He turned to Angelica, saying, "Robert wants to marry you, but sometimes men find expressing their feelings difficult, if not impossible."

"A man who says 'I love you' too easily is not to be trusted," Aunt Roxie agreed.

"Be patient with Robert," Duke Magnus continued. "Despite our wealth, my oldest son has had a difficult time. As a boy, the prospect of living up to his father's and his ancestors' high standards worried him. Then Robert lost his brother to a riding accident, and Louisa's suicide a few months later devastated him."

"How can I compete with a dead woman for his affection?" Angelica asked.

"Robert felt no great passion for Louisa," the duke told her. "Theirs was an arranged marriage."

"What was she like?"

"Gentle and timid, Louisa possessed none of your fiery spirit," Duke Magnus answered with a smile.

You look like your mother but possess none of her gentle-

ness, Angelica recalled her father's final words to her.

His words rang true, but there was nothing to be done for it. She couldn't change who she was.

"Will you marry my son and make him happy?" Duke Magnus asked. "Or shall I step into the chapel and call off the ceremony?"

"I'll marry him," Angelica said, smiling for the first time that day. "Beyond that, I can promise nothing."

"That's good enough for me," the duke said, offering his arm. "Roxanne, tell them we're ready and take your place in the chapel."

Angelica looped her arm through the duke's. Together, they stood at the top of the aisle. When the organs and violins began to play, the duke gave her an encouraging smile and guided her down the aisle toward his son.

Hundreds of flickering candles lit the chapel, casting dancing shadows on its walls. Bouquets of red and white roses adorned the altar, reminding her of the day Robert had stood outside her cottage and tried to make amends with her.

Angelica suffered one bad moment. When the sea of mostly unfamiliar faces turned to watch them, she spied Venetia and her father. Both wore such expressions of hatred that she hesitated for a fraction of a moment.

"Focus on Robert," Duke Magnus whispered.

Angelica took his advice. Blocking out everyone else, she fixed her gaze on her groom, who stood with the bishop at the altar. Robert looked magnificent in his midnight blue attire; but, more importantly, his smile on her held the promise of love.

Reaching the altar, Duke Magnus placed her trembling hand in his son's and joined her aunt and sisters in the front pew. Robert lifted her hand to his lips before turning with her to follow the bishop through the mahogany gates into the sanctuary.

Suffering from a queasy stomach, Angelica felt relieved that the ceremony was short. Its only tiny glitch came when she gasped out loud at the first sight of her wedding band. Topped with an enormous diamond, the band was yellow, white, and rose gold braided together.

"I assume you like the ring," Robert whispered.

"Is it real?" Angelica asked, making him laugh.

The bishop cleared his throat. "Shall we continue?"

In a few short minutes, the bishop pronounced them man and wife, and Robert was escorting her down the aisle. An army of bodyguards surrounded them before they stepped outside, reminding her that someone wanted her husband dead.

Angelica felt shy on the short ride to their wedding breakfast at the duke's town house. The man beside her was her husband, but she couldn't think of anything to say to him.

"You make a beautiful bride," Robert said, lifting her hand to his lips. "One thing puzzles me, though."

Angelica looked at him. "What is it?"

"Why wasn't Jasper sitting with your relatives?" Robert asked, making her smile. He reached into his waistcoat's inner pocket and withdrew a folded white handkerchief. Wrapped inside the handkerchief was a piece of dry toast. He passed it to her, saying, "You look like you need this."

Angelica smiled and began eating the bread. "Where have you been for three weeks?" she asked, the words slipping out before she could stop herself.

"I've been avoiding you," Robert answered matter-of-factly.

His honesty surprised her. "Why?"

"I knew if you saw me, I would aggravate you," Robert told her. "Then you would cancel the wedding."

"That isn't true."

"I wouldn't aggravate you?"

"Yes, you would aggravate me," Angelica answered, making him laugh, "but I wouldn't have canceled the wedding."

Their coach halted in front of his father's home. The driver opened the door, and Robert climbed out. He turned to assist her just as the duke's coach pulled up behind them.

The next three hours passed in a blur. Angelica met more aristocrats than she cared to and smiled until her face hurt. She felt certain, though, that no one could suspect her marriage to the marquess was loveless.

Two incidents irritated Angelica. Against her protests, Robert had forbidden Daisy and Colin from attending the reception.

And then there was Venetia.

Leaving the celebration, Angelica excused herself and went to the ladies' resting area. She needed to compose herself before facing her husband alone in his town house, her new home.

Angelica sat down and took a deep, fortifying breath. A moment later Venetia walked into the room. Sacred sevens, this was all she needed to make the situation worse.

"Are you following me?" Angelica asked, looking in the mirror at the other woman.

Venetia inclined her head and smiled at her, but Angelica knew the gesture was forced. A chill of apprehension ran down her spine.

"You will never be mother to the Campbell heir," Venetia told her. "My father promised me."

Anger swept through Angelica. She rose from her chair and faced the other woman. Almost nose-to-nose with her, Angelica said in a scathing tone of voice, "You tell your father that he may be able to cheat a decent man out of his family's fortune, but he has no control over who will be the Campbell heir's mother."

"What do you mean by that?" Venetia demanded.

"Ask your father." Angelica brushed past her to the door but paused to add, "By the way, I am already with child." Then she quit the chamber.

Angelica slipped into her chair beside Robert's. He turned to her with a smile, and then his expression became concerned. "What's wrong? You look pale."

"I feel tired," Angelica lied. "How much longer do we need to stay?"

"We'll leave now." Robert gestured to the majordomo. "Tinker, have the carriage brought around."

"Tinker, wait," Angelica stopped the man. She looked at Robert, asking, "Do we really need the carriage? It's only two doors down, and I could use the fresh air."

Robert inclined his head. "Tinker, cancel the carriage."

"Tell the marquess's bodyguards we are leaving through the garden door," Angelica instructed the majordomo. She looked at Robert and added, "Though your demise would leave me a wealthy woman, I have no wish to become an eighteen-year-old widow."

"That's a relief to know," Robert teased her.

After saying good-bye to their guests, Robert and

Angelica stepped into the duke's garden. A small army of bodyguards surrounded them instantly.

Reaching his town house, Robert scooped her into his arms and carried her across the threshold and into a kitchen filled with servants. "Your aunt instructed me to do that for luck," he said, setting her down on her feet.

Robert turned to the servants, saying, "This is my wife, Lady Angelica. Serve her as you serve me."

The servants applauded. Robert inclined his head, accepting their approval, and then escorted her up the stairs to the foyer.

"Would you care to rest now?" he asked.

"Yes, I would."

"I'll show you to your chamber."

Her chamber? Angelica wondered, disappointed. Didn't a husband and wife share a chamber? She understood that he'd married her to legitimize the Campbell heir, but he could at least pretend he cared for her. Had he and Lousia shared a chamber?

Robert escorted her up the stairs. When they reached the second-floor landing, Angelica noticed the portrait of a pretty blond woman dressed in a blue gown. She stopped short and stared at the woman she'd seen sitting in the marquess's garden.

"Who is that?" Angelica asked, her gaze on the portrait.

Robert remained silent. Angelica glanced at him. His expression was grim.

"Louisa Emerson," he answered.

"That is the woman I saw in the gazebo," Angelica told him.

"Impossible."

"Her spirit is restless," she added.

"I do not wish to speak about my late wife today," Robert said curtly.

"Very well, my lord," she acquiesced, following him up the stairs. "We'll speak about it tomorrow."

Her bedchamber was larger than the whole cottage near Primrose Hill and decorated in gold, fire red, and sky blue, with touches of cream and black. The door was located at one end of the room. On Angelica's right was the hearth, on her left an enormous canopied bed complete with curtains. Along the opposite wall were four windows, and on the wall to the left of the bed was a door.

"I had it redecorated for you," Robert told her. He smiled, adding, "Which is what I've been doing for the past three weeks. If you don't like the colors—"

"The colors are fine," Angelica said, blushing. She'd thought of him doing many things during the past three weeks, but decorating a bedchamber for her wasn't one of them.

"I thought vibrant colors suited you more than pastels," Robert said. "The sky blue reminded me of your eyes, and the fire red matches your personality."

"Is that a compliment or an insult?" Angelica asked.

"A compliment."

"In that case, I thank you." Angelica pointed at a side door, asking, "Where does that go?"

"To the nursery."

"Is that decorated in vibrant colors too?"

"I thought I would leave the nursery to you," he answered.

"Where does that door lead?" she asked, pointing again.

"To my bedchamber." He ignored her blush

and said, "Turn around and I'll unfasten your buttons."

Angelica showed him her back. Her thoughts fixed on the day she'd been in his house and he'd unfastened her buttons.

"You are being unusually pleasant," Robert said, turning her to face him.

"I had the same thought about you."

That made Robert smile. He planted a kiss on her forehead and said, "Enjoy your rest, and I'll see you at supper."

Angelica watched him cross the chamber. Without thinking, she called out, "What do I do?"

Robert turned around, a puzzled expression on his face. He walked back to her.

"How do I pass the hours when I'm not resting?" she asked.

"How do you usually pass your days?" he asked, clearly amused.

"Cooking, cleaning, playing my harp, practicing cards and dice, and gambling."

"Except for the harp, those activities are inappropriate for the Marchioness of Argyll," Robert told her. "What did you do at my father's?"

"Plan my revenge and play with Daisy," she answered.

"I'll take care of the revenge," he said. "After today you will confer with Cook about the meals, play your harp, care for Daisy, and—Do you read?"

"I know how but don't like it," Angelica answered. "There's no action."

"Spoken like a true gambler." Robert put his arm around her, saying, "Let's not worry about all the days of our lives. Let's concentrate on today."

Angelica smiled and nodded. She would speak with her aunt at the first opportunity and consult her about a lady's household duties. Clearly, her husband was ignorant about such things.

"Take your nap," Robert said. "I'll awaken you for supper."

After he left, Angelica undressed down to her chemise and carefully lay her mother's wedding gown on the chaise near the hearth. She removed the wreath of orange blossoms from her hair and placed that on the dressing table.

Pulling the coverlet back, Angelica lay down on the bed. She held her left hand out in front of her to admire her wedding band and stared at the diamond winking at her from its setting of gold. Did the size of the diamond reflect Robert's feelings for her? Or was he playing his role as the Marquess of Argyll?

Angelica's thoughts drifted to the woman whose portrait hung on the wall of the second-floor landing. Why hadn't she noticed the portrait the first time she'd been here? Perhaps she'd been too nervous.

Louisa looked sweet and biddable. How could she compete with that? Sweet and biddable were qualities noticeably lacking in her character.

Bull's pizzle, Angelica thought. She'd rather eat dirt than be sweet and biddable. She could never compete with a dead woman, nor did she wish to be something she wasn't.

Angelica slipped the band off her finger and peered inside to see if he'd had the date engraved. The inscription read: A MA VIE DE COER ENTIER.

What did those words mean? she wondered, her eyelids growing heavy. How like the marquess to hide his sentiment in a heathen language.

"*Angel . . .*"

Angelica drifted up from the depths of unconsciousness. Depleted of energy from her pregnancy and the excitement of the past weeks, her body wanted more sleep.

Opening her eyes, Angelica saw Robert sitting beside her on the edge of the bed. She noted his black silk bed robe and smiled at him drowsily.

Leaning close, Robert planted a kiss on her lips and asked, "Are you ready for supper?"

Angelica yawned and stretched. "Give me a moment to dress."

"There's no need to dress," Robert told her, holding up her ivory silk bed robe. "We're supping in my chamber."

Angelica rose from the bed and let him help her into her robe. She felt his arm go around her shoulder as he escorted her through the doors connecting their chambers.

A table had been set up in front of the windows, which were open to allow the evening breeze inside. Fine linens, crystal, china, and silverware lay on the table, lit by two candles.

Angelica sat down and looked over the evening's fare: tomato soup, potted mushrooms and chicken, slices of toast, a glass of wine for him, and milk for her. She lifted the glass and sipped the milk.

"Warm milk?" she asked. "I am celebrating my wedding with warm milk?"

"I thought you would prefer to eat lightly after this morning," Robert said. "If you want something else, I can order it." He smiled and added, "You are carrying my child, though."

"You believe the babe prefers warm milk?"

"The milk will be better for him," Robert answered.

"Better for her," Angelica corrected him.

"I am relieved you didn't hang wolfbane over your door," Robert said, ignoring her comment.

Angelica smiled. "I never thought of it."

"That sounds encouraging." Robert changed the subject, saying, "We'll be leaving London mid-morning tomorrow and arrive at Campbell Manor in the early afternoon."

"And will Daisy be accompanying us?" Angelica asked.

"Sweetheart, telling you who isn't accompanying us would be easier," Robert answered. "Our families and invited guests will be arriving in a week."

Angelica nodded. She had only one week to plant the bud of a relationship between father and daughter before others claimed some of her husband's attention. His relationship with Daisy took precedence over her.

"Angel, did you hear me?"

"I beg your pardon?" Angelica said, fixing her gaze on him.

"What were you thinking?"

"I-I was thinking about the baby," she lied.

Robert smiled at that and then repeated himself. "I said, we'll be married for a long time. Will you give us a chance?"

Her husband sounded as if he cared for her. If that was true, why couldn't he profess his love?

Angelica reached across the table and touched his hand. "I intend to give us more than a chance," she told him. Was it relief she saw in his expression?

"I have a gift for you," Robert said.

"And I have one for you." Angelica stood and hurried to her chamber. When she returned, she carried two boxes. On the table in front of her chair, Robert had placed three boxes.

"Open mine first," he said.

Angelica opened the largest first. A diamond choker lay on a bed of black velvet.

"Sacred sevens, is it real?"

"Yes, angel, it's real," Robert said, a smile lurking

in his voice. "I bought you the choker so you could wear your pendant with it."

"That was thoughtful of you," Angelica said, touching her diamond pendant. She opened the second box. This contained a diamond bracelet. "Can we afford this?" she asked.

Robert laughed. "Open the last one."

The smallest box contained diamond earrings that matched the choker and bracelet. "You bought me the whole damned set," Angelica said.

"You have a wonderfully refreshing way with words," Robert remarked. "If you don't like them—"

"I love them," she told him, "but I cannot help wondering how many poor we could feed with the money they cost you."

"I promise to make a charitable donation equal to what I spent," Robert said.

"Thank you, my lord." Angelica passed him one of her gifts.

Robert opened the lid. Inside lay a ring of gold shaped like a lion's head, its eyes two rubies.

"What a handsome ring," Robert said, lifting it out of the box. He slipped it on the third finger of his right hand. "It suits me."

"I thought of you when I saw it."

"I'll take that as a compliment." Robert lifted the lid of the second, larger box and withdrew a sterling-silver covered pot dressed with a ribbon.

His expression told Angelica he didn't know what to make of it. "The gift is inside," she told him.

Robert lifted the lid off the pot, peered inside, and shouted with laughter. "Strawberry jam?"

"I knew how much you liked it," Angelica said, a high blush staining her cheeks. "My aunt couldn't understand why I wanted to give you strawberry jam for a wedding gift."

Rising from her chair, Angelica pulled a sachet out of her pocket and asked, "Where will we sleep?"

"In my bed."

Crossing the chamber, Angelica drew the bed-curtain aside. She lifted one of the pillows and hid the sachet beneath it.

"What's in the sachet?" Robert asked, standing behind her.

"Valerian root is for harmony," Angelica answered. "Burr is for faithfulness."

"No wolfbane?"

Angelica shook her head.

"Nothing for love?" he asked.

"Faithfulness covers love," she answered, staring at his chest.

Robert tilted up her chin and waited until she raised her gaze to his. "Are you telling me or my chest?"

"Love is not a requisite for marriage," Angelica said, blushing.

"My parents married for love," he said, his face inching closer to hers.

"So did mine," she said in a whisper.

"Our children's parents married for love, too," Robert told her, his lips hovering above hers.

Angelica stared at him blankly, and then realized what he was saying. A smile touched her lips, and she hooked her arms around his neck to draw his face even closer.

"I love you," she said.

"And I love you," he told her.

Robert pressed his lips to hers in a slow kiss that seemed to last forever. Angelica returned his kiss in kind.

"Shouldn't we disrobe?"

"I thought you'd never ask," he said.

Robert unfastened her robe and pushed it off her shoulders. Next came her chemise. He shrugged out of his own robe, letting it drop to the floor to mingle with her chemise, even as they would mingle their bodies.

His mouth hovered above hers for the merest fraction of a second, and then his lips claimed hers in an earth-shattering kiss. An urgent need to join their bodies overpowered them, and that single, devastating kiss melted into another and then another.

With a groan of mingling emotion and need, Robert dropped to his knees in front of her. He wrapped his arms around her hips and kissed her belly.

Robert slashed his tongue across her moist female's crevice, and Angelica gasped with pleasure. He cupped her buttocks and held her steady while his exploring tongue made her squirm with hot desire.

Up and down, Robert flicked his tongue in a gentle assault on her womanhood. He kissed and nipped her dewy pearl while his fingers teased her sensitive nipples.

Surrendering to the exquisite sensations, Angelica melted against his tongue. She cried out and clung to him as waves of throbbing pleasure surged through her.

Robert stood then and, lifting her into his arms, placed her on the bed. Then he lay down beside her and poured all his love into a single, stirring kiss.

"The babe?" he asked.

"Will be fine," she answered.

Robert rose up between her legs and plunged deep inside her. He withdrew slowly and then slid forward, teasing her over and over again until she trembled with rekindled need. Holding her hips steady, Robert rode her hard, again and again grinding himself into her throbbing softness.

With mingling cries, Robert and Angelica exploded together and then lay still as they floated back to earth from their shared paradise. He moved to one side, pulling her with him, and cradled her in his arms. Long moments passed in silence.

"The sachet worked," Angelica said.

"I'll never doubt your aunt again," Robert said.

And then they drifted into a deep, sated sleep.

When she awakened the next morning, Angelica was alone in the bed. Two pieces of dry toast and a single red rose lay on a dish on the bedside table.

How kind of her husband to remember her queasiness, Angelica thought. Even more important, he'd professed his love, and she finally belonged somewhere. Her revenge didn't seem so urgent this morning; her husband would take care of that. All she needed to do was concentrate on her unborn child and foster a loving relationship between Robert and his daughter.

He walked into the chamber while she was eating her toast and sat on the edge of the bed to give her a lingering kiss.

"What a lazy wench you are," Robert teased her.

"Thank you for the toast," she said.

"Cook packed us a basket," he told her. "You can eat something more on the way. The carts are packed, and we leave in an hour.

"What about Daisy and Jasper?"

"Both are ready to go." Robert smiled, adding, "That bird has more cages than the king has coaches." He rose from the edge of the bed, saying, "An hour, my lady."

After he'd gone, Angelica returned to her chamber. She hadn't felt this happy since the day her father had lost his fortune. She felt young again.

Angelica dressed in a white muslin morning gown. She paused for a moment to gaze at her wedding band, its diamond winking at her, and sighed. How could Louisa Emerson have committed suicide? What incited her to do it? Not Robert, certainly.

Grabbing a shawl, Angelica left the chamber. She started down the stairs to the foyer.

When she reached the second-floor landing, Angelica passed her predecessor's portrait and said, "Good morning, Louisa."

Good morning. The words sounded like a sigh on the breeze.

Angelica stopped short and stared at the portrait. Chills ran down her spine, and the fine hairs on the back of her neck stood on end. Had she heard someone whisper? Or had she imagined it?

"Angelica!" The voice belonged to her husband.

"I'm on my way." Angelica stared at the portrait for a moment longer and then turned away.

Chapter 17

"*Angelica.*"

She heard her husband calling her name again and, with one last look back at Louisa's picture, continued down the stairs.

"There you are," Robert said, his booted foot on the bottom stair as if he'd been about to come after her.

"I was just—" Angelica broke off and glanced over her shoulder. Her husband wouldn't appreciate his first wife speaking to her. "Never mind."

"Angelica Campbell, you are the most beautiful woman I have ever seen," Robert said, lifting both of her hands to his lips.

Angelica blushed, but his words pleased her. "Are we ready to leave?" she asked.

"The coaches are parked in the alley," Robert answered, reminding her that his life was in danger.

Hurrying her along, Robert grasped her arm and escorted her down the corridor to the rear of the house and then outside to the garden. Angelica hesitated as they passed the gazebo.

"Do not tell me you see ghosts," Robert said, as if he knew her thoughts.

"I see an empty gazebo," she assured him.

Angelica stopped short in surprise when they reached the alley. She saw two coaches with the Campbells' boar's head insignia, ten carts filled with their belongings, and twenty-five armed guards.

"How did I ever travel around London with nothing but myself?" Angelica asked, making her husband smile.

"We do resemble a parade," Robert said, leading her to the first coach. "The damned bodyguards and bird are ruining our anonymity. Jasper's cages and toys fill two of those carts."

"What a spoiled bird," Angelica said.

Robert opened the coach's door and started to help her up. She pulled out of his grasp, asking, "Where is Daisy?"

"She prefers riding with Sweeting, Webster, and Jasper," he told her.

"I think not." Angelica gave him an irritated look and marched back to the second coach. When she opened its door, the macaw shrieked, "Hello."

"Hello, Jasper." Angelica smiled and said, "Good morning to all." She held out her hand, adding, "Come, Daisy."

"Lady Allegra wants to ride with Jasper," Daisy refused, shaking her head.

Angelica felt relieved that her husband had spoken truthfully. "Lady Allegra may ride with Jasper if she wishes, but you must ride with me."

She watched the girl glance at Robert, who stood behind her, and realized the child was frightened.

If only her husband had passed a few hours with his daughter.

"I want to tell you a story," Angelica said, trying to coax the girl out of the coach.

"Come, Daisy," Robert ordered in a voice that brooked no disobedience, holding out his arms for her. "We're wasting time."

Though she appeared close to swooning, Daisy obeyed in an instant. Still clutching the doll, she let her father lift her out and carry her to the other coach.

"Sit over there," Robert said, and then turned to assist Angelica, who was smiling at him. "What do you find so amusing?"

"Thank you, my lord," Angelica said, and planted a kiss on his cheek.

Robert inclined his head and helped her climb into the coach. Angelica sat beside Daisy and put a comforting arm around her. She knew her husband wanted to be alone with her, but this was a good opportunity for him to become acquainted with his daughter. Someday he would thank her for doing this.

Once their entourage left London behind, full-bodied summer landscaped the scenery. Rich, robust scents wafted through the air, and lush greenery colored the land. In the fields and along the roadsides goldenrod was beginning to appear, splashes of yellow that would blaze in the coming days.

Angelica stole a glance at Daisy. The girl's enormous dark eyes were fixed on her father, who seemed oblivious to her presence.

"My lord, what do you have in the basket?" Angelica asked, trying to make conversation.

"Cucumber sandwiches," Robert answered, peering into the basket. "Would you like one?"

"Yes, I would," she said. "What about you, Daisy?"

Daisy said nothing. She shook her head but kept her gaze fixed on the man sitting opposite her.

"What about Lady Allegra?"

Again, Daisy shook her head.

"Do you speak?" Robert asked his daughter.

Daisy nodded her head, bringing a smile to her father's face. She smiled when he did.

"Would you like a drink?" Angelica asked her.

"No drinks," Robert said. "If she drinks, we'll need to stop for her."

"In my condition, we'll need to stop for me," Angelica told him.

"What's a condition?" Daisy asked.

Angelica looked at her husband for help, but he said, "You handle this."

"I have a baby growing inside me," Angelica said, putting her arm around the little girl. "In a few months, you will have a baby brother or sister."

"Oh." That seemed to be the only explanation the girl needed. She looked at her father and asked, "How are your boils?"

Robert looked surprised. "My what?"

"Lady Angelica said you were angry because you suffered from boils," Daisy told him, "but you smiled, so you must feel better."

"Thank you, Daisy. I do feel better," Robert said with a wry smile.

Daisy returned his smile. Hers was filled with love and adoration.

"Thank you for Lady Allegra," she said, apparently encouraged by his kind words.

Robert gave her a puzzled look.

"Lady Allegra is her doll," Angelica explained. "You know, the doll you sent her."

Robert sent Angelica a grateful look and said to his daughter, "You are very welcome."

"I love Lady Allegra," Daisy told him, "but I wish you had brought her yourself." She held up her hand like an adult woman, adding, "I know you are a busy man and very, very important, but I waited such a long time to meet you."

Through tear-blurred eyes, Angelica watched her husband's expression change. Was it regret she saw on his face? Only a monster would be unaffected by the little girl.

"Come over here and sit on my lap," Robert invited his daughter. "I want to tell you a story."

Daisy didn't need a second invitation. She climbed onto his lap and gazed up at him through enormous dark eyes.

Angelica felt like weeping. A lump of raw emotion formed in her throat, and tears welled up in her eyes.

"What's wrong?" Robert asked her.

Angelica shook her head. "Nothing."

"It's her condition," Daisy said, making her father smile.

Robert gave her his attention, asking, "Do you like ponies?"

"I love ponies," the little girl answered.

"I have ponies at my estate," Robert told her.

"Do you have monkeys?" she asked. "I love monkeys, too."

"No monkeys," Robert said. "Do you want to learn how to ride a pony?"

"Will you teach me?"

Robert nodded and flicked a glance at Angelica, who quickly brushed a tear off her cheek. "Once upon a time there lived a rich boy."

"What was his name?" Daisy asked.

"His name was Robert Roy," Robert answered.

"In spite of all his money, the boy was very unhappy because nobody loved him. One day he went to a fair and met a girl. She was dressed in rags but wore flowers in her hair."

"What was her name?" Daisy asked.

"Do you want to hear the story or not?" Robert asked her.

In answer, the little girl pretended to button her lips. Then she gestured for him to continue, which made him smile.

"The boy challenged the girl to a game of dice," he told her, "and the girl won because she cheated."

"Cheating is very bad," Daisy told him.

"That is correct, poppet." Robert went on, "Anyway, the boy kissed the girl, and she turned into a beautiful princess who fell in love with him."

"Did the witch put a spell on her?" Daisy asked.

"No, sweetheart, a bad wizard named Emerson had cursed her," Robert answered, "but the boy's kiss broke the spell. The boy and his princess lived happily ever after."

"Oh, I love that story," Daisy gushed, clapping her hands. "Did the boy punish the bad wizard?"

"Yes, he did."

"I know a story, too," Daisy told him.

"I would like to hear this story," Robert said.

"This is the baby," Daisy said, holding up her thumb. "This is the mommy." Up went her index finger. "And this big fellow is the father," she ended, sticking her middle finger into the air.

Robert laughed out loud and then asked, "Who told you that story?"

"Lady Angelica."

"I'm not surprised," he said, and then encircled her in his embrace. "Lean against me and nap."

"No nap," Daisy said, but leaned against him anyway.

"You don't want to be too tired to ride the ponies, do you?" Robert asked.

Daisy snapped her eyes shut, which made Angelica smile. The little girl fell asleep with a happy expression on her face.

"What do you have to say for yourself, wife?" Robert asked.

"Thank you, husband," she answered, raising her blue gaze to his. "I'm tired, too."

Angelica switched seats and cuddled beside him. Robert put his left arm around her and pulled her close against his body. Like Daisy, Angelica fell asleep with a smile on her face.

An armful of family, Robert thought, content. A month ago he'd had nothing. Now he had a wife, a daughter, and a babe on the way.

. . . tea today, dinner tomorrow, and marriage before Parliament broke for grouse hunting.

His father's plan had worked. The old fox must certainly be happy now. And damned if Robert didn't like the feeling of a pregnant wife at his side and a child on his lap.

"Wake up, angel."

Angelica opened her eyes and sat up straight. She smiled at the sight of Daisy still sleeping on her father's lap.

"How long did I sleep?" she asked.

"Almost two hours," Robert answered. "Look out the window. We're home."

Their coach traveled down the estate's curving drive of mellowed plum-red bricks. In the distance a two-storied red brick mansion stood in the midst of perfectly manicured lawns that carpeted the grounds between lines of yews that had been clipped to form high hedges.

When their entourage halted in front of the mansion, Angelica climbed down and turned in a circle to scan her husband's estate. Her eyes lit with excited pleasure when she saw the three water terraces, complete with statuary and fountains.

A mermaid, spouting water from her tail, reclined in the middle of the smallest water terrace. The second terrace held Neptune, his trident spouting water. Venus, rising from the sea, graced the third and largest terrace, her shell spouting water.

"What an ingenious idea," Angelica said, turning to her husband. "Did you think of this?"

"I'm not so talented." Still carrying his sleeping daughter, Robert led her toward the mansion, saying, "I'll deliver Daisy to her room while you settle Jasper. Then I'll take you on a short tour of the grounds."

Angelica dropped her mouth open at the first sight of the foyer, which rose two stories high. It boasted a curving grand staircase on the right that led to the second floor. On the balcony overlooking the foyer was an enormous statuary of the Three Fates.

"How do you like the cottage?" Robert asked.

"This bears no resemblance to my cottage," Angelica answered with a rueful smile.

Two lines of servants stood at attention in the foyer and waited to greet the marquess. Webster, who'd been speaking with the head footman, turned to them and said, "The servants wish to welcome you home, my lord, and wish you and the marchioness a long, prosperous life."

"Thank you," Robert said, addressing the entire staff in a clear, strong voice. "This is my wife, Lady

Angelica." She smiled, but he continued, saying, "That is my wife's pet macaw, Jasper. Do not put your fingers near him or you will lose them."

Angelica thought he was finished, but he stunned her when he added, "This girl sleeping in my arms is my daughter, Lady Daisy. Please assist my wife and daughter in whatever they need."

The servants stared in surprise. Apparently, they hadn't expected that scandalous piece of information.

"Return to your duties," Webster instructed them. "Several footmen will be needed to unload the carts. Shall I enlist someone to carry Lady Daisy to her chamber?"

"I think I can manage my own daughter," Robert replied. "Be certain the footmen bring Jasper's cages up first."

"Very good, my lord."

Angelica's smile could have lit the whole mansion. "Thank you, husband."

"I hope you'll be as grateful tonight when we retire," Robert said, and then winked at her.

Robert led the way upstairs to the second level and then down a long corridor toward the rear of the mansion. Mrs. Sweeting followed behind, waiting to take charge of the child.

"We'll leave the rest to you, Sweeting," Robert said, gently placing Daisy down on the bed.

With Jasper in tow, Angelica and Robert walked farther down the corridor. He led her into an enormous chamber as richly appointed as their rooms in London.

"Are we sharing this chamber?" Angelica asked, turning to him in surprise.

Robert nodded.

She smiled. "How convenient."

Robert pulled her into his arms and planted a kiss on her lips, whispering, "Welcome home, wife."

"My home is wherever you are," Angelica whispered back, entwining her arms around his neck and pressing her body against his.

"I've instructed the footmen to put a cage in most of the rooms," Webster announced, interrupting them. "Where do you want this one?"

"Set it near the hearth, but not too close," Angelica answered.

"Do you want to rest or tour the grounds?" Robert asked her.

"I want to tour the grounds, of course," Angelica said, looping her arm through his.

Robert escorted her out of the bedchamber, but when she started down the corridor in the direction they had come, he stopped her. "Come this way," he said.

Angelica spied a door in the corner of the corridor. When her husband opened it, she saw a wrought-iron landing and stairway leading to the lawns below. Angelica stepped outside and paused on the landing to gaze at the scenery. What she saw resembled a painting more than reality.

Directly below the wrought-iron stairs was a rectangular expanse of lawn, bordered on the long side by a stone wall and an iron gate leading into a garden. The rioting colors of chrysanthemums, fuchsias, peonies, azaleas, and rhodendrons set against the backdrop of an indigo sea of bluebells filled the garden.

Angelica followed Robert down the stairs. Hand in hand, they crossed the lawn, and he opened the garden's gate for her.

"How do you like my handiwork?" he asked.

"You created this beauty?" she asked in surprise.

"Gardening relaxes me," Robert told her.

Beyond the garden was a maze created from clipped yews. At the back of another, larger expanse of lawn sat a gazebo bordered by woodland trees.

"This looks like paradise," Angelica said.

"Paradise is a person, not a place," Robert said, raising her hand to his lips.

Angelica smiled at that. "I like a well-planted man."

"Do you want to try the maze?" he asked.

"I'll leave that for another day," she said, looping her arm through his. "How about the gazebo?"

Robert led her around the maze, and they crossed the lawn toward the gazebo. "It looks like yours," she said.

"I patterned the one in London after this one," Robert told her.

For a long time, Angelica and Robert sat in the shade of the gazebo and enjoyed the summer afternoon. The perfumed scents of the flowers wafted through the air, along with birdsong.

"I never realized a place like this could exist," Angelica said. "What a wonderful setting in which to raise children."

"Decorate the nursery however you want," Robert said with a smile. "We can spend as much time here as you like."

"Won't your businesses suffer?"

"No, we are only a few hours from London."

"A few hours and a world away," Angelica said with a sigh. "I always wanted a tree house. Could we build one for Daisy?"

Robert grinned. "I'll build one big enough for Daisy and you."

"Thank you for being kind to her," Angelica said.

Robert looked away. "I couldn't bear the fear

and the longing I saw in her eyes when she looked at me."

Angelica lifted his hand to her lips and kissed it. "What lies beyond those trees?" she asked.

"There's a path through the woodland leading to a waterfall and pool," Robert told her. "Beyond the waterfall lies James Armstrong's property."

"Let's take a walk and see it," Angelica said. In spite of the reluctance she read in his eyes, Robert stood and led her toward the trees and then to a path into the woodland.

Peace pervaded the air along the woodland path. Thick hedges carpeted with wildflowers grew along side it. The distinctive songs of swallows, warblers, and turtledoves filled the air.

And then Angelica heard the faint chuckling of a brook. The farther they moved along the path, the louder the noise grew, until the faint chuckling became a roar.

Emerging from the path, Angelica saw a crystal-clear river bordered on both sides by willow trees. Robert kept a tight grip on her hand as he led her down the bank of the river.

Angelica looked at him, puzzled. Her husband was hurting her hand, and his expression grew tense as they neared a precipice.

"My hand hurts," Angelica told him.

"It's a waterfall," Robert said, loosening his grip but refusing to release her.

Angelica peered over the edge of the precipice. The rocks formed terraces, though the fall itself was relatively small, perhaps thirty feet. Sharp, jaggard rocks stood like sentinels at the bottom of the fall, and beyond them was an inviting pool of water.

"What's wrong?" Angelica asked, feeling his grip on her hand tighten again.

"Louisa leaped to her death from here," Robert told her, staring at the rocks below.

"I'm sorry," Angelica said. "If I had known—"

Robert pulled her close, saying, "Promise me you'll never—"

Angelica placed a finger across his lips to silence him. "Do not speak the words," she said. "Do not even think the thought."

"Promise me."

"I promise if you ever take a mistress," Angelica said, giving him a smile filled with sunshine, "I'll take *your* life instead of mine."

Robert relaxed visibly. "I believe you."

"The water looks inviting," Angelica said, her blue eyes sparkling. She decided to try to wash the bad memories away by making a pleasant one. "Let's follow the path to the pool and swim."

"What about the babe?" he asked, concerned.

"The fact that I'm carrying a child doesn't mean I am impaired," she told him.

Hand in hand, Robert and Angelica followed the path leading down to the pool. The afternoon sun shone there still, sparkling beams dancing across the top of the water.

They sat down on smooth boulders near the edge of the pool and removed their boots and stockings. Robert stood, pulled his shirt over his head, and then unfastened his breeches.

Angelica couldn't tear her gaze off what belonged to her now. She admired his broad shoulders, his well-muscled chest with its light matting of black hair, and his tapered waist. She dropped her gaze lower.

"Were you planning on swimming?" Robert asked, turning around, his hands on his hips. "Or just admiring my beauty?"

"I didn't know you wore black silk drawers," she

said, raising her gaze to his, a soft smile flirting with her lips.

"There are many things you don't know about me," he told her, "but you'll learn more over the next forty or fifty years."

Angelica stood then and showed him her back. "The buttons, my lord?"

"This feels very domestic," Robert said, unfastening her gown and then dropping a kiss on her shoulder.

After removing her chemise, Angelica took his hand. They waded into the sun-warmed water and swam toward the waterfall. Holding on to the large boulders ringing the bottom of the falls, they paused to rest.

"Are you all right?" he asked.

"I've never felt better," she answered.

"If we swim to the edge over there, we can walk behind the falls."

Robert led the way. When they reached the jagged rocks where the falls met the pool, he took her hand and helped her up. Behind the falls, the tops of the boulders had been smoothed from the constant beating of the water.

"Looking at the falls from the back feels strange," Angelica said.

"The falling water provides complete privacy," Robert said, drawing her into his arms.

Angelica recognized his desire when he dropped his dark gaze to her breasts. She entwined her arms around his neck and pressed her body against his.

"I want you as much as you want me," she whispered, sliding her hand down his body to his groin. She stroked him and smiled when she heard his breath catch in his throat.

"Your nipples are large and dark," he said, cupping her breast. He flicked a thumb across one nipple, making her moan at the sensation.

Robert drew her close against him, savoring her incredible softness. His mouth covered hers in a slow, soul-stealing kiss.

Running his hands down the side of her body, Robert cupped her buttocks and lifted her. Instinctively, Angelica wrapped her legs around his waist and sighed when he entered her.

Holding her steady, Robert buried himself deep within her. He backed her against one of the boulders for support. And then he moved, enticing her to move with him. Angelica caught his rhythm and moved her hips, meeting each powerful thrust with one of her own.

Waves of pleasure flooded Angelica, carrying her to heaven and beyond. Only then did Robert release his own need, joining her in ecstasy.

They stood, joined as one, for long moments. Finally, he let her slide gently to her feet.

"I feel like Adam and Eve," Angelica said.

"Sans fig leaf." Robert took her hand in his and led her around the waterfall. They swam to shore together. Still wet, they dressed and stood to leave.

"How do you feel?" Robert asked, planting a kiss on her lips.

"Wonderful but tired, a contented countess."

Robert scooped her into his arms and kissed her again, lingeringly. When he started walking, she cried, "What are you doing?"

"I am carrying the mother of my child home," he told her.

Angelica protested, "I'm too heavy to carry such a long distance."

"Lady, I will carry you home or die trying," he vowed.

"Oh, don't do that," she said. "I have no wish to become a widow."

"When I tire, I'll save my arms by throwing you over my shoulder like a sack of barley," Robert teased. "Like this." He turned her in his arms, placed her gently over his shoulder, and began running down the woodland path.

The sound of Angelica's laughter mingled with the song of the turtledoves.

Chapter 18

Sacred sevens, Angelica thought, staring at herself in the mirror. Her breasts had grown and were almost too swollen for her low-cut petal-pink silk gown. Her husband would certainly enjoy a grand view of her cleavage at dinner.

"Come in," she called, at a knock on the bedchamber door.

Angelica smiled when Daisy walked into the room. The little girl also wore a petal-pink dress that perfectly complemented her dark hair and eyes.

"Hello," the macaw shrieked.

"Hello, Jasper," Daisy said.

The little girl looked at Angelica and giggled, her enormous black eyes gleaming with excitement. "Our dresses are the same color."

"That is correct," Angelica said. "If you're hungry, let's eat."

"Eat," Jasper called, making the girl giggle again.

"Jasper, your food is in your cage," Angelica said, leading the macaw across the chamber. She opened the door for the bird and then closed it behind him.

"Your father, you, and I will eat dinner like a real family tonight," Angelica told Daisy. "Jasper is not invited."

"Won't he be sad and lonely?" the girl asked.

"Jasper will be fine for one night," Angelica assured her, holding out her hand. "Perhaps tomorrow we'll take him on our picnic."

Daisy clapped her hands in excitement. Then she grabbed Angelica's hand and kissed it, saying, "I love you, Lady Angelica."

"Good night," the macaw called.

"Good night, Jasper," both called over their shoulders as they headed for the door.

Hand in hand, Angelica and Daisy walked the length of the corridor to the stairs. Reaching the foyer, Angelica looked toward the footman for directions.

"Please follow me, my lady," the man said.

Angelica and Daisy walked into an enormous dining room. The chamber was a hundred feet long, and a forty-foot dining table stood in the center of the room. Above the table hung three gigantic crystal chandeliers.

"Sacred sevens, I never saw such a big room," Daisy exclaimed.

Speaking with Webster near the sideboard, Robert turned at the sound of his daughter's voice. With a welcoming smile, he crossed the room and escorted them to the table, saying, "I never saw such two perfect roses."

"Thank you, my lord," Angelica said.

"Thank you, my lord," Daisy imitated her.

The three of them sat at one end of the long

mahogany table. Robert sat at the head, with Angelica and Daisy on either side of him.

Under the majordomo's supervision, two footmen served them from the sideboard. The main dish was roast beef and potatoes, accompanied by a tomato and bean salad with a vinaigrette dressing.

Silence descended upon them as they began to eat. Angelica watched Robert who, in turn, watched his daughter. Angelica couldn't contain her happiness at the heartwarming sight of the father and daughter enjoying their first meal together.

Eating her roast beef with gusto and her fingers, Daisy looked up and caught her father watching her. She smiled at him and popped a piece of beef into her mouth.

"Do you like the beef?" Robert asked.

Daisy nodded. "I'm lucky I have teeth to chew." She leaned forward, as if divulging a secret, whispering loudly, her mouth filled with beef, "Sweeting has problems with chewing."

"Is that so?" Robert said with a smile. "I don't see you eating your vegetables."

In reply, Daisy tossed several pieces of tomato into her mouth, saying in a garbled voice, "Mmmmm . . . good tomato."

"Don't put too much food into your mouth," Angelica said. "Ladies take small bites."

Daisy did exactly what Angelica thought she would: The little girl spit the glob of chewed beef and tomato into her hand. She stared at the glob and then looked at her father for help.

Angelica watched Robert hold out his hand, and Daisy passed him the glob. He dropped it in his napkin and handed the cloth to Webster, who gave him a fresh one.

"Use your fork to eat those vegetables," Robert ordered.

"Are those beans?" Daisy asked.

"Yes."

"I don't eat beans."

Robert looked surprised. "Beans are good for you."

"I don't like them."

"I promise you'll like my beans," he coaxed her.

"Lucille said don't eat beans," Daisy refused, shaking her head for emphasis. "I make vulgar noises and foul odors when I eat beans."

Angelica burst out laughing, and Robert joined her. Daisy laughed because they did.

"I give you permission to make vulgar noises and foul odors," Robert said, lifting a bean out of her salad. "Close your eyes and open your mouth." When she obeyed, Robert put the bean into her mouth and then asked, "Do you like it?"

Daisy nodded.

"Eat as many beans as you like," Robert told her.

"You'll be sorry," the little girl warned.

Angelica succumbed to a fit of giggles, and Daisy laughed, too. Never had Angelica seen the child so happy. The bruises on her arms had begun to fade, and her sweet expression had lost its pinched look.

The remainder of their dinner was uneventful, a relaxed feeling swirling around them like a magic spell. Daisy yawned as dessert was served, and Angelica signaled Webster to fetch Mrs. Sweeting.

"Daisy, go upstairs with Sweeting," Angelica said when the woman appeared. "I'll be along shortly to tell you a story."

Daisy went without argument, weary from her exciting day. When she reached the door, the girl turned around and called, "Lady Angelica!" She blew Angelica a kiss, and then looked at her father, saying, "This is for you." She blew him a kiss, too.

When the footman opened the door for her, Daisy said, "Thank you, my lord."

Once the child had gone, Angelica turned to her husband and said, "We should adopt her legally in the event Lucille comes around again."

"I'll speak to my solicitor," Robert replied.

His easy acquiescence surprised Angelica. "No argument?"

"Do you want one?"

Angelica smiled. "No, my lord."

"Have you considered how difficult gaining her acceptance into society will be?" Robert asked.

"A thousand scandals will have occurred by the time Daisy reaches that age," Angelica said. "No one will remember this one."

"Don't count on that," he told her.

"Would you care to make a small wager?"

"My lady, I have already experienced your cheating," Robert said.

"That really is too bad of you," Angelica replied. "Speaking of wagers, when will you ruin Emerson?"

"I haven't given that any consideration," Robert answered, "but I will concentrate on it tomorrow. Would you care to walk outside?"

Angelica shook her head. "I promised Daisy a story before she goes to sleep."

Robert rose from his chair and offered her his hand. "I'm going to step outside for some air while you tend to your maternal duties."

Hand in hand, Robert and Angelica walked down the corridor to the foyer. Angelica paused before going upstairs, saying, "Thank you for being kind to her."

"Being kind to Daisy is easy," Robert said. "She's a charming sprite. I only regret—"

Silencing him, Angelica placed a finger across his lips and said, "No regrets." Then she hurried upstairs and stepped inside the little girl's chamber.

"I told you Lady Angelica would come," Daisy told the nanny. "She never breaks her promises."

Angelica smiled at the older woman and sat on the edge of the bed. "Mrs. Sweeting, why don't you go downstairs and have yourself a cup of tea?"

"Thank you, my lady."

Angelica lifted the nightcap off the little girl's head as soon as the woman left. She tossed it on the floor, saying, "No nightcap tonight."

Daisy clapped her hands in approval. "Will you tell me a story now?"

Angelica leaned back against the headboard and put her arm around Daisy. "Once upon a time a poor girl lived with her aunt and two sisters. This girl had a special talent for gambling and went to the fair one day to win money for her family's supper."

"They had no food?" Daisy asked.

Angelica shook her head. "Not even a single bean."

"What happened?"

"A handsome but poorly dressed man stepped out of the crowd and challenged the girl to a game of dice," Angelica continued.

"What's dice?"

"Dice is a game of chance," Angelica told her. "I can teach you how to win every time. Anyway, this handsome man let the poor girl win lots and lots of money. At the end of their game, the man insisted on escorting the girl home. When they arrived at her cottage, the girl kissed the man, and he turned into a handsome prince. They married and lived happily ever after."

"What was the man's name?" Daisy asked.

"Robert Roy Campbell."

"The same as my father?"

Angelica kissed her forehead. "Your father is the prince."

"He doesn't have a crown," Daisy told her.

"Princes don't always wear crowns," Angelica said. "Your father is a prince among men."

"And are you the poor girl?"

"Yes, I am."

"I like that story."

"I'm going to see my prince now," Angelica said, standing and drawing the coverlet up to Daisy's chin. "If you need me, I'll be right down the corridor."

Angelica turned to leave and saw Robert, standing in the doorway. She crossed the chamber and whispered, "Come to bed, husband."

Following her out of the room, Robert said, "Please, call me Your Highness. . . ."

Long after Angelica had fallen asleep in his arms, Robert lay awake and watched her. His wife considered him a prince, but how wrong she was. If he had been a real prince of a man, Louisa would never have committed suicide, nor would he have hurt his young daughter by ignoring her existence for all those years.

He couldn't do anything about Louisa, Robert knew, but he could change his ways. He would shower his daughter with belated love and spend all the days and nights of his life making his wife happy.

Robert planted a kiss on Angelica's head and

smiled when she sighed in her sleep. Then he joined her in a deep, dreamless sleep.

Awakening early the next morning, Robert washed, shaved, and dressed in his oldest clothing. The rosebushes needed pruning, and he wanted to finish the job before Angelica and Daisy awakened. Today was theirs, and he intended to devote every moment to them.

Robert worked outside for several hours, tending his plants with infinite care. With his hands resting on his hips, he stepped back to inspect his work before starting on the next rosebush.

His shadow caught his attention when another, smaller shadow, with hands on hips, stood beside it. Glancing to the left, Robert spied his daughter standing beside him.

"Good morning, Daisy."

"Good morning, you."

"What do you think of my roses?" Robert asked, gesturing to the plants.

"I like them," Daisy answered.

Using his shears, Robert snipped a rose and handed it to her, saying, "For you, my lady. Roses guard against ill humors."

Daisy sniffed the rose. "It smells good, too." She looked around and said, "Wait one minute." Racing across the lawn, the little girl stopped and picked a daisy before running back to him.

"Lean down, you," she ordered. When he obeyed, she placed the daisy under his chin, exclaiming, "Oh, I see you adore butter, too."

Robert grinned. "I certainly do. How did you know?"

"Lady Angelica says if the daisy re—re—shows yellow under your chin, then you love butter," Daisy told him.

"Did Lady Angelica tell you about my flower fairies?" Robert asked.

"You have flower fairies?" Daisy asked in a whisper, her dark eyes gleaming with excitement.

Robert took her hand in his, led her into the main garden, and walked her around to admire his flowers. "Every single flower has a fairy that holds its spirit," he told her.

"I don't see any fairies," Daisy said. "Do you?"

"Flower fairies are difficult to see," Robert said with a smile, "but they speak to us all the time."

Daisy looked doubtful. "I don't hear anything either."

"Have you ever caught a flower's fragrance as you were walking by it?" he asked.

"Yes," she answered, lifting the rose to her nose.

"The flower's fairy is greeting you," Robert said. "Have you ever thought how lovely a flower is?"

Daisy nodded.

"That means the fairy caught your attention," he said.

Finished with their tour of the garden, Robert walked her back through the iron gate onto the lawn where the rosebushes grew. "The rose is a special flower, one the angels love," he told her. "The red rose fairy helps you gain love."

"How do you know?" she asked.

"Webster told me," Robert answered. "When you have a favorite flower, its fairy has something special to share with you. Do you have a favorite flower?"

Daisy nodded and held up the rose. "This is my favorite."

"Why is the rose your favorite?" Robert asked.

"You gave it to me."

Robert felt a lump of raw emotion form in his throat, and his eyes filled with unshed tears. He nodded his head in understanding, afraid he would lose control if he spoke. Regaining his composure, he asked, "Why did you call me 'you'?"

"I don't know what I'm supposed to call you," Daisy answered, looking at him through enormous dark eyes that mirrored his own.

Robert knelt on bended knee in order to be at eye level with her. "Call me Daddy," he told her.

"My wish came true," Daisy cried, throwing herself into his arms.

Robert smiled. "What wish was that, sweetheart?"

"I wished upon a star for a daddy."

"And now you have one," Robert said. "If you climb on my back and put your arms around my neck, I'll take you for a pretend pony ride."

Needing no second invitation, Daisy ran around behind him and wrapped her arms around his neck. "What now?" she asked.

"Don't let go."

"I won't."

"When I stand up," Robert said, "wrap your legs around my waist."

Robert stood slowly, and Daisy did as she was told. Making neighing sounds, he began galloping around and around the lawns while his daughter giggled and encouraged him onward.

"Good morning," called a voice.

Robert stopped his prancing and turned toward the mansion. "Madam, I believe morning has aged almost to afternoon."

"Lady Angelica, look at me riding my pretend pony," Daisy called.

"I see you."

"Oh, no, let me down," the little girl cried.

Robert lowered her to the ground and watched

her run a short distance away. She stared at the lawn and then burst into tears.

Crossing to her side, Robert saw a dead sparrow. He reached for it, saying, "I'll throw it away."

"No, Daddy, we need to bury it," Daisy whined.

"Wait one minute," Angelica called. She disappeared inside and then reappeared a few minutes later. Throwing him a small box and a cloth, she ordered, "Wrap the bird in the cloth and place it in the casket. Then come inside the house while I fetch the other mourners."

The casket? Robert thought, amused. The other mourners? Were they now hosting a funeral for a sparrow?

"Daddy, wrap the bird in the cloth," Daisy said. "The mourners are waiting."

Robert covered the sparrow with the piece of linen and lifted it off the grass. Then he set it inside the jewelry box-casket and closed the lid.

"Where is his grave?" Daisy asked.

Robert paused. That was a good question. The family crypt was definitely out of the question.

"Do you see the lawns beyond the maze?" Robert asked.

"Yes."

"On one side of the lawn near the woodland lies a garden of wildflowers, because flower fairies love to play in wildflowers," Robert told her. "On the other side of the lawns lies my butterfly garden. Which place do you think the deceased would like?"

"Daddy, what is *deceased*?"

"Dead."

Daisy's bottom lips quivered at the word *dead*. "I think the butterflies would be better."

"Let's go inside," Robert said, offering her his hand. "The mourners are waiting."

Daisy gave him a sad smile. "Thank you, Daddy."

Robert and Daisy returned to the mansion. Angelica had managed to assemble a small group of mourners consisting of Jasper, Mrs. Sweeting, and Webster who carried a spade.

"Hello," Jasper called when the little girl appeared.

"I'm sorry your cousin is deceased," Daisy told the macaw.

"Great grunting shit," the macaw shrieked, making the adults smile.

"Everyone is here," Angelica announced. "Where is the final resting place?"

Robert struggled against a smile and managed to keep a somber look on his face. "Daisy decided that—" He looked at his daughter and whispered, "What's his name?"

"Chirp."

"Daisy has decided that Chirp will spend eternity in my butterfly garden," Robert told them.

"A wise choice," Webster said, earning a nod of agreement from Sweeting and Angelica.

"Would you like to carry Chirp?" Robert asked his daughter.

"No, Daddy. I want you to carry him."

"I am truly honored."

"Everyone take your handkerchiefs out," Angelica instructed, playing the funeral director.

The mourners held handkerchiefs in front of their faces and formed a line behind Robert. Daisy, Jasper, Angelica, and Sweeting walked in that order. Webster followed behind. Slowly, their group marched outside. They crossed the lawns, skirted the maze, and made their way to the butterfly garden.

Robert turned to face them, and they formed a semicircle in front of him. Setting the box down on the ground, Robert began, "We are gathered here today—"

"Wrong ceremony," Angelica called.

Robert nodded. "We have come here to bid farewell to Chirp. Though we didn't know him very well, we listened each morning for his song and enjoyed the pleasant sight of him flying by. Each one of us will miss him." He turned to his daughter and asked, "Would you like the last word?"

Daisy nodded and announced, "Chirp was a very good bird."

"Amen," Webster said.

"Amen," echoed Angelica and Sweeting.

"Great grunting . . . hello," Jasper called, making everyone but the little girl smile.

"Come, Daisy, we'll prepare lunch while your father buries Chirp," Angelica said, taking the little girl's hand in hers. "Then the three of us will picnic. Won't that be fun?"

"What about Chirp's grave?" Daisy whined. "How will I find it?"

"I'll find something to mark the grave," Webster said.

"Thank you, Webster," Daisy said, and blew him a kiss. Then she walked away with Angelica.

Robert had buried Chirp by the time Angelica and Daisy returned to the butterfly garden. Marking the grave were two small statues of praying angels crafted of resin. Serene and regal, the graceful angels knelt silently in prayer.

Daisy gazed at the makeshift monument and said, "Chirp would be pleased."

"Bookends," Robert whispered to Angelica. "Where is Jasper?"

"I left him inside," she answered. "Where shall we picnic?"

"The pool?" Robert asked.

Angelica nodded in agreement. Yesterday, he'd been reluctant to go there, and today he was suggesting the pool as a picnic spot. She hoped his emotional scars would fade in time, until the thought of Louisa's death would merely be a bad memory.

"I'll carry Daisy," Robert was saying. "You carry the lunch, the blanket, and your harp." He turned to his daughter, adding, "I'm taking you to a secret place."

"I love secret places," Daisy said, clapping her hands.

Robert lifted the little girl into his arms and led the way to the woodland path. Angelica was glad she'd left the macaw behind; the bird would only have slowed them down.

"I smell the flower fairies, Daddy," Daisy said. "Do you?"

"Yes, I do."

"Lady Angelica?" she called over her father's shoulder.

"I smell them, too," Angelica answered.

Reaching the path that led down the side of the waterfall, Daisy cried, "Sacred sevens, what is that?"

"That is a waterfall," Robert told her. "It's very pretty but *very* dangerous. Never stand near the edge."

Angelica felt insistent tugging on her heartstrings. She prayed that one day her husband would recover from his first wife's untimely death.

With Daisy's help, Angelica spread out the blanket on the grass. Then she put down the basket and her harp.

Robert sat down and removed his boots and hose. Then he rolled up his trouser legs, saying, "Daisy, take your shoes and stockings off. We'll dunk our toes in the water while Lady Angelica unpacks the food."

Daisy plopped down on the blanket and did as she'd been told. Hiking up her gown, she ran to the water's edge, calling, "The grass tickles my feet."

Angelica watched her husband and his daughter wading ankle-deep in the pool. She smiled when she heard the little girl cry, "Look, Daddy. That is a fish."

"Do you want to fish with me some morning?" Robert asked. "Fishing is fun."

"I don't know how," she told him.

"You stick the worm on the hook and then toss it in the water," Robert explained. "Then along comes a fish, who tries to eat the worm but gets caught on the hook."

Daisy stared at him in obvious surprise. In a disgusted tone of voice, she said, "I bet the worm and the fish don't have fun."

Robert looked over his shoulder at Angelica and shrugged, saying, "I suppose I'll need to wait for a son."

"Daddy, how does the fish live under water?" Daisy asked, tugging on his sleeve to get his attention.

"Those little moving flaps are its gills," Robert explained. "The fish breathes through them."

"Oh."

"Do you understand?"

"No . . . Why don't people have gills?"

"People don't live under water so we don't need them," Robert told her.

"But Daddy—"

"Let's eat lunch," Angelica called, saving her husband from another question.

Hand in hand, Robert and Daisy walked back to

the blanket. They had cucumber sandwiches, sugar cookies, and lemon-barley water.

"I wish you were my mother," Daisy told Angelica.

"I am your mother," she answered with a smile.

Daisy looked confused. "What about Lucille?"

"Sweetheart, you have two mothers," Angelica told her. "When I married your father, I became your stepmother."

"What's a stepmother?"

"A stepmother is like a fairy godmother."

Daisy threw her arms around Angelica and said, "You're my fairy godmother."

"Lie down on the blanket with your father and watch the cloud pictures while I play my harp," Angelica said.

Robert lay down on the blanket and put his arms behind his head. Daisy imitated her father.

Angelica plucked the strings of her harp, conjuring a soothing, atmospheric sound, transporting them to a mystical world. Her notes imitated a river winding its way through a serene valley in springtime, filled with wildflowers, hummingbirds, and nightingales. Soon her tune became a duet with the waterfall.

Glancing at her new family, Angelica smiled to think that for once she had righted a wrong. Both father and daughter were asleep. Her husband needed his daughter as much as the child needed him, and she needed both of them.

Her own life had taken a road she'd never imagined existed. The only thing left was to get her revenge and see that her parents were buried on their own land.

Angelica watched her sleeping husband and recalled her father telling her as a child that she couldn't be a princess. She would need to content herself with a duke's son. Oh, she was more than content; she was happy. And when her sisters married and had children, there would be an enormous extended family, with many cousins for Daisy and her unborn babe. If only her parents had lived to see this day . . . .

Much later, Robert carried Daisy piggyback, down the shaded woodland path to the mansion. Walking behind them, Angelica smiled at their conversation.

"I still smell the flower fairies," Daisy said.

"I'm going to give you culture when we get home," Angelica called.

"What's *culture?*"

"Culture is stories about people and places and all sorts of things," Angelica answered.

"I like stories," the little girl said.

"So do I," Robert called. "Will you give me culture, too?"

"There is nothing I would rather give you than culture, my lord," Angelica answered.

"Nothing?"

"Well, almost nothing," she amended herself.

At Daisy's insistence, they stopped at Chirp's grave and said a prayer. Then the little girl turned to Angelica, saying, "I'm ready for my culture."

"I'm ready, too," Robert said.

Angelica led them across the lawn, around the maze, through the garden, and into the mansion. They walked down the corridor to the grand foyer.

Pointing to the statuary, Angelica told them, "Those are the three Fates, who rule the past, the present, and the future. All three ladies were weavers. Clotho is the spinner of life, Lacheses is the measurer, and Atropos is the cutter of life's thread."

"That means you die," Robert told his daughter.

"I don't like culture," Daisy said, looking frightened.

"The three Fates are everyone's fairy godmothers," Angelica said. "Come out to the front drive."

Angelica led them outside to the water terraces. She pointed to the smallest of the terraces, saying, "That is a mermaid, a virgin of the sea. She has the tail of a fish. Mermaids receive the souls of men who drown." She gestured to the middle terrace. "King Neptune is the god of the sea." Finally, she pointed at the largest of the three terraces, saying, "Aphrodite is the goddess of love and the queen of the sea, where she was born."

"Aphro was born in the sea?"

"That is correct, sweetheart."

"She got no gills," Daisy said.

Robert and Angelica looked at each other and burst out laughing. "I think we've had enough culture for one day," Robert announced.

"My lord, I think you are correct," Angelica said, turning toward the mansion,

"Great grunting shit!" Daisy cried, pointing toward the distance. "Look at the parade."

Chapter 19

"Bull's pizzle," Angelica cursed, realizing what the parade of carriages meant.

"Daddy, what's a bull's pizzle?" Daisy asked.

"Never mind," Robert answered. He whispered to Angelica, "Guard your tongue around her."

Ignoring him, Angelica stared in dismay at the parade of coaches and carts wending its way up the red brick drive toward the mansion. Sacred sevens, she wanted more time alone with her husband and daughter.

"I thought your father was going to give us a week," Angelica said, glancing at her husband.

Robert looked unhappy. "He did say that."

"They are five days early," Angelica complained. "I suppose we won't be swimming at the pool for a while."

Robert winked at her, saying, "I'll do my best to hurry them along to Scotland."

"I recognize your father's coaches in front," Angelica said, "but whose are those behind them?"

"Apparently, the Emersons accompanied them," Robert answered.

"If we take care of the Emersons now," she replied, "we won't need to think about them again."

"Wouldn't that be pleasant?" Robert said noncommittally.

"Lady Angelica, what's an Emerson?" Daisy asked.

"A monster," Angelica said dryly.

Daisy looked frightened. "The monsters are coming?"

"Don't tell her that," Robert said.

"How else would you explain it?" Angelica countered.

Robert smiled. "A point well taken, my love."

"Don't worry about the monsters," Angelica said, putting her arm around the little girl. "Daddy will protect us."

The first of the coaches bearing the boar's-head crest on the door halted in front of the mansion. The coachman jumped down and opened its door. Duke Magnus alighted and turned to assist Aunt Roxie, Samantha, and Victoria.

"Think of the fun we're going to have with my sisters," Angelica told Daisy. She took the girl's hand in hers and followed her husband to the coach.

"How wonderfully radiant you look, my darlings," Aunt Roxie gushed. "The three of you must be so happy together."

"We were happy until unexpected guests arrived five days early," Angelica said, making her husband laugh.

"You told me you'd be here at the end of the week," Robert said to his father.

Duke Magnus shrugged. "Venetia was making noises about taking Colin north."

"Colin is here?" Daisy asked.

"How is my favorite granddaughter?" the duke asked, turning his attention to the girl, who gave him a thumbs up. "Here is Colin now."

Daisy turned around to see Colin alighting from the second coach, with James Armstrong and Adam St. Aubyn. The little girl would have made a dash for the boy, but Aunt Roxie grabbed her hand.

"Always let the man approach you," Aunt Roxie told her. She looked at the others, saying, "It's never too early to learn strategy."

"Tinker is here, too?" Angelica asked her husband, seeing the duke's majordomo and the boy's nanny alight from the third coach.

"Tinker will accompany my father to Scotland," Robert told her. "Webster will remain here with us." He greeted his friends with a handshake, saying, "Are you grouse hunting, too?"

"We're going our separate ways to our own estates at the end of the week," Adam St. Aubyn answered.

"We couldn't possibly miss the fireworks here," James added.

Angelica watched Charles and Venetia Emerson step down from their coach. "Daisy, take Colin and Mrs. Honey inside to find Mrs. Sweeting."

Daisy took Mrs. Honey and Colin by the hand and led them toward the mansion. "We had a picnic and a funeral," the little girl told them in a loud voice before disappearing inside.

As the Campbell footmen began unpacking the carts, Charles Emerson and his daughter advanced on the group of adults. Emerson shook Robert's offered hand and then nodded at Angelica.

"Alexander remained in London?" Robert asked. "How disappointing."

"My son had urgent business and will join us by the week's end," Emerson explained.

"I do not want to see my son playing with that girl," Venetia said by way of a greeting.

"Then you are welcome to leave," Angelica replied, making her sisters giggle.

Duke Magnus cleared his throat. "Why don't we go inside and settle ourselves?"

"Come, sisters," Angelica said, looping her arms through theirs. "I'll help you unpack, but only five days' worth of clothing."

Four hours later, Angelica smoothed an imaginary wrinkle from her peach gown. She wanted to spend as little time with Venetia as possible and had delayed going down to dinner until the last moment. Too bad time couldn't sprout wings and five days pass by in the blink of an eye, she thought.

"Come, Jasper," Angelica called, walking toward the door. She held the door open for the macaw, smiling to think of the fun she could have scaring the elder Emerson with her pet.

Pausing at her stepdaughter's chamber, Angelica opened the door and saw Daisy, Colin, and their nannies just beginning to eat dinner. "Daisy and Colin, come with me," Angelica ordered. "You are eating with the family in the dining room."

"Lady Venetia won't like this," Mrs. Honey said, a worried expression on her face.

"I am the Marchioness of Argyll," Angelica reminded the woman, giving her an easy smile. "Lady Venetia has no voice here."

"Hello," Jasper called.

That got the children out of their seats. "Hello," both called and dashed across the chamber to the door, apparently the idea of eating dinner with the macaw being too exciting to resist.

Like a woman on a mission, Angelica marched

into the dining room, calling, "Good evening, everyone."

Daisy, Colin, and Jasper followed behind her. She kept her gaze on her quarry and watched his reaction to the new arrivals.

"Hello," the macaw shrieked as it passed the elder Emerson on its way to the cage.

"Keep that bird away from me," Emerson said, looking apprehensive.

"You aren't afraid of a bird, are you, Chuck?" Aunt Roxie asked.

"Don't call me that," Emerson snapped.

"Is the dining room now a nursery?" Venetia asked. "The children should be eating with their nannies."

"Families, including children, dine together," Angelica told the brunette, seating Daisy between herself and Robert.

"Come here, Colin," James Armstrong called, beckoning the boy. "Sit with Adam and me."

"Speaking of children, darling, how are you feeling?" Aunt Roxie drawled.

"I feel wonderful," Angelica answered.

Tinker and Webster supervised the serving of dinner. There were roasted Cornish hens with rice and mushroom sauce, shellfish soup, dressed dandelions with vinaigrette, and French rolls with butter, as well as wine for the gentlemen and lemon water for the ladies and children.

"Will you be joining us in Scotland?" Duke Magnus asked.

"Angelica and I are still honeymooning, Father," Robert answered. "We'll pass on the grouse hunting this year."

"Honeymooning with your illegitimate daughter?" Venetia said snidely.

Stunned silence descended upon everyone at the

table, broken only by Daisy, asking, "What's *illegitimate?*"

"Never mind," Angelica said. She glanced at her husband, who opened his mouth to speak, but she touched his hand. When he paused to look at her, she said, "I'll handle this."

Angelica turned her attention on the brunette. "Lady Venetia, never mention that word in any of its forms in my home again or I will order you to leave," she said in an overly polite tone. "After which, assisted by my aunt and sisters, I will spread a rumor that you stuff napkins in your unmentionables."

Robert and his friends laughed out loud at that. The children joined them but, obviously, had no idea what was so hilarious. Even Duke Magnus struggled against a smile and needed to cover his mouth with his hand.

Venetia opened her mouth to reply, but her father said, "Drop it, Venetia."

"I want to stay with Daisy," Colin announced.

"You are riding north with us," his mother informed him.

"If Colin wants to stay, then he can stay as long as—" Duke Magnus glanced at his son.

"Colin is very welcome to remain with us," Robert said.

Angelica nodded in agreement. "We'll have so much fun. We'll picnic every day and study the cloud pictures."

"I'll have a fishing companion," Robert added. "You'll come fishing with me, won't you, Colin?"

"Don't go," Daisy told him. "First you'll kill the worm, and then you'll kill the fish."

"I don't want to go fishing," Colin said, looking appalled.

"Don't be squeamish," Robert said. "I'll bait the hook for you."

"What's *bait the hook?*" Daisy asked.

"Baiting the hook means tormenting the unfortunate worm by sticking it on a sharp point," Angelica explained.

Colin shook his head. "No fishing, Uncle Robert."

"Thank you for explaining that," Robert said to his wife.

Angelica gave him a puckish smile. "I believe in always telling the truth."

"Speaking of truth, Parson Butterfield stopped by the duke's house yesterday afternoon to see how you were getting on," Venetia said, a snide edge to her voice.

"How would you know?" Angelica countered, refusing to panic, though her sisters looked ready to swoon on the floor. "You don't live there."

"I had just arrived for a visit with my son," Venetia answered.

"Dear Parson Butterfield is an old family friend," Aunt Roxie lied. "I should have written him as soon as we arrived in England. Actually, the man is a distant cousin of my late husband."

"Which one?" Venetia asked.

"I beg your pardon?"

"Which husband? You have had several."

"I can't even remember which husband," Aunt Roxie said with a throaty chuckle. "Some women are fortunate enough to attract any number of gentlemen, while others—poor darlings—have trouble with one."

Venetia bristled visibly beneath the implied insult. She looked at Angelica again, saying, "Prince Rudolf will be joining us in Scotland. What a pity you won't be there."

"Scotland and Prince Rudolf hold no appeal for me," Angelica said, glancing at her husband. She slid her gaze to the elder Emerson, saying, "My lord, would you care to finish that game of chance we began a few weeks ago?"

"I'm sorry, my lady," Emerson said by way of a refusal. "I've sworn off gambling for a while."

Angelica felt like screaming with frustration. She pasted a polite smile onto her face and said, "Another time, perhaps."

When dinner ended, the adults walked upstairs to the drawing room. Angelica paused in the corridor to hug Daisy and Colin, promising the little girl, "I'll be along shortly to tell you a story."

"What about me?" Colin asked.

"I think your mother might like to tell you a story," Angelica said.

"No, she won't."

"How do you know?"

"She's never told me a story before," Colin answered. "Only Nanny Honey tells me stories."

What kind of a woman didn't tell her own child bedtime stories? Angelica smiled through her irritation and said, "Then I will tell you a story, too."

Turning away, Angelica headed down the corridor to the drawing room. Apparently, Venetia was as horrid a mother as Lucille. Not only that, if Venetia had met Parson Butterfield, then she and her father knew where the Douglases had been for the previous ten years. Was that why Emerson had refused to dice with her? Did he have an inkling that she had revenge on her mind?

Angelica paused outside the drawing room, took a deep breath, and pasted a smile onto her face. Then she stepped into the room.

"How long is that Dubois girl going to remain here?" Venetia was asking Robert. "Her presence in His Grace's home is scandalous and could affect Colin's social standing."

"My daughter will be living with me permanently," Robert replied, his irritation evident in his tone. "My wife and I plan to adopt Daisy."

"This whole situation is unseemly," Venetia protested.

Tossing caution aside, Angelica reached her husband's side and told him, "I'll handle this." Then she turned on the brunette.

"Venetia, you and your family stood on the fringes of society until ten years ago, when your father swindled my father out of his fortune," Angelica told her. Then she threatened, "Keep your lips shut regarding Daisy, or I'll tell society about how disreputable the Emersons really are."

"How dare you," Charles Emerson snapped. "I am the Earl of Winchester."

"I don't give a fig who you are," Angelica shot back. "Whatever you have has been stolen from others. I fully intend—"

"I would love a madeira," Duke Magnus interrupted in a loud voice.

"I'll pour it for you, darling," Aunt Roxie said, rising from her chair. "Chuck—I mean Charles—would you care for a glass?"

The Earl of Winchester nodded.

"Come with me, darling," Aunt Roxie ordered, grabbing Angelica's hand. "I could use some help."

Angelica turned away and saw her husband's smile. She glanced at his friends, who were also smiling, as were her sisters.

Fuming, Angelica walked across the drawing room with her aunt. She watched her pour madeira into five glasses, one for each gentleman, and then flip open the secret lid of her ring to drop herbs into one of the glasses.

With one finger, Aunt Roxie stirred the herbs into the madeira. Then she wiped her finger on a linen napkin and passed the tainted madeira to Angelica, whispering, "This is for the Earl of Winchester. If he doesn't wish to gamble, we'll get our revenge another way. Please do not drop it."

"I'll be especially careful," Angelica assured her, smiling brightly.

Angelica crossed the drawing room and, for a brief moment, suffered the urge to pour the madeira on top of the earl's head. She handed him the madeira and then sat with her sisters on the couch. Purposefully, she refused to look at Emerson or his daughter.

The conversation swirled around Angelica for a time. The gentlemen spoke of grouse hunting and business.

"Arghhh," Emerson groaned, and doubled up as if in pain.

"What is wrong?" Venetia cried.

"My stomach pains me," Emerson panted, his complexion white.

Robert was at the earl's side in an instant. "Can you make it upstairs?"

Emerson shook his head.

"Let me move you to a couch then," Robert said, his two friends at his side, ready to assist.

"No, the pain—" Emerson called weakly, "Venetia, I've been poisoned."

"That is ridiculous," Aunt Roxie said. "All of us ate the same food."

"You poisoned his madeira," Venetia accused Angelica, turning to glare at her.

"Don't be silly," Aunt Roxie scoffed. "I was standing right beside her."

"I don't care where you were standing," Venetia screamed, hearing her father moan again. "She has a motive for murder and contrived to poison him."

Angelica mustered as much dignity as she could and rose from the couch. Instead of denying the accusation, she said, "Assume a more respectful tone when you address the Marchioness of Argyll." At that, she turned and walked toward the door, followed by the macaw shrieking "Good night," Venetia screaming "Murderess," and Charles Emerson groaning in pain. The sound of his discomfort brought another smile to her face.

Reaching her bedchamber, Angelica put the macaw into his cage and covered it. Then she changed into her nightgown and sat on the settee in front of the darkened hearth to wait for her husband.

The bedchamber door crashed open suddenly, and her husband marched in. When he stood before her, Angelica raised her gaze to his and saw the anger in his expression.

"What did you put in Emerson's madeira?" Robert demanded.

Angelica stared at him in surprise. Did he actually believe she would murder the man? Sacred sevens, she wanted Emerson to suffer as her father had; why would she offer him an easy road to oblivion?

"I'm waiting for your answer," Robert said, his hands on his hips.

"Do you actually believe me capable of murder?" Angelica asked, rising from the settee to challenge him.

"Do not answer my question with a question," Robert said. "Tell me what you put in the man's madeira."

"Aunt Roxie slipped Emerson a purgative,"

Angelica answered. "He will recover by tomorrow morning."

Robert nodded, and his lips twitched into a smile. "I apologize for doubting you," he said.

"Take your apology and stuff it in a dark place," Angelica shot back. She whirled away and climbed into bed.

"Are you angry with me?" Robert asked.

Angelica answered by turning her back to him. She refused to speak to a husband who believed her capable of murder.

"Should I take that as a *yes?*" he asked.

"Whoever said the Campbells weren't perceptive?" Angelica asked rhetorically.

Silence greeted her sarcasm. Then she heard the door click shut.

The Emersons had been in residence for less than a day, and already she and her husband were arguing. On the other hand, her husband could have assumed she wouldn't stoop to murder. His confidence in her would have been appreciated.

A long time passed before Angelica drifted into a fretful sleep. She awakened the next morning to find the bed beside her empty but then heard a noise on the opposite side of the chamber. Rolling over, she saw her husband shaving.

"Where are you going at this hour?" she asked drowsily.

"I'm going fishing," he answered over his shoulder.

"This early?" Angelica sat up and drew up the coverlet. "Do you want to be certain no one hears the screams of the worms and the fish?"

"Precisely." Robert wiped the excess soap off his face and crossed the chamber to sit on the edge of the bed. "I've left some dry toast on the table and a bowl of nuts for Jasper. Be sure you eat the bread before you rise.''

"Thank you," Angelica said, feeling guilty because he was being so nice and she had behaved badly the previous evening.

"I apologize for considering you capable of harming Emerson," Robert said.

"I am perfectly capable of harming the man," Angelica admitted. "However, poisoning is too easy a death for that villain."

Robert smiled and leaned close. He planted a kiss on her lips and then said, "I won't return until early afternoon."

"How many worms and fish are you planning to murder?" she asked, arching a blond brow at him.

"I'm going to Armstrong's estate to look at a pony for Daisy," he said, rising from his perch and walking toward the door. "Try to stay out of trouble until I return."

"Yes, my lord," she called. "Your wish is my inconvenience."

Angelica ate her dry toast, lay back on the bed, and slept peacefully for another three hours. After dressing and feeding the macaw, Angelica walked downstairs to the dining room.

The hour being late, Venetia sat alone at the table, and Angelica hesitated for a brief moment. She decided not to let the other woman bother her. After all, *she* was the Marchioness of Argyll.

With as much graceful dignity as she could manage, Angelica crossed the room to the sideboard. She helped herself to a buttered scone, a slice of ham, and a spoonful of scrambled eggs. Turning around, she sat at the opposite end of the table from the brunette.

"I saved you *The Times,*" Tinker said, setting the newspaper down beside her plate.

Angelica gave the majordomo an easy smile. "Thank you, Tinker."

Angelica began to read the newspaper while she ate. Feeling a presence beside her, she looked up to see her nemesis sitting in the chair beside hers.

"May I speak with you?" Venetia asked politely.

Wondering what caused this change in attitude, Angelica stared at her for a long moment. Finally, she nodded.

"I want to apologize for my outburst last night," Venetia said, a pretty blush staining her cheeks. "My father's sudden illness panicked me, but he's much better this morning. You know, my father and I are close, much closer than he is to Alexander."

The father preferred the daughter to his only son and heir? That was odd. Her conciliatory words put Angelica on the alert, however.

"I forgive you," she said, and then turned her head to continue reading the newspaper.

"May I speak frankly?" Venetia asked.

Angelica looked at her again. "Speak, then."

Venetia inched closer and dropped her voice to a mere whisper. "My behavior to you has been unforgivable," she began, "but I would like to explain why I have been so despicable. After my sister died, I assumed that Robert and I would eventually wed. It seemed inevitable, since both of us had suffered a heartbreaking loss. And then you dropped into our lives."

Venetia shrugged. "Naturally, I became upset, especially since—" She broke off and stared at the opposite wall.

"Especially since what?" Angelica asked.

"I suppose you may as well know the truth," Venetia said after a long pause.

Angelica felt the first stirrings of panic beginning

to swell in her chest. "What truth?" she asked in a small voice.

"Colin is Robert's son."

Those four words hit Angelica with the impact of an avalanche. She leaped out of her chair so quickly that it toppled over. "Another Emerson lie?"

"I am sorry," Venetia said, looking decidedly insincere. "If you don't believe me, ask your husband."

"I won't insult my husband's integrity by repeating such a monstrous accusation," Angelica said in a scathing voice. With her head held high, she marched out of the dining room. Returning to her chamber, she dropped onto the settee in front of the hearth.

It wasn't true, Angelica told herself. Her husband was too good a man to have made love to his brother's wife. How dare that Emerson bitch—!

Angelica's head throbbed with troubling thoughts. Perhaps Colin's father wasn't dead; perhaps he was at the Armstrong estate looking at ponies. Was Daisy Colin's sister instead of his cousin? She lay down on the settee and closed her eyes, escaping her thoughts by falling asleep.

"Alexander Emerson just arrived." Angelica heard these words as if from a distance.

"Are you ill?"

Angelica opened her eyes to see her husband standing beside the settee. He wore a concerned expression on his face.

"I feel much better now," she said, then yawned and stood to stretch. Venetia's shocking revelation came rushing back to her.

"Is Colin your son?" Angelica asked, before she could swallow the words.

Robert stared at her for an agonizingly long

moment and then answered, "I don't know. Does it matter?"

His words stunned Angelica, who had expected a different answer. "I mind very much if the man I married made love to his brother's wife," she replied.

"I cannot deny or confirm Colin's paternity," Robert told her. "Once, *only once,* a long time ago, I was drunk and—" He shrugged, seeming at a loss for words.

Angelica couldn't speak. She plopped down on the settee and stared at him. She had married a stranger. Yes, he was the duke's son, promised to her by her father all those long years ago. But he was a stranger to her.

"Say something, angel," Robert said in a choked voice.

Angelica tilted her head back to stare him straight in the eye and said, "I want a divorce."

Chapter 20

An expression of unspeakable pain appeared on her husband's face, making Angelica doubt her resolve. She watched him banish the emotion and, turning away, walk toward the door.

Was he dismissing her feelings? Angelica wondered, her anger swelling again. Had he nothing else to say to her?

"I meant it," she said. "I want a divorce."

Robert paused. When he turned to face her, his hurt had been replaced by a look of contempt.

"Don't be ridiculous," he snapped. "No one divorces."

"I do," Angelica told him, her voice rising in anger.

Robert ignored her and walked out of the room. The quiet click as he shut the door was more deafening than if he had slammed it.

"I do," Jasper shrieked from inside its cage. "I do."

"Shut up, you dumb bird," Angelica snapped.

"Dumb bird," the macaw repeated.

She marched across the chamber and covered the bird's cage, saying, "Good night."

Angelica remained closeted with her troubled thoughts for the rest of the afternoon. When her anger subsided, she began to doubt herself again. Perhaps she'd been too hasty, demanding a divorce. She loved her husband, only . . . She wanted the man she married, not the one who had made love to his brother's wife.

Tears welled up in her eyes and ran down her cheeks. What was she supposed to do now? She had spoken the word *divorce* on impulse and needed to live with it.

"Lady Angelica!"

The chamber door swung open, admitting Daisy and Colin. Both children dashed across the chamber to her, and she greeted them with a sad smile.

"Hello," the macaw called.

"Ignore Jasper," Angelica whispered. "He's in the doghouse."

Daisy looked confused. "That's a doghouse?"

"I meant that Jasper irritated me, so I banished him to his cage," Angelica explained.

"What did he do?" Colin asked.

"The dumb bird mocked me."

"Dumb bird," the macaw said, making the children laugh.

"Lady Angelica, will you tell us the story about the poor girl at the fair and the prince who rescued her?" Daisy asked.

At that, Angelica burst into tears.

"Why are you crying?" the little girl wailed, her own bottom lips begining to tremble.

"Your daddy—"

"What's wrong with my daddy?" she cried.

Angelica realized she was frightening her step-

daughter and set her own misery aside for the
moment. She put her arm around her and assured
her, "Your daddy is well. Do you want to live with
him or me?"

"I want to live with him and you," Daisy
answered, obviously puzzled by the question.

"We may be divorcing," Angelica said, and
instantly regretted her words.

"What is *divorce?*" Colin asked.

"Divorce is when a married couple becomes
unmarried," Angelica tried to explain.

"I don't want a divorce," Daisy said.

Colin shook his head. "Me neither."

"Well, I don't want a divorce," Angelica told
them.

"Then we won't divorce." Daisy grabbed her
hand, saying, "Let's go and eat dinner now."

Angelica nodded. She rose from the settee and
followed them to the door.

"Hello," Jasper called.

Angelica crossed the chamber, removed the
cage's cover, and opened the door. "Come, Jasper," she said. "Let's eat."

"Eat," the macaw repeated, making the children
giggle.

Angelica and the children reached the dining
room just as the others, including newcomer Alexander Emerson, took their seats. "Daisy and Colin,
you sit in those two chairs," she instructed them,
glancing at her tight-lipped husband. "Beside
him." After escorting the macaw to his cage, she
sat on the far side of the children, away from her
husband.

"Lady Angelica, you look tired," Duke Magnus
remarked as the footmen began serving. "Are you
feeling well?"

Angelica opened her mouth to reply, but Daisy

was faster, announcing, "Daddy made Lady Angelica cry."

"But we made her smile again," Colin added.

Everyone at the table looked at Angelica, who blushed, and then shifted their gazes to Robert. Angelica glanced at her husband to find him staring coldly at her. His expression told her that he was not pleased.

"You made Lady Angelica smile?" Duke Magnus said to the children. "How did you manage that?"

"My daddy wants a divorce," Daisy began.

"*Divorce?*" Aunt Roxie cried, looking ready to swoon.

Ignoring their stunned audience, Robert tossed his napkin on the table and rose from his chair. "I told you there would be no divorce."

Angelica bolted out of her chair. "You cannot leave me sitting at this table and stalk off in anger," she told him. "I am leaving in anger first."

At that, Angelica tossed her napkin at him and marched toward the door, leaving a silent audience in her wake. She glanced over her shoulder before stepping out of the room and saw her husband watching her, the hint of a smile flirting with his lips.

Of all the unmitigated gall, Angelica thought as she climbed the stairs to her chamber. How dare he admit to making love to his brother's wife and then become angry with her!

Angelica sat on the settee and realized she'd left Jasper behind. Well, she had no intention of returning to the dining room to fetch him.

A few minutes later, Angelica heard a knock on the door. She knew it wasn't her husband and hoped it wasn't her aunt or sisters. She didn't have the energy to argue and refused to tell the world what the problem was.

"Lady Angelica?" The voice belonged to Tinker.

Angelica rose and crossed the chamber to open the door. "Yes?"

"I believe you forgot something," the major-domo said.

"Hello," Jasper said, walking past her into the room.

"Thank you, Tinker." She started to close the door, but the majordomo held up his hand to stop her.

"Your presence is requested in His Grace's study," the man told her.

"Requested or required?"

"Required."

Angelica nodded and began to close the door again.

"Immediately," Tinker added.

"I'll be there in a minute," she assured him.

The majordomo left, and Angelica closed the door. No matter what, she refused to tell the duke what this shocking problem was.

Angelica summoned her courage and counted to ten slowly. Leaving the macaw behind, she left her chamber.

Walking into the duke's study, Angelica stopped short. Not only was the duke there but also her grim-faced husband and her aunt.

"Sit down, child," Duke Magnus said. "I want to speak to you and my son."

Angelica crossed the study like a woman going to the gallows. Three against one was unfair, but it was so like her husband to send for reinforcements. These Campbells cared nothing for her; they cared only for the babe she carried.

Angelica settled herself in one of the chairs in front of the desk. Her husband remained standing, his arms folded across his chest. Keeping her face expressionless, she looked at the duke and waited.

"Usually, I refrain from interfering in other people's marriages," Duke Magnus said. "However, you are carrying the Campbell heir."

"I'm positive Venetia engineered this whole situation," Aunt Roxie interjected. "Whatever this situation is."

"I would like to know what the problem is," Duke Magnus said. He smiled at her. "Four heads are better than two, my dear."

"With all due respect, Your Grace, my problem is of a personal nature," Angelica replied. "You could do nothing to solve it."

"The fault lies with me," Robert spoke up.

Angelica snapped her gaze to her husband. His admission surprised her.

Duke Magnus inclined his head, acquiescing to their wish for privacy. "For the sake of my grandchild, will you stay here and try to work out your problems after the rest of us leave for Scotland? If you still want a divorce later—" He let his words hang in the air.

"Yes, of course." Angelica rose from her chair and left the study. Robert walked directly behind her and touched her shoulder once the study door had closed behind them.

When she turned around, Robert said, "Thank you for not telling my father the truth."

"You are welcome," Angelica replied, and then continued walking down the corridor.

Angelica didn't speak to Robert for three days, and there was a hole in her world where he had once stood. Though the entire household was aware of the rift between them, no one mentioned it, only watched them ignoring each other.

On the afternoon of the fourth day, Angelica sat

alone in the gazebo. She plucked the strings of her harp in a melancholy tune and watched her husband and her stepdaughter in the distance. Robert had purchased a pony for Daisy and, at the moment, led her around on the lawn near the mansion. Colin sat on top of his own pony, the reins being held by Alexander Emerson. James Armstrong and Adam St. Aubyn stood watching them, calling occasional encouragements to both children.

Too bad her husband hadn't really been Robert Roy instead of a Campbell, Angelica thought. She would have been happy living with him in her modest cottage.

She loved him and had overreacted to Venetia's revelation. After all, he had made that mistake before he even knew she existed. But how could she reconcile with him? Could she plead her condition as overemotional? That would be untrue. Perhaps the duke was correct; when the others left for grouse hunting—

"How do you feel?"

Angelica focused on the owner of that voice, Venetia Emerson Campbell. Without bothering to reply, she looked down at her harp and began plucking its strings again.

"May I speak with you?" Venetia asked.

"Why?" Angelica asked, raising her gaze. "Shall we compare our experiences with my husband?"

The brunette blushed. "I-I want to apologize for causing problems for you."

"I find that impossible to believe," Angelica remarked.

"Please?" Venetia asked again. "Let's take a walk through the woodland."

Angelica shifted her gaze to Robert, who had paused and now watched them. She inclined her head and, setting the harp aside, rose from her seat, saying, "Very well, Venetia. Lead the way."

The two women started down the well-worn path that led to the waterfall and pool. The afternoon was warm, and the tree-shaded path offered more cooling comfort than the gazebo had.

"What did you wish to speak about?" Angelica asked.

"I prefer to wait until we get to the river," Venetia said over her shoulder.

At the river, Venetia began to walk in the direction of the waterfall. Angelica fell in beside her.

"I would like us to be friends," Venetia began.

"Isn't it a little late for that?" Angelica asked.

"We are in the same family now," Venetia said. "Please set your anger toward Robert aside. Think of your child."

Leaning against the solid trunk of an oak, Angelica wondered why the brunette was suddenly concerned for her and her child. When she did not reply, Venetia turned away and walked toward the edge of the rocks at the top of the waterfall.

"This is where my sister—" Venetia broke off, raised her hand to her face, and began to weep softly.

Sorry for her loss, Angelica pushed away from the tree and walked over to her. She placed a hand on the other woman's shoulder in an effort to offer comfort. Without warning, Angelica felt a hand on the small of her back, pushing her forward.

Caught off balance, Angelica went over the edge of the thirty-foot waterfall. Instead of panicking, she wrenched her body forward in order to miss hitting the boulders and kept her body vertical, feet first and squeezed together.

Clenching her buttocks against the shock of the impact, Angelica dropped her hands to her stomach to protect her baby. She hit the water but ignored the sharp pain she felt in her ankle. Trying to keep from plunging to the bottom of the pool, she spread her arms and legs wide and moved them back and forth.

Within seconds, Angelica surfaced and heard the brunette's shout as if from a great distance, "Help! Help, there's been an accident."

Thankful that her dress was light, Angelica swam to shore. She dragged herself onto the grass and lay still, trying to catch her breath.

Venetia tried to kill me, Angelica thought. *Venetia murdered Louisa, her own sister.*

Angelica put her hand under her dress and felt between her legs. No blood meant the babe was well. She tried to stand then, but her left ankle wouldn't hold her. Slowly, she lowered herself to the grass and closed her eyes, praying that help would come soon.

"She slipped," a sobbing woman said. "I tried to grab her, but—"

Venetia.

"There she is!" That voice sounded like Alexander Emerson.

"Help, I've hurt my ankle," Angelica called.

"She's alive," her husband said, his voice closer than the others'. A moment later, he crouched down beside her and examined her leg and ankle, saying, "I don't think it's broken, probably just a bad sprain."

"Venetia pushed me off the edge," Angelica told him, her voice strong and clear.

"That's a lie." Alexander Emerson leapt to his sister's defense.

"She slipped and—"

"Venetia murdered Louisa the same way," Angelica interrupted the brunette.

"My sister would never have murdered her own—"

"I'm not your sister," Venetia snapped, her hatred for her brother apparent. She looked at her father, asking, "How long must we keep up this charade?"

"You stupid chit," Charles Emerson shouted at her. "Keep your mouth shut."

"I was the eldest," Venetia protested. "I should have been the duchess. I would have been the duchess if this one hadn't shown up."

"You were the mother of the Campbell heir," Emerson told her.

"I want to be the duchess," Venetia shrieked and stamped her foot.

"You're not my sister?" Alexander echoed, his shock apparent in his voice and expression. "What do you mean?"

"Louisa and you are bastards," Emerson told him. "What else could it mean?"

Alexander Emerson stepped back as if he'd been struck. "I am your heir, Father."

"I suffered you calling me that name for twenty odd years," Charles Emerson said, an unholy hatred shining in his eyes. "I thought when I hired those—" He broke off, realizing what he had almost said.

"Whom did you hire?" Alexander asked.

"I hired men to rid myself of you," Emerson answered.

"Are they the same men you hired to get rid of me?" Robert asked, standing to face the elder Emerson.

Charles Emerson clamped his lips shut, but Venetia shrieked, "How could you do that, Father? You knew I wanted to marry him and become the Duchess of Inverary."

"Would you have awaited my father's death or rid yourself of him, too?" Robert asked. Without waiting for a reply, he sent his friends a pointed look.

James Armstrong positioned himself beside the elder Emerson. Adam St. Aubyn inched closer to Venetia.

"I'll see both of you hanged at Tyburn," Robert told them.

"Nobody is going to hang," Duke Magnus announced, surprising them. "We do not need a scandal."

Robert flicked a glance at Angelica. "Venetia tried to kill my pregnant wife," he said to his father. "Charles tried to kill Alex and me. Will you allow them to go free?"

"If he wants to live, Charles will sign his estate and title over to Alexander," Duke Magnus said. "Then we will transport him and Venetia to Australia on board one of the Campbell ships."

"I want them hanged," Robert insisted.

"Be reasonable, son," the duke said, touching his shoulder. "No good can come from creating a scandal."

Robert finally nodded. He gestured to his friends to escort the two Emersons back to the mansion.

"Wait," Alexander Emerson said. He stood in front of Charles and in an anguished voice, asked, "If you're not my father, then who is?"

"You'll need to discover that for yourself," Charles Emerson sneered.

Alexander's expression crumpled. It was then Angelica realized there were worse things in life than having one's father lose his fortune to a swindler.

"You can't tell me?" Alexander asked. "Or you won't tell me?"

"Both," came the reply.

With his fist clenched, Alexander struck the older man, who toppled to the ground. "That was for Louisa," he said in a voice filled with contempt. He turned away but stopped in front of Robert to apologize, "I'm sorry I tried to ruin your businesses."

"Did you pirate *The Tempest?*" Robert asked.

"No, that wasn't me," Alexander answered, and then walked away.

"Take them back to the mansion," Duke Magnus ordered James and Adam. "Be sure to lock them in separate chambers."

"I'm sorry I endangered your life," Robert said, lifting Angelica into his arms. "I don't know what I would have done if—" He broke off, unwilling to complete the thought. "If you still want a—"

"I don't want a divorce," Angelica told him, wrapping her arms around his neck. "I love you."

"I love you more," Robert vowed, and poured all his love into a single kiss.

"My ankle hurts," Angelica whispered against his lips. "Can we go home now?"

Robert smiled.

"Are you smiling because my ankle hurts?" she asked.

His smile grew into a broad grin. "No, angel, I was thinking of how much bed rest you'll need to recover."

"Will you keep me company?" Angelica asked in a seductive voice.

Robert laughed out loud. Echoing her own words, he answered, "Whoever said the Douglases weren't perceptive?"

* * *

Summer died in a flourish of color, making way for autumn's Michaelmas daisies and riotous orange, red, and gold leaves. All too soon nature slept beneath a powdery blanket of snow that melted into spring's herald, the courageous crocus.

Content with life, Angelica watched the seasons passing from the gardens tended lovingly by her husband. At first she looked for signs of her husband in his nephew, but that passed away. She couldn't love Colin any more if he were her own flesh and blood, and the boy found an attentive mother in her.

The Campbell heir arrived on the first day of spring, and his father named him Douglas, in honor of the family that had given him his wife. Surprising the entire household, Douglas's sister arrived thirty minutes later, and her mother named her Amber Louise for her reddish-gold hair and the unfortunate young woman who had died by her own sister's hand.

The following afternoon Robert and Angelica remained closeted in their bedchamber and watched their babies sleeping. Angelica sat up in bed and held her daughter in her arms, while Robert leaned against the headboard beside her and cradled his son, the future Duke of Inverary and Campbell laird.

"I'm going to remove all of the portraits of the Campbell lairds from my father's house," Robert said, without taking his gaze off his son.

"Why?"

"I know from personal experience how daunting the sight can be to a small boy," he answered.

"You might not have grown into such a prince

of a man without those illustrious ancestors keeping you on your best behavior,'' Angelica told him.

"Thank you, angel."

A knock on the door drew their attention.

"Come in," Angelica called.

"Hello," a familiar voice shrieked as the door opened to admit their relations.

"That damned bird," Robert muttered.

"Jasper is part of this family, too," Angelica reminded him.

Duke Magnus, Aunt Roxie, and Victoria walked into the chamber behind Daisy and Colin. "Sacred sevens," the little girl exclaimed. "I see two babies."

"Do you like your brother and sister?" Angelica asked.

Daisy nodded.

"What about you, Colin?"

The little boy shrugged. "Can they do anything?" he asked.

Robert smiled. "Your cousins eat, sleep, cry, and poop."

Colin appeared wholly disgusted. "You mean, they don't do anything?"

"Great grunting shit," the macaw shrieked. "Drink, drink, drink."

"Lady Angelica, Jasper said a bad word," Daisy whispered.

"He doesn't know any better," Angelica told her.

"Your parents would be so proud," Aunt Roxie said, dabbing her eyes with a handkerchief.

The thought of her parents brought a well of tears to Angelica's eyes, and a lump of aching emotion formed in her throat. She managed to regain her composure within seconds.

"What do you think, Tory?" she asked.

"I think they are the most beautiful babies I've

ever seen," her sister answered. "I only hope they
haven't inherited my reading ability."

"I wish Samantha was here," Angelica said.

"How divinely romantic to be abducted by a
prince," Victoria gushed.

"Ruined by a prince, you mean," Aunt Roxie
said. "Between the prince and her limp, we'll never
find her a husband."

"Don't worry, Roxanne," Duke Magnus said.
"My investigators will find them, and then we'll
see them wed. Your niece will be a princess."

Aunt Roxie brightened. "Oh, my, just think of
how in demand we'll be."

"I wonder where he could have taken her,"
Angelica said.

"I almost forgot," Duke Magnus said, passing
his son a missive. "This arrived from London."

After their visitors had gone, Angelica watched
her husband as he read the letter. When he raised
his dark gaze to hers, he appeared displeased.

"Is there a problem?" she asked.

"Charles and Venetia Emerson arrived safely in
Australia and promptly disappeared from my sur-
veillance," Robert answered. "This doesn't bode
well for Alexander. I'll send him a note."

"That doesn't bode well for any of us," Angelica
said.

Without disturbing his son, Robert put his arm
around her and drew her close, saying, "I'll protect
you with my life, angel."

When she cuddled against him, Robert dropped
a kiss on the crown of her head. "How did I manage
to tempt an angel into becoming my wife?" he
asked.

Angelica smiled and drawled in a perfect imitation of her aunt, "Darling, you seduced me."

"Oh, but you were *so* cooperative."